FALLEN
STAR

Also Available From This Author

This and other works by the author are available from:
RedPetalPress.com
Order from other fine bookstores

FALLEN STAR

BOOK THREE OF
THE MACMASTER CHRONICLES

a novel by

Jason Lord Case

NEW YORK

First edition copyright ©2010 Jason Lord Case

ISBN: 978-0-9825616-4-5

Published by Red Petal Press, New York.
RedPetalPress.com

*Book and Cover Design, and Cover Photographs
by Red Petal Press*

This book is a work of fiction. Names, characters, businesses, organizations, places, events, and incidents are the product of the author's imagination or are used fictitiously. Any resemblance to actual persons, living or dead, events, or locales is entirely coincidental.

Printed in the United States of America

For Alexander Lloyd.

Chapter One
What Price Damage Control?

Half the room was in darkness, including the desk; the other half was bathed in a harsh, glaring light. The only furniture on the lit section of the floor was an old kitchen chair, occupied.

"What exactly is it you want, George? I'm not sure I'm reading you right." The man at the desk glanced sideways, closing one eye.

"Well, Frank… Can I call you Frank? What we need is a certain person or persons to disappear, quietly and permanently."

"Permanently is easy; quietly costs more." The hint of New York City was not left in the man's accent deliberately but it was there nonetheless.

"Yes, I understand. What do you suggest?"

"I know some gentlemen in New York, New Jersey and Pennsylvania who can make this sort of thing happen. They are effective and efficient. I will stress that they do things quietly; permanently is a given." The tall man in the gray suit crossed one leg over the other and picked at an imaginary piece of lint on his hand-tailored suit.

"You don't know anyone locally?"

"Of course. I know everybody. I know you, though you didn't know that until now. I know your boss, too."

George felt his ass cheeks tighten.

"You don't need to worry about this. I am a professional and the men I work with are all professionals, though they vary in methods. As I said, I know everybody. I know, for instance, that your boss would be ruined if he were implicated in this. In fact, he would probably be ruined if you were implicated in this. The likely result of that would be a quiet and permanent exit for you. Am I wrong?"

"Oh, I don't think he would…"

"Do not presume to tell me what I already know! You may think you are an indispensable cog in the congressional process, but I assure you that you are more like immediately replaceable." Frank Hicks snapped his fingers for emphasis and pulled out a notebook. "The very fact that you are sitting here in your underwear means that you want something done that you are not man enough to accomplish for yourself, and for that you need me. You are George Arridagio, uh… here we are, third generation Greek and Italian. Your grandfather was a shipbuilder, your father still owns a moderately successful winery up by Sacramento. Your brother will probably inherit that on his death since he still works it for the old man. You went to the University of Michigan in Ann Arbor majoring in political science. You work for Henry Cabot, Congressman of the, uh… the Twentieth District. That's the State's Congressional District Twenty. Does that cover your father's land too?"

"No, his land is in the north end of the valley." George Arridagio had lost every speck of arrogance and every hint of power he had entered with. He sat stripped to his underwear before a man who knew everything about him, a man he would never allow his employer to meet with. He had been stripped further than his clothing now and it seemed suddenly as if Frank Hicks could see right through him, watching the stomach acids churn in his belly and the muscles of his neck all but spasm.

"Relax, George. I mean you no harm, nor do I mean to harm the congressman or any of your family. You are among friends here. Once again, I apologize for insisting we speak this way. You understand, I'm sure." Frank's gestures caused his right hand to enter the light and his ring sparkled.

A knock on the door announced the return of the advisor's clothing. It had been thoroughly inspected for listening devices of all sorts. George was more than happy to regain his business armor and was, in fact, happy for just the physical work of dressing himself.

"Shall we get down to business then? I will need specifics if I am to work with you and yours. I need who, how many, and I need a time frame. I need a policy for collateral damage as well. Possible women and children on the scene can cause a messy situation, not to mention bad press. Nobody cares if a few gang bangers get plowed under but women and children bring out the left wing. Do you want it clean as well as quiet or do you want to leave a message to someone? As I said, I am a professional and the men I work with are professionals. I require the entire amount we decide upon in cash and I expect to never see you again. If you attempt to cause any trouble for me or mine, I will make sure that we take care of another action quietly and cleanly. Nothing will ever be found."

George knew then that he had just made the worst mistake of his career, possibly his life. His superior had a clean record and did not paddle in the dirty end of the pool as far as money and favors were concerned, but like so many married men his wife did not provide everything he needed from a woman. George had procured many different services for Henry Cabot over the years and through the utility of darkness and the occasional mask, kept the congressman's face out of the tabloids. As with anything done often enough, a fly was inserted in the ointment.

Henry had gotten a hankering for a Mexican woman and George had gone to a different area to get what the congressman needed. The lesson was to be long, harsh and potentially expensive as the lawmaker was filmed having his way with a thirteen-year-old Hispanic girl. The girl ended up in the hospital with a bleeding colon but there was no DNA evidence to process from what was investigated as a rape. A copy of the grainy, mostly infrared recording was delivered to the congressman's office a week later. The men who had made the clandestine video wanted money and a lot of it.

Henry and George knew that the payments would never end and that the only way to stop the extortion would be to kill the men who were demanding payment, so George took it upon himself to clear up the situation.

The one express goal of Cindy Anderson's life was to find a movie star or producer and marry him. Children, while detestable to her, would be necessary since they represented the financial settlement necessary to maintain a lifestyle that would amuse her for the rest of her life. The competition was fierce and getting worse all the time. In the city where you could look young well into your fifties and beyond, it takes a special something to be worthy of snaring the big prize.

Nobody who worked on the same block of Lexington Avenue as Cindy could afford to live in that neighborhood. The men who owned the businesses could if they chose. The lofts above the stores were rented out at exorbitant prices. Cindy did not want to live in a loft. She wanted to move into one of the mansions in the hills. She wanted to become American Royalty, but the best she had done so far was to sniff the rarified air of the upper crust as she worked in a coffee shop where they might visit from time to time.

Being a natural blonde was an advantage, even in an area that was full of blondes. There was not a single pound of excess fat on her body; adipose tissue was something she could not allow. In a culture obsessed with the automobile she rode a bicycle most of the time and took the bus in bad weather. She ran on the beach as often as she could get there, the sand providing the kind of resistance that increased balance and muscle tone. A breast enhancement had set her last boyfriend back a fortune since she had insisted on the best plastic surgeon in the area. Once she had gotten what she wanted from him and sent him off to bankruptcy court, she moved on. He had been generous and gullible, not the kind of man who could hold on to a prize like Cindy.

The coffee shop opened early, before the morning sun had burned the dew off the land. This simple fact kept Cindy sober on weekdays. Riding her bicycle all that way with a hangover had little appeal. On the weekend she tended to hang around with a couple of friends she had made from the area she worked, or her roommate Shelly. They were in the same financial situation she was, but they all looked good enough to get in the clubs and they never paid for their own drinks. Boyfriends came and went with this group but never lasted. These girls were high maintenance and the men who didn't get chased away left for other reasons.

Cindy did not chew gum, she did not smoke, she did not drink more than one cup of coffee in the morning and she did not eat meat. She was not a strict vegan as she found this too restrictive and expensive and she did eat eggs from time to time. In short, her choice was not from some sense of moral obligation that she felt but from a practical one. Meat was expensive and made people fat, she did not have much money and she had a burning desire to stay thin. She actually preferred a man who ate meat. Vegetarian men all ended up looking starved to her. Drugs were all right with her but they were an extravagance she would not pay for, and she would not get involved with a man that did a lot of drugs. She did not want to be enslaved by narcotics as so many are.

One of the problems with hunting in the restricted zone was that so many of the prey were homosexuals. More than once Cindy had cast her net thinking she could haul in a prize only to find that the man preferred other men. She did not understand since she could do anything a man could do and more, but she was forced to accept the situation. After all, she was in California, working between Hollywood and West Hollywood. It came with the territory.

Initially, there was no question of the tall blond with the accent being gay. He came in early one Tuesday and wanted a large cup of straight black coffee. He looked her straight in the eye and told her he needed to come into this neighborhood more often. Then he introduced himself as Jerry Kragon. Cindy's name was on her shirt. Cindy couldn't help but think about him the rest of the day. He may not have been a rich movie star but he had everything else a woman looked for in a man: tall, blond and muscular, with a foreign accent to lend some mystery. His simple attire was clean, name brands, obviously new and he carried himself with an unconscious air of self-confidence that spoke of breeding and money.

It was two days later the man returned to the coffee shop where Cindy worked and asked, "Hello darling, what say you let me pop for some tucker?"

Cindy managed to keep the sneering California girl attitude out of her voice when she asked what he was talking about.

"Dinner. I'd like to buy you some dinner. After work, of course."

She told him she would love to allow him to buy her some dinner, but that she got off at three and would not be ready for dinner until later. He countered with an offer to take her for some drinks before dinner. She refused, knowing that drinking without eating was a sure recipe for disaster.

"Well, where can I fetch you then?" he asked.

She gave him the address of another coffee shop, a block from her house and told him to be there at six. When she arrived at the designated shop, half past six, he was waiting comfortably in a tailored three-piece suit and black tie.

"I'm sorry I'm late. I was relieved late and needed to get home and get fixed up."

"You look darling, dear. And don't worry. It's the woman's prerogative. I'm parked around the corner, unless you want to eat here?"

"No, no. Let's go down to La Grande Chateau on Highland."

"Capital."

Around the corner was a Mercedes with a new car smell to it. Cindy knew it was a rental but she knew the cost of renting a car like that. She also knew the cost of a meal at La Grande Chateau, regardless of the fact that no prices were listed on the menu. The manager believed that if the diner must ask, the diner should eat elsewhere. In fact, the only reason Cindy and her new friend were seated was that a man had just called to cancel his reservations. Ordinarily dinner was by reservation only.

Cindy enjoyed an overpriced salad with fresh greens, artichokes and fruit. The man paying for the meal ate a steak with mushrooms and shallots and chased it down with a couple of bottles of Guinness Stout. Before the meal started he had told her he was an entrepreneur who was looking for opportunities in the area north of Los Angeles. She countered with questions about specifics; how far north was he looking, Palisades, Malibu or Oxnard? Maybe he was looking the other way, Hollywood, San Fernando or Santa Clarita? He was evasive about it, saying that he needed some help in determining where the best opportunities arose.

Cindy's sharp eye picked out that Jerry Kragon was thirty or thirty-five, ten or fifteen years older than she, but in no less fine physical condition. He was not the kind of thin that comes from starvation or disease but from exercise that built long whipcord muscles. His skin was tanned, but it was a different sort of tan from the beach bums of California, as if a dryer sun had seared him. It was not a detriment and went well with his sharp, piercing blue eyes and blond hair. If she looked close enough she could see small scars on his face, as if he had been in a lot of schoolyard fights and had lost often but not drastically. In all, he was a very handsome man and his looks coupled with his accent made him a very attractive catch, for the short run. She would need to see how well off he was before she looked at anything longer than a weekend romp.

From a man's perspective, Cindy looked delectable. She was dressed in a short skirt and a tight blouse that accentuated her breasts. Her high heels were black patent leather, open toes with two ankle straps and a three-inch spike heel, uncomfortable for her to walk in but the look was worth the trouble. She had a toe ring on one toe, and a large amethyst on one finger that matched her stud earrings. She had not been relieved late from work; she had spent the extra time working on her hair which was thrown up in a swirl over her head.

They had a few drinks after dinner and Cindy was surprised when he said good night without trying to get into her apartment. She was very careful not to sleep with anyone on the first date and seldom on the second. Cheap women were dismissed without consideration everywhere and she did not wish to be seen as a cheap woman.

Unfortunately for her, Cindy had little acting talent. This was unfortunate because she had the look; her naturally blonde hair framed a soft and articulate face, kind-looking eyes and a sensuous mouth shaped like the arch of a bridge. Jerry Kragon kissed her moist lips softly before he got into his rented Mercedes and drove off leaving her to her own devices.

Thinking for a second that he might be gay, she slipped her key into the lock and walked in on her roommate Shelly and a man Cindy did not know, unclothed on the couch.

"Shel, you're such a slut. You couldn't wait till you got him in bed? Go on. I need a real drink and I'm going to watch television."

"Sorry, Cin. I didn't expect you home at all."

"You know better than that. Take your five-dollar

foot-long upstairs and let me have a drink."

Once Shelly had gone, she poured herself a strong rum and cola and sat on the couch without turning the television on. What had happened? She was ready to fight off his advances and insist that he take her out at least once more before giving him what she knew all men wanted. Well, some men, she admitted to herself, given that she lived about five miles from West Hollywood. It had been years since a man had kissed her at the door and left. Maybe it was just because he was a foreigner. She had heard of how gentlemanly the British could be, but she had never heard the same of the Australians.

The fish did not know they would be called denizens of the Paleocene Epoch. They only knew what fish have always known, that the fast live and the slow die. They knew that the deeper water held enough draught for the larger predators and the warmer, shallower waters closer to the coast were not quite so dangerous. The genetic memory that constitutes instinct led some fish to spawn in the shallower, warmer water near the coastline. Some of these fish spawned in the warm and shallow inland sea that formed when the Pacific Plate was beginning to subduct under the North American Plate. At first the area was just a huge, shallow spawning ground fed by the rivers that cascaded out of the newly formed mountains to the east but after a while, the coastal ridge asserted itself and began to block it off from the ocean. For sixty million years the fluctuating sea level alternately flooded and marshified the land inside the protective barrier, changing the nature of the fish that made it their spawning grounds but never truly blocking it off from the sea. Life was beginning to assert itself again after the global extinction and the remaining species required a safe area to reproduce. The billions of fish that made their way to this area created a spawning and feeding frenzy. The marshlands made a magnificent refuge from the larger ocean-going predators though; as life reasserted itself on land, birds and mammals came to the area to partake of the bounty. Year after year, century after century, the inescapable circle of life played out as they young ate the old and the old ate the young and new species of fish and birds and amphibians evolved out of the furnace of the Pacific Rim.

The bones of the fish and the scat of the birds, the shells of the eggs and the skins of the crocodiles all floated to the bottom to become the digesting and fermenting soil at the bottom of the pool. For sixty million years the detritus of life formed itself into a rich salty soil at the bottom of this cleft in the earth, waiting for the next epoch of life.

The land continued to rise as the magnificent Rocky Mountains were pushed up from below. Earthquakes, eruptions, avalanches and volcanic explosions changed and formed the land. Life not only thrived, it erupted as well. Then came that age when the sea level began to drop along with the temperature. The land had raised itself to the level where the salt water no longer invaded over the coastal ridge and fresh water began to replace the salt water that had provided so many millions of generations with life. Some species adapted and swam into the brackish flow to the ancestral breeding grounds. Some species found alternate spawning fields. Those who could not adapt died off and their bodies contributed to the rich soil of the marshlands.

For two-and-a-half million years the fresh water poured off the mountains into what had been an inland sea and transformed it into a huge and magnificent lake that poured into the ocean below. The variety and volume of species was extraordinary, the massive lake veritably boiled with life. Then came the recent ice ages.

The water that had constantly and seemingly permanently rained down on the land and sea alike was being captured and solidified. The sun was not giving the planet all it needed to maintain a steamy Paleogene climate. The Indian plate had rammed into the Asian plate with enough force to thrust the mountains of Tibet twenty-five thousand feet into the air. The Earth's orbit was disrupted and the volcanoes vomited ash from the belly of the planet. Cooling and drying weather shrank the magnificent lake and then the super volcano on the far side of the mountain range erupted. Enough ash was thrust forth to cause the sun to dim and to blanket the North American continent in yards of ash. Death walked the land, once again reaping the glorious resurgent life that had been fulfilling its destiny and as the water froze, millions of tons of flowing glaciers ground into the bones of the planet.

When the glaciers once again relented in their implacable march to the equator, they left what men would call California's Central Valley. The southern section was to be known as the San Joaquin Valley and it was some of the best, most fertile land ever created. Many men had known this wonderful, ancient valley by many names. Congressman Henry Cabot knew it as California's 20th Congressional District. He also called it his Congressional District and was willing to do anything to keep that piece of paradise under his control. When he felt himself under attack he responded with all available resources.

Chapter Two
Love's Labour's Lost

"Colonel, I had a look at your proposal. It seems that the American Las Vegas is so heavily surveiled that they have you on film as you drive into the city."

"Ah, yes. Surveiled?"

"The whole place is one big gambling arena and a good part of the population is paid to watch the rest of the population. By the time I got to what I was looking for I would have been recorded for hours. I do not like having my face on film."

"I understand, Mr. Glasgow. You have a phobia about being recorded." It was difficult to pick up on the laughter in Colonel Richter's voice because of the German accent. Everything he said made him sound like he was a villain in a second-rate horror film.

"Aye, the days of simplicity have passed and it takes a special kind of entrepreneurial spirit to keep up with the times. Things have become so complicated that retirement looks better and better."

"Well, my friend, you and I both know that you will never retire until you end up as I, in a wheelchair or worse. I have a hard time believing you would ever feel fulfilled sitting in the park feeding the pigeons."

"I suppose it would depend on the park."

"You know you are right. I was in a park one time that I found particularly appealing. Of course it will never match the parks in the Fatherland, but I liked this one in my travels."

"Really, there were pigeons there that would pick up the crumbs?" It was not difficult to pick up the laughter in Gordon MacMaster's voice. He was obviously enjoying the clandestine wordplay with his old friend.

"Ya, I believe so. It was in Indianapolis, Indiana. It

was called, let me see… It was called University Park and it was situated between New York and Vermont Streets. A very appealing place. I liked it much. It is very near the Ivy Tech Community College so there is many young women in the park at all hours of the day. That has always made the most attractive of settings more appealing to me."

"Aye. And I suppose, being the young man you were at the time, there was a particular young bint you cast eye upon?"

"A bint? Yes there was a woman. I don't suppose she is still there. She worked as the librarian of the Ivy Tech. I believe her name was Carmilla Schiffer. Anyway, enough reminiscences. I did think to ask about your latest conquest. Was there any trouble getting north. Your affair with her was, shall we say, torrid? At least, from all accounts."

"The materials provided were of high quality and my new bride and I had no trouble taking a vacation to America."

"This is good. I am gratified that your travels were successful and I wish you good sailing, as they say."

"I was thinking of visiting once we return to the EU. Are you still on Wendigo?"

"Ya. I look forward to seeing you. We will drink schnapps, no?"

"Yes. I will give you a call when our vacation is concluded. Good day."

It was actually night in Germany but Colonel Richter did not make a point of it. He picked up the phone and began dialing another international call.

Gordon MacMaster hung up the pay phone in the restaurant and returned to his seat. He and his ersatz wife were at a table away from the door. The receptionist wanted to put them in a booth, but neither of them would sit with their back to the door, although they did not state this as a reason the seat was unacceptable. From the table they could both watch the door that faced Bee Line Drive in DuBois, Pennsylvania. Anastasia Viuda could see the back of the Cadillac in the parking lot and Gordon MacMaster could see the entrance to the parking lot. It was not that anyone knew them or why they were there but old habits die hard.

"We have a job."

"Oh. It is not the one in Las Vegas? I think that would be a very bad idea." Anastasia put the coffee cup down and licked her lower lip, making it shine.

"No. It is something different. We will need to go to Indiana. The city is Indianapolis and the place is the library of a community college. If we look at the job and do not like it, we walk away no questions asked."

"*Bueno.* Though I still think we could do better in, say, Colombia or Panama."

"No. I had enough of running through the jungle, fighting diseases. Besides, it will be a while before they stop looking for us down there. If we had consolidated some power while we had the reins, we might have been able to put something together but now, we would only be in the way. We would end up dead within days."

The waitress brought more coffee and they suspended their conversation as she put the bill on the table.

"Gordon my love, you underestimate me."

"Ah, I love the way you say my name; so sensual."

"*Que no.* We must move on. It was your plan that we go to… get to Cleveland today. Is that not what you wanted?"

"Plans can change. I look at your tight, beautiful body and your full, wet lips and all I can think about is…"

"I know what it is you think about and we will both be thinking much about that later today, but now we must drive that silly big thing you bought back to the highway."

"Anastasia, I thought you liked the Cadillac." Gordon pronounced every letter of her name, in Spanish style, rather than the Russian pronunciation.

"Oh, I do and I thought that everybody drove these big barges in America, but I see that it is a different thing now. We are sticking out like iguanas on a termite mound. I see all the people looking."

"They are admiring your dark Argentine beauty, my dear. They would still be staring if you were driving a bicycle. Well... even more on a bicycle."

"I still think we are being flashy without need."

"You are worrying too much, now. Would you like to drive for a while?"

"*Sí.* You are better with the map."

"Alright. It's a straight shot to Cleveland anyway. I'll probably just take a nap."

Once they were in the car and Gordon was settling back and feeling sleepy he felt compelled to tell Anastasia, "Remember, you can't shoot the police just because they pull you over."

"Ah, you are so silly. I would not shoot the police," she replied and then, with a smile and a whisper, "It is too noisy on the main roads. I would take them off into the woods and cut their throats."

"Just keep your speed down and there will be no problems, okay?" The twinkle in his eye belied his gruff tone.

"G'day mate. You doing any heavy lifting of your own these days?"

"I'll be damned. I haven't heard from you in, what... two years?"

"'Bout a year and a half I guess. You still up there in frozen country?"

"Yeah."

"No problem with the last job?" Terry Kingston had not been sure his contact in Michigan would recognize his voice though he was pretty sure there were no other assassins in America with Australian accents.

"I'll say not. Everything turned to shit in this town though. GM pulled out, shut the plants down and bulldozed 'em. The whole state is sinking into its own asshole. We got the Democratic President they all voted for but it didn't give them what they wanted. Anyway, I'm sorry to say that I don't have any work in this town."

"Well, I wasn't fond of Flint when I was there. I thought we might have something on the West Coast I could pick up."

"Oh. Well, I can make some calls. I might be able to pick you up something. I get a finder's fee though. From you. Before I make any introductions. The same as before."

"Well, mate, that's not the same as before. The company paid you last time."

"True but that one was on my home turf. This is an outside job so you ship me the money and I will get you a contact."

"Ah... no deal. Given the quality of the last job, I would think you had more respect. If you want a professional job done, hire a professional."

"I'll make some inquiries. It will take longer and there are no guarantees, but I might have something."

"I'll call back in a week." Terry hung up the phone and almost unconsciously, wiped down the receiver with a bandanna which he returned to his back pocket. He did not need the money, but inactivity was boring for him. He smiled slightly as he thought back on some of the things he had done in the past. Things that could bring in some cash. He wondered if he still had the finesse he had acquired while he was younger.

The spring foliage was in full bloom in Indianapolis. It was that lovely time of year where the air conditioning had not been turned on but the heat had been off for a couple of weeks. Classes were in full swing and the students were either acclimating themselves to society or returning to school after the recent economic disasters in the manufacturing sector.

One could never accuse Carmilla Schiffer of being a clothes horse. This surprised no one since the salary of a librarian at a community college was nothing to boast of. She dressed in sensible clothing that might not have been out of place in the mid 1940s. It made her look like the stereotypical spinster and did nothing to outline her highly toned body, rather it hid the unexpected.

The exercise room at Ivy Tech Community College was under-served and underutilized and as such almost worthless to the students and staff. Carmilla used a health club instead, where she taught aerobics on the weekends in exchange for free range of the facilities. While she did not make much of a living, Carmilla had inherited her parents' home and had no automobile. She had no need or desire for spiritual fulfillment from a church or mosque and seldom contributed to charities.

The chance meeting in an airport lounge had introduced Carmilla to a man who gave her the opportunity to make a few dollars extra on the side without putting forth any more than a normal effort at work. The scheme seemed too good to be true but it had been a much needed if sporadic boost to her income. The Ivy Tech Community College received shipments of books from a variety of sources, often they were not new books. Except for the technical books and manuals, the works that arrived came frequently from other libraries, sometimes collections or bookstores that went out of business. It was not unusual to get a book in the U.S. Mail addressed directly to Carmilla Schiffer and these books went directly in her desk drawer without being opened. When a man or woman arrived at the library and asked for the latest printing of whatever book had recently arrived, she would deliver that package and the next arrival would be more liquid in nature. Cash delivered by overnight mail. The one thing that this system demanded, aside from not getting curious, was that Carmilla be at work on time every day. She didn't find it necessary to have a car for the parking space reserved in her name. On good days she walked and she took the bus when it rained or snowed.

It was a Wednesday in the spring and Carmilla was half torn between getting a workout and going to a bar to find a man for the evening. Regardless of which she decided on, she would not be leaving until five o'clock and she would be going home for a quick dinner first. If she decided on the workout, and that looked more and more likely, she would put on a riding suit and ride her bicycle to the gym. If sex won out, she would put on the tight-fitting red dress and high heels then call a cab.

There had never been serious thoughts in Carmilla's mind about sleeping with other women, but the tall Hispanic woman that strode into the library that day could have seduced her. The visitor was almost six-foot tall and her high heels made her well over that. Black hair barely reached her strong neck, focusing the observer on her wide eyes, straight nose and self-assured movements. Her dark stockings ran up her long thin legs and disappeared into the short black skirt that covered her posterior tightly. Her large chest pushed at the sweater covering it as though yearning to be free. There was something about this woman that made Carmilla think of sex, hot, sweaty, multi-orgasmic sex.

"I'm looking for <u>Love's Labour's Lost</u>," the woman breathed.

Carmilla actually shook her head to get her mind off the subject and back on track. "I'm sorry, you'll find that in the Shakespeare section, aisle 4."

"I think I need the latest printing of this book."

"Actually, dear, it's a play."

The temptress smiled like a tigress, showing a mouth full of even white teeth rimmed by full lips, painted red. "Of course it is. A play. Do you have the latest printing?"

"Why yes, I believe I just got one in." Out came her keys and she unlocked the drawer. It would have seemed unusual for her to have handed the book to a visitor without opening it, so she did take the book out of the package before handing it to the woman.

"Yes, I think this is the one. Thank you."

"You have a beautiful accent. May I ask where you're from?"

"No," she breathed, "you may not. Knowledge can be power but there are some things you do not want to know. I am one of them."

Carmilla watched as the mysterious woman stalked out the door of the library. She thought, "That woman will make some man very happy or incredibly miserable."

In the diner down the street, Gordon MacMaster was having a cup of coffee and reading the local newspaper, the Indianapolis Star. It told of more shootings across the country. People who were law-abiding citizens one day and mass murderers the next. There was a school shooting in Boise, Iowa, a postal employee killed a family in Arizona, and a police officer went to town on a street gang in Los Angeles. The latter was the most interesting story since the officer's daughter had been raped by one of the gang members. It made Gordon think about Terry Kingston, the Australian who had become his closest confidant. They had played a revenge game in Sydney that had brought the two of them together. They had recently left South America after some action there but the Australian had chosen the West Coast. Gordon MacMaster and Anastasia Viuda had flown into Newark, New Jersey.

Gordon wondered briefly if the officer would have reconsidered his rampage if he had been given a viable option. It did not matter now, the officer was dead and the department had listed it as lost in the line of duty. He was on duty when he gunned down the fourteen gang members, killing six of them. There was nothing to be done about it now.

The short order cook licked his lips when the door opened. He was a skinny man without much of an appetite, but he could have generated some hunger for the tall black-haired woman who strode in on her high heels. He went back to the grill when she sat down with the huge redhead man. The cook would have fancied a toss with her but he knew when he was outclassed.

"This is the latest printing of <u>Love's Labour's Lost</u>. I guess it is a comedy."

"And you think it would be more appropriate if we used a tragedy?" Gordon signaled the waitress for more coffee and some for his companion.

"Oh, I think it will turn out a tragedy for someone."

Gordon used his best fake southwestern accent when addressing the waitress, in truth not really very convincing. "Dear, could you bring us a couple of Denver omelets, rye toast and some orange marmalade."

"We don't have any marmalade, just jelly," she replied.

"All right then, just put some butter on the toast and leave it as that." The waitress went away and Gordon flipped through the book to be sure the added material was present. He did not take it out but told Anastasia to put it in her purse.

After breakfast, the couple drove to a department store. The object was to get some clothing that did not reveal their bodies so much. Gordon was the more difficult of the two to fit. Since he was six-foot four and bulged with muscle, the local Whale Mart had little that would fit him. Anastasia had better luck in the exercise department and managed to cover her curves by dressing in a sweatshirt and running pants. She tried several pairs of sneakers before deciding that they had nothing she could be comfortable wearing. Gordon laughed and asked if the stiletto heels were comfortable. She smiled and said that she did not wear them for herself.

MacMaster bought a hat and a pair of sunglasses at the Whale Mart and they drove to the nearest mall. The oversize store had a much better selection. Gordon bought three charcoal gray suits and a cream colored one, then inquired about the location of the nearest tailor. He had been on vacation in Brazil so none of his more formal attire had been with him. If it had, it would have remained in Brazil anyway. He also bought a set of exercise clothes that blended with Anastasia's. She bought some sneakers that fit her and a set of guitar strings.

The internet terminal at the county library gave Anastasia access to maps of Kansas City at the intersection of Interstates 70 and 35. The city also straddled the confluence of the Missouri and Kansas Rivers and held prominence in both the State of Kansas and the State of Missouri. She could not understand why the Capital of Kansas was Topeka, not Kansas City. The satellite views fascinated her and with a little practice she was able to zero in on a particular business or residence. She did not request that the program go to the target for fear that someone could back trace it but it was easy enough to go to an address down the street and move over from there. The program did not track in real time, so there was no way of really spying that way but the views did give a good idea of the terrain, the distances involved and the foliage around the target.

While Anastasia was taking care of directions and potential routs of ingress and egress, Gordon was making a phone call from the pay phone in the foyer. The number, address and instructions had been slid between the pages of the book. After confirming there was no trouble or change of plans, he hung up the receiver, surveyed the library's parking lot, the road and what he could see of the interior. He could see no unusual or out of place individuals. He knew he was being too careful and that there should be no one interested in him yet. He shrugged it off as an occupational habit.

Inside, Anastasia was paying for printouts of some maps and turn by turn directions to a Whale Mart in Kansas City. Once they were back in the car, she revealed that Kansas City was about 750 kilometers from Indianapolis, around 465 miles. Then she asked, "Why do they insist on using the old method of calculating distances. The entire world understands that kilometers make more sense. Yes?"

"Yes, perhaps, but they are working on it slowly and only when they need to. They have gone to liters from quarts and gallons because the rest of the world already packaged in the metric uh, packages. Bottles and cans and the like. But, look at the number of signs on the road in America. It isn't like any other country in the world. It's virtually impossible to get lost."

"So there are a lot of signs. So what? It would not take that much to change the ones with distances on them."

"Oh, my love, I think it is more complicated than that. You see the numbers of the exits depend on how far they are from the beginning of that road. In miles. They would need to rename all the exits as well. Until all the signs were changed and the system, you know the maps and the address programs and all, until they all got in line and revised, everything would be complete chaos."

"Ah. I see some of it now. Is everything set with the... how you say, ordnance?"

"Yes, dear, we will be outfitted. I do not know the man involved but he comes recommended. After all, this is America. You can get anything you want here if you have the funds to pay for it." Gordon's words proved prophetic. Twenty-five miles outside of Indianapolis, on a straight shot down State Road 40 was the Hamlet of Stilesville, surrounded by farmers' fields. It was just over five miles from the interstate so it was just out of range for any stopover traffic from there.

Stilesville had a used furniture store that did not seem like much of a place until a customer got inside. The store was deeper than it looked, with four subsequent additions to it. The front held beds and sofas, the middle section had tables and chairs and the like. The third partition hid office furniture and filing cabinets, though it did not look as though there would be a large market for it in this town. The last addition was the smallest but the most valuable to its newest customers. This room was filled with military equipment.

Gordon introduced himself to the aged proprietor of the shop as Glasgow. The man received him well enough but looked askance at his partner. He took Gordon aside and asked if he was sure the woman was trustworthy. Even after Gordon assured him of Anastasia's qualifications, the man was reluctant to allow her past the front rooms. It was only after Gordon's insistence that he allowed the two of them to pass into the office furniture section.

The old man was undoubtedly good at one point in his life but he no longer had the speed or flexibility of a young man. He moved to the side a little too much and a little too slowly so that when he tried to spin around with the silenced 9mm in his hand, his guests were ready. Anastasia's foot came up and hit his forearm to drive his hand up. Before he could bring it back down, Gordon had his wrist. There was no question about holding on to the weapon after that; MacMaster would have broken his trigger finger.

The old man dropped the pistol; Anastasia caught it on the way down. She had the clip dropped, the chamber emptied and the slide pulled in a heartbeat. She set the pieces on a filing cabinet.

Gordon dropped his fake accent and growled in a

genuine Scottish brogue. "Now, why on Earth would you be wanting to do that? I am a legitimate customer who comes to you with not only the proper references but with a wad of bills that barely fits in me pocket. I came as a legitimate customer and you decide it's time to shoot me? Ye'll not get much repeat business that way."

"All right, you got me. The guns are in the back."

"Lead the way."

"You're not going to handcuff me?"

"Who is it exactly that you think I am?"

"I figure, you come in here with a woman in tow, you must be BATFE or FBI."

"Should I kill him, love?" Anastasia asked.

"No, I don't think so. It was a simple misunderstanding. Right?"

"Uh, right," the old man replied, looking at his female customer with a different set of eyes. Women in Stilesville did not casually speak of murder. Nobody had been killed in Stilesville since the 1800s.

The back room had no windows and was secured with a steel bar set into a steel frame. Inside were shotguns and rifles along with quantities of ammunition. The really interesting equipment was held inside a secondary enclosure welded together out of plate steel. As tall as a man and about eight feet wide it held Semtex, C-4, hand grenades, detonators, blasting caps and rocket propelled grenades, though there was no launcher.

"How old is the Semtex?" Gordon asked.

"That comes from before the 1991 addition of the taggant. They can't detect that stuff very well."

"But it is still over twenty years old. That makes it unreliable."

"It's still in the original plastic. Look at it, a nice rich orange color. If it was unreliable it wouldn't have that nice color to it; it would look bleached out. If you like the C-4 better, it's not quite as old."

Gordon was browsing through the explosives but Anastasia could not relax. She knew for a certainty that as soon as the old man had a second to spare he would find a way to kill them both and worry about the bodies later. She considered that he was probably senile and it would have made her relax considerably if MacMaster would simply allow her to kill him. She would not terminate the man without her lover's approval however. They had a tumultuous and vibrant relationship and each knew that there was a fine line that the other would not stand to see breached. Physically, there was nothing the nameless man could do but it was clear he had been in the business a long time, and he probably had a few more tricks up his sleeve.

A pound of C-4 and one of Semtex, detonators and timers, some smoke bombs and a remote trigger all went into a dusty box along with a thousand rounds of ammunition, two Smith and Wesson .357 Magnum revolvers and a compact Taurus .380. Then he watched the manager while Anastasia looked around. She chose a Ruger P94 chambered for .40 caliber S&W rounds and 400 hollow points. She found a couple of extra clips to go with the Ruger and then selected a Beretta 21 Bobcat with a couple of hundred-round boxes of .22 caliber long rifle rounds for it.

The shop owner smirked when he saw her choice but he said nothing. He had been in the business for many years, much of it legitimately. Now he just wanted to get rid of his inventory without the trouble associated with the government.

Lastly, Anastasia grabbed two Mossberg 88s and half a case of 3-inch buckshot before seeing the Serbu Super Shorty. The grin on her face was unmistakable. The Serbu would only hold three 12-gauge rounds but it had a six and a half inch barrel and a pistol grip. At sixteen and a half inches total length, she could strap it to her leg under a long dress as long as she did not have to walk too far. She licked her lips in appreciation, grabbed the one she saw and hunted for another.

"That one ain't legal in most places, you know."

"Neither is Semtex," she replied. "Have you another?"

"No. Sorry. That's the only one. I got a couple of pistol grips for the Mossbergs though. You know they hold eight rounds. It looks like your going to outfit an army so you might want the increased capacity. If it's concealment your after, swap them out for the 500 and saw the barrel off. You'll only get five shots but it'll be that much shorter if that's what you want them for."

"It is not your concern why we want the firepower. I would think you should be thanking the saints that you are still alive. However, if my man tells me I can kill you I will make it quick and painless."

Gordon almost cracked a smile. After some negotiation, they paid for the supplies with cash and loaded most of them into the trunk of the Cadillac. They both felt safer now that they were armed.

Chapter Three
Kansas City

"So, this guy kissed you at the door and left? How friggin' gay!"

"Shelly! Just because you would have pulled him in the door by his dick doesn't mean I will. Besides, it's nice to be respected for once. You know, the old fashioned values."

"He's gay and doesn't want anyone to know it. That's what it is. Come on, a hot, young, Australian man takes you to dinner in a fine restaurant and then kisses you on the cheek at the door?"

"No, well, he kissed me on the lips. I thought it was romantic. A lot more romantic than what you had on your lips when I came in." She tried to look morally superior for a moment and then asked, "How was he anyway?"

"He's got a stud in his tongue and he doesn't mind using it. Hey, you gonna see the guy again?"

"Jerry? I don't know. If he asks, I'll go out with him. I like him, he's nice. I don't know. He didn't show up for a coffee today. I don't think he liked me all that much."

"What's not to like? You're a thin blonde with big tits, even if they are fake. You should have grabbed him by the balls and hauled him in."

"Well, he'll call if he's interested."

Jerry Kragon did call the next afternoon, Saturday. He asked Cindy if she would like to see a movie. She accepted and they went to a rather early showing of a romance. This was as much a surprise to Cindy as the kiss at the door. She began to suspect that Shelly was right. Dinner afterward went well as he relayed humorous tales of shark fishing.

Before the night was over, Cindy got suspicious as to the real reason Jerry was courting her. He asked if her boss owned the whole block of businesses or just the one she worked in. She confronted him with her idea and he laughed.

He explained that all he needed to do to get that kind of information was to go to the Hall of Records and ask. He explained that he was making small talk about what he knew of the area and that he didn't know much. While he had her a little off balance he asked if she opened up in the morning or if the manager was there. It was to let her know he was interested in what she did, not just what he did. He already knew she opened up in the morning.

After dinner they had some drinks in a mid-level nightclub. It was not the sort of place that had a line to get in but it was upscale. She discovered that he was a very good dancer and after rubbing her posterior against him, she discovered that he was not gay. That relieved her a great deal since she was sick of men who wanted to be friends. They made a date for the following night as he drove her home. At the door that night, he kissed her again but did not leave as readily as he had the night before. She told him good night and slipped inside.

Sunday night would ordinarily have been an early night but Jerry insisted they go drinking and dancing. He promised he would make sure she made it to the coffee shop for opening time. It was some time after the fifth drink that Cindy started feeling queasy. There was no thought that she had been drugged, her date was too much of a gentleman for that. She told him she was feeling ill and that she wanted to go home. Before they got to her apartment she was unconscious. He picked her up, along with her purse, and carried her to the stoop where he kicked the door to announce his presence. Shelly answered the door and wanted to know what happened. Jerry explained as he got her into bed that she had one too many and took a header. He caught her on the way down and brought her home. Shelly commented on the fact that he did not look very drunk and he assured her that he did not drink much when he was planning on driving. After turning down her offer to have a drink there, Jerry left.

Shelly decided that if Cindy was going to act stupid about it, then Jerry would be Shelly's in no time. Not to have and to hold till death do us part, but for a weekend, anyway.

"Well, if you don't know who the fuck they are, then how the fuck are we supposed to know?" The man was wearing a very expensive suit but his speech denied any education.

"That will be arranged." Frank Hicks was looking comfortable and at home despite the fact that the entire group of men in his office were armed.

"So what are we supposed to do until it's arranged, go to Disney World?"

"Disney World is in Florida, Disney Land is in California."

"What the fuck do I care? Do I look like I'm going there? What the fuck?"

"Relax, Rocco. I got reservations for the bunch of you at a place on Sunset Boulevard. You'll love it. I got women lined up in your hotel rooms, you can take 'em to dinner if you want. They'll be there when you get there. Okay? Just relax for Christ's sake and wait for the word. You'll get the location in two days and then you can earn your money and go back to New York with pride."

"I already got pride. Come on boys. Let's go see what the hotel rooms look like."

Frank Hicks picked up the telephone once his less than civil guests had left and called the offices of Henry Cabot to let George Arridagio know that the team had arrived and would be ready for the drop.

This was the first time that Jacqueline had worked with Jerry Kragon. She admitted to herself that she liked the man's style. She did not like the fact that there had been witnesses that could identify him and, by extension, might lead to her. If she had been running the operation she would have made sure that Cindy was found in bed with Bruce Babbage. That would have tied things up a lot nicer for her. Upon reflection she decided that it was not so much Jerry's working style that she liked as his personality.

Jacqueline had never worked with the man who had dropped off the money and commissioned the job either. She suspected he was nothing but a courier for someone who wanted to remain nameless. If she had known that Congressman Cabot was behind this operation she might have asked for a larger finder's fee.

Though it was not the first time Jacqueline had orchestrated a killing, she was never all that comfortable with meeting the killers. Jerry was smooth and charming but after he had the money in hand, Jacqueline might become superfluous. Ending up a victim did not fit with her long-term plans.

Jerry Kragon entered the diner and glanced around. Finding Jacqueline sitting in a booth, he joined her. There was a little strained conversation, Jerry ordered a cup of coffee that he did not drink, threw a couple of dollar bills on the table and walked out with the manila envelope full of cash.

The house was not unusual except that it was a quarter mile back in a set of woods in the largely deserted triangle formed by Interstate 70 to the north and train yards to the south. It was not visible from the road and was a square, two-story wooden building, sixty or eighty years old. Gordon did not look happy upon inspection. Anastasia ventured the opinion that the man was an idiot.

Half a mile away sat a trucking concern with a parking lot, half full of the employees' cars. The trailers were docked on the far side of the building. Gordon dropped Anastasia off near the driveway heading in and parked the car in the parking lot. The operation would have been more difficult if the leaves were not in bloom. The cover would be spare after the leaves fell in the fall and almost nonexistent in the winter. As it was, Anastasia walked through the damp leaf clutter without a sound and slipped right up to the tree line near the side of the house without encountering any resistance. It would have been a misnomer to call the plot of ground around the building a lawn but it was an area free of trees. A couple of sheds sat on the east side of the house, the kitchen was to the south and the driveway to the north. She noted the railroad tie barrier that had been erected across the driveway, WWII style.

There was a man with a shotgun on the front porch watching the driveway. Every ten minutes or so a man would walk around the house, not the same man every time and not in the same direction, but it did not take long to time the rotation. After an hour the sun went down and Anastasia slipped around to the back of the house. The back door was where the men walking their rounds came from. She assumed it was the kitchen and was proven right when she climbed a few feet into a tree and looked through the window. Two scruffy-looking men were in the kitchen, playing cards at the table. Two more came in and set their shotguns down in the corner. Ten minutes later two of them got up, took the shotguns in hand and made their rounds.

The wind began to get chilly after the sun went down and Anastasia was grateful that Gordon insisted she wear a coat. It was more to conceal the holstered pistol under her arm than to keep her warm but she appreciated it more as night descended. It was not quite dark when she heard someone approaching from behind and move away. She had assumed it was Gordon and she was right. He had been involved with making the car inconspicuous and had been required to move it more than once. It had ended up behind a deserted house off the west side of South 68th Street. The two of them moved far enough away to confer and make a plan of attack.

The worst time of night for a guard has to be between three-thirty and four-thirty in the morning. Consequently, it is the best time for an attack. It takes training and a certain temperament to sit quietly until that time of the morning, without falling asleep or being stirred to action. MacMaster was better at the waiting game than Viuda; while he sat quietly, she was fabricating something with rope and rocks. She would have sprung earlier than he, though she may have had the same results.

At ten-thirty, two of the men in the kitchen went upstairs, presumably to go to bed. The lights came on in two rooms and then went off again. From then on only one man made the rounds while one sat in the kitchen and the rotation was more like every fifteen minutes. While the front of the house was being watched by the man on the porch, and the back of the house had two men in the kitchen, there was no one watching the sides.

Anastasia grinned and whispered in her man's ear that it was too easy and asked if he wanted her to show him how it was done. He replied no, that he had some sympathy for the guards and that she did not.

The man left the back door with a shotgun and a flashlight and walked around to the side of the building. If his finger had been on the trigger, it would have most likely ignited a round and served as a warning, but it was not. He was struck in the midriff by a thick branch as he rounded the corner of the house. His feet came up and he landed heavily on his back. In the blink of an eye he had the crotch of another branch shoved under his chin, pinning his neck to the ground. His mouth was stuffed with a bit of rag and then was covered with duct tape. One second later he was flipped over and trussed like a Christmas goose. The large man that had come out of the darkness growled in his ear that the consequence of noise was death.

The man on the porch was expecting a man with a flashlight to come around the corner about the time he did. He did not expect the flashlight to be pointed in his face and he raised his left hand to try to keep the light from temporarily blinding him. It did not work. Before he could make out that it was not the man he expected, someone had joined him on the porch, and stuck the point of a knife next to his Adam's apple. He got the same message about not sounding a warning as he was being bound and gagged.

The man in the kitchen could not make out that it was not one of his partners when he heard, "Hey, get a look at this." When he stepped out, shotgun in hand, all he saw was the back of a man moving around the house so he descended the three steps to the ground. He never saw what hit him. It wrapped around his neck in a spinning motion and smashed into his face. The rope of the bolos closed around his face and prevented him from yelling. The stones all but knocked him out. Before he could remove the offending weapon he had two people tying his arms and legs. The rope was so effective that he would have been choked to death if his attackers had not removed it.

The rest of the assault was easy. The two bedrooms had been noted and the guards awakened to shotguns in their faces. They were neutralized without a sound except to identify which of the other four bedrooms the final target was in.

"Cindy, wake up girl. You're going to be late for work."

"Ah, shit, what time is it?"

"Five-thirty. If you get going right now you can get there in time to open."

"Fuck. What happened last night? I remember having

a couple of drinks and then, nothing. Did he bring me home?"

"He carried you through the door and tucked you into bed. You were so drunk you were passed out cold."

"I never drink that much. You know that. I don't even remember what happened."

"So you probably gave it up and don't even know it. What a shame."

"Oh, shit. Go away. I mean, help me get my shit together. Oh, God, I feel so sick."

"Maybe you should call the boss and tell him you can't make it in."

"No. He'll fire me if I do that. Help me do up my hair. I'll do my makeup when I get there. Where's my cell phone? Okay, I got everything." On her way out the door she found her keys on the walkway. She cursed again, picked them up and headed for work.

It did not surprise Cindy that Jerry Kragon did not call her again. After all, she thought he had some modicum of class and she had undoubtedly acted like some kind of drunken slut. She tried hard to remember what had happened but there was no memory. The days went by one at a time, and it was about ten days before she first smelled the foul odor that seemed to be coming from upstairs.

"You're dead boy. All your guards are dead and so are you."

The man in the bed awoke when Gordon turned on the light. As soon as he saw it was not one of his guards, he had started scurrying backward as if he could push himself through the head of the bed and out through the wall behind it.

"Relax, Homer. If I had been your enemy you would never have opened your eyes."

"Holy shit! Who are you?"

34

"You can call me Glasgow but my name is of little importance. What is of major importance is that you do what I say and when I say it. I have been contracted to protect you against some unsavory elements that would like to see you dead. Are we in agreement?"

"Uh, yes. I have some…"

"I do not care who and I do not care why. What I do care about is you had a pack of idiots guarding you."

"You mean you…?"

"No. I did not kill them although it would have been less trouble than squashing a mosquito. I don't know where you got these men. I'm going to need to send them back there."

"I was told they were professionals."

"Whoever told you that, lied. I would not trust these men to guard my dog house."

"Well, who… uh, what are you going to do?"

"I would think the first thing to do would be to get you out of this death trap. An old wooden structure like this would burn in minutes. You would never make it out alive."

Anastasia stepped through the door with the Serbu in one hand. "We seem to be clear," she said surveying the room. "You, sir, are a lucky man. You have someone who cares about you. If we had gotten the call from the other parties in this thing, you would not see the dawn."

"Yeah, I got that. So where are the guards?"

"Get dressed and I will show you."

Once he had pulled on his pants and a shirt, Homer Sullivan laced up a pair of logging boots and followed his new guests to the other upstairs bedrooms where two men were bound to the bed and gagged. Outside, three more men were in similar circumstances in various locations.

"So how many men did you bring with you?"

"You are looking at it," the redhead replied.

"What? One man and one woman came in here and…

and not killing them, tied up all five guards?" He turned to the trussed men. "You assholes call yourselves professional? A good dog and a Tennessee teenager could have done a better job than this. You're fired. Get the fuck out of here." His statement was incongruous because, until they were untied, nobody was going anywhere.

The three walked back into the house together and Gordon released the two men upstairs. They were angry but unarmed as well as unclothed. They were allowed to go outside to release the other members of their team. Ten minutes later the spokesman for the team came back through the back door, trying his best to ignore the twelve-gauge shotgun pointing at him from the table top.

"We want to get paid. We want a week's pay," he said.

"You want what? You'd be better off getting the hell off this property right now before I shoot you myself." Homer was clearly upset.

"Now, hang on a moment. I say it would be best to pay these men for their three days," Gordon interjected. "There are appearances to be maintained. They did what they could; they simply did not have the level of expertise required. You will be paying me more than you pay them, but you will not refuse them their pay."

"Who do you think you are coming in here and telling me what I'm going to do?" Homer asked.

Gordon's demeanor became deadly serious. "I'm the man who prevented my Valkyrie wife from killing all five of these men. I suggest you do as I say or the men will all walk out of here and I'll leave you here with her."

There was no doubt in Homer's mind that the tall, silent, black-haired woman would do whatever the redhead asked. He looked between the two of them, gauging the situation and weighing his options. He did not seem to have many.

"All right. I'll give you the three day's pay."

The fallen guard did not look happy.

"And I promise not to tell anyone about the circumstances of your release. Your reputation will be secure. I haven't got the cash here. You'll need to come back for it." Homer finished.

"If we can't have the cash then we can't leave."

Gordon stood up and stuck out his chest. "Look friend, I got you your money but I think your pushing it too far now. I think you had best take your leave and return with the dawn. My word is my bond and I swear you will get what is owed to you. I don't think you want the story of your night to be spread all over town, would you? Ah, I thought not. Return when the banks are open and you will be recompensed. Return before that and you will be decommissioned. You will return alone or you will be decommissioned. You will return unarmed, as a show of faith."

Gordon and Anastasia followed the leader out of the house. The pair was armed to the teeth. They spent the next few hours in the woods around the house, never returning to the interior until the leader of the mercenary guards showed up at nine-fifteen.

Chapter Four
New Moon

First it had been the County Health Inspector responding to a complaint of unsanitary conditions at the coffee shop. The shop was clean and orderly. There was no explanation to be found for the stench that permeated the air. Cindy had already called the owner on it but nothing had been done as of yet. The police were the next to arrive.

"No, officer, I don't have a key for the downstairs door. Yes, it does lead to the back stairs."

"So, this guy locks the downstairs door and the upstairs door?"

"Oh, he's a total freak. He never comes down the stairs. He has his food delivered to the back door, newspapers, I never see him. I can't say for sure that he locks the upstairs door but he can."

"Does he ever have company?"

"I've seen a woman come out of there in the morning a couple of times. She looked trashy. I mean she was pretty and all but she was dressed like a hooker."

"And aside from that?"

"No. We can't see his back door unless we're out back, you know, taking out the trash. I can hear footsteps on the stairs if I'm in the back room but they usually go down and then back up. I almost never see him and I don't even remember what he looks like but he's costing us business with whatever he has up there making that stink."

"And this has been going on for..."

"It started a week ago and it's getting worse."

The officer and his partner knocked on the back door but got no response. Cindy had called the owner when the Health Inspector had arrived that morning. She called again when the police arrived. At that point he was only a couple of blocks away. He got there before they forced the door and presented the officers with a key, but the deadbolt had been changed and the key did not fit. Next they tried the padlock on the inside of the business. Oddly enough, that had been changed as well. The only way that could have been done was from the back room of the coffee shop. Cindy volunteered to go a couple of doors down the street and buy some bolt cutters and they gained access to the hallway that way.

The smell was apparent in the hallway and the officers opened the outside door. They took the keys and shooed the owner and employee back into the downstairs establishment. They recognized the smell even if the others didn't. It was the smell of decomposing flesh.

The drop had been set for the middle of the day, at a sidewalk restaurant off Oceanfront Boulevard, near Venice Beach. The weather was typical Southern California warm and dry and the regulars were out on the beach. The men waiting were unshaven and looked like flotsam among the sea of tanned, almost nude flesh. There were three of them, dressed in shorts and beach shirts and drinking domestic beer. They sat at a formed wire table under the awning. All three had sunglasses on and at least two of them were armed.

George had suggested a leather fanny pack but that had been vetoed by the professionals from New York. They insisted that the money be delivered in a briefcase and that the denominations be small enough that the money made a significant bundle. They were not trying to make things convenient for the extortionists. In an unexpected gesture of largesse, Frank Hicks had provided the cash for the transfer. He gave the justification that it would keep Congressman Cabot out of the loop and help maintain his unimpeachable reputation.

George approached the table with none of his usual swagger. He was wearing a casual tan suit without a tie and carrying the deep brown leather briefcase. He paused for a second and one of the men motioned him over. He sat on the edge of the fourth formed wire chair and set the case on the table.

The men insisted that George crack open the case, to make sure there was no bomb inside. There was not. They turned it around and looked inside, charmed by the used, low value bills. They turned over the disk as promised and assured George they would never be in touch with him again. Then they asked that he remain where he was until they were well out of the neighborhood. George had no thought of following them, that was someone else's job. He sat right where he was and ordered a Greek omelet, some orange juice and an English muffin. He tipped well when he left and made sure the waiter noted the time by looking at his watch and exclaiming, "Twelve-thirty! I'm going to be late!" It was crude but effective.

The three men returned to their upstairs studio with stupid grins on their faces. The upstairs studio was used for pornography on a regular, if not daily basis. The sign on the door read New Moon Productions. The downstairs apartment was living space. They had other apartments set up around the area for prostitutes who did not know they were being filmed. Most of that footage was scrapped as being useless but every once in a while they got a movie star or politician in the room and then the fun started. They squeezed and squeezed until the subject was unwilling to pay any more and then they simply stopped. Once they started the squeeze, the apartments were abandoned. The arrangement worked for the most part though they became good at relocating their talent. Sometimes they were forced to relocate them to Death Valley.

Looking through the peephole revealed a lovely, tanned woman, looking a bit nervous. The pornography industry had blossomed so much, with the advent of the internet that women often showed up uninvited to make a little money. It was not that unusual any more.

Once the door opened, however, nothing was business as usual. Five men in business suits and carrying weapons invaded the studio. The men inside did not stand a chance even though they were armed as well. The last gangster in flipped the woman a hundred-dollar bill and she slipped away with a smile.

"All right, you slimy little pieces of shit, come up with the tapes, all of them. Everything you have, if you want to survive."

One man picked up the briefcase full of cash while another threw a canvas rucksack on the table. The studio had a vast collection of disks; they ran a distribution company from that location as well. The rucksack barely contained everything they stuffed in it.

"Is that all of it?" The speaker was obviously in charge of the operation.

"Yeah. That's all we have. You're running us out of fucking business."

"I think you're lying."

"No. That's all of it."

The spokesman and leader did not ask again. He pulled out a silenced .40 caliber pistol from under his arm and shot the other man in the head three times. "That is what happens when I think someone is lying to me. I really don't like liars and I hope I don't need to do that to anyone else."

The other two men would have given up their sainted grandmothers if they had been hiding them. They hunted around and came up with a few more disks, unlabelled stuff, undoubtedly surreptitious recordings. They also pulled out some old style tapes from a dusty box in the closet. They were doing anything they could to be compliant. It did them no good. Once the New York gangsters were convinced they had everything they were going to get, they executed the pornographers and left them lying in pools of their own blood and brains.

Frank Hicks offered the opinion, "That sure was an expensive piece of ass. It's no wonder the State of California is bankrupt."

His East Coast associates had been well compensated and returned to their usual haunts. The pornography was the usual stuff for the most part; professional women and men with oversized equipment in revealing positions but the quality was not all that good. There was quite a bit of stuff that did not look anywhere near that commercial. Some of it was obviously clandestine recordings. That was the truly interesting stuff. Frank was careful to find an extra copy of Congressman Cabot's recording and send it to his office. With the note, *You owe me a favor.* He was not going to squeeze the congressman for money; he knew that the connection was worth more than any cash payoff. Some of the other inadvertent porn stars would not be so lucky.

Sean Warren had made his fortune on his talent because he was certainly no poster child. He had been losing his hair since he was thirty-two or so and had shaved it all off five years later. He had started in television and graduated to movies, becoming an action star and a valuable, bankable commodity. By the time he was fifty he could have retired in luxury for several lifetimes, but he was in good shape and had many years more in front of him. Sean had divorced a couple of women along the way and paid them off in fine style as well, but not so much as he could not live an elevated lifestyle with his upper crust friends and high maintenance girlfriends. Sean did have a small quirk, however. Every once in a while he liked to go into the city and associate with some of the city's less affluent women.

The now deceased pornographers had squeezed him for a while, while he was married to a very popular actress.

Revelations of infidelity could be grounds for a ruinous divorce. The divorce had occurred anyway for different reasons, and once he had no real stake but his reputation, Sean had stopped paying the extortionists. Strangely enough, they let it go as well. Now, a few years later, Sean Warren was enamored of a sweet young thing who had amazing star potential and was still naïve enough to believe that Sean was completely innocent of all the nasty things printed about him in the tabloids. If the tape of Sean during one of his less conservative moments was to surface, it would have a real effect on his current relationship. He intended to marry Melissa his pretty young girlfriend, and if the recordings came out after that he would be paying her big money forever and not enjoying the fruits of his finances. Sean knew the recordings were out there but did not know who had them, or he would have contracted to end the extortion years ago. He was more than just an action star;; he was the kind of man who took charge in the real world as well.

Since he had not heard anything about his indiscretions for a couple of years, he assumed that the person or persons involved with extorting money from him had died or moved away. Things looked good for him right now as his second sequel to the immensely popular "Blaze of Glory" was almost done filming.

He got home that particular evening to find a bubble wrap envelope with a familiar movie disk inside. The note simply told him he had one week to come up with half a million in cash. The squeeze was going to begin again, but this time, Sean was not going to pay.

"Ice Cream?"

"Yo. Who dat?"

"Sean Warren."

"Sean, my badass white-boy brother. What can a rapper do for you my man?"

"I got a guy here says he wants money for something

he has. He took a movie of me and a woman some time back and now he wants money."

"Aw hell no. You just getting into one o' yo' bitches and now he says you gotta pay?"

"I was just wondering if you still had any connections on the street, maybe find out who this asshole is and we can take care of him, you know, old school."

"Old school. That's what I'm talking about. Ice Cream the motherfucker."

"I think you know what I'm saying."

"I know, but now, let me tell you what else I know. I know you halfway through the "Blaze of Glory" thing so I can't get no lead role but you can give me a nice walk on..."

"I can do that. I'll talk to the director and producers."

"Then, I want a role, a big one, in your next film."

"I don't know if I can do that but, hang on a minute. Johnny Lee is making a movie about inner city gangs in the new century..."

"I already got me a starring role in that one. Who do you think they come to when they want the real street? Ice Cream, motherfucker. I want the main street. I wanna work with Sean Warren. I wanna be the man all over the town. I wanna be the Ice Cream all the bitches wanna lick."

"All right. You find out who this is and take care of my little problem and I'll make sure you get a nice, juicy role in the next major film I do."

"That's what I'm talking about. I need a copy of the film. I gotta see who knows this bitch and I need to know where it was shot." Suddenly Ice Cream was much more businesslike. "I can find anybody in this town." The clownish voice got deadly serious.

"That's why I came to you. I need the best."

The first thing Sean did was take the disk to Stranger Than Fiction Studios on Fountain Avenue to have his face completely obliterated. His good friend Roger ran the place and took good care of him for a nominal fee. They had known each other for years and Sean had thrown enough work his way to make for a thriving business. Roger was not one to forget a favor.

Once he was no longer the star of his own porno, Sean had the recording sent across town to the offices of Ice Cream Inc.

Not wanting to create too much interest, Ice Cream offered $1,000 to anyone who could find the woman in the movie. She was a cute young Mexican woman with blossoming breasts, leaking milk. It was obvious she had recently given birth. That helped to narrow it down a little. The location where the footage was shot was another clue. It only took the street crowd a couple of days to locate the woman, who denied ever having been filmed. She obviously didn't even know about it. She didn't know much about anything, being primarily concerned with where her next fix was coming from. The men who confronted her were happy to supply that for her if the information she provided was of commensurate value.

Since the prostitute was a bit hazy on the facts, Ice Cream's posse hunted down her pimp instead. Rock Hardey was a well known figure in the area. Black and overdressed, he had an eclectic stable of black, Hispanic and oriental women working the streets for him. His headquarters was the old Alexandria Building, a once opulent hotel on West 5th Street. He was surprised to see the film, as if he had never contemplated earning extra money after the dirty deed was done. The posse did not buy it. They took him up to the roof of the hotel and hung him off the edge until he spilled his guts.

It was Rock's contention that the men who had made the tape were dead as of a couple of weeks ago. They had run a porno studio on Ocean Park Boulevard and had been butchered like cattle. It seemed the men used Hardey's girls once in a while, taking them to an undisclosed, classier location than the Alexandria. They paid well and did not abuse the women so he had no problem with supplying them. Until the men turned up dead.

So, the real questions that remained were: who had shot the men on Ocean Park Boulevard? Why had they shot them? And who had the clandestine footage now? Rock Hardey was of no help in this regard. They called Ice Cream and he told his men not to throw the pimp off the building, that he might be useful yet.

Inquiries into the investigation being conducted on the slaughtered pornographers yielded nothing of substance. The method was obvious and the opportunity presented no mystery but the motivation was unclear. Yes, the studio had been stripped of movies but there was scarcely enough market for these films that it would be worth a multiple murder. Yes, the hard drive had been removed from the computer and taken but that might mean nothing more than a group of thorough individuals making sure to cover their tracks. There were no fingerprints on the scene that the police could not account for and that put it in the range of a professional hit. Also, the men had been armed yet had not fought back. They had not gotten off a single shot, which usually meant that they knew the person or persons who killed them or they were surprised and disarmed. The police suspected that someone had been unhappy with the services rendered, but without evidence they had no suspects and without a suspect the case would be relegated to the cold case file in short order. They considered the pornographers to be in the same category as the paparazzi, one step up from pimps.

"Yo, Sean."

"I.C. what it be?"

"Look, man, you got something really strange going on here. The white bread that got you on film is no more."

"You mean you…"

"Hell no. I didn't have anything to do with that. This happened a couple weeks back. I tracked 'em down but they was already dead. Way I see it, whoever snuffed them got your cameo appearance and now they wants to get paid for it. If they weren't putting the squeeze on you, I'd say you might be a suspect."

"You know better than that. I might be a tough guy on screen but I'm a pussy cat when the lights are off."

"Right. Well, I got no access to the crime scene but I do know a thing or two. The three guys that borrowed the little mamasita with the leaky tits all got lead poisoning two weeks back. Whoever did that deed is the one trying to pull a number on you. When did you get the contact?"

"Yesterday."

"That means they didn't know what they were getting until they had it home. They needed to look at the film before they knew who was on it. The original guys were killed by someone else they were pulling this shit on. That's who you need to talk to. Whoever it was they were sliding it in on now."

"So, who…?"

"I don't know. Look, Sean, I can get all there is from the street but I can't get what's not out there."

"Yeah, I see."

"So, we good?"

"Yeah."

"I still got that cameo?"

"Yeah, I got you a role as one of the bad guys. It's a speaking role. Call the studio for a schedule, I think we'll shoot that one next week."

"All right, my man. I'm gonna keep working on this one for you. I still got a game or two they ain't seen yet."

"All right, I.C. You call the studio today. I got your part."

Sean hung up the phone and stared at it for a minute, wondering what to do. It was as if the rules of the game had changed. He had no idea who the men that were found dead were working for or if they were independents. He did not know if there was anything at the crime scene that could implicate him. He couldn't even be sure that the dead men were really the same ones who were responsible for the tape since the recording was not found.

Booting up his computer for the first time in a couple of days, Sean accessed a browser and requested murders in LA. He got so many hits he needed to narrow his search considerably. It seemed the Ocean Park Boulevard murders had occurred in the New Moon Productions studio. The studio had been stripped of its entire stock of movies. Any one with information of any persons selling large quantities of New Moon films was encouraged to call the police and collect $1000 reward.

Calling his butler to fix him a drink, Sean searched further into the New Moon catalogue. New Moon Studios had a number of the high profile female porn stars working for them from time to time and a lot of unknowns. It was no secret that a lot of the pretty, fresh-faced young girls who headed for California with dreams of Academy Awards often ended up on the streets, or in films that did not show on television. He did not pity these women. Sean had made his money and reputation on his talent. He knew that most of the women who made it in Hollywood made it on their backs. He also knew that porno was the fastest way to finish a movie career.

Chapter Five
Prometheus

The City of Los Angeles was home to lots of private investigators. With well over ten million people in Los Angeles County alone, there was lots of business. There was also a large rift between the haves and the have-nots. Archimedes Prometheus Chamberlain was one of the private investigators that had earned some respect in a town where respect was a truly valuable commodity. He had retired as a Los Angeles Police Department Captain but had missed the action so badly that he returned to the streets in private practice. He had connections any other PI would kill for and they were not just among the police. Archie had street credits, he had judicial friends, he even had connections with lawmakers. Movie stars called Archimedes P. Chamberlain from time to time when they wanted some discreet surveillance or if a fan was getting too chummy. Archie took care of business and he was not always politically correct about it.

One of the things Archimedes did well was research. He took to the streets to find things out that could only be found on the street, but he left the longer-term research to his assistant, Jacqueline Vandenberg. What he knew of her was she was a young woman with a degree in programming but no stomach for it. She was much happier in Archie's office looking up school records, arrest records, military records, credit reports and the like. She seldom saw her boss and could take a break when she wanted. The money was not great but she loved her job and it paid enough for her to get a cottage. Unlike so many others she had not come to California to try her hand in the movie industry, she was going to program. She had more or less fallen into her present position and fully intended to keep it until the job was no longer there which, given Archie's age and unhealthy diet, might not be all that far off. Jacqueline was a bright girl and learned quickly. She had picked up contacts that even Archimedes did not have but she played those very close to the vest.

When Sean called, Archie had given his case high priority. After all, Sean paid top dollar and this was the second time he had contacted Prometheus Investigations. The first time had been in the case of the first wife who had been having an affair with her producer's assistant. Archie had produced photographs and bank card records proving the affair and the wife had settled out of court for much less than she would have gotten otherwise. It also cost much less in negative publicity.

"Mr. Warren?"

"Archie. Please, call me Sean."

"Sean, then. Is there someplace I can meet you that we can discuss your proposal? I do not favor telephone lines, they are so unsecure."

"Well, maybe they need some self-worth seminars."

Archie chuckled politely.

"Look, Archie, I really do need to talk to you but I can't pull myself away right now. We're filming some particularly vital action sequences and I need to be here."

"You don't have a body double to do that stuff for you?"

"Arch, have you seen any of my films? You can see my face in all of them. I'm the one sliding down the fire escape, jumping into the pickup at fifty-five miles an hour, getting blown out of the burning building. Come on by, you can see me get run over by a garbage truck today."

"All right. I've got something this morning but I'll be by between noon and one."

"Good. I'll try to schedule lunch for that time."

Archie managed to get into the studio because the guards around the set expected him. He was a half-hour early and he did get to see Sean drive a car through a brick wall and get out with guns blazing. Archie thought to himself *"If only it were that easy in the real world."*

Noon came around and Sean and Archie were able to get some face time. Sean explained what he knew and what his problem was. Archie asked him why they had not spoken before, when the problem had first arisen, and Sean told him that it had been before they had been acquainted. There had been a private eye retained for the same problem at an earlier time but he had been inefficient and ineffective. Archie took notes, called Jacqueline and reassured Sean that it would be handled in short order. He wanted to know as soon as contact was made and he would be taking care of things from then on. Sean agreed to let his PI handle it all and also promised to stay out of the seedier sections of town for a while. Archie spent the rest of the day taking care of some loose ends while his assistant did some research on the filmed footage.

"What'cha got for me, Jackie?" Archie asked as he walked through the door the next morning.

"Morning, Arch. I'm not sure you really want to get mixed up in this one."

"Why is that?"

"Well, on top of the fact that all three of the men working at this studio, apart from the swinging dicks that is, got shot a couple of weeks back, and it looks like the owner got rubbed out too."

"You meant the guys who got shot didn't own the studio?"

"That's what I said. The owner was a Bruce Babbage from Lexington Avenue near Highland. He was shot a couple of days after the guys on Ocean. I got the whole story here. He lives above a coffee shop on Lexington. The girl in the coffee shop calls the cops cause it stinks up there, lo and behold, the guy is dead and stinkin'. It must have been the

same guy that killed them all, but the cops got no leads."
Jacqueline repressed the smile that threatened to curl her lip.
She was happy to have the killings lumped together. She may
have c2oordinated the owner's demise but she was curious as
to who was commissioned for the others.

"Interesting."

"Want the address?"

"I want the address of the coffee shop the address of
the girl who called it in, the names of the officers who
responded to the call, the name of the ME cutting on the
corpse, and everything you have on Bruce Babbage since he
was found under a cabbage."

"Okay. I'm not sure about the cabbage though."

"You know, Babbage, cabbage. Oh, I guess you're too
young. They used to tell kids the stork brought you, you
were found under a cabbage, you were dropped off by the
nuns, all sorts of things to prevent having to tell kids about
sex and stuff."

"Okay. I get it. I'll get you what I can."

"I'll start with the local precinct. You start with the
cops on the job and call me when you get it. Good work,
Jackie."

It turned out the officers on the job were young
enough not to know Archimedes Prometheus Chamberlain
personally but he had a reputation almost as long as his name.
He knew the desk sergeant and the precinct captain and used
his friends to get an informal appointment with the officers
on the scene. The Medical Examiner was an old friend,
actually older than Archimedes, and he was happy to be in
touch.

"Archie, you old scoundrel, you only come around
when you want something."

"I've been busy, Joshua. You know I'm still working
and you know that business is booming. I never got the time
to write my memoirs the way I always said I would. I'm too

much in demand. I'll tell you what, I'm meeting a couple of the fine young lads from your precinct after hours. You're welcome to come along."

"Are you buying?"

"Ah, yes. The client is buying."

"And he is?"

"You know I can't reveal that, you old goat."

"Heh, as long as somebody is buying."

"Well, what have you got?"

"You know I can't reveal that." Joshua lowered his voice to a whisper and said, "Meet me at the Casting Call Lounge for lunch, eleven-thirty."

"Right," the PI whispered back

"Then get out of here and never darken my door again," he said in an overly dramatic fashion.

Eleven-thirty rolled around and Archie and Josh were sitting across a table from each other having a couple of drinks. Archie wanted to know if they were bugging the morgue and why. The Medical Examiner could not tell him why but he said that they had installed cameras and microphones some time back, and there was no sense in taking chances. Archie kept his own counsel, knowing that Joshua was an alcoholic and always looking for someone to buy him a drink.

"So what is it?"

"This guy was executed. He was shot through the head while he slept. Two slugs, 9mm. He never even woke up as far as I can tell," Joshua confided.

"This is the owner... uh, Bruce Babbage?"

"Right. The stiff from the coffee shop."

"That's all you can tell me?"

"What else do you want to know?"

"Nothing I guess."

"Okay then. The rest of it you can get from the cops on the scene. All I do is chop up the bodies."

"I know. I just wanted your opinion."

"Well, you got it. He was executed in his sleep. He didn't suffer."

Joshua had a couple more drinks and wobbled back to work. Archie called Jacqueline to see if there was a name for the girl in the coffee shop, but the Health Department, not the counter girl, had called the police. She had the owner's name and phone number for him, however.

Archie was halfway through dialing the number when it suddenly struck him. He hung up and called Jacqueline back. "Jackie, tell me, why does a guy rent an apartment above a coffee shop on Lexington if he owns a studio on Ocean Park Boulevard?"

"I don't know, boss."

"Give me the address on Ocean Park."

When he got to the New Moon Productions studio, the mystery only deepened. The property included the three-bedroom lower apartment, the upstairs studio and the two-car garage. The garage alone would have made an apartment if someone took the time to put in a bathroom and some dry wall. As it was, there was a late seventies Corvette, old furniture and exercise equipment stuffed in there. It did not look as though anyone had bothered to intrude on its dusty existence in quite some time.

Archie snooped around for a while, took some digital pictures and then drove back toward Hollywood. He had no close connections at the Ocean Park Precinct and had already learned whatever that group was willing to make public. He felt it more likely something of interest could be gleaned from the death of the owner.

"So, gentlemen, can you explain to me why a man who owns a film studio complete with living quarters would rent an apartment from someone else?"

The blank look on the officers' faces indicated that they had no idea what Archie was talking about.

"Okay. I know you guys aren't in on the investigation, I just wanted your impression. I don't expect you to breach protocol."

One of the pair looked as though he was ready to talk; the other had a sour expression on his face showing a lack of respect for private investigators in general and Archimedes P. Chamberlain in particular. Neither of them said anything for a moment, addressing themselves to the drinks that Archie had provided. They were both in street clothes so they were off the clock and probably annoyed that they had been asked to be there, gratis.

"What was your impression of the crime scene?"

"In and out. Nobody knew this guy was there until two weeks later." The younger of the two officers was speaking, the older gave him a dirty look. "The place was locked up tight but the padlock on the inside door had been duplicated and changed. This guy did not want anyone to know he had been there. If it hadn't been for the smell, we wouldn't have known either. This was no crime of passion; this was a hit, plain and simple. Professional hit."

"Got any suspects?"

"Can't say. That's part of the ongoing investigation. I couldn't comment if I knew. You'll need to talk to Detective Packard about that." The older of the two was clearly pleased with his partner's response to that question.

"Look guys, we're on the same side here, looking for the same thing. I spent thirty-two years on the job, right here in LA. Can't you give me something?"

The police everywhere are protective of their proprietary advantage in society. They know they are not the same as the rest of the population. They know that everybody has a secret or two that they don't want known. Even spouses were often secretive and the divorce rate among police officers was horrendous. A suspicious nature comes with the job and the job requires a suspicious nature.

It is a self perpetuating cycle fueled by the need for self preservation. So it was that even a long-term veteran of the department has a hard time breaking through the crust and getting some trust.

Archie plied the officers with more drinks and they loosened up some. He told them outrageous stories about his time on the street and some of the better times. He told them about the 1992 riots and how he had been attacked in Korea Town. Neither of the young officers had even been on the job when the riots had occurred. He told them about getting shot walking into a liquor store holdup by mistake. He told them about his three ex-wives and his two sons. By the time he was done talking, the men could not help but like him, identify with him and respect him. He also kept buying them drinks. After a few drinks, their own personal feelings about the case came out.

"This guy was a slick professional," the younger one said. "He worked it for three days, working on the dumb blonde in the coffee shop, convincing her he was the next Errol Flynn or some-such from Australia. He took her out a couple of times and then dopes her and steals her keys. He didn't even fuck her. That's how good this guy is. I would've fucked the bitch. Anyway, he steals her keys, lets himself in, goes upstairs and bing, bing. Two nines to the head. Nobody saw him go in and nobody saw him go out. Nobody heard the shots. No fingerprints. Sure, we got a composite picture from the girl but that ain't worth a shit. This guy was so good he even took the keys back to the bitch and dropped them on the sidewalk. The only real suspect we got is the blonde but she didn't do it. She was at home all doped up at the time. At least that's what her roommate says. I believe her."

"So, what we got here is a guy who owns a studio and an apartment but rents another, smaller one, from someone else. He never goes out and has everything delivered, even his groceries. He's gotta be witness protection. There's no other answer. But somehow the word gets out and whoever it is he's hiding from finds him and takes him out. Am I right?"

"That sounds reasonable." The younger of the two was still the spokesman but by now, the older was nodding his head in affirmation.

"Thank you, gentlemen. This is all off the record. I never spoke with any of the officers on this case. We're just a couple of guys having a couple of drinks."

The patrolmen left but Archie stayed for a while, drinking and thinking. He knew he shouldn't drive home in the condition he was in, but he did anyway.

Morning came with all the subtlety of a rusty ice pick to the eyeball. The dead rat that had replaced his tongue sometime during the night was flayed by a shot of mouthwash, but the demon with the jackhammer inside his skull would take a bit more time to subdue. The gremlin kicking him in the kidneys would need to be addressed someday but he needed to subdue the wildfire in his stomach first.

Opening the refrigerator did not help Archie's current condition. The curdled milk and green bacon hinted at the age of the eggs. He had not cooked for himself in weeks and could not have safely eaten anything he had. In the freezer was a half-pint of Old Crow and unlike Poe's famous bird, this one was beckoning to him. He closed the freezer door once and then opened it again, losing the fight this morning. He did not usually drink in the morning, and he did not usually get as drunk as he had the night before, but there was work to be done. He justified it as a part of the job.

With a shower and a few shots under his belt, the day looked a bit more manageable. Squinting through the front window allowed him to see that the Crown Victoria was still in the driveway. Brushing his teeth reminded him that he needed to see his dentist.

Jacqueline Vandenberg was already on the job when he called. She had the address of Cindy Anderson, the girl who worked in the coffee shop. The patrolmen would not give him her name, but Jacqueline dug it out of somewhere along with her address.

Driving to Cindy's place blew the last of the cobwebs out of Archie's head. The Old Crow had pecked the little demon with the jackhammer to death but had done nothing for the wildfire in his belly. He stopped on the way for a bottle of bismuth and a pack of mints.

"Cindy Anderson?"

"Yes."

"My name is Archimedes Chamberlain. I'm a private investigator hired to look into the murders that surround New Moon Productions. Do you think I could take up a little of your time?"

"Sure, come on in. I've got nothing better to do. Boss says it will be a couple of days before I can go back to work."

"So they shut down the coffee shop?"

"The boss said he did, but by the time he finally got around to taking care of the place, the cops had already been there and I think the Health Department shut the place down."

"When did this happen?"

"What? The…"

"Let's start from the beginning."

"I told the cops all about it."

"I know, but I'm not an officer, I'm a private investigator and they don't always like to tell me what's going on. I was on the force for thirty-two years but now that I'm retired, I actually need to work harder to make the same amount of headway. You don't need to tell me anything. I'm not here in an official capacity, but I am here to help."

"Okay. You want some coffee? I'm going to have

one." Cindy took her time. They had coffee and went over the meeting and the romance, or lack of it. She explained that there was really no evidence linking Jerry Kragon to the murder but that she knew he did it. She went through the time line from the minute she had met him to that day. It was currently Tuesday. The body had been found the previous Friday, and if the owner of the place was efficient, the cleaning crew would already have been in to take care of the stink.

Archie did not get the impression that he was hearing from a woman scorned. She claimed she had hardly met Bruce Babbage and had never dated him, explaining that he hardly ever left his apartment. She further claimed that she had never slept with Jerry Kragon. He didn't know if he believed her on that score, but he did not think she was the shooter. There was nothing more to be learned from her; he needed to be investigating the deceased. He called Jacqueline and asked her to get into the history of Bruce Babbage.

Rather than get in touch with the investigators on the Babbage case, Archie got in touch with the men working the New Moon murders and offered to buy them lunch. They declined the lunch offer. It was an obvious ploy when partway through the call, the detective spoke to his partner without cupping the receiver. He said, "Hey, Joe, we gonna get some drinks after work in the Blue Button?" Then he returned to his previous conversation where he told Archie he had nothing to say.

Archie's stomach was finally feeling up to some food so he went to a Big Boy and had some lunch. The chicken salad sat well enough in his stomach initially and made him a lot happier. Jacqueline had printed out a ream of information on Mr. Babbage, and Archie stopped by the office to go over it.

The majority of charges were on a debit card, taken directly from a checking account. All the usual stuff was there: telephone, cable television and internet, gas and electric, insurance, rent and grocery bills. There was a recurring charge for movies delivered through the mail. There was a monthly notation for the mortgage on New Moon Productions along with the power and water for that location. The monthly deposits came from that enterprise and were substantial but not overwhelming. They might have justified his living elsewhere since he rented the lower apartment to the three men living there. The arrangement made him money. There were some things notably absent from the financial report. Bruce had no car payments, no gasoline charges, no auto insurance or garage payments. He obviously walked wherever he went, or took the bus, but the reports of a reclusive individual didn't fit with that. It was possible that the man took to the streets after six when the coffee shop closed. He certainly didn't have a day job.

There were a couple of things that did not fit properly with the perceived personality of the deceased. There was a membership to a gym a few blocks away. It was a little outside the regular walking distance parameters but could have been accomplished on a bicycle. Archie decided he would be looking into that possibility. There was also a membership at a shooting range that had been paid six months earlier, but there were no charges for ammunition or firearms. The range was miles away, on the slopes of La Tuna Canyon and could not have been accessible even by bus. The membership was for a full year, but there were no further charges at that location.

The personality disorder, if it can be called that, seemed to be borne out by what was not there, more than what was there. There were no charges from taverns, strip clubs, liquor stores, restaurants, or after hours clubs. There had been no ATM withdrawals, no cash withdrawals from the bank, no charges at clothing stores, shoe stores, post offices or sundries stores. If Bruce Babbage wanted it, it got delivered to him.

Archie took a small shot of Seagram's from the bottle in his desk drawer and told Jacqueline he was going back out. Before he made it out the door, his cell phone rang. Sean Warren was calling to tell Archie that the extortionists had just called him up and told him where to deliver the money and that he needed to move now.

Chapter Six
A Big Bag of Money

"Well then, Homer, what is it you did that makes you think there are people who want you dead? You don't strike me as the type to be flouting the law." Gordon MacMaster sat facing his new client and lighting a mid-sized cigar.

"I'm not. Well, that is to say, not really. I don't come from around here."

"Why is it then that you feel they will be hunting you here if this is not your usual area? How did you get here, why are you here, and how did you find that bunch of fools that were parading around the house like clowns in the circus?"

"I don't think they are hunting me here."

"Well then, why have you retained us? I assume you know what it costs you?"

"Yes, I know. Look. I saw a deal go bad, a bust of some kind, I don't really know. I was down in Miami with my cousin when he tells me that he's got something to do down by the docks. So I'm just in the car and he goes to this place near the docks and goes inside. I'm outside in the car listening to the radio and all of a sudden, these three cop cars pull up next door. The whole place turns to shit and bullets are flying everywhere. The cops are getting shot from the building, these greasers are coming out of the woodwork like cockroaches and my cousin comes running out of the building like his tail's on fire. I'm trying to make myself as small as possible in the car, you know, 'cause I didn't want to get shot. So bang, my cousin gets shot in the neck and he's holding on to it like he can stop the bleeding and the blood is just flying everywhere and he tries to get in the car but the door is locked and by the time I get the door unlocked, he gets shot again as he's opening it. Okay, so this other greaseball gets in the car with me but he's been shot in the guts, you know, right in the stomach. He starts the car up and we drive out of there but he's all fucked up and we only make it a couple of blocks before he drives tight, right into a dumpster. Oh, I forgot, this guy's got a bag, like a canvas bag with him in the car and he's bleeding like a pig and it really stinks, like he shit himself and then he runs tight into the dumpster and I think it knocked him out. So I get out and I'm gonna run away but I don't know what's going on and then I see that the car's still running and he's too fucked up to drive it so I open the door and I pull his ass out onto the pavement and I get in the car and I drive it away. I didn't even see the bag he threw in the back seat until I got away from the docks and then I'm like, 'what's this?' And the bag's full of money and I said 'Holy shit, where did this come from?' and I'm thinking my cousin threw it in the car and then I'm thinking this other guy threw it in the car and I don't know what to do about it. And then I think 'What the hell, nobody knows I've got it and I could just keep it.' But I can't stay in Miami 'cause, well, my cousin is dead, at least I think he's dead and all those cops that were getting shot and, shit, all them greasers. Who knows who the fuck they are and I'm scared and running away in a car that was at the scene of the crime, you know? So I said, what can I do to get the fuck away from here and keep the skin on my ass? So I get on a bus and come up here to my uncle's place in Kansas, thinking they don't know who I am and don't know where I live and my uncle just died and so nobody expects him to be here. And I put the money in the Bank of Am... In the bank. And that's about it." Homer took a deep breath, his high speed explanation having drained him.

"Let me get this straight then," said Gordon as Anastasia rolled her eyes. "You picked up a bag of money from a gunfight in Miami and brought it north to Kansas City, Kansas?"

"Right, I took a bus..."

MacMaster held up his hand to forestall another

avalanche of words from his client. "This house belonged to your uncle?"

"Yes, he was my father's brother."

"And you were in Miami visiting his son, your cousin?"

"No, not his son. He was my cousin on my mother's side of the family. Uh, he was my mother's brother's son, Ralph."

"Okay. So you thought it would be appropriate to leave the rest of Ralph's family in Miami while you came north with your bloody bag of money?"

"There wasn't much blood on the bag and none on the money."

Gordon looked at the ceiling of the motel room and took a deep breath through his teeth. Anastasia threw the shotgun on the bed, tossed a windbreaker over her shoulder holster and stepped out the door.

"Look, I know I fucked up when I took the money but…"

"Homer, how much money did you get from the bag?"

"I don't think that's your business."

"Lookit here, ya wee tube, I'm not looking for a specific number, I'm trying to protect you from your own stupidity. That is why I'm here. Primarily to protect you from the men who want you dead, and second to protect you from your own stupidity. Now, tell me, have you called your cousin's mother? That would be, what, your mother's brother's wife?"

"Uh, no, why would I have done that?"

"To see if she is still alive. Homer did you think they would not be able to identify your cousin? Were you staying there with his family?"

"Yes."

"Perfect. How many people live there?"

"There's, let's see, Ralph, his mother and father, his sister and three kids, her husband left her but her boyfriend

64

stays sometimes."

"Spare me the soap opera. What I'm thinking is that they need to get out of there and to take any trace of you, that you left behind, with them. They will probably be getting a visit from men who want to know where the bag of money went."

"Oh." It was as if it was the first time Homer had thought of the danger he had put his family in. "Then I'd better…"

"Wait before you do anything. Think the plan through before you do anything that will get you in a pail of hot water. I already know the money is in the Bank of America. Did you put it into an account or did you have a safe deposit box there?"

"Uhh."

"Look, you poor dolt, you hired me to keep you from harm. Do I need to explain myself?"

"Well, yes. You need to explain why you need to know about the money."

"Very well. That's fair. You picked up this money in Miami. I'm thinking drug money. I'm thinking that it is a substantial amount of money that would make the men who lost it come looking for you to get it back. This is backed up by the fact that you have hired guards to protect you, twenty-five hundred kilometers away. Now, by extension, this means that you not only think they will be hunting you, you think they will be hunting you here. So, perhaps you are only acting so stupid and really you've got a plan in that little head of yours after all. So, that leads me to explain that you will need to rely on the money that you stole from the drug dealers in Miami to survive for a while. The length of time they actively chase you is determined by how much money you actually stole from them. Now, to access this money in, say, New York City, it would need to be in a bank account but if you tried to deposit this much money into a bank account, the government might be a wee bit interested in what you thought you were doing and where the money came from. Am I making a case for myself?"

"Uh, yes. I put it in a safe deposit box until I could figure out what I was going to do with it."

"Good! I can see you are not as bit of a ring as I first assumed."

"I, uh, I wish you would stop calling me stupid."

"I will, when you prove to me that you deserve it."

"And how am I supposed to do that?"

"You will decide where it is you want to be." The Scotsman assumed an air of long suffering. "You must know that you cannot hire guards forever and that the very fact that you hire guards makes people wonder what you are up to. So what you really need, and what you want us to do for you, is to change your identity and set you up with a history and a location that will leave you as an unimpeachable member of society in some androgynous sector of society where you can live out the rest of your life in comfort and security. Am I right?"

"Yes." His new protector's calm confidence was as reassuring as his Scottish brogue was exotic.

"Good then. Where is it you were thinking of disappearing to then?"

"California."

"You'll be joining the party that paid this contract then?"

"Yes. Jacqueline Vandenberg. She lives in Los Angeles, she's a programmer, I think. I don't talk to her much. She's my half sister. My dad left my mom and then got married again in Arkansas. We got the short end of the stick but things got better after we moved north. I got acquainted with Jacqueline a couple of…"

"I'm sorry, but I never heard of her and don't really care to know her. Does she have a place you could stay in

Los Angeles? Is that what she expects?"

"Probably. You know, LA is huge. I could hide there forever and they would never find me once I change my name."

"California it is then. Call your sister from this phone." Gordon handed him a cell phone. "Tell her you are coming to LA and that you're going to need an apartment. Make sure she doesn't think you need a back-alley jacksey and not a palace, neither. Something in a reasonable range. Tell her you need to rent it in a name other than yours. Then we call your family in Miami."

"G'day mate. You doing any heavy lifting of your own these days?"

"Ah, good morning. I was hoping you'd call. I managed to pick up a number that would require the sort of finesse you managed to display in Michigan."

"Tell me about it." Terry Kingston knew that he had done quality work on that last job but the nature of the job still bothered him a little.

"Remember what we discussed regarding the finder's fee?"

"Of course. One hand washes the other."

"Good. This is the wife of a prominent businessman. He is going to…"

"Hold up there, mate. I don't do women. Not my style. I love women too much to enjoy putting a cold hand on 'em."

"A cold hand. Yes, well, it's the only job I can get you on the West Coast."

"No good. Don't want it."

"Someone will pick this up and you will be out the cash."

"Not a problem. I'll call back again. Until then, I think I'll just enjoy this wonderful weather." Terry Kingston hung up the pay phone and wiped down the handle. He'd had enough of sunning himself on the beach and picking up women in the bars. It was entertaining but it did not have the jolt of adrenaline that he had come to crave. He needed something to get his blood pumping hard.

A little research taught him that Compton was one of the most violent cities in America. There would be plenty of action there but there was a bit of a problem, Compton was 58% Hispanic and 40% African-American. Non-Hispanic whites made up about 1% of the population. Terry Kingston was much too fair-haired to blend in there; he would be singled out in a heartbeat.

Turning to a different location would yield better results he decided, and investigated the breakdown in Inglewood. The computer gave him some contradictory data leading to more than 100%, but it also made it clear that a six-foot two inch blond Australian would look quite out of place.

Turning to some of the areas outside Los Angeles, Terry started getting frustrated as he found the crime statistics for the white neighborhoods to be lower than the national average. He began to feel that the infiltration techniques he learned as a young man in Sydney would be useless in California. Then he looked to the north and decided that Van Nuys looked like a place where he could stir up some trouble. It was far enough from the border that the INS wasn't focusing their spotlights on it. The gang presence was not so great that the FBI was interested. North of Hollywood hills, Van Nuys seemed to have enough of a white population to allow Terry to blend in but enough crime to allow him to get his hands dirty. There was also the money factor. A lot of people who worked in Hollywood could not afford to live in Hollywood. Van Nuys was ten miles away, over the hills, so it was a completely different neighborhood without the elaborate security and armed guards demanded by the movie stars.

Taking his time, Terry packed a few possessions into a bag and strolled away from the hotel. Venice Beach was still mostly empty since it was still early. He walked a few blocks just to enjoy the neighborhood and the view. The Aussie was looking for a car being sold by an individual. Used car lots needed paperwork, insurance and all the accompanying need for subterfuge on his part, and Terry was unwilling to play the game that day. A few blocks off the beach, there was an Acura for sale. He made the owner an offer that was rejected. The owner seemed to think he had something special and Terry disagreed with him so he politely told him that he wouldn't pay that much and he walked off. A few blocks further, a 1976 Gran Torino station wagon caught his eye. There was nothing sporty about it, but it did not seem to leak oil. A knock on the door got no response but he could see someone inside so he knocked again, louder. This time an older woman came to the door.

"Hello, my dear, I was wondering about this old wagon."

"Oh, my, yes. It was my son's project for my grandson. You know how it is when you worry so about your kids? You want something that will protect them."

"Ah, yes, ma'am."

"You have a lovely accent."

"Thank you, ma'am. I find yours charming as well."

"But I don't have an accent."

"No, ma'am, of course not."

"Oh, my. Well, yes, my son wanted a car that would run well but couldn't be used for racing, you know?"

Terry said nothing.

"So he got this old station wagon and he put this, uh, Cobra Jet engine in it and then did something with the transmission…"

"Might I have a look at it, then?"

"Oh, my, let me get my house slippers on then. I know

I don't get many kids asking about this one. I guess it wasn't a very popular model."

Once Terry had the keys in hand he verified that the engine under the hood was a big block crate engine with twin 4-barrel carburetors. The valve covers announced it was a Cobra Jet. There had been extensive work done for the transmission as well, since it was originally an automatic. Somebody had hung a third pedal and chopped a hole in the firewall to accommodate a four-speed manual transmission, also an aftermarket assembly. The work looked less than professional, but everything was locked in solidly and the parts were new. The aluminum radiator was full of antifreeze and had an electric fan cinched up to it.

A naturally cool customer, Kingston did not let his enthusiasm show immediately. He let the old woman know that there was no telling how much abuse the engine had taken since it had clearly belonged to a younger man.

"Oh my, no," she said. "Bobby never drove it. No, he was only ten years old. Andrew, that was my son, Andrew. Andrew was building the car for Bobby for when he got his driver's license. He got it all done about a year ago and then they got caught in one of those awful forest fires in the hills. They were cut off and they… they died. Died of smoke inhalation."

"My goodness, dear. I'm so sorry to bring up your grief. It must have been horrible."

"I'm sorry. It still brings on the tears." She looked distraught but the actual tears did not flow.

"Well then, can I start it up?" he asked awkwardly.

"Oh my, yes, I… I'll need to get the keys."

"I have the keys already."

"Oh, that's right. Well, feel free."

Terry did not know if the aged woman was making a sympathy play or if the story was real but he gave her points for the attempt. When he had the keys in the ignition, he was very disappointed. The battery was low but had enough juice to turn it over and get it started, such as it was. It ran terribly. The crankcase had clean oil in it and the transmission was full, but the engine popped and backfired as if it were only burning on half the cylinders. It did not seem like a viable ride.

The last thing Terry needed was to be left at the side of the road in a car that he did not intend to register and for which he had no license. The station wagon stood out enough as it was since it had been so long since full-sized station wagons had been built. He almost walked away but the aged woman offered him what would have been a really good price if the car had run properly. Even then he almost walked away but decided at the last minute that he would take it. He paid for it in cash and drove it until he saw a run-down garage that looked as if the owner asked no questions he didn't want to know the answers to.

The Mexican mechanic was efficient. Within twenty minutes he had corrected the two spark plug wires that were crossed, smoothed out the idle on the carburetor and set the timing. There was no need to set the dwell since it had an electronic ignition instead of points. A little brake fluid in the reservoir and some air in the tires and the old granny mobile was ready for a road test.

Before he let the car out of the bay, the manager spoke with Terry. "You know, *jefe*, this was the first year you got to have emissions certified on it?"

"No, I didn't know that."

"I'm afraid there is no way this monster is going to pass in a regular shop."

"Why would that be?"

"Is got no catalytics on it, is got no emissions controls at all. There's no way this thing gonna pass. It all goes in on the computer, direct to the DMV. I see you got no sticker for the registration and you ain't gonna get it registered without the smog check. That's why this baby been sitting down the street for so long. It needs lots of work if you gonna drive it. If you just gonna drag race it, I can put a set of gears in the back and a couple of bottles of squeeze in the back seat. Tub it, put some slicks in it and she'll pull the front wheels."

"So I can't get the bloody thing certified for, say, five hundred?"

"I'm sorry, I don't do the certifications. In the past I could hook you up but not now. Is all computer shit." The manager did seem genuinely sorry that he could not help.

"I'll tell you what. I don't need the tubs and slicks in the back but I would like a posi rear end."

"It's a Ford, *jefe*. They call it a traction loc."

"I don't care what they call it. Get me a limited slip differential, something about three-seventy-eight or so."

"For the gear ratio?"

"Yeah, I don't need the four-eleven in something this heavy, too likely to break it. Something in a high three-to-one ratio is fine, limited slip."

"Okay. The good news is, she already got the big axles and the nine-inch differential so she can handle all that torque. The bad news is the factory Ford LSD unit can't handle the torque that engine gonna make. I gotta go with an aftermarket gear and that's gonna cost more."

"Right. Go with the aftermarket."

"That's a good move. Otherwise you gonna be picking up pieces of your rear end off Ventura Boulevard."

"Right. Do it. I tell you what, a couple of bottles of nitrous oxide sounds like a winner too. Look, stuff 'em in here, where the spare tire goes. Run your lines up front from underneath and put a couple of perimeter plates under the carbs. Can you do that?"

The smile grew on the manager's face as he asked when the work should be done.

72

"I want it done right away. This should get you started." Terry pulled out a wad of hundred dollar bills and peeled off five of them. I'll be back tomorrow and I expect to see some progress. Clear?"

"*Claro*. I get the juice bottles in today. I'll see if anybody got gears, too."

"Two. Two bottles of nitrous in a two-stage perimeter plate system."

"Okay. You know I gotta run eight lines for that with the two carbs?"

"Just do it. I'll be checking in about this time tomorrow."

"We get started on this one right away." The mechanic was grinning.

Terry walked away from the garage and waited at a bus stop. There is no way to get a feel for the people in an area like riding the mass transit systems. He started conversations with young women of all colors, his mastery of Spanish dialects greatly improved by the contact. He had no agenda for the rest of the day so he simply rode around for a while.

Around midday, Terry got off the bus in a place called Walnut Park. He walked a few blocks looking for the park but found there was no park, just more people. Ducking into a tavern he ordered a draught of beer and some lunch. He had finished three beers by the time his lunch was served. He didn't leave the waitress a tip.

Another half mile down Pacific Boulevard he found himself in Huntington Park. This time he was not surprised there was no park. On directions from a young man on a bicycle he turned down East Slauson and found Augustus Hawkins Natural Park, a tenth of a mile on a side. He stood there with his lower lip between his teeth thinking of different lands and different times. The immensity of Los Angeles was finally sinking in. He had seen it on the map, but the true density and size could not be conveyed any other way. He sat in the tiny park and smoked a cigarette, commenting to himself that the only green plot for miles around was covered in litter. He thought that people should have more respect for the park. Then he noticed that the metal hoops where the garbage baskets were supposed to sit were empty. Somebody had stolen them and there was no place for people to throw their trash.

Since he was on foot, Terry figured to be inconspicuous but such was not the case. On the main avenues, the foot traffic was negligible. On the side streets and residential neighborhoods he felt somewhat uncomfortable. It was early afternoon and the porches of many of the homes were filled with young black men drinking, playing cards and offering to sell him drugs. Young children of eight or ten years old were running around with almost no clothing on. Some of them offered to get him whatever he needed. It was not long before he decided that he was walking through much too dangerous a territory. On foot and alone he represented too much of a target regardless of the fact that he was armed. He decided to stick to the main streets until he got transportation. After he hit South Central Avenue and got a bus heading north he smiled ruefully and admitted to himself that despite the fact that he had been raised to be a killer of men, there were simply too many men in Southern California that had been raised the same way. The difference was that Terry Kingston had been trained to follow a personal code and the gangs of LA had no such upbringing. The gangs of LA had no honor, no education and no conscience. Terry was an assassin, but these men were more like rabid animals savaging and fouling everything around them including their own homes and families.

In Sydney, there had been one major organization headed by a pair of twins that made a visible target. In California, it was more like warring tribes of well-armed savages. There would be no attacking from within. Even if he were able to infiltrate a gang, it was only a small part of the greater evil and he would have made enemies out of every other gang. He felt he was a very small fish in a very big pond.

In the half hour it took for the bus to get five miles into downtown Los Angeles, Terry searched his mental archives for a scheme that would work against the violent and savage street gangs without exposing himself to the danger and notoriety involved with actually consorting with them. He got off the bus at North Hill Street and First Avenue when he noticed a sign for the metro rail. The subway system was nowhere as extensive in Los Angeles as in other cities. Terry decided that it may be because of the threat of earthquakes. After all, California is part of the Pacific Ring of Fire, a major seismic activity zone.

The subway was much faster than taking the buses but the rail riders were not the same sort of friendly that the open air travelers were. Nobody wanted to talk to anyone else and the armed security on each rail car stood like prison guards. After fifteen minutes Terry disembarked at the famous Hollywood and Vine, expecting a visual assault of the Hollywood film industry history. What he got was a mix of glitz and decay, building and destruction. A hotel was being built directly over the subway station. The Universal Pictures Building was in its last stages of being demolished after a fire had damaged it extensively. Sections of the iconic Walk of Fame were torn up badly. Some of the buildings were deserted and boarded up. He was virtually assaulted by four young people who claimed they were homeless and needed money for food.

Terry listened to the refugees from society and thought it incredibly ironic that in a city of such excess, in a country that had so much, that there would still be beggars. He told them to sod off and learn a profession. They quickly moved to a family with children and got much better results. Terry thought about finding something for them to do but then rejected the idea. They were obviously not underfed; their only real need was work ethic and they did not have any. In all, he was not impressed with the area but he did appreciate its diversity and wealth.

After soaking in some of the ambiance, Terry decided that he had seen enough and took the bus back to Santa Monica. The area was still buzzing with activity near the beach and all manner of unusual clothing and hair styles were visible. He walked onto the beach and stared out over the water, his eyes glazing over as he remembered the day his father had been killed off the coast of New South Wales. The vision naturally, painfully transformed to the hospital room where he had seen his mother's brains blown all over the wall and his Uncle Ginger shot. He knew the thoughts would haunt him for life regardless of the vengeance he had wrought upon those responsible. He shook his head and headed down the beach toward Marina Del Rey. He did not want to drink in the hotel he was staying in.

Chapter Seven
Grandma's Station Wagon

There was no doubt that only the most inexperienced blackmail men would ever allow the victim a week to prepare himself. A week is long enough to change your mind, or set up contingency plans. Sean Warren had not known this, thinking that the week was merely to allow him to acquire the large sum of cash demanded by the caller. Archie knew this however; he had dealt with this sort of pressure before. Once they had discussed it, they were both grateful for the set-up time and Archie had convinced his client that their target was an amateur.

Archie insisted that Sean act the way he would if he were going to accede to the extortionist's demands. The action star was to go to the bank and make a huge cash withdrawal, slipping the tracking chip into one of the bundles of money. There was another chip in the locked briefcase he kept the money in and another in the heel of Sean's shoe. The briefcase was chained to Sean's wrist in public. Archie was taking no chances with him disappearing or the money getting out of hand.

Sean filmed every day until he received further notice from the extortionists. Everybody knew that the show must go on but none of the staff understood the passion the star brought to his role that week. Some of the footage was unusable because the character's laconic demeanor was ruined by the actor's apparent fury.

Sean got the call on set and was forced to tell the director he needed to leave. The director was furious because they had the scene ready. The camera man was furious because the light was right and the shot needed to be taken right then and there. The special effects men were furious because they had set up the stunt men for the burning man scenes and Sean's co-star was furious for personal reasons.

He managed to calm everybody down when he pointed out that they did not need him for the burning man scene, the exploding cars or the kidnapping scene. It was already two in the afternoon and the light would be perfect again at that time tomorrow. He had to go. He stuck the microphone in his pocket and the receiver in his ear and headed for the Hollywood Forever Cemetery.

Whoever was on the other end of the cell phone connection must have seen every spy, abduction and thriller film ever made. First of all, his voice was disguised electronically so that it sounded like a robot. Secondly, he wanted everything done on a particular time table so that Sean would need to run to get to where he needed to go for the next contact. It was melodramatic and infuriating.

"You will leave your car in the cemetery and run to the bus stop at the corner of Santa Monica Boulevard and Van Ness," the voice said. "There you will get on the south bound bus. You have two minutes."

"You're crazy, it's more than a half mile!"

"Then you had better hurry."

The bus driver saw him running down the sidewalk and waited the extra couple of seconds it took for him to get to the bus stop. A minute later his cell phone rang again.

"Get off the bus at Vermont and remember, I'll be watching."

Sean wondered how his nemesis could be watching him and dismissed it as a scare tactic. He exited the vehicle at Santa Monica and Vermont and stood on the corner for a second before realizing that there was a railway station right on that corner. Assuming that would be his next destination he walked toward it. True to form the phone rang again and directed him into the cool recesses of the underground and to a bank of pay phones on the wall. Cell phone reception was almost impossible underground. He only waited a few seconds before one of the phones rang. Assuming it was his contact, he picked it up but instead of the electronically altered voice, a woman was making the call.

"Sean, they took me and threw me into the trunk of a car. They forced me off the road in the hills and they grabbed me."

"Oh, God, Melissa. I... I didn't know. I... Let me talk to the sons of bitches."

Again the electronically altered voice came on the line. "You have nothing to be concerned about. The plan is the plan and nothing has changed. We will release your pretty little girlfriend unharmed when you deliver the money to us. However, if there are bugs in the cookie dough all deals will be off and we will kill her in horrible and memorable ways. Have I made myself clear?" The completely dispassionate way the altered voice sounded made the threats all the more horrible.

"Yes, perfectly clear. If you hurt her I will hunt you down."

"Mr. Warren, you are in no position to be threatening us. This is not some movie where you can come to the rescue. If you do nothing stupid, she will not be harmed. Now get on the train and head for Union Station"

"The train for Union hasn't arrived yet."

"It will and you will be on it. Toss your cell phone in the garbage can next to the newspaper vendor. Remember, I am watching."

As he walked over to the newspaper vendor's stall, he tried to find anyone watching him but it seemed as though it could have been anyone or everyone. He reached the trash can but did not throw his cell phone in. A grubby little urchin ran up to him from down the platform and handed him another cell phone, with some electronic device taped to the back of it. As soon as it was in his hand it rang. Sean tried to tell where the boy had come from but could not, and the child melted back into the crowd the same way.

"You have not thrown your phone in the trash. I told you to throw the phone in the trash and you have not done so. Would you like your little girlfriend so much if she only had one ear?"

"You bastard, don't hurt her. There, the phone is in the trash."

"That's better. The train is arriving, get on it."

Sean got on the train, watching every other person on the car carefully, thinking he could spot the one who was watching him but it was impossible. They all looked suspicious. Then one of them noticed that they were sharing a rail car with Sean Warren and he was mobbed by requests for autographs. It was nothing he hadn't gone through before. It was why he had needed to move into the Hollywood Hills after his first successful film, between the overzealous fans and the paparazzi, they made his life difficult. This time, through force of will, he maintained his gracious persona, signed notebooks and T-shirts, using his briefcase as a table and even signed one woman's bare breast. He turned down several offers of a drink and the offer of a blow job before the new cell phone rang again.

"Sean? Your girlfriend is glad you are still popular. It must be gratifying to hand out all those autographs. Now, how do you think she'd feel if she saw the pictures of you and this little street tramp?"

"Fuck you, asshole. You just don't touch her. Put her back on the phone."

"In good time. You haven't earned the right to talk to her again. You can talk to Melissa when I tell you that you can. Now, take off your shirt and your jacket."

"What are you talking about?"

"Take off your shirt and jacket. I know you are wearing a wire. So disconnect the briefcase from your arm and take off your jacket and shirt."

"This is bullshit."

"You might as well take that little hearing aid out of your ear as well. Remember, I am watching you. I know everything you are doing and thinking and you will never double-cross me or I will fill your girlfriend full of GHB and give her to the Crips."

That was it. The caller really was watching him. Unless…

Sean had his shirt off and the ladies were gawking at his chiseled physique. As a last minute thought he dropped his ear piece into the shirt pocket, signed the shirt and gave it to the girl who had offered her personal services. She was ecstatic, literally jumping up and down, making Sean think the offer was given in good faith rather than in collusion with his extortionist. He would have loved to grab her and find out for sure but there was no place and no time. But…

She latched onto him and planted a kiss full on his mouth. He hugged her and whispered that she was to get off where he got off but to exit the other door. He told her to be discreet and to follow him, that he needed her help.

Hollywood is full of men and women that would like to be actors. Every waiter and street vendor north of the Mexican border is an out-of-work actor, even if their only role was in a toilet paper commercial. Most of them will never make it into another commercial let alone a feature film but some have the talent required. The fan with the oral obsession did not have the talent to make it in the film industry but she had enough talent to make it off the train without being detected and enough savvy to know that she was playing an unexpected role.

"Jacqueline. Turn on the base unit. Warren is going into delivery man mode. I'm gonna need to get with him somehow so keep in contact. I'll put this bluefish in my ear so you can tell me what's going on."

"Okay, boss. I'll get the connection set. You know, it

wouldn't have cost much more to get it relayed to you directly, so you could talk to him?"

"Okay, okay, I'll make the investment eventually. It's too late for this one. I'll call you in a minute. I need to make a call and I'll get right back with you."

By the time Archie was done with his call, he was sitting in his Crown Victoria with the engine running.

"Okay, boss, he's turning into the Hollywood Forever Cemetery."

"I can get there in minutes."

"Wait, he'll be leaving his car and running for a bus. Do you want me to get the car taken care of?"

"No. Somebody may be watching. Let the city impound the car if they want to. It keeps it real."

"Right. Keepin' it real. All right, he's running down the street to catch the bus. Now he's on the bus heading east on Santa Monica. This guy has a voice scrambler and he said go south but the bus doesn't go south. It goes east and west."

"I'm just a couple of blocks back."

"All the bugs are active and still together."

"Is it approaching Vermont?"

"Aye, aye, cap'n."

"That's the one then. I'm right behind it."

"Oh. It looks like he's getting out."

"Shit. They're gonna make him get on the fuckin' train."

"Yeah. It looks like it, boss. I'm gonna lose the signal if he goes down there."

"Shit. I'm gonna need to get down there." The horns blared at him and people cursed as he moved his vehicle into the left-hand turn lane. The light turned green and he jumped the gun on the oncoming traffic, screaming the tires and whipping the back of the car around in the street. He parked it in the parking lot on the northwest corner and got out, running to get to the train station entrance on the southeast corner. Not only did Jacqueline lose the signal from the tracking devices, she also lost Archie's cell phone signal; it came on and then she lost it again. She could not maintain the connection.

Archie saw Sean get into the railway car and stepped into the next one down. He could see through the window at the end. His client was perfectly visible at the near end of the other car. Sean did not turn around and look at him, and Archie wished he could let the man know he was right there but he could not risk it. He observed the women on the train mobbing Sean, and he saw the signatures being handed out. Then Sean was on the phone. He was surprised that Sean could get cell phone reception in the subway. As far as he knew, nobody else could.

After a few seconds on the phone, Sean took off his jacket and threw it on a seat, then he removed his ear piece and put it in his shirt pocket, took off his shirt, signed it, and gave it to an admirer. The young blonde woman he gave it to was obviously overwhelmed by the gift because she threw herself at him and kissed him full on the mouth. He hugged her for a second and then let her go. The train was stopping and the action star was moving toward the exit.

"Yeah, boss, I got you again. I'm getting something from the mic but it's garbled. I was getting something until he was in the subway, but I can't make it out now. I tried to talk to him but there's no way I can tell if he can hear me."

"Look, Jackie, we got off at the Pershing Square Station. He's walking away. I think I got some woman wearing his shirt following him around. I don't know what happened to his bluefish ear piece. I... yeah. He's buying a T-shirt from a street vendor. Crap! Now he's coming back this way."

"Look, little darling, you want to help Sean?" Jacqueline listened to Archie growling in somebody's ear.

"Turn around and walk with me."

"Who do you think you are?" came clearly through the other connection.

"I'm Sean Warren's bodyguard, and I'm trying to keep him from getting killed. Now are you going to help me or are you gonna be responsible for getting him snuffed?"

"Okay," the vapid female voice responded.

"Boss, I can hear you both ways. You got the mic?"

"No, it's attached to the shirt."

"Well, get the shirt."

"I'll try in a minute. Give me a second, Jackie. I think this is going down, now. Yeah, he's going into the parking garage underneath Pershing Park." Archie muttered a string of curses that ran together unintelligibly. He knew the signal was going to be lost again.

"Look, sweetheart, if you wanna help Sean, stay right here and talk to my secretary. Her name is Jackie. The microphone is right here in the collar. I'm going down into the parking garage. Can you do that for me, sweetheart?"

Jackie heard the unidentified voice answer in the affirmative, then she was treated to both voices speaking simultaneously.

"Hello, Jackie, my name is Candy and I'm supposed to talk to you while… this guy follows Sean Warren into the parking garage. They both went into the walk down at the uh… Fifth Street side of the park. I'm feeling pretty stupid standing here and carrying on a one-sided conversation but that's what he told me to do."

"Jackie," came the deeper voice of her boss, "keep an eye on the transponder signal. I don't know what's gonna happen now, but I'm going underground. I'm betting this is where they set up the drop. If he drives out of there I'm fucked."

As was to be expected, the transponder signals were the first to drop out, almost simultaneously. Archie's satellite signal dropped out next and the only thing remaining was the microphone on Sean's shirt, and that was spewing out chatter from someone named Candy.

"Y'know what? He said to stay there, by the door to the walk up, but that doesn't make any sense. I'm gonna walk over to the corner, 'cross the street from the Biltmore. That way I can watch the drive out too. I don't know if that's what I wanna do, but it's what I think I should do and so that's what I'm gonna do. I really don't know what's going on so I don't know what I'm supposed to be doing, but he said to watch the walk in door and..." The chatter went on in this vein, unceasingly, a veritable fountain of one-sided conversation. The verbal equivalent of white noise. Aggravating, but the only signal Jackie could get. The wireless ear piece in the shirt pocket was in play, but Candy could not hear it when Jackie tried to communicate. Candy did not seem to know it was there.

Archie pulled his gun as soon as he was out of sight of the street. It seemed to him that the men making the swap had picked a pretty smart spot. They were in the heart of the downtown area with unlimited escape routes, underground where trackers and communicators were useless. They had already made him get rid of his wire, almost as if they knew he was wearing it. Maybe they didn't know it would be useless down there.

Looking through the window of the stairway, Archie could see Sean talking to someone on the cell phone he had gotten in the subway. The one with the device taped to it. He decided that the device must be some kind of walkie-talkie. That, he thought, meant the extortionists were close enough to use a short-range communicator. He watched his client walk down to a four-door BMW and stand behind it, still talking on the phone. Sean set the briefcase on the trunk of the car, unlocked it from his wrist, turned, faced away from the car and took two steps into the drive.

The doors to the car opened and three men in business suits got out. There was no sign of Melissa, but Archie did not know that they had kidnapped Melissa so he was not looking for her. One of the men carried what looked like a hand-held antenna, which he passed over the briefcase. There must have been a signal detected because the man waved a gloved hand at one of his compatriots and that man opened up a nylon bag, obviously for the money. The third man retrieved the cell phone from Sean's hand.

Things got complicated when the first man tried to open the briefcase and could not. It was locked. A true professional would not have allowed this to upset him but this man became enraged. Rather than asking Sean to open the case, he swung the case by the handle and smashed it into the side of Sean's head. Sean fell to the ground with a cry. The second man pulled a revolver from inside his jacket.

There was no way Archie could have known what was going to happen in the next second. As far as he could tell the swap had gone bad, and Sean Warren was about to end his last performance. He opened the door to the stairs and yelled "LAPD."

The one man who had already pulled a weapon was as surprised as the others, but his surprise caused him to move the barrel of his pistol upward toward the sound of the newcomer's voice. It was an unfortunate move on his part, though not entirely conscious. His hand pointed to where his eyes had moved. It cost him dearly. Archimedes Prometheus Chamberlain shot him twice in the chest.

The remaining two men in business suits reached into their jackets and without a second's hesitation, Archie shot the nearest of the two. The man had no protection. There were no other vehicles between himself and the stairwell. Before the first victim hit the floor, the second man had two slugs in his chest. The third man was on the other side of the

German automobile, and the two rounds Archie aimed at him took out the back window but did not damage him.

In all the years he had been an officer of the law, Archie had never needed more than six shots. He relied on his .38 revolver now as he had for all those years as a cop. This was the first time it caused him a problem. The man behind the car had a 9mm semi-automatic with fourteen rounds in the handle. As soon as he saw that Archie was fumbling with a reloader, he opened up. The only thing that saved Archie was the fact that the man was not much of a shot and he was scared half to death. The third round he fired caught Archie in the outside of the right thigh, spun him around, and dropped him to the ground. Seeing what he thought was a detective for the LAPD go down, he jumped into the BMW, started it up and nailed the gas. Sean barely got out of the way in time as the wheels smoked and then bounced over the fallen man directly behind the car. Archie could not get his revolver reloaded fast enough to put a bullet into the driver. As if in final insult, the license plate on the rear of the vehicle was obscured by a plastic cover and unreadable in the dim light of the parking garage.

Jacqueline was almost to the point of shutting the feed off from the microphone. The insipid blather that came from Candy's mouth was beginning to drive her up the wall. She drank seldom but was about ready for a shot of something strong when she heard the voice say, "Oh, I think I heard someone shooting something. Yes, that was definitely gunshots and they were coming from downstairs, that is they were coming from the parking garage under the park. Oh, I hope Sean's all right. I hear more shots. I'm pretty sure they're shots. They sound like bang, bang, bang. Here's a car coming out now. Oohhh! He drove right through the gate. License plate QRT233. It's a beamer. He's driving like a maniac. Okay, he's gone. I think somebody should call the police."

Chapter Eight
Follow the Money

Terry revved it up, released the clutch and stomped on the gas. Both rear wheels began to smoke and stink as the street radials spun over and over without catching traction. The engine was everything it was supposed to be; all it had needed was a tune up. Even without the nitrous oxide, the Ford was a hell of a sleeper. Terry was heading for Van Nuys in a vehicle that made him look like he had borrowed it from his mother. He thought it was perfect.

The job had taken longer than the manager had expected, but the lines were finally run. The new gears were in the rear end and the clutch was nice and tight. The license plates were stolen and it was impossible to certify so getting stopped was not an option. Terry transferred his residence from the pricey but luxurious hotel by the beach to a sleazy motel on Sepulveda Boulevard. The parking lot was behind the motel so it could not be easily seen and there was a friendly tavern next door where some of the local youngsters came to drink. The room came with a kitchen space but he did not use it much.

Within a couple of days Terry had found some young hot-rodders in the neighborhood who had told him about cruise nights and invited him to ride along. Terry was astonished that first night by the number of old vehicles registered and running the roads. They had nothing like this in most of the places he had been, or he had never seen them. What he was really interested in was street racing and in a couple of days he was in with that scene. All the younger crowds were driving light, souped-up, front wheel drive foreign cars. When he mentioned his smog era station wagon he got laughed at and, in truth, he began to wonder if he could compete against the more modern machines. What he was looking for was the sort of no-holds-barred autocross that was as much like a demolition derby as a road race. This sort of unofficial smash 'em up was common in Australia and he had assumed he could find them here as well. It was a great disappointment to find such a different racing culture in Southern California where looking good was every bit as important as being good.

Unable to get his adrenaline fix on the road, Terry called his connection in Michigan. "G'day mate. You doing any heavy lifting of your own these days?"

"I don't do any heavy lifting."

"Well perhaps I can lend you a hand then."

"I'm thinking you can. I found something on the left coast that might be of interest to you. High profile case, lots of potential."

"Run it out. I'll give it a peep."

"Okay. A movie star had his girl kidnapped. He hired a PI and went in like a cowboy. To make a long story short, the PI got himself shot last Tuesday. The movie star lost the money and the girl. She showed up three days later, yesterday actually, full of heroin and raped to death in Compton."

"She was raped to death?"

"Well, yeah, raped and beaten and then overdosed, I think. I got a call from LA. She was asking for someone smooth, efficient and effective. I thought of you, naturally."

"It sounds like a winner. I'll need particulars, a down payment and, I expect you'll need a finder's fee."

"The client will be paying the finder's fee. You are in no situation to contact the client in any way. This was made very clear."

"Bloody right. It makes for a better slide. Plausible deniability, I believe it's called. 'No sir, I never met Mr. Moviestar. No sir, I was never paid anything.'"

"Right." Terry's contact in Michigan wanted to get the transaction over as soon as possible. He was certain that someone else would be contracted to do the job if he were unable to come through soon. He did not want to chat.

"So where is the package?"

"Go to Torrential Motorsports on Olympic and Stoner and tell the man at the counter that you want a 1956 Indian. When he tells you that he doesn't have a 1956 Indian, you are to respond that you will be going to India and want to fit in. Is that clear?"

"Check, mate. Torrential Motorsports on Olympic and Stoner. I want a 1956 Indian. When he tells me no Indians, I need to go to India. Tell me though, what is an Indian?"

"It's an American motorcycle."

"Oh, right. They started making those again."

"Don't worry about that. That's not important. Remember the 1956."

"Well, what if he has a 1956 Indian?"

"They didn't make Indians after 1953 so there is no such thing."

"Right then. We'll talk again."

Terry hung up the phone and wiped down the handle, thinking about movie stars and Indians. Then he thought about a young woman raped and beaten to death in Compton. He was a killer, an assassin and a murderer but he was still amazed at humanity's capacity for inhuman acts. A scene flashed across his mind. He had the man who had killed his mother tied to a post and he was firing up an acetylene torch. He was not exempt from the inhumane, but he still felt justified in his actions that day. He took a deep breath and thought that he had not tortured that man enough.

The trip to Olympic Boulevard was a little over eleven miles as the crow flies and it took him over an hour on the buses. He appreciated the fact that it was impossible to tail a bus effectively and that waiting at bus stops gave him the opportunity to observe everything around him. He was certain that nobody knew he was in California and nobody in

California knew who he was. That was going to change, the moment he walked into the shop and asked for the non-existent model.

The parking lot was full of motorcycles, new and used, with a smattering of all-terrain vehicles. It made him slightly uncomfortable when he thought about it. He had set the bikies in Sydney up in fine style, despite their objections. Inside, the place was well lit and the floors were clean. Harley Davidson and Indian Motorcycles had the premier spots on the floor with some of the larger displacement Japanese offerings shouldering up to the back wall. The service counter was empty, but there was a man with long hair and a beard behind the parts desk, leafing through a copy of American Iron.

Mexican was the most common of all the foreign accents in Southern California but it did not fit well with Terry Kingston's blond hair and blue eyes. On top of his complexion, he was taller by a head than most Mexicans and while he could speak a good Spanish after the last couple of years practice, he did not have the Mexican dialect down perfectly. He opted instead for his German accent which was much more convincing.

"Good day, sir. I was thinking that I might perhaps be able to find a classic motorcycle here."

"Sure. We got all kinds. What were you looking for?"

"I was thinking of perhaps a 1956 Indian."

"Sorry, bud, we got no 1956 Indians here. We got some new ones."

"Ah, I see. Well, I was hoping in vain then. I was actually looking for one because I am to be transferred to the Indian continent and I was hoping it would help me fit in."

The sheer absurdity of the statement combined with the German accent would have made almost anyone laugh. The man behind the parts counter did not laugh; he reached under the counter and pulled out a manila envelope marked

BSA and handed it to Terry.

Resisting the urge to click his heels and bow like a true Nazi, Terry took the envelope, thanked the man and walked out of the shop.

The restaurant had the kind of lighting calculated to defeat photographers and the drapes were permanently pulled over the front window. There was no way of telling if this attracted movie stars or love birds, but it made a good spot to peruse the 8x10 glossy photographs. Terry pulled the little candle in a jar in front of him and went through the pictures that, while crime scene standard, were horrifying. The one picture taken before the episode showed her to be a beautiful young girl with an impish smile and perfect skin. The crime scene photos revealed that she had been tortured before dying.

Terry wondered how his mysterious client had gotten a copy of the homicide report but did not waste time speculating. The report revealed a massive dose of heroin in her system and listed that as the preliminary cause of death. The Medical Examiner's initial report was attached to it and clearly stated that the cause of death was a myocardial infarction caused by an overdose, but it also stated that the girl did not look as though she was a regular user. Terry lit a cigarette and thought to himself that the overdose was a blessing at that point. Some of the mutilation had been done post mortem, but not most of it, and there was evidence that she had been raped after she was dead as well as the multiple raping that occurred before she died. Without reserve, he decided that the men who did this deserved to die.

After reading the report Kingston returned to the photographs. He stared for a minute at the professional head shot. Melissa had been California movie star beautiful, with flawless skin and perfect teeth. An impish smile hinted at a playful personality and the gleam in her eye was a reflection of her wit. The crime scene photos set Terry's jaw. His face became florid and the smoldering fire that he kept banked behind his eyes threatened to run up his forehead and singe his hair.

The waiter appeared and asked if Terry would please put out the cigarette, that the whole state had a strict no smoking policy. The look that the waiter got was such that the waiter physically took a step back. Kingston stuck his smoke in the melted wax of the candle and told the waiter to bring him another cup of coffee, a steak and chips and a fruit cup. The waiter went away to fill the order.

That was when Terry first foresaw some trouble. There was no target name or photo. There was no address. There was only a telephone number. He exhaled heavily out his nose and stared at the number wondering if he was being set up. He sat there and drank his second cup of coffee, memorizing the contents of the envelope as best he could. When the waiter showed back up it was with a plate full of potato chips and an overdone steak. Terry told him to feed it to the dogs, paid for his meal and left without tipping the waiter. He was losing his feel for California but he had gained a sense of purpose. Whoever had beaten this beautiful young woman to death was going to pay and it was not going to be the tender mercy of death from afar. This man deserved to die a horrible death.

The bank of pay phones outside Santa Monica Place, a block from the beach, was a good spot to call from, though it was a long way from the motel. There were three major routes of exit, and the beach to the west. There was a good view around, though all the glass might make for observers hidden behind reflective surfaces. Terry had to remind himself that nobody knew he was here. He was a stranger, a tourist, a ghost.

"Prometheus Investigations." The woman on the phone did not have a California accent; it was more like something from New York City, but Terry did not have the experience to pick it out.

"Good day, ma'am. I got this telephone number from a man with a beard," he said, using a southern American accent.

"Lots'a guys got beards, they just kinda grow. Can you be more specific?"

"He stood behind a parts counter."

"And you were looking for a 1956 Indian, am I right?"

"Yes. I'm to be transferred to India."

"We've been expecting your call."

"I am calling."

"Well, Archie's not out of the hospital yet. If you wanna talk to him, you can visit him in room 412 of the new wing of County General. That's on Marengo between State and Chicago. Downtown."

"I'm sure I can find it. Where's your office?"

"It's in the Rampart Building between North Curson and North Stanley on the north side of Melrose Avenue. Second floor. Name's on the door."

"And what might your name be?"

"I'm Jacqueline Vandenberg. I'm in charge while Archie's indisposed."

"Then perhaps I should speak with you, after all, you sound so much more appealing than Archie."

"No, I don't think so. Arch said to send you there if you called. He has a special kind of assignment for you. I'm not supposed to know about it."

"But you do, don't you?"

"That is unfounded speculation on your part and cannot be proven."

"I'll tell you what, you sound like you could use a drink. Why don't you and I meet somewhere and knock back a couple?"

"Look, you sound like a nice guy, but mixing business

with pleasure is out of the question. Maybe after it's all over we can go out and have a drink or something, but not until after this thing is taken care of."

"Very well. I will give Archie a call. What is the number?"

"Oh, I don't think this is the sort of thing Archie is going to want to do over the telephone."

"I'm sure you're correct. I'm looking forward to meeting you Jacqueline. Please call Archie and tell him I will visit him tomorrow."

"Sure thing. What should he call you?"

"Don't call me anything, I'll call you." Terry hung up the phone and wiped off the handle, then he pulled out a map of Los Angeles from his back pocket and a bus schedule. He had to admit that it was getting to be a bit annoying to ride the bus but it was the most anonymous method of travel he had ever encountered. He had never even seen the same bus driver twice, let alone the same passenger.

Halfway to County General he regretted not eating lunch, and so stopped off for a hamburger and french fries before continuing. It took two and a half hours to get where he was going and when he got there he was faced with it.

Terry had a problem with hospitals. His experience at the tender age of eight had left him with traumatic stress disorder related to hospitals. He almost had a nervous breakdown in the hospital where he had finished his Michigan assignment. This time he was sure it would not be so bad.

It seemed logical to Terry that he go in through the emergency room entrance but he was stopped short at the door. The metal detector at the emergency room door made this entrance unfeasible. The next choice was the parking ramp doors; these too had metal detectors. He was looking for a clandestine alternative when he realized he could walk in through the front doors without incident.

The air conditioning felt good but it was not the temperature that kept him sweating. There was no chance he was going to use the stairs, the elevator was the only option reasonably open to him. His memory of hiding in the stairwell of the Goulburn Community Medical Center, with his mother's killer hunting him, still haunted him.

As uncomfortable as he was, he forced himself to reach the fourth floor and find room 412. It was a private room containing a bed, a television and an older gentleman with a heavily bandaged leg. There was also a brace of uniformed police officers in the room with him. They looked at Terry with the suspicious eyes that belong to officers all over the world. It did nothing to relieve the anxiety.

"Archie?" he asked with a smile plastered on his face and his best southern accent.

Without a hitch, Archimedes asked the officers if he could have a minute with an old friend. He made it look sincere, even though they had never met.

Once the officers had left the room, he asked, "You the guy? Jackie said you'd be here tomorrow. I didn't expect you today."

"I'm the guy with the '56 Indian." Terry was hoping his American accent would pass.

"You don't look too comfortable."

"I'm not. Look, I'm not here for small talk, to pass the hoppers, I'm here to find out what the job is. I know why but I don't know where and I'm beginning to feel a bit like a square peg in a round hole. Why the bronze?" He finished with a toss of his head.

"If you mean the cops, they're friends of mine. I spent 32 years on the force. They want to get this shmuck that shot me as much as I do. Here, put these in the bag." Archie brought some sheets of paper out from the bedding. "It's good to have friends."

A quick look convinced Terry that he was getting

somewhere and he stuffed them into the manila envelope with the photographs and reports. "All right, ma… Archie, I'm going to need legal transportation and a down payment."

"Down payment is in the safe in the office. Tell Jackie you're there for the round table discussion and she'll get that for you. I'll have a registered vehicle for you to drive delivered to wherever you are. It'll be a company car, so to speak."

"I think this is concluded then. I will be in touch soon."

They shook hands and Archie grabbed Terry's wrist with his other hand. "These motherfuckers put me down. I'll never be able to do the job again. I'll need to shut down the office but not before I see their fucking heads on a spike. Understand?" His head fell back on the pillow.

"Yes. I understand fully. I'll stop by the outfitter on the way back and pick up some spikes." If Terry's eyes could have projected the cold that Archie saw in them it would have frozen his face. It gave Archie a feeling of warmth in his belly even as it sent a shiver up his spine.

The feeling of relief that suffused Terry's mind as he left the hospital was akin to a narcotic. He actually sat on a bench outside and breathed deeply for a couple of minutes. Hospitals would never be a place of healing for him. Then, in his more relaxed state, it struck him. His connection in Michigan had said 'She. She was asking for someone smooth, efficient and effective.' The secretary had called for a professional, not the investigator. He filed it away for the moment but realized that there was something wrong with the outward appearance of Prometheus Investigations.

As he waited, he looked at the documents Archie had given him. They were the police reports of a couple of crime scenes. Three men had been murdered at the New Moon Studio and another had been executed in his upstairs apartment on Lexington. There was no explanation of what these crimes had to do with Archie being shot or Melissa being kidnapped. Terry scratched his head and lit a cigarette. He did not know how effective he could be with such a dearth of information.

Chapter Nine
1956 Indian

One of the things the circuitous trip to California did for Homer Sullivan was make him lonely. The first night the three of them had shared a motel room, but the second night they had taken adjacent rooms and the noise of wild, thrashing sex through the wall had depressed the young man. He had no illusions that he could bed the woman he had been told was named Rio, but it made for a good fantasy.

When morning came, Homer awoke to the man he knew as Glasgow standing at the foot of his bed. His guard had insisted on keeping the room key himself, as if he didn't trust Homer not to do something stupid.

Within minutes, the trio was on the road. Homer was sick of sitting in the back seat and had asked to sit in the front. There had been no objection.

It seemed as though every time something was done that Homer Sullivan didn't understand it was almost second nature to the other two. He asked about their selection of roads, knowing they could have made it a lot faster if they had taken the expressways and probably been noticed less. He had not taken into consideration the cameras and speed traps in place on all the major highways. He mentioned that the best way to LA from Kansas City was to go south on Route 35 to Oklahoma City and get on Route 40 West. He was told that Homeland Security had set up roadblocks on major highways in New Mexico and Arizona. They were looking for illegal immigrants. He had answered that he was not an illegal immigrant and his associates had looked at him as though he was stupid.

The Cadillac performed flawlessly throughout the beginning of the trip, as long as they kept the fuel tank full. Its big engine did drink a lot of gasoline. The first day they cruised comfortably across the flat lands of Kansas and

Eastern Colorado. The second day they turned north before hitting Denver, angled over and went up Route 25. Homer thought that was stupid since LA was in Southern California, but when he asked, he got a friendly lecture on how to keep himself alive when being hunted. When he said he didn't think he was actually being hunted, a purring voice from the back seat told him that it was always better to assume the worst. When he complained they were wasting time he was told there was nothing but time. Then he got a strange lecture from the Scotsman.

"Man, born of woman, has but a short time upon this Earth," Gordon began. "And during the time he has been given by our lord there is little that he may do that is seen as good and pure, save the praising of the Lord. So it is, that all returneth to the soil in its time, ashes to ashes, dust to dust and what hope may a man have for his life but to be seen as good by the Lord? Yea, though many wonder what will be said about them after their passing, such is not the true measure of a man but whether he has lived his life to be a good and pure individual, according to the scripture, for he that is so, shall dwell in the house of the Lord forever."

Homer stared at his guard who did not look back at him. He looked into the back seat at Anastasia who was looking out the window with a calm and unconcerned look on her face. He turned back to ask Gordon what that was all about when he heard Anastasia's purring voice from the back seat, "Even the Devil can quote scripture." Homer Sullivan said nothing for a long time after that.

Without explaining why, MacMaster stopped at the memorial for George Armstrong Custer's 7th Cavalry at the Little Big Horn. They had negotiated Wyoming and were about an hour into Montana. He stood and smoked a cigar for a while, looking past the mass grave and out over the field. Neither Homer nor Anastasia asked what he was doing and all three were consumed by their own thoughts as they headed north to where Route 90 turned west.

There had been options when tooling across the Great Plains but those options were less plentiful at the Rocky Mountains. The only way over was to get in line where it was necessary and pass the freight trucks when one could. Homer was quick to point out that if they had gone south on Route 25 they could have gone west on Route 10 and avoided the mountains altogether. Gordon did not reply as he was maneuvering between two semis at the top of a hill where the left lane disappeared. There were few police officers on the roads in the mountains and they were concerned with overheated vehicles and stranded motorists. To pull anyone over for a routine traffic stop was unheard of and immensely dangerous with all the big trucks straining their way up one side and trying to restrain themselves on the way down.

Gordon pulled off the expressway at Fort Ellis just east of Boseman, Montana and parked the Cadillac in the lot of a family restaurant. There were not a lot of customers and the men who were eating were trying not to stare at Anastasia. After eating, Homer asked Gordon if he didn't mind them staring at his woman. Gordon gave him a lopsided grin and lit a cigar as they pulled back on the highway. He explained that there was no way to keep men from looking unless he wrapped her in a burka. Then he asked how many of the men in the restaurant would be able to identify who was with her. How many had even looked at Homer? Homer acceded the point.

They continued through Butte and turned south on Route 15, stopping for the day at a motel in Dillon, Montana. Homer found it humorous that they were in Beaverhead County but his escorts did not understand why. Dillon was a charming little college town. Anastasia stayed with Homer while Gordon walked about. When he returned he brought bags of take-out food, beer and liquor. They ate and drank and watched the people. Nothing thrived in Dillon that did not appeal to the college crowd or service them in some way. It made for a young and refreshing local culture.

Route 15 went across the tops of the mountains in Idaho and Utah. The towns were small and the valleys barren. Homer was amazed that anyone would live there but Gordon was of a different mind. He appreciated the solitude and the views were marvelous when they could be seen over the ridges. The Scot understood that the high mountains were no place for a young man in this day and age, but he truly enjoyed soaking in the ambience. He said nothing about it for his mind was working on plans for the future. When a man needed to disappear, these valleys could provide the cover.

When they hit Las Vegas, Gordon took Truck Route 215 around the city, giving them a view of the glitz and neon but not subjecting them to the chaos and cameras of the strip. He had already turned down a job in Las Vegas for just that reason. Howard complained that he had wanted to stop in Vegas and gamble some of his ill-gotten gains, but he was overruled. Gordon would not even let him visit one of the notorious ranches outside town. He was going to deliver his charge and then, perhaps, he would learn to surf.

"Please have a seat, Mr....?"

"Just call me Indian," Terry said as he sat down in the outer office of Prometheus Investigations. He had come here the day after visiting the owner and founder in his hospital bed. He sized up the woman behind the desk, the woman behind the man, so to speak, and liked what he saw. Jacqueline was about five-foot six with brown hair pinned tightly behind her head. She had wide, brown, doe-like eyes that gave her a look of innocence and vulnerability that belied the severe hairstyle and out of date business attire. Her skin was strikingly smooth and she used little makeup on it. Her lips were painted a coppery color that went well with her outfit. For jewelry she wore a single pair of small emerald studs and no rings.

"Well then, Mr. Indian, what may we do for you this morning?"

"I was told to ask you about a round table discussion."

"And I was told you would visit Archie today. Instead, you visited him yesterday and here you are this morning. I have a problem with that. I have seen enough men who want to get paid for something they have no intention of doing. Are you such a man, Mr. Indian?"

"No, I assure you. This job may take longer than some others due to the unknown nature of the subject, but when it's all done, he'll be a bulldog eatin' porridge."

"A what?"

"Uh, never mind. Look, I'm not here to talk to you about how I work, just to collect a down payment for my services and an auto to use while I'm working."

"Okay, I'm gonna give you Archie's car since he isn't going to be using it for a while. You'll need to get it out of impound, okay?"

"No. That is not okay. I am neither an errand boy nor a chauffeur. I will not be getting anyone's car from impound. Rent me a vehicle if you must but have it here by the end of the day and get me my down payment." Terry was not usually so short with women but this one was clearly going to get on his nerves. His initial impression had been one of efficiency and candor, but her demeanor had quickly changed to suspicion and distrust, rankling him somewhat. He knew better than to worry about anyone doubting his professionalism. After all, he did not come with a resume and signed letters of reference; however, to all but insult him upon initial meeting was not what a man in his position would expect. It was as though she was looking down her nose at him.

Jacqueline stood and went through the door into the

back room, returning a few minutes later with a stack of bills. "Here's the cash. I hope you're better than you look."

Terry dropped his pretense of an American accent. She was actually insulting him now. "When all's said and done perhaps we'll take the ferret for a run. But until then I'll pass on the fun and step out of the sun. Man's not a camel. Rent me a car and deliver it to the pub down the street."

Jacqueline shook her head once and blinked twice. She had no idea what he had just said but it had jolted her. She watched silently as the blond man walked out the door and she did not smile until the door had closed behind him. A few minutes later, she picked up the telephone.

"Something does not seem right, my love." Anastasia seldom smoked, but she was enjoying a few puffs from Gordon's cigar.

"What? Is it because we're not callin' the priest?" Gordon looked at his woman's sweaty face on the pillow next to him.

"I do not know. I am not comfortable with the assignment, this is true. Let us look at what we have. This boy saw something and got a lot of money a thousand miles from where we picked him up. He is being guarded by a bunch of farmers. His half sister from a thousand miles away contracts us to guard him instead, and yet it took him time to think he wanted to go to her. The men he is sure are not following him probably have no idea where he is. He could have driven himself to California without all this drama and expense. I do not like it and I do not like him, and I will be glad when this assignment is over and we can go back to doing what I like to do."

"I thought we were just doing what you like to do," he said stroking her bare breast.

"You know what I mean." She slapped his hand. "Decommissioning a man is a simple and final assignment, without all the stress and personality of being a guardian."

"Right. Like General Modiano?"

"Ai! Are you going to bring that up forever?"

"I'm sorry," he said with a smile.

"It was much more than the general's death that caused the trouble in Rio."

Gordon took the cigar from her hand and drew on it, inhaling the heavy smoke and blowing it out with a satisfied look on his face. He did not have the same sense of foreboding that Anastasia did. He thought it was an easy job for good pay. They were taking their time on the trip, and it was more like a vacation than an assignment. They were armed to the teeth but needed almost none of it and would likely finish the job without a single shot being fired. The first half of the purse had been paid, what more was there to worry about?

Terry sat in the bar for about an hour and a half, nursing a couple of beers. The cash felt good in his pocket, but he did not like to meet the principals in an operation. He much preferred the anonymity of the outsider, the freelance solver of problems. When the parties that had most at stake could identify you, it led to more than just trouble. What he was mulling over in his mind, however, was not that he had met two of the principals, but the fact that he had been told that he would never meet the real principal, the movie star whose fiancée had been so brutally murdered. He had accepted Archie's act and had seen it as sufficient motivation to wreak vengeance on the culprits, but he knew the real motivator was still anonymous. It would work better that way. He realized, just as he was feeling self-satisfied, that he had intended to ask the secretary what the significance of the earlier murders was. He had allowed his feelings to upset his agenda. A voice came into his mind from the past. It was his Uncle Ginger telling him that emotions and munitions had no place in the same room, or something like that. He hadn't written to Ginger in a long time and made a mental note to do so soon.

The driver of the rental car double-parked in front of the tavern and the young man ran in looking for Mr. Indian. Terry threw a tip on the bar and grabbed the keys and the receipt. Within a minute he was in the rental and pulling off while the driver got into another vehicle.

His new transportation was not a police car but it had the police/taxi package in it. The heavy duty suspension would have been appreciated on the deteriorated roads of the northeast but California's highways were not so broken. He mused as he pulled off that the vehicle did not have a fraction of the horsepower that the station wagon he had bought did. He would have liked to have driven the old wagon; after all it had cargo space, ground-pounding torque, and it felt solid. If he could have made it legal, or even made it look legal, he would have been driving it. The young hot rodders he had been consorting with had no idea how to get something like a 1976 Ford emissions tested. They would never have considered trying.

It wasn't until later that day he saw the tabloid headlines "*Sean Warren suspected of killing his fiancée.*" Every one of the star-status pseudo newspapers ran the story. Terry had to buy one of each and read about it. The photographs of Sean's love interest were difficult to use as identification for the tortured face in the autopsy photos because she had been beaten so badly. It was the same woman however. The "Blaze of Glory" star had definitely been questioned, but he was not a suspect. He had been released. Terry had no need to speak with the man. He had already decided the merits of the case. In his younger years he might have finished the man who did this on principle alone. Terry Kingston did not hold with wife beaters or child molesters. He might kill people for a living but he considered that a necessary evil, a legitimate service. Raping and mutilating women and children was worse than an animal and the perpetrators of such crimes deserved to die.

Jurgen Schrimple was in a state of agitation that could not be called unjustified but might be characterized as insensitive. His aggravation was compounded daily by circumstances, some of which were beyond his control. He was the director for "Blaze of Glory", but Sean Warren had gone underground when his fiancée had been brutally murdered, and the production schedule was threatened. Jurgen had been obliged to work with a rapper named Ice Cream who had little previous acting experience and only a modicum of talent. The entire block outside the set had been flooded with reporters and photographers from scandal magazines who were constantly trying to infiltrate the set and bothering all the workers, even the grips and designers. Jurgen did not think he was going to be able to finish the film and certainly not within budget. It was like seeing the second coming of the Lord when Sean walked on set, five days after the murder of his woman.

It was embarrassing to watch the normally rigid and controlled German fawn over the star. No one who knew Jurgen could believe the way he was acting, though they could understand it. He did everything in his power to thank the action star for returning.

Sean devastated him when he said that he was only on set to confer with Ice Cream. The meeting set off a whole new set of rumors.

"IC, my brother from another mother. What did you find out?"

"I got yer back, Jack. Have I ever failed you?"

"No, Ice, you always been there for me. Now you know I'll always be there for you too. What is it?"

"It was the South Alley Bloods that took possession of

your woman. They in Carson. Only Bloods in Carson. They were the ones what done the real shit. I got nothing on who took her though. Those fools ain't got the sense to organize a gang rape in prison let alone kidnap a smart girl like 'Lissa. You looking for somebody else, someone with the smarts to put up all those little cameras and watch you movin'. The South Alley Bloods did you dirty, but the real power is someone else, and you're gonna need to sweat the capo of the neighborhood to get the power's name. Capo's name is Bash."

"Bash?"

"Yeah, street name. I can't find his real name but it don't matter. You go into that neighborhood and Bash is all you need to know."

"Brother, you just got a part in every film I ever make. I need to know how to proceed from here."

"Hey, I'm not the power I was then, y'know. I can get some men willing to do some gang banging but they ain't no smarter than the SAB. If you want to get your hands on Bash I suggest you get some professional help. I'm talking the SWAT team, now. These guys is armed like the Waco Wackos. I ain't goin' in against 'em."

"I'm already working on that. I'm going to talk to Jurgen and Central Casting. You just got yourself a bigger part."

What Sean did first however was not to call Casting, but to call Prometheus Investigations and tell Jacqueline Vandenberg what he had discovered. She was skeptical, as was her wont, but promised to relay the information to the appropriate personnel.

Jacqueline actually wore a big smile now. She had not liked the man retained to hunt down and eliminate the kidnappers. It was more than just the fact that he was a killer; that made him rather exciting to her; it was his attitude. She got the feeling he was looking down his nose at her. And then, there was his changeable accent. She was more than happy to relay this latest bit of news. She was betting it would take the wind out of his overblown sails.

It was a pity, Jacqueline thought, that she could not have used Jerry Kragon to do the job, but Jerry had left town and she did not want Archie to know Jerry existed. Jerry did jobs for her exclusively. As far as she was concerned, Archie would never meet the man.

Chapter Ten
Go West Young Man

"Have you made any progress?"

"It's only been a day and a half and I had lizard shit to work with." Terry's feelings toward Jacqueline had not softened. Something about her really annoyed him and the fact that he could not pick out what it was annoyed him even more. He had dropped his fake accent half because of his feelings. He watched her mouth as she spoke; it had an unpleasant, condescending sneer.

"Technically, it's been two days. Forty-eight hours, y'know."

"So, you decided to help me out and give me something more than reports of killings? The New Moon killings were professional and they took tapes, right? Pornos? So I'm thinking Sean Warren was on one of them and the new owners decided to take advantage of the one film he did not want released. I got no connection to the man killed on Alexander. So, if they got this guy on film with whatever it was, they didn't need to kidnap his woman except as a backup so he wouldn't go in like a cowboy. He decided he really was John Wayne and got her killed for it. Am I right?"

"Archie told you this?"

"No, Archie just said he got shot. I haven't seen that police report. It should have been the only one he had, but it was the only one he didn't have."

Jacqueline realized her mouth was open and closed it. She been prepared to reveal some of that to him, but she suspected that he had already known it. He was either smarter than she thought or a better liar. She decided that she would treat him with more respect than she had planned on originally. He was obviously much better than she had given him credit for.

"So, we got something new?"

"Uh, yes. Our contacts on the street tell us it was the South Alley Bloods out of Carson that are claiming the responsibility."

"Why would they do that?"

"You obviously don't come from LA…"

"Neither do you, luv."

"Look, I'm here to help. Let's stop picking at each other and work together like civilized human beings."

"That would assume a modicum of civilization on my part that has not yet been established. I might be nothing but a barbarous outlander."

"I'm sure you are, but we can still find a middle ground where some semblance of civility may be practiced."

"I'll try to keep my savage instincts in check."

"Thank you. Now, as I was saying, it's all about respect and among the gangs, the most outlandish crimes get the most respect. The police will investigate but they won't find anything, they never do. The gangs have gotten sophisticated, not like the mobs of days past. They have lookouts and secret codes and signals. The cops are scared in the gang neighborhoods. They don't get fucked with much, but they don't like to get out of their cars."

Terry said nothing but he noticed some elevated angst in her voice as she spoke. That was the first time he had heard her swear.

"So, the South Alley Bloods out of Carson are claiming the job. As near as I can tell, there are about a hundred of them. Their local leader is called Bash. It is imperative that he be taken alive as he is the man who will know who brought Melissa to them. He is the key to finding out who took her."

"And by extension, who is blackmailing Sean Warren."

Jacqueline knew there would be no hope of hiding the clients name now, so she just went with it. "I don't think that is going to occur any more. Sean would never give them any more money now."

"But they did get some from him."

"Yes, they got some money, but they also lost two men in the process. Archie shot two of them."

"And that would have been useful information. Why am I being misdirected?"

"It was decided you did not need to know."

Terry lit a cigarette and exhaled out his nose. He was regretting having taken the down payment and was feeling increasingly uncomfortable. Jacqueline was more than she appeared, and they were continuing to play games with information. He could not walk away now without sullying his reputation among those that mattered. He decided on the spot that if things did not improve, he would leave Archie and his lovely, carnivorous secretary six feet under. Without another word, he stood and walked out the door. The whole thing felt like a setup.

It was only ten miles to the downtown hospital, but the traffic jam on County Route 170 brought him to a virtual standstill and raised his blood pressure even further. By the time he reached County General he was furious, the adrenaline overwhelming the reaction he had developed for hospitals.

"Why is your woman fucking with me?"

"You mean Jackie?" Archie was looking little better from the day before. The painkillers gave him a droopy look to his already sagging face.

"That's right. I don't know how you work it here in the land of plenty, but I expect to be told who I need to attach and if there is anything extra I need to know, I need to know it. What I'm getting here is go and find somebody but you have no clues. Then you tell me to pick the leader of a street gang and force a name out of him. Then I'm told about the men you shot while they were shooting you. Is there anything else I need to know that I don't?"

"Uh, I don't know."

"Where is the police report?"

"I gave them to you."

"You dribbler. The one where you got shot."

"Oh, Jackie has that at the office."

"That's it then. You and your woman are playing a game with me. Our contract is terminated. I'm keeping the down payment for my trouble, but I'll be tossed before I'll do a job this way."

"Wait, wait, wait, wait, wait. I'll call Jacqueline and we'll get it all straightened out. I need this job done."

"No, you want this job done, or are you in commerce with someone else that makes it more worth your while?"

"You get a good recommendation and you are from outside the area. I assume you are leaving the area after the job?"

"I can't wait. This town is corrupted."

"It has its corruption but it has its enticements as well."

"As any place."

"Look, Mr. Indian, you seem to have gotten out on the wrong side of the bed this morning. I'll call Jacqueline and insist she give you all the pertinent information. We must have gotten some wires crossed. I've been a bit off my game what with being shot and all the drugs they pumped into me. Relax and give me a minute to gather my thoughts. I think I can give you everything you need. There's a notepad in that briefcase, take it out and write down any questions you have. We can still do this right. I can understand why you might think we were hiding something but we're not, really. Honestly, we didn't expect to get the kind of response we got. I didn't expect to see you for at least a week. I did ask for outside talent."

"Right, and I am. I happened to be here at the time so we both got, um... lucky."

"Let me begin at the beginning. First of all..."

The smell of antibiotics and industrial cleaners invaded Terry's sinuses, snapping his head back and transporting him to a time long past when he was nothing but a terrified child. His surroundings closed in on him and he felt everything he felt when huddling under the bottom of the stairs in a different hospital on a different continent. The back of his throat closed off and he could neither swallow nor breathe. He needed to get out of there and it was all he could do to get to his feet on wobbly legs.

"Mr. Indian? You look terrible," went unnoticed as Terry stumbled out the door and down the hall. He did not see the elevators and could not have waited for them anyway. He was in full flight syndrome.

The door to the stairwell twisted on its hinges like a living thing before his assaulted mind. He forced himself to open it and tore down the steps, his feet touching only the outside edges of the steps as he hurtled down the flights to the ground floor and tore out of the building. He was two blocks away before he slowed to catch his breath. He would not be going back in there again that day. He did not see the eyes watching him as he ran.

"I'll be going in first. I will give you a ring if the place looks safe. Rio, drive around the block. We were not followed into town, but a moving target is always harder to hit." MacMaster stepped out of the driver's seat and Anastasia slid over. Homer was hunkered down in the back seat.

While his woman drove the Cadillac off, Gordon strode into the building and up the stairs. The office door read Prometheus Investigations. When he stepped into the office he had one hand in his jacket pocket.

"I'm terribly sorry, my dear, I had thought we were directed to a software company. I was told that Jacqueline was a software developer."

"I am Jacqueline and I am a programmer, but I'm doing this for right now. Is there something Prometheus Investigations can do for you or are you looking for a software developer. I know some good ones if you have a job for them."

"Ah, well then, it would seem I am in the right place. I was, in fact, looking for your brother, Homer."

"I ain't seen Homer in years. Last I heard he was in Florida. I can't help you."

"Oh, but I'm sure you can."

"Mister, I don't know who you are, but I want you to know that I have a .45 caliber Glock pointed directly at your balls, and if you decide to get froggy I'm gonna blow them all over the wall behind you."

"Well, that certainly makes a statement. Why would you pull a big gun like that on somebody who just stopped by with a polite inquiry?" MacMaster's tone did not change and a smile twisted his lips.

"You want Homer. Nobody who wants Homer is polite. Now get your hand out of your pocket and put both of them on your head."

Gordon slid his hand off the revolver in his pocket and raised both hands in the air but the look on his face was still amused. "So, I assume you want Homer as well, since you are being so much less than polite?"

"I don't know what you are talking about. He is on the other side of the country and he can stay there. He's nothing but trouble."

"Then why did you contract me to protect him?"

Jacqueline wavered visibly and pulled her .45 auto from the holster secured under the desktop. "I didn't hire anybody. Who the hell are you?"

"If you allow me to make a telephone call, I can prove this to you, dear." Gordon now had his most winning smile on his face. He reached for the breast pocket of his jacket.

"Hold it. Two fingers. One wrong move and you're gonna look like a bagel."

Gordon reached into his pocket with two fingers and pulled out the phone. He pushed a few buttons and got an immediate answer. "Drop the boy off at the front door and find a place to park."

Jacqueline stiffened back up and looked nervous. Her eyes darted from Gordon to the door. It was obvious she was not used to this sort of tension. The door opened and she relaxed as if a spring had uncoiled. Homer walked in with his bag in his hand.

"Whoa, sister, can the firepower. Shit. She got the drop on you, huh?"

"I allowed her to believe she was in charge to find out if she was truly who she said she was. One can't be too careful; she might have been replaced. She is your sister and as such, might have been targeted by your enemies." Gordon had lowered his arms.

"And what were you going to do then?" Homer asked.

"I would have shot her."

Jacqueline was sitting there, still pointing a loaded, large caliber weapon at them, amazed that they were talking about her as if she was somewhere else. "Hey, if anyone was gonna get shot, it was you."

Gordon's eyes twinkled as he said, "If that is what you wish to believe, milady, who am I to dissuade you?"

"A better question is, who are you?"

"You may call me Glasgow. I was asked by what must be a mutual acquaintance to keep your brother Homer from the consequences of his ill conceived actions."

"Hey Jackie, this guy takes care of business. He and Rio tied up six guys I had watching me without making a noise. I woke up and boom, there they were."

"Who is Rio?"

"Oh, Rio's his wife. Is she coming up? Oh, here she is

now."

Anastasia was stalking down the hallway with her arm inside a newspaper.

"Rio," Gordon said "this is Jacqueline. She is our erstwhile employer and if you shoot her we will not get the rest of our paycheck."

"Then why is she pointing a gun at you?" the Argentine woman asked.

"I think it would be a good idea if we all stopped pointing guns at each other," Homer decided aloud. "I could really use a drink."

"I think we all could," Gordon opined.

Anastasia closed the door behind her and stalked over to the desk, pointedly waiting until Jacqueline set the pistol on the desk top before she dropped the newspaper and stuffed her Beretta in the back of her tight jeans. The grip was pushing her burgundy leather jacket against her spine. She never took her eyes off Jacqueline.

"Homer, would you go in the office and get a bottle of something? The glasses are behind the mirror."

"If you don't mind," Gordon said, "I would prefer scotch." He sat down on one of the chairs, off to the side. Anastasia moved to the opposite corner but did not sit down.

Homer came out with four glasses and a bottle. He poured four drinks. Gordon did not drink until after Jacqueline had and Anastasia did not drink at all, setting her glass aside.

"God, sis, too much tension. Pay the man and let him get his ass out of here."

"Homer, would you be so good as to return this bottle to Archie's office and stay in there for a minute with the door closed."

"Uh, yeah, okay. Jackie, is something going on here I need to know?"

"No. You don't need to know and that is why I want

you to stay in there."

When Homer had closed the door behind him, Jackie opened the drawer on the right side of her desk, held her right hand in the air, flapping the fingers against her thumb for a second and then picked up the .45 by finger and thumb and put it in the drawer. When the drawer was closed, she took a large drink of scotch then clasped her hands together in front of her.

"Tell me, Mr. Glasgow, are you in the market for a more lucrative assignment?"

"It all depends on what you had in mind. And you still have not paid us the balance of the agreed upon babysitting money."

Jacqueline fought a smile. "I have a very wealthy client who has had a bit of bad luck lately. I will give you the details before you take the assignment. This will not be a babysitting job." Her mouth then made an expression of distaste.

"I am willing to take a look if there are no objections."

Anastasia smiled a tight smile and nodded twice.

"I feel I must tell you that I already retained one specialist for this assignment, but he proved woefully inadequate and might need to be eliminated."

"Will this be a requirement?"

"No. However, if he causes any problems for you, feel free to decommission him with malice aforethought and extreme prejudice."

"I see. He upset you."

"He is unstable, and though he came with the highest of recommendations, he has acted like a freak. He freaked out in the hospital and went running out for no reason. I saw it happen."

"Why was he in the hospital?"

"He was visiting Archie. Archie got shot."

"Is this part of the assignment?"

"Let me begin from the beginning."

This time, Jacqueline started with the murder of the three men in the New Moon Studio on Ocean Park Boulevard and segued to the assassination of the owner on Lexington. She did not prevaricate with her new acquaintances. Perhaps she had learned something about dealing with professionals, or perhaps there was a different motive. She told them about Cindy Anderson and the Australian man who had wooed her and then drugged her for her keys. She did not see the look Gordon and Anastasia exchanged. She explained the importance of the murders because the disk delivered to the movie star had led to the New Moon Studio. But these murders happened before the blackmail attempt. The obvious conclusion was that the man or men who had killed the owner and operators of the New Moon Studio was the blackmailer and the man responsible for the kidnapping and murder of Melissa. Cindy Anderson had called the chief suspect Jerry Kragon and described him as six feet tall with blue eyes and blond hair. This time Jacqueline saw the look that passed between her newly acquired assassins. She did not know the significance of it. She did know that she felt a lot more comfortable with this pair than with the blond man, Indian. She did not consider that she had expected to retain Jerry Kragon and that her feelings toward Indian were those of frustration. She would have rejected the idea if it had been put to her. As far as she was concerned she was perfectly well adjusted, sexually liberated, and detached from any Freudian dilemmas. She simply did not like Indian and that was all there was to it.

The police reports from the scene of Bruce Babbage's execution did not include Cindy's statement, merely the fact that a statement had been taken. Cindy was officially the only one to have seen the Australian man.

The photos of Melissa's battered body were the money shot. Even Anastasia's usually taciturn face was twisted by the images. MacMaster ground his teeth together. His nostrils flared and his usually florid face blossomed. The nature of Melissa's death had a way of making the job personal.

Jacqueline described the payoff and how Archie had shot two of the three men in the underground parking structure. She gave them the license plate number that had been read from the getaway car and the fact that it had been reported stolen a few days earlier and had not yet been found. The dead men had been identified as opportunistic hoods, extortionists and drug runners with no known affiliations to any of the larger organizations.

Gordon wanted to know if any shots had hit the vehicle, if the man who had driven off was injured, if the victim was in the trunk at the time and why Archimedes had jumped the gun. Jacqueline deferred any such questions to her boss who was recuperating in County General.

When describing the information she had gotten from the client, that Melissa had been killed by the South Alley Bloods, Gordon got very interested in how the information had been obtained. There was no way he was going head-to-head with an LA street gang unless there was some further proof of malfeasance on their part. The risk was too great. Jacqueline was insistent that the intelligence was good but would not reveal the source. Gordon picked up a notepad from the corner of the desk and wrote on it for the first time.

Anastasia finally took a drink of her scotch and asked with her thick accent, "What is it you think we would be doing then? We will not be killing a whole street gang on your say so."

Jacqueline said nothing for a moment and studied the woman from Argentina. Until now she had been a totally unknown quantity, now she seemed to represent an elemental force, like one of the jealous and vengeful Greek Goddesses. The way she casually spoke of killing a street gang, as if she was discussing getting a tire changed, was chilling. It made her seem more than human.

"I'm thinking," Anastasia continued, "that if we need to kill that many people that we need more money."

Jacqueline broke out of her reverie and explained that the gang had been responsible for the woman's actual death but that Bash, the captain of the group was the one responsible for making the deal with whomever had kidnapped Melissa. He was the one who should be taken alive and interrogated. He was the one with the knowledge of the instigators. He was the central target. His soldiers could be taken care of by local talent, but kidnapping him, from under their noses, was a job for professionals.

"Wait, now," Gordon spoke up. "Now, we are not being contracted to assassinate anyone, now we are to be kidnappers and torturers?"

"I thought that would be a natural part of your repertoire. I didn't know hired killers had qualms against kidnapping, or are you stepping on someone's toes? Is there a murderers' union? Is it outside your job classification?"

Gordon was grinning hugely. He appreciated a bit of New York City sarcasm and her accent came through stronger as she spoke.

"We can do this but to do this alone will be extremely difficult," Anastasia said. "And I am unsure what we will be gaining. From what you tell us it is the Australian man who killed the owner of the sex shop. Is he not then the man who shot the workers in the sex shop?"

"The MO was different. Both looked like professional hits but the Australian that killed Bruce Babbage was patient and disciplined and quiet. He dated this... uh, Cindy Anderson three times without putting a hand on her, even when she was drugged and out cold."

"How can she be sure?" Gordon asked.

"A woman can tell. Anyway, the New Moon killings were done during the day and the door was left open, you know, kind of old school. Nobody even knew Bruce was dead for a week and that was only because of the smell. I don't think it was the same man and neither do the police. The goons who worked the exchange in the underground garage don't have the brains for the operation that got pulled. They were strictly bottom feeders who took the job that was presented. We need to know who presented the job to them. Who ordered Melissa kidnapped and who ordered her killed?"

"And then what? Are we going to pick him up as well and have him tortured to death. Is that the plan?"

"I don't know and I don't care. I have no personal stake in this. I did not know this woman and I do not know the man. I am only here to assist Archimedes Chamberlain in the completion of his contracted duties. This is the most recent photograph we have of this Bash character. If you like I can get it blown up."

"And this Archimedes is in the hospital now. May we visit him?"

"Of course. Are you going to take the job?"

"I'll let you know about that. I need some time to think about it. If I do accept the commission, I will need some street soldiers so calculate that in with your expenses."

"All right then." Jacqueline stood abruptly and then froze as Anastasia whipped her pistol from her waistband. "Easy there, Annie Oakley, I'm just getting you the remainder of your commission for saving my degenerate brother's skin. I will take it out of his hide later."

"I do not think that you will need to sell any of his body parts," Anastasia said with a perfect dead pan. "He has a large satchel of money that he can assist you with."

After paying Gordon the agreed upon cash for delivering her half brother, Jacqueline turned to Homer and spitted him with her eyes. She then flayed him verbally, telling him how lucky he was to be alive and how stupid he was to mess with drug money from whatever cartel it came from. She was merciless in her condemnation and ended up by telling him he should leave the money with her.

Homer was cowed, but he was not about to let his half sister manage his money. He declined shyly and cringed when she unleashed her formidable invective toward him again. They began to argue and eventually Homer picked up his bag and walked out the door.

Sitting behind the large desk, Jacqueline was upset at herself. She opened the drawer and put the .45 back in the holster under the desk, checking to make sure there was a round in the chamber.

The first thing that upset Ms. Vandenberg was the way she had mishandled Homer. She had not seen him for quite a while and while she had always been able to browbeat him into having things her way before, it had not worked this time. He must have known that once she got that cash she would never have given it back. That was something she needed to work on soon. The second thing she thought about was not as upsetting. Sean Warren had been almost frivolous with the money. The stipend in the safe that was to serve as the remainder of Terry Kingston's payment was a substantial lump of money. Once Sean had heard there was trouble with their initial choice for the job he had simply come up with another, larger amount and told them to find someone else. That left a full paycheck for more than one team. Jacqueline looked at her empty glass and licked her lips. When it was all done she was going to be taking home one of those paychecks. Her percentage was adequate for the administrative role she enjoyed, but it was nowhere near what the professionals took home. Let one of these hired killers take out the other and she would simply pocket his share. Archie would never know about it if she took care of most of the financing. Before she was done she was going to have Homer's bag of money as well. She hadn't decided how that was going to happen but it would.

She tapped a pencil against her lower lip as she started thinking of other ways the situation she found herself in might be turned to her advantage. Information was a powerful thing and there were men who would pay for information about this sort of operation. A small pang of conscience raised it feeble little head when she thought about selling out her brother but she squashed it before it could nurture and grow. She hadn't figured it out yet, but there was more money to be made and she was determined to make it.

Chapter Eleven
Contract Contact

The blocks across Marengo Street from the hospital were a quarter of a mile around and Terry had walked around four of them before he was done smoking and thinking. His usual devil-may-care demeanor had been shattered by the smells of the hospital environment. He had not felt quite so assaulted when he stepped in the building, but it had hit him like a hammer and he panicked like a child. Like a child. He spit on the sidewalk and headed back toward County General with a purpose, but his purpose went no further than the driveway and he stopped before going through the door. The feeling was gnawing at him as if he drank wart remover. He turned and walked grimly to his rental car in the parking ramp, and left. He needed to get away from there and he was not sure if he could ever go back. He could not remember ever being so embarrassed in his life.

A block north of the hospital was the entrance to Route 5 South. From there he took the San Bernardino Freeway to the Hollywood Freeway North. The gridlock had broken and while they did not move fast, the cars moved. He pulled off on Santa Monica Boulevard without knowing exactly why and toyed with the idea of visiting Jacqueline Vandenberg again but decided against it. He was more likely to leave her lying in a pool of her own blood than accomplish anything at this point. He kept driving until he got to West Hollywood and pulled off into a residential neighborhood, parking by the side of the road. He ignored the 'No Parking' sign, considering the street wide enough to accommodate any necessary traffic. Then he walked back to the boulevard. He was in the mood for some whiskey.

The tavern had only a couple of patrons at that time of day and nobody said anything to him as he sat at the bar and sipped one bourbon after another. The patrons began to filter in about an hour later and more than one eye landed on him questioningly. A tall redhead with long curls sat next to Terry and asked for a light in a smoky voice. He lit the cigarette but did not seem in the mood to make small talk. The next patron that approached him was wearing a muscle shirt and had obviously spent endless hours lifting weights. He was bulging with muscles and had shaven every hair off his body and his head. The only hair he had was brows and lashes. His effeminate voice belied his masculine body.

"Hey, stranger, what part of town you from?"

Terry automatically assumed that the man was talking to the redhead next to him so he said nothing. Then the redhead put a hand on his shoulder and said "Hey, honey, Butch asked you a question."

Terry looked over at the redhead and saw the Adam's apple in his throat, the webbing of the wig and the thick pancake makeup covering the roots of the hairs. His eyes went wide as he realized he was looking at a man.

"What the fuck are you?" he asked drawing away from the transvestite's touch.

"Oh, honey, I think you got it all wrong."

"A fucking poof. Get off then, you sick fuck."

The body builder took offense at this point and said, "You can't talk to her highness like that."

"Her highness? Oh, you've gone and done it now. I oughta make you wish yer dad settled it at a blow job."

"You want a blow job?" the body builder asked, obviously trying to diffuse the situation but it was the wrong thing to say at the wrong time. With the man in a dress seated at his right, Terry spun to the left with his whiskey glass in his hand and smashed it into the body builder's face. The man was hard and strong but he did not know what was coming at him. Terry punched him in the throat and broke his nose before he took another breath and then kicked him in the back of his knee, driving him to the ground. The transvestite got off his bar stool as his friend went down but he never even took a step further as Terry kicked him between the legs and kneed him in the face as he doubled over.

The whole exchange happened so quickly that nobody had a chance to make a move. Before they could decide not to get involved, the bartender was bringing a shotgun from behind the bar. He never got it clear of the beer taps before Terry had a revolver shoved into the man's face and was warning him, "You got one chance to go home to whatever it is you go home to tonight. Put the shotgun down or I'll ventilate your noggin."

The bartender decided on the better part of valor and Terry pulled a couple of hundred dollar bills out of his vest pocket. He tossed the bills on the bar and told the bartender, "Get the flamers on the floor looked after." By the time the police arrived, the perpetrator was long gone.

Terry drove back to Van Nuys feeling a bit better. He knew conceptually that it was unhealthy to take your embarrassment and frustration out on somebody else, but it had felt so good that he was willing to forgive himself. After the incident in the hospital, he should have known the only reason he stepped into a bar was to get in a fight.

The one visitor from the police department had gone for the day and Archie was watching some inane talk show on the television when he got his next visitors. The first filled the doorway, almost brushing each door jamb with his massive shoulders. The second made him sit up and take notice. His secretary had called to tell him they would visit and that they had been briefed on the situation, but that they had not accepted the assignment as of yet. She urged him to convince them, having been convinced herself of their innate ability.

"Archimedes? Please call me Glasgow. This is Rio, my

executive assistant."

"Please, call me Archie. Thank you for visiting. What is it I can do for you?"

"Oh, I think it more likely we may do something for you. I do not like conversing in this public edifice however. The cameras noted us on the way in and who knows but we may be under surveillance as we speak. When will you be released?"

"Tomorrow I think. They had some issues with getting the bleeding to stop but they have it under control now. I hope so. I been in here two weeks. I should have been out ten days ago."

"Yes, well, gunshot wounds are unpredictable. So, you will be in the office tomorrow?"

"Yeah, I should be," Archie replied, nodding.

"Tomorrow is Saturday."

"I got too much to do. I ain't been there in two weeks. I'll be there Sunday too."

"Okay, we'll call and set up an afternoon appointment."

"Fine. Are you going to leave the chocolates?" Archie was eyeing the large, red, heart shaped box Anastasia was holding against herself.

"Ah, no. You might break your teeth." She had emptied out half the chocolates, inserted her Beretta under the top layer and cut a hole in the bottom of the box for access.

Archie was indeed released the next morning and could not wait to get to work but there was an issue. After climbing the stairs and letting himself into the office he needed a shot of whiskey.

Between the painkillers and the remains of a bottle of bourbon, he slept in his chair for two hours. When the phone rang to announce the imminent arrival of his visitors he was feeling drained. He was wearing a new suit but one cannot sleep in a suit and expect it to look fresh.

MacMaster did not care if Archie looked fresh or not. He was interested in the details of the job at hand and wondering how much a complicated plan such as this would pay. After all, the Hollywood movie industry paid its stars well.

"Mr. uh… Glasgow, Ms. Rio, please come in. I hope you will forgive my not rising. It may be some time before I am spry again."

"That is perfectly all right. We seldom stand on ceremony. Have you any more of that tasty scotch we had the pleasure of sampling yesterday?"

"Yes, I believe it is still in the cabinet. The glasses are dirty, however."

Anastasia smiled that smile, the one that sent men gladly into the Valley of Death, and took a pull off the bottle. "I usually prefer brandy," she said. "It warms me better."

Archie was much too old a hand to play any of that sort of game. He was able to appreciate the potential in a variety of ways, however. Prying his eyes off her flat, exposed belly, he looked MacMaster in the eye. "Are you interested in the assignment or am I to look elsewhere?"

"From what I understand, we were the second choice. There was another man?"

"Yes, well, he, uh … yes. He came well recommended and was right on hand when the call went out, but it seems he is too unstable to trust with a job of this delicacy. He panicked in County General and ran out of the room, presumably out of the building, because he did not come back."

"Could you describe him to me?"

"Sure. He was six-foot one or two, blond hair parted on the side, not long. He was clean shaven and had a good tan. His eyes were blue. He was of medium to large build, not like yourself, of course, but he had good shoulders."

"Did he have an accent?"

"It was not so much that as he uses unusual phrases like 'pass the hoppers' and 'the bronze.' Maybe he thinks he's Mel Gibson, I don't know. But no, he didn't really have a definable accent. Maybe he was trying to hide one, you know, like a Yankee in Georgia."

"Ummm. So let's go over the real job. Your secretary did a good job, but I would like to hear it from the man paying me."

"Well, I am not technically the man paying you. That is coming through me from a client of mine who has taken a dramatic loss of late. He has asked to remain anonymous, but a man such as yourself will be able to figure it out. I assume you have seen the pictures and the police reports?"

"Yes, but they are old and they tell me little. The owner of the New Moon was killed a month ago. Same with the other three. I doubt, in a city such as this, they are even looking for the killers any more. And yet, the problem of the tapes remains and that is what really drives this bus, isn't it?"

"No. In the beginning, yes, but not now. Whoever kidnapped Melissa is also responsible for the hole in my leg. It's not these idiots in the parking garage. They're just hired punks. I don't care about them and neither does Shhhhh shit. Neither does my client. We both want the man behind the affair. Now, don't get me wrong, the Bloods that did the deed belong in Hell, prison is too good for these scum-sucking pieces of shit, but the only way to identify them is to get their captain, Bash, into a room alone. I think that is everything and if you will pardon me, miss, I could use a shot off that bottle now."

Anastasia poured two fingers into the glass that lay on the table in front of Archie and then took another short pull herself. MacMaster was not drinking and he was saying little. He wanted to get all he could from Archie before the man got overwhelmingly drunk. Unfortunately, it looked as though that point was not far off and Archie was in a hurry to get there.

"We need to find some wogs we can trust to do some preliminary work. Do you know any?"

"There's no shortage of 'em. You mean blacks, right?"

"Yes."

"Well, we got plenty of 'em but how many I would trust…" He made a rude sound with his lips. "The only ones I would trust are cops. The rest of 'em are all looking to sell dope to your kids and fuck your wife."

"Spoken like a true officer of the law."

"Hey, you don't need to be a cop to see what the fuck is going on in this town. The blacks and the Mexicans are staged for an all-out war over the business from the suburbs. The Koreans are laying low 'til they can spawn enough of them to have a chance, but you know them bastards. They spawn like rats. Even worse than the Mexicans. No offense, ma'am."

"There is nothing you can say to change my opinion of you," Anastasia said with a smile that only partially hid the menace behind her words.

Archimedes held up his glass again and Anastasia poured him another couple of shots. MacMaster watched her carefully. He could see what Archie could not. Those shots disappeared in a heartbeat and Archie held his glass up for more before his throat was done working it down. She poured him another and then locked eyes with her lover. It was obvious that she was uncomfortable with the arrangement.

"I don't usually drink so much but the pain in my leg is killing me," sounded like another excuse for the actions of a drunk.

Anastasia Viuda took a long deep breath through her nose, making the nostrils flare. It was obvious what that meant to anyone watching closely. MacMaster knew what she meant. She took another sip from the bottle and screwed the cap on.

The drunker he got, the more Archie's eyes wandered over her body. She had deliberately worn a skimpy halter top and a tight fitting pair of daisy dukes. A pair of four-inch spike heels were strapped to her feet, giving her well over six feet of height and showcasing the curve of her back. Her hair was swept up and spiked, making her even taller. There was no place to hide a pistol in that outfit but her man was carrying two in what looked like a fishing vest that was worn over a tie-dyed tee shirt with a surfboard logo on it.

"If I can't get some trustworthy men from around here, I'll need to bring them in from outside and that will be expensive. Understand that my base of operations is not in the states. I usually work elsewhere."

"And the sort of work you do is commenshurate with thish operashun?" Archie was beginning to slur his words as the bourbon and the painkillers tag-teamed him.

"Yes. We can take care of this for you. What is the job worth to you?"

"I'm not sure yet. I need to communicate with my finansheer. Call me again tomorrow. No better yet, enjoy the weekend and get back with me on Monday. I'll be in better shape to give you a number then. Don't worry, my man hash plenty of cash." He shook his head to try to get some of the cobwebs out. "Forgive me if I don't get up to shee you out. I'm a little indeshposhed."

"Monday then. We will see you in the morning."

Anastasia stalked out of the room with the grace that comes from long practice on high heels. Gordon followed her out of the office suite and down the hall. He kept his distance, not wanting her blocking his range of fire. They moved across the front of the building and down the driveway to the small parking lot in the back of the building where the Cadillac was parked. Once they were back on the street they felt safe to speak freely.

"I don't know about this *borrachon*. I don't think we can trust him."

"He certainly likes his liquor."

"Gordon, it is more than that with him. I like my liquor, you like my liquor, I mean your liquor…"

"I think you got it right the first time."

"Be serious, *mi amor*. There is no telling what a man may do when he is drunk, no telling what a man may say. Despite his words, this man is a long-term drunk. He has not been out of the hospital for a day and he is already in his soup."

"None of this means he does not have a job that needs to be done. How many people in this world would be willing to try a job like this, let alone succeed?"

"I do not like it. There is a not so good feeling I get."

"Is that thing in your head active again?" Gordon's sudden concern was apparent.

"No. I have felt nothing since it was shorted dead. I am just thinking now that it is not good to work with drunks, it is not good to go after street gangs without backup, it is not good to go into unfamiliar territory with such a, how you say? With an amplified agenda."

"Ambitious. An ambitious agenda. I tend to agree that it will be a bit of a challenge, but I have seldom shrunk from a challenge and I know you never have."

"Still, there is the thought that this may be more than we contract for."

"We don't know what the contract is for yet."

"*Si*. But a man cannot spend money from the grave."

"I'll try to remember that. Do you still think the woman is the real force behind the company?"

"*Si*. She knows more and sees more. I want to know why she did not tell the *borrachon* that the other man she hired was Australian. I am thinking she hired him. This one did not seem to have a clue. Is this where your friend Terry Kingston came?"

"Yes, I think so, but Terry is much the glacier-hearted man. He is cold and hard and does not panic in any situation I've seen. Whoever they got in touch with, it was not Terry. He may have done the other job though. The owner of the sex shop."

"That is why I chose you. He is cold and hard, you are hard and hot."

"Not yet I'm not, but it won't be long."

Chapter Twelve
War

Ginger,

I hope the weather is agreeable.

It has been a while since I wrote. I was doing a job in Brazil and it kept me quite busy. Don't bother replying to this address, I took another job here in the colonies that will keep me moving around.

Things are different here. I got propositioned by a man in a dress! Can you believe that? The poofin' blighter was wearing a dress.

Anyway, I know you have no truck with the telly so you probably never heard of Sean Warren but he's a movie star. He was courting this lovely young thing when his past popped up and somebody was demanding money to bury it. Well, you know how complicated that sort of thing can get. Anyway, a couple of bad men got shot and then they killed Sean's mistress. It seems they kidnapped her to make sure nothing happened with the payoff, but it happened anyway. So I get commissioned to pick up this black fellah that was responsible for the killing but not the kidnapping. It seems that Sean Warren is going to beat the truth out of him. We'll see. I'll write again soon.

Terry

Terry put down the pen, folded the single sheet of paper and slid it into the envelope. Terry had not heard from Uncle Ginger for about a year and it was well past time they got in touch. Ginger was no longer in the business but he had taught his nephew more than could ever be repaid. As he addressed the envelope, Terry could picture Ginger's grin as he said, not for the first time, "There are no old assassins, boy. You reach an age where you lose your edge and then you retire or somebody retires you."

Jurgen Schrimple was in a state of bliss. Sean Warren had reappeared halfway through Saturday and had attacked his role with renewed aggression the following day. The anger behind his eyes was real and Jurgen, being an adept director, made up for it by filming the scenes that required raw, fierce emotion. Sean was not the prima donna sort. He was not yet popular enough to demand the unreasonable and probably never would be anyway. Actors could be difficult, though, and Sean had suffered a huge, debilitating blow. The fight scenes went exceptionally well that day.

There had been massive speculation and untold pages of blogs regarding the movie, the culprit, and everything regarding it, but the consensus of opinion was that the movie would never get made. Jurgen had feared this greatly because he had a large financial stake in it. He was not just the director, he was also one of the producers. Sean's return to the set was as gratifying as it was unexpected.

It was late on Sunday when Ice Cream showed back up on set.

"Chocolate Ice Cream, what do you say we get out of this sun before you melt." Sean was directing his friend toward his trailer and motioning for Jurgen to take five.

"You got it set up?"

"Check it out, my vanilla brother. I got fifteen badass motherfuckers set up with all the latest street sweepers. They just waiting for the word and they go in like the charge of the light brigade."

"I knew I could count on you."

"Who got yer back, brother?"

"All right. I'll call you and we'll get together elsewhere on this."

"Respect."

"Respect. Oh, you might like to know that the Light Brigade all died."

"Oh, well. Them niggahs on the street don't know that. I'll keep it in mind though, in case anyone ever calls me on it."

"Okay. Hey, if there is a number four "Blaze of Glory"

I got you a big part in it."

"Respect. Oh, hey, I gotta tell ya something went down this morning, down in the Southtown, that might throw us a curveball or it might help, I dunno."

"What?"

"Well, one of the West Carson Crips got taken out and it looks like the South Alley Bloods did it. We lookin' at a gang war maybe. The boundary is Route one-ten, always has been. Crips to the west, Bloods in Carson, east of the line. As long as nobody gets outta hand, they got no problem. This morning, someone got outta hand on Jay Street, west of Vermont."

"It wasn't just some robbery?"

"Pay attention when I say this, my man. It makes no difference why they did it. When a Blood kills a Crip and leaves a flag, all hell gonna come loose."

"He left a rag?"

"Blood red rag left on the corner. Everybody knows what that is. They may negotiate first or they might get right ta killin' each other. Don't know."

"Okay. Keep your men on standby and I'll be in touch. I got some professionals from out of town and I need to find out what they are going to do before I can make a call. For right now, I got a movie to make. We'll be shooting a night scene when the sun goes down. You may as well stick around, I think we still gotta get another take of that scene with you at the dumpster."

The sun was coming up over the Rocky Mountains and most of the church-going citizens were stirring, but the victims of their own excesses would be sleeping in. The first service was generally at eight and the second was about eleven. That gave a good hour when nobody on the street was a solid citizen. The worst thing you could do in this sort of setup was to shoot a solid citizen.

The fire escape was on the opposite side of the building

and had been an easy climb once it had been brought down. The wide, flat roof would not get hot until the middle of the day. The warehouse was one of two identical buildings set between a medical clinic and a stamping plant. The roof gave a good view of the street but the activity was nothing like the night before. Saturday night on Jay Street was like the Roman Bacchanalia with liquor flowing, women dancing and drugs enough for an army. The police had been nowhere in sight and would probably have ended up dead if they had been. Terry had not taken a target then, he wanted to wait until he had a clear look at whomever he was going to kill. While run down, the neighborhood still retained some middle-class workers. It would do him no good to decommission a factory worker or a bus driver.

Shortly after eight that morning a man, naked under a terry cloth robe, walked into his front yard with a joint dangling from his lips and a blue head rag tied around his hair. He might have survived if he had not walked to the edge of the dirt that might have been a lawn at one time and pissed on the corner post. He was shaking off his unit when the slug slammed into the back of his neck. It took him directly through the spine and with such force that it blew his jaw off. His tongue ended up in the gutter on the other side of the street. A cat took the tongue under one of the neighbor's porches and ate it later that day.

Terry left the ejected shell and a torn piece of red head rag on the roof. He slipped the Weatherby Mark V into a nylon bag and headed down the fire escape from the roof. Back on the ground he took one second to determine if there was anyone after him before walking to his car. He had the bag slung over one shoulder and his other hand under his vest, gripping his .38 revolver. Nobody saw him that would admit to it. He left the red head rag with the piece missing on the corner of the building and drove off. He felt no joy, no excitement and no remorse. This was the job and he was very good at it. He had hoped to get some sort of adrenaline rush but with the exception of a few thumps in his chest as he pulled the trigger, there was nothing. A few blocks away he pulled over and took the brown paper bags off the license plates. He drove north on Vermont then got on Route 110 North.

It was too early to find an open bar but he felt his day was over with and he wanted a drink. He thought of the bottle of gin he had left in his motel room but knew he didn't want to drive that far. Eventually he simply headed west, parked a couple of miles from the beach, left his guns in the trunk and jogged down to the ocean. He spent the rest of Sunday alternating between running on the beach, sunning himself and watching the bikini clad women. Later in the day he convinced one of the oil-covered ladies to have dinner with him in a posh restaurant near the beach. After dinner, drinks flowed with abandon and Terry, who had wanted a drink in the morning, finally got around to getting drunk. He woke the next morning in a hotel room off the beach with a naked brunette that he barely remembered. She was not the one he had taken to dinner and he did not know her name. He cursed himself for losing control and hoped he had not done anything he couldn't remember, that he would regret later.

A hot shower loosened him up a bit but his head still hurt. His escort from the night before swore upon seeing the time, did a quick freshen up and raced out the door, late for work. Her car was in the parking lot. Terry hoped his was where he had left it. When he put his pants on he found a couple of two-ounce bottles of gin and a small bag of cocaine in a hip pocket. He drank both bottles of gin and felt better almost instantly. He left the cocaine for the cleaning staff and headed downstairs to check out. He had signed in as Terry Garreth, a native of Arkansas. His driver's license bore out his identity and his credit cards were legitimate, though automatically paid through a credit union account. This had been the first time he had used the credit line. He took a moment to think about who could trace him back to his year in Little Rock and decided that there was no danger. He had never worked in Little Rock.

The Ford that the agency had provided him with was still in the spot he had left it in the day before. It had a parking ticket on the windshield. Terry almost threw it away but stuck it in the glove box instead.

As he drove off, he could not help wondering what he had told the woman. He did not know who she was or where she worked and did not care much, but he had gotten sloppy and in his line of work sloppy often equated to dead. He thought about the man he had shot the day before. If everything went the way it should that would start a local war, weakening the South Alley Bloods, and opening opportunities for Terry to get inside. Once inside, he would take the gang leader for a little ride.

Searching through his memory, the owner and CIO (Chief Investigating Officer) of Prometheus Investigations could not recall the last time he had been in the office on a Sunday. Truly, he worked seven days a week, but he seldom made it to the Melrose Avenue office building.

The pain from the gunshot wound was less severe today than it had been. He was taking it relatively easy as a result of his decreased mobility. Waking in his chair for the second time on Saturday, he swore to himself he would stop drinking. Then he swore to stop taking painkillers. Then he swore never to do the two together again. When all was said and done, there he was, Sunday morning with a glass of bourbon and a belly full of pills. Even Archie would not have said he was uncomfortable.

Most of the day was spent on the phone, talking to old friends of his on the various police forces on the West Coast.

He had always been a friendly man, even when drunk, and it had stood him in good stead with his contacts. His street contacts were often less available through the telephone since they changed numbers and addresses often.

By mid afternoon he had heard about the killing of Ignatious "Barrow" Brown, on Jay Street in Carson. The local police departments had requested that the State Police remain on alert to back them up in case a gang war erupted. Of course, Archie was behind the times on the gang tactics which were constantly evolving. He had been used to picking up white cocaine customers and getting them to turn over on the dealers. They folded easily and had no loyalty for the black gang members they got the drugs from. Things had changed since then and gotten less personal and friendly. Crack had come into town and changed the scene forever. Nobody knew who they were buying the drugs from and the delivery was done by children so the prosecution was immensely difficult. The gangs needed little reason to shoot someone. It came as second nature to them after a while. The culture of violence had inured an entire generation to violent death and taught them the proper response was more violence.

The sun set on Los Angeles and the West Carson Crips were ready for blood. They had no real strategy, no battle plan; they would simply drive down Doloros Street in a caravan and shoot anyone wearing red. They had a case of Hennessy and an arsenal of guns representing various designs and descriptions. They rolled mostly in older American cars here, though this was far from ubiquitous. It was a regional preference.

The Bloods on Doloros Street had been warned there was a problem, but they did not suspend business on a rumor or a whim. They were on the street and dealing in what they always dealt. Women and drugs and guns were sold and traded like on any other day. If the Crips were coming, let them come. The Bloods were ready for them. And come they did.

Five full-sized automobiles on air bag suspensions with big wheels and skinny tires came rolling down the street. The windows sprouted gun barrels and the lead began to fly. For all their bravado and bluster, none of the men attacking their rivals that night had much experience with their chosen weapons. If they had, there would have been a lot more blood spilled.

Andrew "Trooper" Sykes caught a .45 in the shoulder as he was running for his front door. Trooper had been in several fire fights and this was the first time he had been shot. He was also the first Blood shot that day. He lay on his front porch unable to move and bleeding heavily.

Percy "Predator" Grimes saw his neighbor shot and all the gun barrels poking out of the windows of the cars, and he ran for home. He didn't actually get shot, though he slashed his arms open when he broke the window on the screen door. He tripped on the front step and went through it hands first. The scars would be impressive but the act had been nothing memorable.

Afeelah "Warbucks" Amboulah took a 7.62 round right through the eyeball that removed the back of his skull. He did not take a step or utter a cry; he simply collapsed like a bag of grain.

Across the street from where Afeelah's life left him, Shaqueenah "Shanty" Jones was struck in the leg with a 9mm round. She was lucky in that her wound did not nick any of the major blood vessels. Her leg went numb and she could not move it properly. It was her cell phone that first called 911 and reported that there was a drive-by shooting going on, and that they were going to need more than one ambulance.

The next person hit was John Abbarealah, a 37-year-old postal worker with three children and a girlfriend. He had lost his wife to heroin addiction five years earlier and had lost a fourteen-year-old son two years before. He had just gotten home from a fast food restaurant with a bag of dinner. He caught a 9mm round through his right hand.

On the other side of the street Marshall "Wyatt Earp" Alloise got three 9mm rounds and then a .45 through his guts. He stood there, uncomprehendingly, looking at his burst intestines and the biological waste painting the door in front of him. He could not feel the area, he did not seem to be bleeding, he could not understand what had happened. He could not hear anything and then, he could not see anything. He fell to the deck and tried to vomit but could not. He was grateful for the blackness that enveloped his mind.

By that time, everyone on the street was either behind a parked car or in a house, and the lead was being returned.

James "Jack" Swaree was shot through the door of the Buick he was in. The round had lost much of its momentum and buried itself in his arm, next to the bone. He could not use the arm after that but continued firing with the gun in his left hand. He was not much of a shot with his right hand and was pathetic with his left.

Arturo "Paco" Brown was driving an Olds Cutlass. The job was done and they were heading out. He was accelerating to get himself and his crew away from the target zone when a .40 caliber round came through the rear window and took off the right side of his head. The car veered to the left. George "Hardtime" Corey was covered with his driver's blood and brains and had smacked his head on the windshield when the Olds crashed into a parked Cadillac. He put the car in reverse and smoked the tires as he tore backward. Ja'Quando "Fireman" Miller was running up to the back of the car, firing his .40 caliber Taurus. It had been his bullet that took out the driver but he miscalculated. He thought he could get out of the way before the car reached him but the rear wheels caught traction and launched the back bumper into his knees. He screamed as his calves went under the car and his thighs bounced off the back of the trunk. He was thrown to the ground and the differential in the middle of the rear axle smashed his head to a pulp while the passenger side wheel shattered his arm. He lay in the middle of the street with his legs at impossible angles and his arm bones poking through his flesh.

More bullets flew but there were no more casualties.

The response had been made, now the ball was in the Bloods' court.

Bash had not been on Doloros Street when the Crips came cruising through; he had been a mile away watching football. The game took second place once he heard the news. He had already been told about the murder of Ignatious "Barrow" Brown over the pipe, as they called the other side of Route 110, but knew none of his men had done it. At least he was relatively sure none of his men had done it. He had not gotten the entire story. The police had determined the angle of entry and picked out the roof of the warehouse as the firing point. When they got to the roof, through the building, there was already a group of Crips there. They had climbed the fire escape. The scrap of red cloth and the spent shell were evidence and the officers were quick to tell the gang members that the items did not mean anything, but the Crips were already convinced of what they suspected and had rolled on what they thought they knew.

Monday's newspapers made little of the incident. The press and their readers had become inured to the gangland killings and the latest Hollywood hairstyle made a bigger splash. That is not to say they ignored the incident, they ran a column on page three describing it. The article concluded that the police suspected it was gang related. Once the statement was made, the LA Gang Unit of the LAPD took over. The Gang Unit was so overloaded, they didn't even send anyone to the scene that day. By the time they did, they had more things to worry about.

D'arniel "Bash" Jamiel was not the kind of man to take such an affront lying down. He let the dust settle on Monday, insisting that there be no business conducted on Doloros Street for the rest of the week. Tuesday he took nine men in a van and they went over the pipe with glass bottles filled with gasoline. Their Molotov cocktails set a dozen fires Tuesday night and they shot one man who tried to stop them. They did not target anyone's house in particular; their violence was devastating, but it was random. They were burning and killing without regard to whom they were hurting. The war was not confined to the participants. War never is. Innocents are never spared just because they are innocent.

Monday morning was another perfect Los Angeles day with the dew burned off before the sun finished rising over the mountains. Anastasia Viuda was in the hallway before anyone showed up for work in the building. Gordon was sitting in the Cadillac when Jacqueline pulled in next to him. She seemed genuinely pleased to see him and they walked up the stairs together. She was decidedly less enthusiastic to find Anastasia in the hallway waiting for her. She said nothing but her body language spoke volumes.

When Jacqueline went into the office's efficiency kitchen to brew some coffee, Anastasia put her hand on her lover's upper thigh and whispered in his ear, "You fuck that woman and I'm going to kill her."

Gordon turned with mock astonishment and said, "I wouldn't think of it."

She replied, "This woman is thinking about it and it will be the last piece of ass she ever gets."

The discussion went no further as the secretary came back into the room and Gordon asked her how the news from Carson was going to impact their assignment. "Surely this latest violence will drive our quarry underground and not even the foxhounds will stand a chance of driving him out."

"This is another example of your not knowing how the gangs in LA work." Jacqueline corrected him. "Bash will not be going underground, he can't. It would mark him as a coward. He needs to make himself all the more visible. He needs to make sure everybody sees him doing business as usual. That is the only way he will maintain respect. That and leading the charge against the Crips that hit them yesterday."

"I understand. This shows no military discipline, no sense of protocol. The leader is the leader because he is stronger and smarter than those around him. If he loses face he will be killed and swallowed by the inexorable machine that makes up the gang mentality."

"Exactly. You must be used to working with an army or something. Things do not work that way on the streets. Out there you feed on the weak."

"It sounds like you spent some time out there yourself."

"Me? No. I never had anything to do with these bottom feeders, but I know what they do and I know how they think. It's a jungle and the monkeys are in charge."

Neither of the visitors said anything at this point. Anastasia had not been exposed to all that much prejudice in her life and Gordon had tried to avoid it in his own life. He knew he might have misinterpreted her remark but he did not think so. He felt the malice but did not know if it was from a hatred of gangs or a hatred of blacks. She seemed to have an issue with black gangs though.

It was still early when Archimedes showed up. To say he looked spry was overstating the case but he looked much better than he had on Saturday. He was walking with a cane and had worn shorts for a Monday, with the bandages in full view on his thigh. He also chose to wear a Hawaiian shirt with bright yellow flowers on a blue background. He looked more ready for the beach that the office and his attitude was commensurate with his dress.

"Good day, Mr. Chamberlain."

"Ah, Mr. Glasgow. I am glad to see you indeed. I received a package by messenger yesterday. I had no doubt that the contents would suffice as a down payment for your services. Come into the office and we shall negotiate."

Gordon got up and followed Archie into the office but Anastasia did not stand. Archie lifted an eyebrow at that but decided not to pursue the question. Jacqueline was not as sanguine about it. She got up and went to the kitchen, coming back with a cup of coffee. She pointedly did not offer Anastasia a cup.

Inside the office, Archie pulled a stack of bills out from his locked desk drawer and slid it across the desk to Gordon. Gordon crossed one booted foot over his knee. He had on cowboy boots with large steel taps on the heels, blue jeans and a blue cotton shirt with a vest over it. He did not move to take the money.

"Now I have a question before we go any further. You took the cash out of the desk drawer. It is a good looking stack but it represents nowhere near what this job is going to cost and you know it. I am going to need a vehicle or two, clandestine and voluminous. I am going to need to hire some street-level soldiers for reconnaissance and infiltration. I may need to pay off some police and I need a place to stay for a while. I am thinking the rest of the down payment is in the safe, probably on that wall, behind that painting. Am I right?"

"That, my friend, is none of your business."

"Ah, but it is. We are negotiating here. You want to give me that little bit and think I should be happy with it, but you have forgotten that we are professionals who command a respectable wage. You are, in effect, insulting me with this paltry stack of bills. If you want some bargain basement gang bangers, you can get them any day of the week, but I will reiterate that you will be getting what you pay for. I'm not certain how much experience you have with this side of the tracks but, in this situation, and in this business, you cannot afford to go low end. You have an upper-class client who has been grievously injured and he will be willing to pay for the upper-class work. I think I can determine in a matter of hours who this man is and I can take my proposal to him directly, cutting out the middleman so to speak. Now if this is the route you think I should take, tell me, but if you wish to retain my services and my good will, then be a more reasonable client. I want to see the money."

Archie sat with his mouth open for a minute and then realized he was staring and shut it. The man in front of him had a look in his eye like the granite of the mountains. He was not fidgeting or moving at all, he was simply engaging Archie's eyes and Archie was the first to look away. He knew when he had been read and there was no doubt in either man's mind that the assassin's assessment had been accurate.

"Yes, let us be reasonable. I have the client and I can make sure you never get near him." Archie could tell it was time for him to show some of the spine that had carried him through his years on the force. "I was injured on this case and I deserve more compensation, sort of a disability policy. I hold the information and I have the contacts. If you try to make a move without me I will shut you down so fast your head will spin. I know all the cops and I know half the pieces of shit on the street. I can get your head sent to you in a box. Are we clear?" It may have been the bourbon and the painkillers speaking. Archie realized after he spoke that he was dealing with a man who actually would send him his head in a box if it was warranted.

"Yes, your point is very clear. You don't want to pay me what I feel I am worth and you have threatened to have me killed if I go against your wishes." Gordon's voice held all the warmth of a katana. "You think that your position is such that you hold the upper hand."

"You could have been a profiler for the FBI." The words were complimentary but the attitude behind them was unmoving. The PI knew he could not waver now; the dice had already been cast.

"Yes, but I am much better at killing people." Archie felt a shiver run up his spine, not at what the Scot said but the matter-of-fact way he said it. "I think you had better assess your own profile before we go any further."

Archimedes Prometheus Chamberlain stared across the room at his potential associate and came to a decision. He had overplayed his hand and the big redhead had called his bluff. Groaning with the effort, Archie stood and limped to the painting on the wall. The painting was on hinges and the wall safe behind it was open in short order. The wounded PI threw another stack of bills on the desk.

Gordon did not move a muscle.

Archie threw a third stack on the desk and Gordon came to his feet in a fluid movement, tucked the bills in his interior vest pocket and smiled for the first time since he had arrived. "As you see, we can come to an amicable arrangement without either of us needing to decommission the other. I will be glad to take care of your little problem. If you would like us to expedite this little effort, it might be good to have a few of the street people you have such sway over. I will reconnoiter today and call again tomorrow."

In the outer office, Jacqueline and Anastasia were sitting like two jungle cats claiming the same territory. If either of them had jumped, the other might very well have killed her. Gordon paused for a second and inhaled strongly through his nose. The scent of competition was so strong the pheromones made his testicles tingle. Nothing was said as they walked out the door.

It was too early for the gangs to be hitting the streets so the couple stopped in a diner for some breakfast before heading to the beach for some sun and salt air. Of all the places they had been, Venice Beach was one where they did not stick out. With all the varieties of humanity visible around the area, even they blended in.

A couple of hours on the beach richened their already deep tans. While the sun was hot, it could not compare with the intensity of the Brazilian sun. They took a swim in the ocean and then showered, retrieved their clothing from the beachside locker and got back into the car. A couple of miles south they had a light lunch and a couple of drinks in a dockside cantina in Marina Del Rey.

After lunch they took the 405 freeway south to Route 110 and the Town of Carson. The east-west roads didn't have names here, they were numbered. West 220th Street, West 221st Street, West 222nd Street were in lockstep as if the planners had run out of ideas for the street names and had gotten lazy. The north-south roads had names and house after house built right next to each other with barely enough room to walk between them. The lawns were bleak and dry where they actually sprouted; most were just packed dirt. They knew they were in the right neighborhood when cars on blocks began to appear by the side of the road and abandoned houses appeared with their boarded-up windows. Some of the condemned houses had people living in them. A few young men were soaking up the sun or playing cards on the porches. They cruised the neighborhood slowly but nobody approached them. They saw different sites where impromptu memorials had been erected to the slain youth of the area.

The southern boundary of Bloods territory was East Bonds Street. Anything closer to Mexico than that was Mexican gang territory. The truce at this line was tenuous as the Mexican population kept growing and the young

150

gangsters from the border were always looking north.

"Are you sure you'll be all right, love?" MacMaster asked as he dropped Anastasia in the parking lot of a restaurant.

"Please! These stupid little men could no more worry me than a Chihuahua. If they give me a hard time, I will step on them."

"All right. Call me if things get out of hand or if you need me. I'm going to spread some seed money to see if we can get this gangster to cooperate." He popped the trunk. "Don't forget your purse."

She leaned over the console and gave him a long, sensuous kiss. "It should only take a couple of days. Be faithful," she said as she stepped out of the car.

MacMaster waited until she was going in the restaurant and then pulled out of the parking lot and headed north again. Once he was back in Bloods territory he pulled up to a stop sign and motioned for a boy of about fourteen to come over to the car window. The boy was trying to look as tough as he could.

"I need to get in touch with Bash. I have something he wants. I want you to give him this card personally. Can you do that?"

"What makes you think I know anyone named Bash?"

"Oh, I guess I got the wrong man. I thought you looked like you could use a Benjamin. That's all right. I can find another who does."

"No, wait, I can get this to him."

"Today?"

The young man licked his lips nervously, "Today."

"Very well. Make sure it goes into his hands and his alone, yes?"

"Yes."

"What's your name?"

The boy looked left and then right, as if searching for a

name.

"You little shite, you plan on stealing from me, don't you?"

"No. I don't even know you. How I'm supposed to do dat? I got you covered. I got a line right to the man. We tight. You'll see."

"No, I won't see. I need a real man." Gordon drove off without giving the boy anything. This scenario was repeated a couple of times before Gordon distributed a couple of business cards and $100 bills. He should be able to connect with one of them; he had created enough of a stir in the neighborhood. After all, a white man giving away $100 bills is nothing they were used to.

Chapter Thirteen
Horatio Hotel

"I would never have given him that much before seeing what he can do."

"Jackie, this man is a real professional. I can see it in his eyes."

"I know. You were LAPD for thirty-two years and you know what makes people tick." She said it like a mantra. She had heard it enough times by now.

"Well, you gave that other freak a stack of bills."

"Look, boss, he came with the highest of recommendations. I didn't like him from the minute he walked in the door. My connections said he was a dependable man and could do almost anything we needed done. How was I to know he was an unstable freak? I told you, I didn't like this guy from the beginning."

"Have you called him?"

"He won't answer the phone. I think we're gonna need to face the fact that he took your cash and headed for the hills."

"I'm not sure. He seemed like such a proven character when I first met him."

"Oh please! A proven character. What's that supposed to mean?" Her New York City accent increased the feel of a statement already dripping with scorn.

"I'm going down to the rental office. We'll see if he left town. Oh, by the way, what was with that woman? She didn't come in the office, what was she doing?"

"She sat there staring at me like I was a piece of meat and she was hungry."

"Yeah. Well, that's what I mean about these guys. They got the look. I wouldn't want them hunting me. And I wouldn't want them hunting you, either."

The automobile rental office was only a couple of

blocks away and ordinarily Archie would have walked it. At least they had parking spots in the lot; walking was very low on Archie's to-do list at this point.

The tracking device in the Crown Victoria that Terry had been given indicated that he was parked a couple of miles from the coast. Archie knew that his secretary would have had the car picked up if she had come down here. She tended to be a little too quick on the draw and judged people before seeing what they could do. She actually made a good foil for his attitude which had mellowed considerably since he had been investigating crimes for the LAPD. He reflected for a second that he had indeed gotten old and maybe getting shot was a sign that he should retire for good. Sit on the beach and drink beer and forget all about the criminals of the world. Then he saw the spot begin to move. The rental car was being driven northeast on Pico Boulevard.

It had taken a while before Terry figured out how he could blend in to the predominately black neighborhoods in South-Central LA. After all, he stuck out like a flare at night walking around the streets, and if he drove through the neighborhoods they would likely figure he was a member of the vice squad or an undercover narcotics officer. He needed a more realistic reason to be there and there was nothing more realistic than the world's oldest profession.

The area immediately south of Compton and northwest of Carson was an industrial wasteland of fuel oil storage tanks, warehouses and injection molding factories surrounded with the houses of the lower-class inhabitants and workers. It was a triangle, bordered on the north and separated from Compton by Artesia Boulevard. It was separated from Carson by Route 405 on its west and South Alemeda on the east. There was an insufficient density of population for a gang to have developed in the neighborhood so the traffic in contraband was controlled by the Compton Crips. This was all a matter of public record if anyone thought to look it up, or it was disseminated by any waitress or bartender familiar with the area.

A fairly well-detailed map of LA had piqued Terry Kingston's curiosity about this particular slice of land. It was not Compton, it was not Carson and it was not Lakewood or Signal Hill. It did not seem to have an identity of its own, but it was a distinct entity, separated as it was by major freeways.

Pulling off Route 110 at El Segundo and Figueroa was close enough to the area without being in it or its neighbors. Terry found a Mexican restaurant and ordered a plate of tortillas. They did not serve beer so he settled for a ginger ale. Sitting in the corner with the map open pegged him for a stranger in town and was an automatic draw for assistance. The waitress told him what she thought she knew about the area he indicated and then asked her husband, the cook. He was much more helpful and explained that the Compton Crips controlled the whole area even though the whole south side of the triangle was technically Carson. He did not mind telling his affable blond customer that the Bloods were in charge of Carson but that the Crips had claimed that side of the triangle. He did not know if there was bad blood about it though. He could not tell Terry if there were any hotels worth staying in anywhere in that area.

The Horatio Hotel had never been an upper-class establishment. It had been built in the mid 1920s to provide rooms for the travelers flying in to Compton/Woodley Airport. It had served its function for many years, but as aircraft became larger and larger the Compton/Woodley Airport was relegated to the status of overflow runways to take a backlog of aircraft in the case of fog or simply too many scheduled flights. Nobody with the means to fly would stay in the Horatio Hotel anymore and it became known as the Ho-Ho-Hotel or simply the Ho-Tel. The Horatio had not degenerated to the point where they rented rooms by the hour, like some others in the neighborhood, but they did not have an upscale clientele.

What the Horatio Hotel did have was an underground parking garage complete with armed guards. It was the only hotel in the area that still provided any protection for its boarders and so it got some out-of-the-area business. This allowed it to survive as a hotel. Policy was strict, nobody but current customers could park in the underground lot. With a room on the top floor, Terry parked his rental car in the dark and damp seclusion underground.

The girl had chosen the name Rabbit for herself. She seemed young enough to be fresh and old enough to be legal and that was what Terry was seeking. He picked her up south of Artesia Boulevard, in the area that intrigued him. Rabbit was by no means the first woman Terry had spoken to that day but he was looking for someone in particular. He rejected those who sounded excited when asked if they wanted to smoke some crack. She had been standing at a bus stop on Avalon Boulevard with her tiny, yellow vinyl shorts and her thigh-high, high heeled, faux leather boots. There had been little question that she was not interested in catching the bus. She seemed relieved that Terry actually had a hotel room, even though it was outside her regular area.

Terry made sure that the desk clerk saw him taking his black escort upstairs. There was no surprise for him there, it happened every day of the week. The one thing that stuck in the clerk's mind was the large aluminum travel case he carried as well. Customers of the hotel who were there for the female company seldom brought luggage with them.

Interestingly enough, once she got upstairs she seemed suddenly shy and unsure of herself. Terry asked her if she would like a drink. He had brought a bottle of vodka and some orange juice up with them. She licked her full lips, obviously interested in a drink but then said that she probably shouldn't.

156

"What's wrong, darling? It's still early. I suspect you would've stood at that bus stop a long time if I hadn't come along."

"What? You saying I ain't got what it takes?"

"No, no, no." Terry grinned at her. "You have everything a man needs and then some. No, I was only saying it was early in the day and that the customers would be stopping by later. I mean Monday is seldom a banner day in your trade, is it? I'm having a drink and I suspect you should to."

"All right, Johnny England. Just one."

"That's right then. What is it you worry about then?"

"Do I look worried? You ain't some kind of a freak are ya?"

"No, dear. I was just thinking that you look the part and you act the part but this is not who you really are. I'm not trying to put you down; my first was plucked in King's College in Sydney."

"What's that mean?"

"I'm just saying you look a little uncomfortable. I'm trying to find out who you are."

"I wouldn't be doin' this if it wuz up to me, Johnny England. I was goin' to community college when my ma got sick. I dropped out so I could care for her and then I needed to borrow some money for her medicine. I got no credit record. The bank says no, you got no credit, you got no job, go home. So I borrow some money from the man and now he got me. You don' wanna hear this."

"Yes, I do. This is exactly what I mean. You belong somewhere else. You're dressed that way but I can see more.

"We still in this hotel room an' I'm getting' set ta do you up." The woman had seemed on the verge of opening up and then had shut back down again.

"Well, I can help a little. I can let you earn a little extra."

"Look, mister, I don' do nothin' weird. I don' do other women, I don'…"

"No, no, no. You misread me. I got some other stuff I'm thinking about and you might be able to help." Terry took his aluminum travel case into the bathroom and set it on the sink. His vest went on the hook on the back of the door and his twin revolvers got locked in the case. Then he stepped back into the bedroom and peeled off his shirt.

"Wow. You got a really nice body."

"Oh, I pull me own weight from time to time."

"A guy like you gets all the women he wants, why are you pickin' up down in South-Central? You want something strange, doncha?"

"No. Nothing strange. In fact, you don't need to do this if you don't want to."

"That's it. You five-oh. I'm outta here."

"No. Sit down." Terry's voice went from a friendly and playful day tripper to a commanding officer in the blink of an eye. Rabbit sat down. Then his voice softened again. "I got no qualms against pluckin' a rose. As I said, the first woman that ever had me was a working girl. Nothing fancy, nothing kinky, nothing painful. We're just gonna have a good time here for a minute, and then we're gonna have another drink and I'm going to ask you some questions."

"Look John, you gonna go home to your wife or your boyfriend or girlfriend or whatever it is you got waiting for you but I gotta live here. I owe money that I gotta pay off or they gonna hurt my family, and if they think I been talking to five-oh they gonna hurt me, so why don't you just keep your questions, get some of this fine young thing and go back home and leave me alone?"

"Sit on the bed." The first thing Terry did was take off the short rabbit fur trimmed jacket from around her shoulders and then he undid the bikini top that was underneath it. Rabbit's breasts were firm and young, not large but perky and cone shaped.

Rabbit lay back on the mattress, her fingers circling her nipples. She did her best to make it look as though she would enjoy what was to come.

The tall high heeled boots had zippers on the outside. With slow, deliberate motions Terry unzipped and removed them, setting them in the corner by the wall. Then he peeled the yellow vinyl hot pants from beneath her bottom and slid them down her legs. When she was lying on the mattress smoothing her hands over her body, he took off his pants.

"Damn. You got a johnson half them niggas wish they had. This is gonna be good. Bring that thing over here and let me get you wrapped up."

Condoms had never been popular with Terry, he found them restrictive and they killed much of the feeling, but when visiting professional women they were indispensable. He coupled gently with Rabbit, at first, but he knew that it would take a long time for him to finish if he didn't pick up the pace. Not that finishing was what was important here, at least in the beginning.

It took over half an hour to consummate the act and Rabbit commented when he was done that he would make good money in the porn industry where they would be paying him rather than the other way around. He replied that while he had enjoyed it a great deal, he was more interested in what she could tell him than what she could do for him.

"I don' know. You sure you ain't five-oh? You talking 'bout 'I suspect this and I suspect that.' That's the way cops talk."

"No. I'm not a cop. They get paid shit and they get shot at for it. I got much more respect for myself than that. I'll tell you what. Here's an extra fifty. Go down to the drug store down the block and get some lubrication and some bigger rubber sacks. We can go again after a while." He peeled a $50 bill from a large wad of fifties and hundreds.

Rabbit smiled hugely, showing the large even white teeth behind her full lips. It looked as though she would take the $50 and run for the hills but if she did not return, then she was not the woman Terry was looking for.

He was almost asleep when the knock came at the door. It was Rabbit, back with supplies including a bottle of Coca Cola and some ice. There was also the unexpected bonus of another woman. Rabbit's friend Swallow strode in on her high heels with a large portable radio. Terry decided it was time to take off the kid gloves and learn how to party LA style.

"Glasgow."

"Yo, fool, I hear tell you been down in my 'hood handin' out Benjamins."

"Ah. You must be Mr. Bash." Gordon was employing his best 'British aristocrat.'

"Tha's what they call me. Y'know why?"

"I can fully imagine. You have quite a reputation."

"Tha's because I earned it. You see?"

"Of course. Now to the matter at hand. I see you have been paying too much for what you are distributing. Your Mexican contacts have been robbing you blind and are in fact giving your competition a much better price than they are affording you."

"What the fuck you talkin' about? I get the same price everybody gets and I don't need no goddamn DEA stooge tellin' me different."

"I assure you sir, I am no government agent, nor do I work for the police of any state, county or city. I am merely a man who sees an opportunity to make vast sums of money from the everyday trade of a large city. I make money for my friends and they make lots of money. I am offering you the chance to cut your overhead. This will allow you to profit even without the requisite street sales and…"

"Now hold on, fool. I don't know what you talking about no street sales. Who the fuck are you anyway?" The conversation was going just the way MacMaster had envisioned it. He knew it would be difficult to get inside. He needed to be bold and he had no time to waste. It was not as though he was trying to set up a sting operation. The money was all it took. The money and the photograph of a young woman, beaten to death.

"As I mentioned, I am merely an entrepreneur who sees the possibility of great profit for myself and all those involved through dropping the overhead and reducing the spillage. There is a great deal to be gleaned from the trade but one must control it more tightly. Your Spanish-speaking counterparts are making a great deal more than yourself and they are doing so with much less risk than you. I understand why you would be suspicious about new contacts that appear from nowhere, but I assure you there is much to be gained. Perhaps if we could meet face to face we could cement our relationship more fully and gain a measure of trust."

"Yeah, I'll think about it."

"Well then, I think this concludes the extent of what may be accomplished over the phone. Perhaps we may meet each other, say four this evening at your, uh, Bubba's Barbecue."

"Yeah. I'll see you at four in Bubba's."

Gordon set the phone down and chewed on the inside of his lip. The site had been chosen to put his quarry at ease but it now seemed a bit too pat. The venue was in enemy territory and if the whole thing blew up, there was no good way out. He needed something to equalize the odds.

D'arniel "Bash" Jamiel had not gotten where he was by being a nice guy. As long as his lieutenants were loyal, they had nothing to fear from him. As long as he thought they were loyal, that is. If he suspected someone of trying to skim off the top or get a little on the side, he made sure they ended up under the ground. His territory was small and he had enemies all around him. He was not paranoid; he knew who his enemies were and did not need to invent any that did not exist. To the north and west he had Crips factions. North Carson should have been Bloods' territory but the various groups of Compton Crips had taken over half the town. Lakewood, to the west, had been taken over by Mexican gangs who were currently in violent competition with the Salvadoran MS13s that were attempting to take over the area. The MS13s were a truly serious threat that was spreading throughout South America and heading north. D'arniel was trying to maintain a power base in the middle of this veritable sea of instability. In his own defense, he was doing a pretty good job by keeping lines of communication open with other Bloods gangs in the city. Unlike the neighborhood Crips gangs, who routinely warred with each other, the Bloods tended to cooperate among factions.

When D'arniel hung up the phone, the two lieutenants who were with him at the time sat back in their seats and looked at him with questioning eyes. Arquila "Moses" Khareem lit a cigarette and said, "You gotta be kidding. You ain't really gonna fuck with this faggot, are you?"

"I don' know, Moses. What do you think, RayJay?"

"He gotta be fuckin' five-oh. Question is, why he fuckin' with us? We hangin' tight but we small beans. This guy, I figure to be DEA. They comin' in lookin' to see what we got goin' so they know if we worth fuckin' with. RayJay say we go in humble. We tell him we can't handle no weight. RayJay say we tell this guy the Dynamite Crips from across the one-ten got all the big business and tha's where he should be talking."

"Look here, Bash," interjected Moses, "we can talk to this faggot and find out what he got to say. If it don' look right we use his ass to setup the Dynamites or the Shotguns or one o' them Crips hoods. The hammer comes down an' we sittin' here sayin' nothin' but smiling like a cat."

"Yeah. I like that. On the other hand, this fool might be on the level. He might have a contact we can't make. He's outside, I mean listen to him. He's outside so maybe he can get a contact we can't because he ain't got no enemies. He probably jus' some stupid white boy that thinks this shit is easy. I seen his ass before. He just gonna end up face down in a fuckin' storm sewer an' we be sittin' here sayin' nothin'."

"Well, Jackie, it looks like you were wrong this one time. I gotta give you that the man is a freak, or a something, I don't know what. He didn't leave town though. He's parked between the Compton Airport and Carson. That tells me he's doing something down there."

"He's probably getting the rental car stolen, or it already got stolen and it's sitting in a chop shop right now. When they go after it, I got twenty that says there ain't nothing but the Lo-Jack left."

"I'll be taking your money then. He's at 1400 West Alondra Boulevard. That's the Howard Hotel or the Horace Hotel, or what-is-it?"

"The Horatio. It's right off the runways. If he don't get the car stolen in Compton, it's a miracle. The bet still stands. Uh, boss, what the hell would he be doing in the Horatio? I mean it's a real shit-hole and it's in Compton."

"Shit, I don't know. He knows the job and he came with the recommendation. I have to assume he knows what he's doing. Give him a call," Archie told her. "See if he has anything to say."

"I did call. It goes right to voice mail. He's either got it turned off or he's on it."

"Okay. Let's not get ahead of ourselves. We already got this guy working it, whatever it is, I say we just let him work. After all, he's a professional."

"Yeah. That's what they all say."

Archie hobbled back to his desk and Jacqueline checked to make sure her desk drawer was locked. As far as Archie knew, she had already given Terry the full payment for his services. He could not have known she had the bulk of it locked in her desk.

Chapter Fourteen
Bubba's Barbeque

"Hey, girl. You sure you wanna live alone in this neighborhood?" The owner of the house was a middle-aged black woman. She never talked about how she had gotten the houses she was now renting to whomever she could. The memories were too painful for her but the rental properties allowed her to stay off welfare. The neighborhood was predominately black but more and more Mexicans moved north every day. She could not have known that her newest applicant came from Argentina.

"I appreciate your concern but I am a big girl and I think I can take care of myself. The doors and windows are bars and I must assume there is nobody else who has a key?"

"Hey, I don' wanna put you off. Like I said first and last month, security deposit and you can move in right now."

"I would expect the first month to be pro-rated. Did I say that correctly, pro-rated? I mean the month is half over now. If I was to take it today then the first month would only be two weeks."

"Sure. I can do that for you. The bus routes go by a block that way if you don't have a car. I ain't gonna involve myself in your private affairs unless you want me to. The rent is due on the first of the month, no excuses, no post-dated checks, no sob stories. If you ain't got the rent, you forfeit the last month's rent and I want you out immediately. We clear on that?"

"*Claro que si*. You will have no trouble from me. I work in the bank as I said. I have no time for gangsters or parties. I have no family and I have no man for right now. I am, as you say, a safe bet. All my luggage was stolen when I moved out here so I don't have much but I can get some furniture moved in by the end of the day. I pay you in cash, today, and then I get a checking account set up at the bank tomorrow. I get it free because I am working there. This will be working very well."

The owner took the cash, showed Anastasia where to sign the lease and gave her the keys. She could not help think that her new tenant would not be staying in the neighborhood for long but she had a couple of months' security to back up whatever happened. She decided to take her remaining child to Ponderosa that night. Her two sons were both dead but her daughter stayed off the streets that had taken them.

Once the owner was gone, Anastasia checked the time and then took out her cell phone and called MacMaster.

"Glasgow."

"This is Rio."

"North meets South again. Have you gotten a place?"

"West Two Hundred Twenty Two Street, number Three Hundred Nineteen."

"Good. Got it. I'm not to be coming around there, so you'll need to come here, but not today. I have a meet at four," MacMaster continued. "Well, it looks like the meet is about two blocks from where you are."

"I will need to go to the store and get a mattress or get one tomorrow instead."

"I'm to be at Bubba's Barbecue at four."

"Do not speak to me if I am there as well. We are not to be known to each other."

"Yes, dear. I think I knew that. I might be forced to stare and drool though. Is that acceptable?"

"Ai! Make sure you have a handkerchief to soak up the slobber."

When Gordon MacMaster pulled his Cadillac into the parking lot of Bubba's Barbecue there was barely a parking spot. If he had been driving a Metro or a VW there might have been room but his body would not have fit in something that small. He pulled back out into the street and

166

parked in front of the building regardless of the 'No Parking' signs, right on the corner of West 220th and South Main. There was an empty parking lot on the other side of the street with no cars in it whatsoever but that was not acceptable to him.

There was a line at the counter but MacMaster was not going to stand, nor was he there for the ribs. He walked through the restaurant without glancing from side to side but still taking in everybody in it and every movement each of them made. What he saw was that D'arniel "Bash" Jamiel was not there; neither was Anastasia Viuda. He turned on his heel and headed for the door without a word. As he exited the barbecue joint, he saw a man standing in front of the place, leaning against the wall. It was instinctive for him to reach inside his jacket for the grip of his magnum revolver but he did not pull it out. The man outside was not threatening him, rather he was fiddling with a toothpick in his mouth. He caught Gordon's eye and beckoned him with a twist of his head. As the man sauntered around the corner onto 220th Street, Gordon started his car and made a right.

"Who you lookin' for?" the man asked when the Caddy pulled up.

"Bash."

"Ain't never heard of him."

"I'm Glasgow."

"Tell you what, go down to Figueroa and take a left. On the corner of Figueroa and Two-Two-Three there's a used car dealership, belongs to my cousin. Stop in, maybe he fix you up."

The used car dealer was less than a mile away but the whole thing looked like too much of a set-up. MacMaster pulled the car into the almost deserted parking lot of Figueroa Motors but did not leave the confines of the vehicle. He angled it for a quick escape onto 223rd Street and left it in drive with his foot on the brake.

It took a minute before anyone came out. They were waiting for Gordon to step out of the car but he did not. Eventually a tall, thin black man in a mechanic's uniform exited the reflective glass building and approached the car.

"Is there something I can do for you, sir?"

"I'm looking for Bash."

"I'm sorry, sir. Something got bashed?"

"Look, you stupid fuck." The mechanic jumped at the sight of MacMaster's revolver. "I am not here to jerk off. I have an appointment with Bash Jamiel and I'm getting run around. Get me the man, now, or he can forget about it."

The man took a pleading look at the building and MacMaster knew the man was inside, but there was too much uncertainty. The reflective glass turned the entire shop into a huge trap, if that was what the gangster had in mind. The only way Gordon MacMaster was going to approach that building was in an armored personnel carrier. He slipped his foot off the brake and jammed the gas, narrowly missing a Honda Accord that was crossing the intersection. He had not gotten two blocks when his phone rang.

"Glasgow."

"Mr. Glasgow, we had an appointment."

"You were not at the meet and then you were not at the alternate meet. I will be doing business in this neighborhood, but I do not think you will be in charge when I do."

"Now that sounded like a threat."

"Nothing of the kind. I have nothing to do with who is in charge, I merely facilitate the cash flow with those I can trust and I must say that I do not feel I can trust you. You can understand that, I'm sure."

"Well shit, my man, you can see my point of view too. You come out of nowhere and decide that I get the pleasure of doin' business wit' you. What that look like?"

"I'll admit to being somewhat unorthodox but that is

the necessity and nature of my business. I concede that without trust there is no forward movement, and that I have not yet earned trust in this section of the city. It is of no further importance. I will do business with your rivals instead. I had thought to work with the Bloods because they are less internally competitive than the Crips, but I can make adjustments. Good day, sir." This was the gamble and MacMaster knew he played a dangerous game. He did not hang up the phone, knowing that if Jamiel did not make a play now he would never get another chance. He thought he had overplayed it and lost the round but then he heard the gang leader's voice.

"Wait a minute. We can still do some business together, come on back and we'll talk. I didn't mean to scare you. You know, I gotta look after number one."

"Change the venue. I need to be in an area I can see what is going on. There is no reason to get holed up behind walls. I suggest we meet in a park somewhere. I will call you back in a while once I have consulted the map. We both need to be comfortable or neither of us is going to come away feeling good and that is what I am here to promote. I will call you in a few minutes at this number." Gordon hung up the phone and pulled onto a side street where he could read the map. A few minutes later he called the number back that Bash had called him from. If his gambit had worked, the gang leader would still be there.

"Bash."

"Mr. Jamiel, I suggest we meet at the baseball yard on Orrick Street. Do you know it?"

"Yeah. I know every inch of my town."

"Very well, then, I will meet you there in a few minutes."

When D'arniel "Bash" Jamiel stepped out of the back seat of his Buick Riviera, Gordon MacMaster was already sitting on the bleachers at the ball field. Gordon was alone while Jamiel was flanked by three of his men. They introduced each other and MacMaster suggested they walk around the field. He wanted to put the gangster at ease first and foremost, to avoid a confrontation that he suspected would be uncomfortable at best. The three junior gangsters followed the two of them around the field but they did not disarm Gordon.

"So, Mr. Glasgow," Bash began with an arrogance and contempt in his voice that the Scotsman found more than just annoying. "What is it you think your white ass can do for me down here in South-Central that we so slow we don' do now?"

"Let me tell you a story. It should be a familiar story to you since it originated from right here in Los Angeles and from the black community no less."

"So I'm here to get a history lesson about black men from a white man?"

"If you want to learn the lessons of the past without suffering the slings and arrows of outrageous fortune, I suggest you listen. We are all condemned to learn the lessons of the past, some of us through the mistakes we promulgate and some through listening to tales of the past and exploits of those who came before."

"You gonna need to speak English if you want me to hear what you gonna say."

"Today's lesson concerns the recent past. You are probably familiar with it. Back in the 1980s, Ricky Ross, known as Freeway Ricky, was moving $2,000,000 a day worth of drugs into LA. Why? Because he was smart and generous and he wasn't concerned with how he looked, with all this gold and diamond foolishness." Gordon waved a contemptuous finger at the chains around Jamiel's neck.

"Ricky dressed like a bum," Gordon continued, "well, like a regular working man anyway. His pants fit him and he didn't bother with status brands. He watched what was going on and who was getting popped, who was getting shot, who was getting their houses blown up and he said 'I'm not going to do that; they're not going to do that to me.'

"You need to know that Freeway Ricky got away with it. At least, he would have gotten away with it if he hadn't gotten bored and greedy. I personally don't think he got greedy, just bored. He had spent so long as the man, running things and running from the cops that when he retired in Cincinnati, Ohio, he didn't know what to do with his days. He could have raced cars or gambled or flown around the world on executive jets. He had made so much money that he never needed to sell another gram but he could not stop. He got bored and started importing cocaine into Ohio and that was his downfall. The question I have for you, Mr. Jamiel, is do you want to retire in some remote location in the plush opulence of a prince of men or do you want to end up the way your predecessor did, dead in the streets of the biggest and most anonymous city in the country?"

"I'm listening but all I'm hearing is bullshit."

"I can turn you into the kingpin of the drug trade. I have studied your history a little and I chose your location as being at the boundary of the Mexican influence. I know the border is south of here, but the influence is so strong that the cultural border is in the south of Carson. Now I can deal with the Sledgehammers or the Shotguns, but they have issues with each other as well as issues with you, and the Balkanization of the Crips will lead to their downfall. Witness Germany. They walked across Europe at will every forty years or so causing so much devastation that they eventually got the entire world to rise up against them and demand that they stop wreaking havoc. Now, a couple of generations after they had the life bombed out of their country, they are on top again. This time they have done it properly, economically. They are not attempting to conquer the continent militarily, they are doing so economically. They

171

got pounded into the European dirt and the Russian steppes time and again because they had not changed their strategy. When they did, it changed everything."

"You talk a lot but I still don' hear you saying anything."

"What I am saying is that you can be a nickel and dime street thug or you can make big money the same way and you don't need to get your hands so dirty. You can be the Seven-Eleven on the corner or you can be the wholesaler supplying them that makes the real money. I can bring it across the border and teach you to do it right."

"An' you gonna do this for me?"

"That was the gist of my proposal, yes." Gordon squinted one eye at him.

"I'll think about it."

"The offer is good for a limited time. I, for one, will not die a tired and broken old man with nothing in my pocket. This country has a fortune to offer to the man with the spine to make it happen."

"I said, I'll think about it."

"Good. Give me a call." The two men went their separate ways amicably. MacMaster knew his prey had taken the bait, but he had yet to set the hook.

The party at the Horatio was swinging. After the first bottle of vodka was gone, Terry gave Rabbit some more money to get more, even though she had never given him his change from the previous run. His largesse was having the proper effect on the ladies. Swallow called an associate to have some to have some weed delivered and Terry got her to call for some food as well. As hard as he tried to stay sober, he knew he was going to get plastered if he didn't eat something.

Rabbit knocked on the door when she got back with the booze. Swallow opened the door, but then Rabbit got thrown into the room, knocking her friend to the ground and leaving the doorway filled with three hundred pounds of Arquebus "Velvet" Johnson.

"What you hos doin' partyin' on my time? This fool lookin' for a good time he gotta pay for it."

Ordinarily Terry would have had little concern. It doesn't matter how big a man is once he's been shot a couple of times, but Terry's weapons were all locked in the hard-sided travel case and he was standing there with nothing but his trousers on. He was not used to being on the defensive end of an argument without an ace in the hole, but thought he could bluff his way through it. "Hey, we got another partier here. Maybe we could have a foursome."

"Shut the fuck up, white boy. I ain't gotta pay ta fuck my hos. They come beggin' ta suck my dick. What I wanna know is why you takin' up all their time without payin'?"

Rabbit tried to placate the enormous Velvet by saying, "I tol' ya, Baby. He payin'". This did little to soothe the man whose rage was mostly artificial. He knew most of the businessmen hadn't even gotten off work for the day and that the chance of the ladies doing much business before then was slim. Velvet was intent on simply extorting every penny Terry had. Rabbit had invited Juggs to join them as well but Juggs had declined. There was no way the girls could have known that Juggs would run to Velvet and tell him about the white boy with all the money.

"Come on in and have a drink, my friend," Terry said with a sweeping, drunken motion of the vodka bottle.

Arquebus Johnson did step into the room and close the door behind him, but he was not interested in having a drink. "How much money you got, bitch," he asked, directing his question to Swallow.

"I ain't got nothin', Velvet. He say he gonna pay me, he just ain't give me nothin' yet. He got done doin' Rabbit an' he ain't ready for Swallow yet."

Velvet Johnson was not in the business of accepting excuses. He took his hand off the pistol in his jacket pocket, stepped forward and backhanded Swallow across the face, knocking her to the ground.

If Velvet had known who it was he was facing down, he might not have stepped into the room. He was a big man and strong but he was more used to beating up women. Any real confrontations were handled with firepower. It had been a long time since he had stood toe-to-toe with someone who could really fight. His hand had not even contacted Swallow's face when Terry Kingston began to move. As Swallow hit the floor, the assassin had stepped across the room. Velvet had not gotten his hand back in his pocket by the time Terry reached him and smashed the vodka bottle across his head. The pimp fell like a marionette with the strings cut.

Terry reached into the man's jacket pocket and pulled the pistol out. His visible intoxication of moments before was gone and he stood unwavering, gun in hand, watching all the members of the little troupe.

Swallow got up off the carpet and cried "Velvet. What's he done to you, honey?" She looked at Terry with hatred in her eyes despite the fact that her face still stung from Velvet's slap.

Velvet groaned and put a hand to his face and Swallow scuttled forward to cradle his head in her hands. Rabbit was not so quick to jump to Velvet's aid but she was also not about to jump ship. There was no possibility of changing alliances yet. The white man was nothing but a customer and as she had stated earlier, she would be staying in the neighborhood when he was long gone.

"Get off me, woman. I gonna fuck this punk up." Velvet did not seem to have a solid grasp on the situation. It only took him a moment to realize that his pistol was in the hands of his opponent, but it did not stop him. He was used to intimidating men, after all he was six-foot-four and three hundred pounds of mostly muscle, plus he was black. He knew that it made a difference to the more urbane members of the white community. Velvet Johnson had never met a white man who could take him and seldom one who would even try.

Launching himself from the floor he rushed right at Terry Kingston with his head down, confident that the man didn't even know how to use the gun and would not have the spine to do so, if he did. If he knew Terry Kingston, he would have run for the hills.

The only thing that saved Arquebus Johnson's life that day was the fact that he did not have a silencer on his gun. Terry did not want to make a lot of noise in the hotel room and chance getting fingered for something before he even got into the proper neighborhood. As the pimp bull rushed him, Terry stepped to the side and smacked him in the back of the head with the barrel of the pistol. Hitting him was actually an act of mercy. If he had maintained his trajectory he would not have stopped moving until he went through the window and took a head dive to the concrete walkway. As it was, the man went head first into the air conditioner but this did not stop him either. Swearing incoherently, the man hoisted himself back to his feet and cast around for something to use as a weapon. The desk had an old wooden chair that could easily split a man's skull, but as he reached for it Terry smashed him in the head again. This was about all the blows to the head the man could take and he collapsed again, banging his head one more time on the desk as he went down.

Terry turned just in time to see Swallow launch herself at him, thinking to jump on his back. He caught her by the throat in midair and slammed her on the bed.

"If you wish to keep the name Swallow, I suggest you lie still. I will crush your windpipe and you'll never swallow again." Terry's voice was calm and dry.

Unlike Velvet, Swallow took his threat seriously.

Rabbit stood by the bathroom door trembling. She flinched visibly when Terry looked at her.

"Don't worry, darling, I won't hurt you. The offer still stands." Terry started buttoning up his shirt while Swallow slid off the bed and started wiping the blood off Velvet's face with a pillowcase.

"What offer?" she asked with a catch in her voice.

"I'll get you out of here and set you up with something else." Terry was opening his case.

"You do that for a woman you don't even know? A street woman?"

"Everybody needs to make a living." The cross shoulder holsters came out of the case with the twin .38s ensconced. Velvet's semi-automatic 9mm Taurus went into the case and it was locked. Everybody was staring at Terry now. "If you're worried about your mother, you can stay."

"Honey, my mother died two years ago."

"Then let's go."

Velvet managed to mumble, "Bitch, you owe me money."

Terry got his vest from the bathroom and slipped it on over his revolvers. Picking up his locked case he stepped to the door, looked behind him and told Rabbit, "Now or never."

Rabbit closed her eyes, sounded a keening tone between her clenched jaws, stepped over to Velvet Johnson and kicked him in the ribs with the pointed toe of her high heeled boots and headed for the door. Terry put a hand to the small of her back and guided her out the door.

Chapter Fifteen
Rabbit Run

Rabbit did not think much of the low-rent motel room in Van Nuys. She immediately decided that she had traded one pimp for another. She had stopped by the building she shared with three other women and started piling clothes in the back of Terry's car. The senior woman was not a madam, she was just the oldest of the whores on site. All she had to say was that Velvet was gonna be upset. Rabbit said nothing until she and Terry were ready to leave. Then she said, "Velvet is gonna be at the emergency room at the Martin Luther King Medical Center. You wanna find out how he feels about it all, go ask him."

The clothes she had taken had included Swallow's who was about the same size. The pile filled the back seat of the Crown Victoria but none of it was what you could wear to a black-tie event. Velvet had equipped his women with a lot of clothing, but it was all revealing and designed to spark the male libido. Of course there was no room for it all in the closet of the motel room, so most of it was piled on the bed.

"All right, Johnny, you got me. Now what are you gonna do with me?"

"I hadn't thought that one through all the way, Rabbit. You can call me Indian, by the way."

"Indian? Indian's no more your name than John."

"That may be true but I am no longer a john."

"True. I guess. That means I no longer a Rabbit."

"I'll buy that. What do you want me to call you?"

"If I'm gonna call you Indian, I should make you call me Pocahontas."

"If that's what you want."

"No. Call me Roberta. My name is Roberta Cunningham."

"Good. Well, Roberta, what do you think I should do

with you now that I have you all to myself?"

She looked at him warily, not knowing what he was really asking and having had and seen enough bad things done to women for little or no reason. "I think you should give me some money."

"Well, that is an option, but the truth is, if I did that, I would go back to being John. I think I have a better idea. Do you have identification?"

"No, Velvet took all my ID so he could keep me down. He does it with all the women. His rationale is that if we can't drive and we can't rent a car or an apartment then we will be doubly indebted to him and we will maintain the status quo."

It was not lost on Terry that as soon as he got Roberta out of her previous environment, her diction and vocabulary improved exponentially.

"This is part of the problem with the system. If you cannot prove who you are then you cannot get identification and if you cannot get identification then you cannot prove who you are. A catch-22 of the highest order."

"Where were you born, darling?"

"South-Central."

"Then city hall has a copy of your birth certificate. Once you get a copy of your birth certificate then you can get a driver's license or at least a photo ID. We will work on that tomorrow. Right now, I'm beginning to feel a little drunk and I never did get the Chinese I ordered. What do you say we go out and grab some tucker?"

"Lead the way, Indian. When we get back, maybe I'll make your feathers stand on end."

"Hey bro, get a look at this ho." Andrew "Trooper" Sykes was half unconscious from the painkillers and half a bottle of Hennessy but he was not so brain dead as to not notice Anastasia Viuda walking down the street.

178

If it was safety she was concerned about, she would have walked east to South Main Street but safety was not on the agenda that day. It was almost the dinner hour on Friday.

Arquila "Moses" Khareem cast an eye on the newcomer to the neighborhood and licked his lips. "Who she workin' for?" he asked.

"I dunno. I never seen this Mexican bitch before. I tell you one thing, she come over here I give her something to work on."

"Trooper, you ain't doin' shit long as you in that cast."

"Hey, the motherfuckers shot me in the chest, not the dick. What I'm supposed to do? Least I didn't get it as bad as Fireman and Warbucks. Shit, Warbucks gonna be closed casket. They shot him through the eye."

"An' Wyatt Earp got his shit blown all over the wall. If he makes it they say he gonna be shittin' in a bag the rest of his life." Moses stopped for a second and waved a young teenager over. "Hey Smallfry, follow that woman to wherever she goin'. I wanna find out where she lives. Take a five. You get twenty when you get back with the address."

"You gonna make a play for that?" Trooper asked.

"Not today. I gonna get drunk today an' mourn my brothers. We putten 'im in the groun' tomorrow."

Saturday was a strain for the reserved and professional staff of the Allen Funeral Home. They were used to mourners but it always caused angst when the deceased were gang members because the other members would show up drunk or with bottles of booze. Funerals have always been for the living but that included the brain dead. Most of the bikers followed a code of solemnity at funerals, but the black street gangs had no such proscription against acting out at the most solemn of events. It was a crapshoot when a member of a Hispanic gang got interred. Sometimes they were mournful; sometimes they were vengeful.

That Saturday, the captain of the South Alley Bloods

kept order among his subordinates and they maintained a calm and serene service. The funeral procession consisted of low riders and SUVs but there was no incident to mar the passage.

The same thing could not be said of the Sledgehammer Crips' funeral held in the Brown Funeral Home. They had buried Barrow Brown earlier that week, he was no relation to the owners of the funeral parlor, and today they were burying his brother Paco Brown and Hardtime Corey. The gang got vociferous and drunken. They did not start ruining things until they got to the cemetery and there was not much there they could ruin. The canopy over the grave site came down and they knocked over a couple of the standing headstones. The police were called but the gang had dispersed by the time they arrived.

After the funeral, business was proceeding as usual in Carson. The perceived level of danger was elevated as would be expected any weekend, but this time it was the Crips not the cops the Bloods were watching out for. They were not watching out for Anastasia Viuda, but they certainly saw her when she appeared.

Word had already spread of the new woman living on 222nd between Rashdall and Kinard. She lived by herself which meant she had left her husband or vice versa. The best thing about this one was that she had no children. It made her a prime target. They all wanted a woman like that in their stable.

"George, what is it I might do for my favorite congressman's aide?" Frank Hicks was looking as dapper as ever in a three-piece, tailored pinstripe suit.

"Frank, I have been authorized to thank you for the generous campaign donation made in your name."

Frank smiled slightly and passed it off with a small wave of the hand.

180

"I uh, I'm here to ask about the request that accompanied the donation," said George.

"I believe the request was straightforward," Frank replied smoothly. "There was nothing about it that needed further explanation. But, I am a patient man and I will indulge you this time since there is so much at stake.

"Where shall I begin? How about the fact that your boss is up for reelection in three weeks, one week after the vote on the decriminalization process goes through? If this bill were to pass before I am ready, it would cost me a great deal of money and that cost would be passed along in a form that I shudder to even contemplate. That is as simple as I can make the issue. Tell me, is there something I left out?"

"No, sir, that is to say, you mentioned all the salient points. What you failed to mention is the fact that if my, uh, that is to say..."

"Let's stop beating around the bush here. We are both here with an agenda, one that may be expedited with mutual benefit to both parties. Congressman Cabot is set to vote on the marijuana decriminalization bill for the state of California, and you are here telling me that he is having second thoughts about our arrangement."

"Frank, may I call you Frank? The congressman is concerned that if he votes against the bill, he will be defeated for the seat in reelection. Most of the district is in favor of the bill. The timing is unfortunate but it may also have been deliberate."

"Your own father owns some land in the valley, correct?" The gangster gestured and his diamond ring sparkled.

"Sure, but I assure you that this has nothing to do with my father or his vineyard. This is coming directly from my boss. I am concerned that he will be unable to secure a reelection if he is to vote against what is so clearly in the interests of the people."

You are afraid? What about the congressman?

George fidgeted and looked at the floor.

"George! You never told Congressman Cabot about our arrangement. You little minx! You slipped away from the scout leader and you were swimming in the deep end of the pool without a lifeguard. Now you don't know how to tell the boss what you did for him, do you?"

"I was protecting him," George replied defensively.

"Of course you were, but now you have gotten your tit in a wringer. Congressman Cabot does not know he owes me a much larger favor than any campaign contribution could ever assure. What do you think we should do about this?"

"I don't know. If he finds out, he'll fire me for sure and then you won't have a friend in his office."

"Ah, those of little faith." Frank Hicks' face took on a look of a long-suffering martyr or an indulgent schoolteacher. "Henry Cabot is going to win the reelection to the Twentieth District, I assure you. His opponent will be forced to recuse himself from the race days before the election. This you will take as a given since I said it and it will happen as I have said. Your boss will also vote against the legalization measure until certain other elements have fallen into place in proper order. You see, there is a certain federal prosecutor who is eager to make the Supreme Court and is willing to go against the will and desire of the public to do so. He intends to make a name for himself by challenging the validity of the vote. It will be his contention that it is unconstitutional for the state to make such a thing legal when the federal laws clearly prohibit any such thing. His little gambit might be defeated but not before the issue gets tied up for months, maybe years in the process. I think he will be forced to resign instead, but that is not in the works yet."

"Ah, yes. I am aware of the man you refer to," George said. "He will be a thorn in the side of the great State of California for as long as he holds office."

"Yes. His self aggrandizement has already become an unacceptable hurdle for those of us just trying to eke out a living in this day and age," Frank said earnestly. "But back to the issue at hand. You will set up a meeting with Henry Cabot and one of my associates. Our position will be explained without exposing your culpability and that way we can still be friends. I assure you and I will assure the congressman as well, that if I do not get my favor on this issue then you and he will be ruined politically. If I stop with your careers it is only because I am in a good mood that day.

"Very well then, I will do what I can to calm the congressman's fears. I'll set up the meeting immediately. It will be a luncheon with a generous constituent and that's all. I won't be there."

"Oh, I want you there. You will advise him on the correct path to take and steer him in the paths of righteousness for his own sake. You will do this for me and for yourself. And for him as well. I assure you, our interests are aligned." Frank held his hands open with his fingers interlaced. "What is good for you and yours is good for us as well and once the time is right, then the bill will be allowed to sail through and we will both reap the vast abundance of our patience."

"I'll be in touch."

"Of course, stop by any time." Frank stood but did not offer his hand.

George Arridagio rose from his seat. In his opinion, the congressman had gotten in way too deep and was way too beholden to this oily snake charmer and didn't even know it yet. There was nothing but trouble to be found in this direction and he regretted the day he ever heard of Frank Hicks.

The worst part was that it had been unnecessary. The congressman had already been dealing with the problem of New Moon Productions through different channels. He had brought in some talent from out of town who was already on the job and had not wanted George's involvement. The outside talent had killed Bruce Babbage so smoothly that it was two weeks before anyone knew he was dead. Of course, once Arridagio had gone to Frank Hicks and arranged the massacre on Ocean Park Boulevard, it was too late. Cabot thought he had gotten the problem resolved already and George thought he had fixed the issue through his unsavory contacts.

"Okay, what's the deal?"

"What is it you are questioning, darling?"

"I wanna know where we going. You beat up Velvet and got my fine brown ass outta there an' now you don' want none of it? It was good enough for you when you was payin' for it." Some of the saucy street attitude tinged Roberta's words; the Rabbit persona.

"Roberta, I respect you. I respect the fact that you don't do drugs. I respect the fact that you want to make your life better and that you are willing to make the change. That takes some spunk and spine. The only reason I have been keeping my hands to myself for the past two days is that respect. I need you to understand that I am not your pimp, your master or your captor. If you wish to stay you are welcome to. If you wish to wander out the door and turn tricks I will not stop you, though neither will I allow you to return. We have been having a good time enjoying each other's company, yes?"

"Yes."

"Have I made myself clear?"

"Yes."

"Good. Rest assured that my celibacy has been extremely difficult to maintain. I find you a wonderful woman and I would like very much for you to share my bed, but I will not force you and I will not expect it of a matter of course. If you want to join me in the sack then that choice is yours and yours alone. I will take a shower now and we will be going to breakfast. Breakfast on the beach all right?"

The situation was nothing Roberta Cunningham was accustomed to. She had been servicing men as long as she could remember. The only thing that kept her from becoming a welfare mother was her infertility, caused by an early abortion. Had she been fertile she would already be caring for a brood of kids. It wasn't that she was a nymphomaniac or even that she enjoyed sex that much, it was a matter of what she thought was expected of her. She had lost her virginity at eleven to an older boy and was pregnant at twelve. She had been both used and abused by the time she finished high school. The story about her mother being sick and her dropping out of community college was true, but her mother had indeed died two years earlier, and she found herself trapped in the cycle of debt and neighborhood. It didn't matter where she tried to hook, if she was working the streets then some man was going to take advantage of her. She had not told Terry, or anyone else for that matter, about the small bank account she had managed to gather and maintain over the past year or so. It wasn't much but it represented something to her. She had planned on leaving South-Central but had no idea how she would do it. She had lived there so long that the idea was terrifying.

A warm glow suffused Roberta's body, centered in her lower belly. It had been a long time since she had actually wanted sex; it was usually just a means to an end for her, but she wanted it now. She took one step toward the bathroom door, trembling, and then her life crashed down around her and her insecurity froze her in her tracks. One hot tear ran down her face, burning and terrifying her. She had not cried since her mother died. She was so far outside her usual realm of understanding that she could not coordinate her feelings. Things were simpler back in the triangle; horrid and brutal but understandable. She wanted desperately to believe that Terry was her knight in shining armor but these things didn't really happen; not to her, not to anyone. She threw a jacket over her shoulders and ran out the door. The jacket did little to cover her exposed skin. The daisy duke shorts and the halter top coupled with high heels gave an immediate impression to everyone who saw her.

Roberta was not the only one confused. When Terry got out of the shower his first thought was that she had robbed him and gone back to her previous life. It was automatic for him to think that she had gone back to what she knew, but he was wrong. A quick examination showed that she had left the case with the guns in it right where he had put it, and that his wallet was left in his pants along with the wad of bills he had been flashing about. Perhaps she had needed to go to the drug store for something.

It did not take Terry long to shave, brush and floss his teeth and comb his hair. It took less time to climb into a fresh set of clothes. He was ready for breakfast on the beach but he was not about to go that far. He had given Roberta a key card for the door, but he was still not certain he could trust her. There was nothing definitive that caused him to mistrust her, but he had not known her that long and his reaction when he came out of the shower showed him that he was getting too comfortable too quickly.

Both breakfast and lunch were taken from local restaurants. Terry began to reassess his next move. Roberta had answered the questions he had pertaining to the two differing quadrants of Carson and the different Crips factions in the surrounding areas. She had lived in the neighborhood her entire life and knew who was doing what with who and why. She knew the names of the gang leaders and, more vaguely, their addresses. He had gotten all this out of her and written most of it down. She had wanted to know what he needed the information for but he would not tell her. That may have been what drove her off. He admitted to himself that he was acting like a cop, or maybe FBI, and that she probably gotten suspicious and decided to bolt for home. This brought up the other potentially dangerous situation. What if she went back to Carson and told her associates about Terry and all his questions? Would they make the trip all the way to Van Nuys to settle the question? Would Velvet be gunning for him? Would they call a local branch of the Bloods and have him targeted from right there? It seemed too dangerous to maintain his position and he was about to pack his things in the car when he heard the lock click in response to the key card.

"Roberta, I'm sorry to doubt you, dear, but where have you been?"

"I got to thinking, while you were in the shower, I..." Her voice caught in her throat and though she had considered herself ready, she found the emotional upwelling to retain some of the morning's intensity. "I wanted to get in the shower with you. I wanted to get in bed with you. I want you. To be with you."

"Well that's all right then.... I waited for you. What, um... where did you go?" Terry found himself at an unaccustomed loss for words.

"I got scared. I ran away." Roberta started trembling. "I got to thinking this is all a trick, some kind of big fucking joke. This sort of thing does not happen to a woman like me. Only in the movies. So I went down the street and then I started thinking 'what could I do if I ever wanted to see the other side of life?', you know, the kind of things regular people do, 'what could I do to make it happen?'"

"And what did you decide?" he asked holstering his revolver.

"Shit, you got a gun out?"

"Again, you'll need to forgive me. I didn't know who was coming through that door. I thought you might have gone back home to get something and been caught by one of your old associates."

"You thought I was gonna betray you, didn't you? You thought I was gonna sell your ass out to the pimps in South-Central."

"Roberta, I thought no such thing, but I do need to be careful. So do you. So, is that what you have done?"

"No. I took my copy of this birth certificate and I went to Planned Parenthood. It took a while but my test records are being sent up from Carter. I… I don't know if you got any tests done in this country but it would be good if you did. I know these things kill a lot of the feeling for you an… I … Well, I wish you would come with me to the clinic." It was an obvious struggle for her to say it and she physically cringed after getting it out, a reaction to having been beaten before.

"I see no harm in that. A bit late in the day now."

The relieved smile that blossomed on her face revealed Roberta's relief about the subject. Men were often touchy about diseases. She knew she had always been careful but things happened along the way that she could not be sure about. She had been to Planned Parenthood a few times, in Carter, when she could make Velvet understand that she needed to see a gynecologist. They were very professional, and she had never forgotten that if she wanted to be tested for diseases she had to ask for the tests. After the first time she had always asked.

Friday morning, at the clinic, Terry needed to take out his Arkansas driver's license to remind himself of his address. They insisted on proof of identification before they would treat and inspect him. He almost walked out the door at that point but decided that he had slept with enough women in his life that it would be a good idea if he got checked out. He did not know that some of the tests were not the sort of thing you could walk out with an answer for. Roberta got a quizzical look on her face when she saw his name and address. He had refused to give her the personal details before, but he had been paying for everything and demanding nothing so she had not pressed him. From that day forward she called him Terry Garreth of Arkansas. It only took a couple of days before the Arkansas address no longer made her giggle.

At about three in the morning, Terry was sitting at the edge of his bed wondering what the devil he thought he was doing. He had never willingly exposed himself this way before. Roberta was a nice girl, as far as hookers went, but he had only wanted to get some information from her. Sex hadn't even been in the original plan and now he was sharing a room with her and she had even talked him into going to the sex clinic. He felt like he had lost control, lost sight of the goal. Smiling ruefully, he decided that women had a way of doing that to a man. A few hours later, Roberta woke him in the most intimate way. He quickly decided that her talented lips made his slight indiscretion worthwhile.

Chapter Sixteen
Commodities

"No, no, no, amigo. Tres kilogrammes por $100,000".
MacMaster's command of Mexican Spanish was not what it
might have been. He sounded like some kind of upper-class
snob to them since his Castilian Spanish was so much more
proper than the regionalized slang they employed. They
could say nothing about it, however, if MacMaster had the
money.

They both knew there was no way he was going to get
three kilos of black tar north of the border for that price, but
they were negotiating. The Scot had been amazed at how
easy it was to locate a major supplier once he was south of
the border. Of course he did not bring more than a token of
the cash with him. A big bag of money carried by a single
man in Mexico was a death sentence. What he did have was a
photograph of a briefcase full of money along with his face
and a recent newspaper. The fact that the money was faked
was irrelevant. Gordon MacMaster did not want to make
that kind of money. He had no problem killing a man for
money, that was simply what was done, but he objected to
the slow descent into Hell that drug addiction represented.

The gist of the conversation ended up being that he
could buy that kind of quantity south of the border for that
price, but once it crossed into the US it was worth a lot more.
MacMaster vacillated, took a telephone number he could call
about it and asked for a sample he could take back with him.
He wanted it wrapped in something quintessentially Mexican
so he took the headline from the Tijuana edition of the Zeta,
the same newspaper that had suffered so many of its
journalists being killed by drug cartels over the years.

On the way back to the border he stopped by the street
vendors booths and haggled a couple of blankets and a nice
leather hat for pennies on the dollar. He bought a Cuban

cigar for the walk back and took the label off. He had not driven across the border; he had walked. The automobile was parked at a local shopping center and he had taken the bus to the border crossing. His passport indicated he lived in New York but if questioned he would say he was a truck driver. As it was, there was no trouble at the border and he walked back into California unmolested. He had tossed the sample into a storm drain before he hit the border but purchased another copy of the Zeta newspaper on the way.

It had been less than an argument when Terry refused to allow Roberta to ride with him back to South-Central. He conceded that she knew the area and the people, but he convinced her that it was not always a benefit to be recognizable. He double-checked on some of the addresses she had given him, the numbers were missing but the street names she was sure of. Some of them she could be a bit more specific about, if they lived on the corner or near the corner. Some of the longer blocks it was more difficult to pin down what house she was talking about.

Terry memorized what he could of the neighborhood from the map and wrote down some street names. His target would depend on the location, condition and situation.

Helmick Street did not look like the neighborhood you would find drug dealing gang members living in, although so much of the Los Angeles residential areas looked alike. The ubiquitous Spanish influence in the one-story houses and the struggling lawns could have been found almost anywhere within the 250 square mile metropolitan area. In keeping with the sprawling, mobile population, the garages occupied half the houses and the view from the street was of the garage door. The truth was that Potter Darnell was not really a gang member. Potter had a job in one of the industrial parks nearby and he had started selling drugs to support his own habit. As time had gone by, he had developed some real connections among the usually closed Hispanic community because he bought a house in their neighborhood rather than gravitate toward the black neighborhoods. Potter was smart enough to take the warning they had given him early in his residence and did not sell out of his house; he instead made appointments and supplied larger quantities to the blacks in their neighborhoods and they in turn distributed the heroin to the streets. Potter knew Roberta as Rabbit and had done some deals with her in the past. Though she seldom did drugs herself, she was not above taking some product in trade if there was a sufficient discount provided. It was just part of the business cycle.

Terry was surprised that there were no bars on the windows and doors as he had seen in the more prominently black neighborhoods. He discovered later that it was because in middle-class Hispanic neighborhoods there were a lot of housewives that were always on the lookout. The men did not want their women working; they wanted them staying home and raising children. The housewives knew every young man that lived in that neighborhood. If anyone heard a window break, there would be lots of reliable witnesses that would say nothing to the police but would tell their husbands instead. These neighborhoods preferred to police themselves. None of the matrons knew Terry Kingston however.

With his license plate covered, the Australian assassin backed into Potter Darnell's driveway. He had seen Potter drive up, activate the garage door remotely and drive inside. He could barely have entered the living space when the doorbell rang. When the door cracked open, Terry kicked it open and forced his way in, pistol first. Potter was not about to be a hero. The barrel of the weapon in his eye convinced him that he was at a disadvantage.

A ski mask covered Terry's features as soon as he got in the house. His victim had seen his face for a second but had not had a chance to memorize his features. Had it been necessary, Kingston had no problem eliminating the witness/victim, but if it was unnecessary, then he could be left alive. The mask had a large hole for his mouth so his words were not muffled.

Using his German accent, Terry asked, point blank, "Where is the heroin?"

Potter had been around a long time and his addiction had given him the ability to lie with a straight face to anyone. "I don't have any heroin. I don't know what you're talking about."

"Your name is Potter Darnell and you sell heroin."

"What are you talking about?"

There had been no ambiguity to the direction he had gotten from Roberta so there was no doubt in Terry's mind that he was in the right house. Add to the directions the fact that he was looking at a black man living in a Mexican neighborhood and all doubt was erased.

"I'm going to say this one more time and then I am going to stab you in the leg." Terry smiled broadly as he said it. "If you resist, I will shoot like a dog. Do I have your attention? Look at me, now. Do I have your attention?"

The man's attention was definitely on the intruder; he stopped casting around frantically and focused on the ice blue eyes staring from the ski mask. "Yes."

"Good. Now tell me where the heroin is or I will stab you." Terry's left hand reached behind his back and pulled out a five-inch tanto blade with a wrapped handle. "I assure you that this sort of knife causes a lot of damage. Observe of the design of the tip. See how it is meant to punch its way in, not slide? Now where is your heroin?"

"I don't have any." Potter's eyes indicated the lie by rolling around again.

Terry was not ready to spend a lot of time with this subject. For all he knew the police were already on their way.

He jabbed the broad tip of the tanto blade about three inches into Potter Darnell's thigh. Predictably, the man screamed but not for long as his masked attacker bashed him across the face with the barrel of the pistol and then stuck the barrel into Potter's mouth. The man's perennially fogged senses came into a much sharper focus and his eyes went wide. Terry grabbed the handle of the blade and twisted it. Potter's mouth opened to scream again and Terry filled it with a red rag from his back pocket.

"Now that I have your full attention, you are going to tell me what I want to know or I am going to shoot you between the eyes. Is there any question?"

Tears ran down Potter Darnell's shiny black cheeks and a mumbling sound came from behind the cloth as he shook his head.

"Good. Now is there any doubt in your mind that I mean exactly what I say?"

Potter shook his head again.

"Good. Now, I have limited time and much to do today so, if you make any noise that is not what I want to hear when I remove your gag, I will shoot you between the eyes. Do you understand?"

This time Potter nodded.

First, Terry pulled the blade from the man's thigh, wiped the blood on the man's shirt and sheathed the blade, then he pulled the red cloth from his subject's mouth. Potter was only too happy to tell Terry that the heroin was in the tea pot in the kitchen cabinet. Terry picked the man up by the collar and hauled him into the kitchen where the man opened the cabinet where the tea pot was. As soon as the door was open, Terry threw the man to the floor. As he suspected, leaning against the inside of the cabinet next to the tea pot was a 9mm Glock. He stuck the Glock in his back pocket and the fist-sized chuck of black tar in his vest pocket.

"Now the money."

"Aw, shit, man, I ain't got no money."

"Do not bother lying to me. Down that road lies pain and disaster." Terry reached behind his back and pulled out the knife again.

"Aw, fuck! You Nazi bastard, leave me something."

"I leave you with your life. If that is not enough then I take that as well. I will leave with the money or I will leave your dead body to rot." He took a step toward him to emphasize the point, but Darnell had already gotten the point.

"Under the sink. It's under the sink. I'm bleeding, I need a doctor."

"You need to shut up unless I ask you a further question." Looking under the sink, Terry found a small fire safe. Given a few minutes he could have cut into it but he did not think he had that kind of time so he told Potter to open the safe. Potter was willing to accede to the request. Inside the safe was a nice bundle of money and another 9mm Glock. It looked like there was about twenty thousand dollars in the bundle, obviously the result of nefarious activities. Terry felt no guilt about sticking it in his pocket along with the other pistol. He considered shooting Potter but decided against it since he knew the man was not a gang member. There were three exits leading from the kitchen, two doors and a doorway without a door. One led outside, the open doorway led to the living room and the third led to the basement. Terry grabbed Potter by the shirt collar and stood him up, took him to the top of the cellar stairs and unceremoniously threw the heroin dealer down the steps.

Now there was no time left to waste. Kingston had left the car running in the driveway. In a matter of seconds he was in the driver's seat and speeding down the block. At the first stoplight he pulled the mask off his face, turned left onto South Central Avenue and was gone. He did not hear any sirens behind him.

Saturday was another California day with the sun crawling over the mountains to burn the dew off the lawns and bathe the coast in sunshine. Anastasia Viuda went running, before the heat of midday made the thought uncomfortable. She was dressed in baggy sweat pants and a sweat shirt that concealed the tight fitting belly holster banded around her midriff. Her hair was tied tight to her head with a silk cloth. It was not her intention to be noticed this morning but to see what the neighborhood had to offer. She turned north on Moneta Street and ran all the way to where it ended with a left-hand turn at a warehouse complex. She turned back and made her way south more passively, back to Carson Street. Turning west again she jogged easily toward Figueroa until she stopped short in front of a local bank.

Using the low brick wall in front of the bank to stretch her legs, Anastasia breathed deeply through her nose to capture the scent that had stopped her. There it was. She walked across the street and through the trailer park on the north side of the street. The trailer park seemed so much more civilized than the ones she had seen in South America. There were no abandoned cars, no pickup trucks with the engine out, no piles of trash. The whole area was blacktopped and had speed bumps every hundred feet. The odor was stronger on the east side street.

Anastasia did not stop moving, even though she was in a hyper-vigilant mode. She missed the adrenaline rush she used to get from the experimental skull implant that was now short-circuited. She was grateful that she no longer got the vibrating feeling in her head or the headaches, but she had liked the artificial adrenaline boost.

That was the one; the trailer with the curtains drawn in the front. The slight vapor was coming from the kitchen vent. They were cooking meth. Anastasia memorized the number and location and jogged off hoping she had not been noticed. She was fully aware of how paranoid meth junkies were and most of the people who produced it used it as well. A side effect of the drug was to induce paranoia. Couple the paranoia, and psychoses caused by sleep deprivation, with the fact that they had a kitchen laboratory synthesizing the stuff and it made for a potentially explosive situation, figuratively and literally. Approaching them was a risky business. There was no cover in the park except the other trailers. There was no real space between then either, other than enough room to slide a car in. Some of them had awnings to protect the cars from the sun but not most. The whole setup seemed overexposed.

Exiting the north end of the trailer park, on West 215th street, Anastasia jogged west across Figueroa. West of Figueroa the homes deteriorated, the lawns were dry patches of scrub and the street dead-ended at a weed and vine-covered wall that hid Interstate 110 from the residential neighborhood. A block north, there was an unused elevated walkway over the ten lanes of expressway and two exit ramps. Anastasia did not investigate the overpass but instead turned south on Figueroa. Before she had gotten back to West 220th Street, she knew that the area between Figueroa and the expressway was full of gangs and drugs. It was too early for the gangsters to be moving around and it was unlikely that they conducted much business on the dead-end streets that comprised the area, but it seemed obvious that they lived there. South of 220th Street there was nothing but factories and warehouses all the way to 223rd Street where she turned east again and jogged back to her apartment. She was surprised that she had seen no bodegas, no corner stores, no convenience stores to speak of. She knew there was a store on the corner of Main Street and 222nd Street, only a quarter mile away, but she was used to seeing corner stores run by widows or the mothers of busy men.

After taking a shower and applying her makeup, Anastasia dressed like the killer she was. A short, silky red dress more appropriate for a cocktail party than a grocery store. High heels with crossed straps up her muscular calves capped her legs and long dangly earrings ornamented her ears. She spiked her hair up with gel and sprayed some sparkle in it. Her purse was red leather, slightly larger than would have been expected for a party. It was unusual inside in that it was split into two small sections. The reason for the lack of room inside the purse was the pocket between them, accessed from one end through a Velcro patch. It could not have comfortably held a J-frame Smith and Wesson but it very satisfactorily concealed the .22 caliber Beretta Bobcat with seven rounds in the clip and one in the chamber.

Those men working Saturday overtime had already reported to work but had not gotten out for lunch yet. The gangsters were thinking about getting out of bed. The younger members of society were out and about or playing with their electronic distractions. Anastasia came close to causing a pile up on the corner of Main Street as she crossed to get to the convenience store. She discovered a symptom of life in LA as opposed to the other major cities of the world. There are sidewalks everywhere in Los Angeles and nobody walks on them. That makes it a novelty when an attractive, well-dressed man or woman is seen walking. People running was not so unusual, though they ran for different reasons.

The high heels had made her feet hurt so Anastasia swapped them out for slippers when she got back to the house. She took a small glass-topped table from the basement, cleaned it up and set it on the porch. She still had no kitchen table or chairs though there was now a bed in one of the bedrooms and a recliner in the living room. The recliner was too unwieldy to bother with but she had no problem borrowing a folding lawn chair from her neighbor who would probably have lent her everything he owned. She invited him to stop over for a shot of whiskey, but his wife was staring at him as if she was contemplating stuffing him in the oven, so he declined. She sat in the lawn chair, on the porch, with a best selling paperback in her hand; a quart bottle of Southern Comfort and a copy of a good Spanish/English dictionary sat on the table.

This neighborhood was predominately black with a smattering of Hispanics and lower middle-class whites. It did not take long for a young man to ask if he would mind if he joined her. She replied that she had no furniture and had been reduced to borrowing the lawn chair that she sat on. By the end of the day there were half a dozen chairs of different descriptions on her porch along with a kitchen table. By the time the second bottle of Southern Comfort was gone and it was time for everyone to leave, only one man objected and his friends hauled him away by his ears.

In vino veritas proved itself accurate again, especially when coupled with an unconquered woman. Every man in attendance was struggling to be the first to answer the mysterious new woman's questions and those that did not get answered came with promises to tell her the next day. Information was given freely that could not be bought on the street. She had learned where D'arniel "Bash" Jamiel lived, Arquila "Moses" Khareem, Andrew Sykes who had been shot in the shoulder on Doloros Street and John "Whiplash" Barton who was an up and coming force in the immediate area. Whiplash had joined them on the porch that day, working his macho as hard as he could, but had been stymied when Anastasia would not let any of the men into the house, not even to use the toilet. She kept the barred storm door locked. They had been forced to walk down the block when they needed to go.

Sunday morning came with only a little pain from the

sweet over-proof whiskey. Anastasia was up and in the shower early and running down the sidewalks before the parishioners left for church. She stopped running at the corner of West Carson and Moneta Streets and breathed deeply for a minute. Then she walked back into the trailer park and up east side of the lot. There was no noise coming from the trailer she had noted the day before and there was no odor coming from the vent stack. They had finished cooking. That meant one of two things. Either they had not done any of the product and were sleeping or they had partaken of the fruits of their enterprise and were somewhere else looking for a party.

The door to the trailer had not been modified in any way which meant any good sized man could have broken it in. Anastasia had more style than to break the door in, she slid a piece of industrial banding out of her belly holster and slid it between the door jamb and the lock. The door was open in seconds.

The chance was that whoever had cooked the drug, the smell inside the trailer confirmed that they had been cooking it. It looked as though they had also packaged the product and taken it to market. It would not have been feasible to deal small quantities from this trailer; it was too close to its neighbors and the traffic would have been intolerable. The cooks took their product elsewhere, but Anastasia was ready to bet her life that they had not taken it all to market.

Anastasia took a few minutes to look around the place. Except for the smell and the lab ware in the kitchen, the interior of the trailer was impeccable. They had not paused to put the equipment away; that might indicate that they had an immediate buyer and sold it as fast as they made it. There was almost no food in the cupboards and nothing fresh in the refrigerator. There was a towering pile of beer cases full of tall necked empties and no full beers in the refrigerator. Anastasia was looking under the bed when she heard the door open and a woman's staccato voice.

"Well, we still got gin. I hate gin. I can't believe they wouldn't sell us beer before noon. Those sons-a-bitches. I could out drink that punk three ways to Sunday and his father too. I tell you what, I'll drink gin for now but I should have kicked that pimple-faced little fucker's ass. I don't know who he thinks he is."

A more even and sane sounding voice broke into the woman's tirade. "How about you just give me a blow job and forget about the gin and forget about the beer?"

The woman's voice took on a less pugnacious tone. "Oh baby, I'll give you some, but a little later. Can't you just let me enjoy my buzz for now without wanting to fuck me all the time?"

"Yes, I can, but I want to get a little hit too and I've been waiting long enough. You know if I hit that shit I'm not gonna be stiff for two days and I want some now."

"All right. Make it quick and let me get back to enjoying myself. I never knew a man that wanted to fuck as much as you do. If it were up to me I wouldn't be bothered with it all. You know I had a boyfriend once that didn't even want me to suck on his dick. He had some kind of religious thing about it and every time I tried he said I was going to go to Hell for it but you know that's a lie because…" Her prattling seemed as if it would go on endlessly except she could not talk with her mouth full.

Anastasia waited, listening to the sounds issuing from the living room. She was glad she had not needed to hide in the closet but the thought gave her a different idea. She opened the bifold door to the closet and found a wrap that she could fashion into an acceptable face mask. After all, she was not living that far from this place and did not want to be recognized.

The sounds of the man groaning as he reached his climax gave her the green light and she stepped out of the bedroom with her pistol in her hand. The woman was on her knees on the carpet and the man was standing in front of her with his pants around his ankles. Neither of them could have mounted a defense from that position.

"Neither of you are going to move or I will be forced to shoot you both." She did nothing to disguise her South American accent. She knew they would not be able to regionalize it.

"What the fuck?" was all the man could say. The woman's dilated eyes went wide as she spit into a paper towel.

"I am here to relieve you of what you have made in your kitchen and I expect you to give it to me without a question."

"Fuck you, bitch!"

"No, sir. That will not be possible. Let me explain that the first thing I will do is shoot your woman in the mouth. It may give you the added bonus of knocking some of her teeth out but it will be a long time before she will be on her knees for you again. This will become um… irrelevant, I think, because my second shot will blow off the balls you are so fond of. Am I making myself clear?" Anastasia smiled inside the wrap as she recognized phrases that Gordon and Terry used in similar situations.

The woman was moving slowly toward the coffee table at the end of the couch. The masked invader popped one round through the floor in front of her.

"I will not give you another chance. Remain still or I will permanently blow your face off." She knew the .22 caliber round would not blow anyone's face off but the phrase worked.

"I was, uh, I was getting the stuff for you."

"Do not take me for a fool. If you move again I will shoot you."

"Can I pull my pants up?" the man asked.

"No. I want your pecker hanging out like that. It is a

good target." Bending at the waist but never taking her eyes off the couple, she opened the coffee table. Inside was a loaded .32 caliber revolver but nothing else. "Where is it?"

"I'll show you." the woman volunteered.

"You'll tell me. Now."

"It's in the bedroom."

"Where?"

"In the bedroom."

"You're lying to me." Anastasia pulled back the hammer on the double action semi-automatic, took it in both hands and pointed it right at the cranked up woman's face. "This probably won't kill you, but it is going to make you very ugly."

"Wait," the man spoke up. "Don't. It's in the freezer."

"A drug dealer with principles, I like that. I will let you live as long as you do nothing stupid."

Inside the freezer was what felt like a quarter pound of homemade crystal methamphetamine. If it was as pure as it looked, there was enough to keep the entire trailer park up for a week.

"Perfect. Now you, get off your knees. Take the extension cord from the television and tie his hands behind his back. I will check your work and if you do a bad job I will know."

The woman tied her man and then Anastasia tied the woman. Using a cord from the blinds, she tied their feet together. This was nothing they could not get out of but it would take them a couple of minutes of concentrated effort. She expected to be home before they freed themselves; in truth she was only on Rashdall Avenue, a block away, when they stood up.

Several men showed up, later in the morning, hoping to party with the new addition to the neighborhood. She sent one down to get some bourbon; it would be a while before she could drink the sweet stuff again. She did not drink much on Sunday but she did work on getting the names and addresses of men who could move a quarter pound of meth. The reason for this was to deflect future suspicions about her actual intention and target. Offering a product for a real discount involved acquiring it in non-traditional ways. There is no telling how Anastasia would have reacted if she knew that Terry Kingston was setting up the same sort of play.

Chapter Seventeen
Needle and Thread

One of the reasons it can be so difficult to get somewhere in the sprawling metropolitan area of LA is the profusion of one block dead-end streets. Some of the streets existed due to the intrusion of the Eisenhower Interstate System cutting them off but many others were constructed that way for different reasons. Dead-end streets are safer for children. The use of right angle turns just before the larger streets makes it possible to squeeze a few extra homes into the area while preventing anyone driving through from using the street as a shortcut. They succeeded in achieving their goal but it made for some problems. Anyone unfamiliar with the neighborhood they were in stood the chance of never getting where they were supposed to be going. For instance, the 400 block of East 249th Street is half a block long and dead-ends. There is no 500 block and the 600 block is a block and a half away but you need to drive three blocks to get there. There is a profusion of short, dead-end streets with the same name, except that one might be 247th Street and one 247th Place. It would be enough to ruin an experienced taxi driver and make him insane. A GPS was almost essential for navigation with the codicil that one must be sure to enter the address exactly.

"Gordon, my love?" MacMaster could not help think, and not for the first time, that he loved the way she pronounced his name.

"Yes, my passion."

"Your new amigo, Bash, lives on the corner of E 230th Street and Anchor Avenue. Is between Rowena and Avalon. On the map it shows that there is only a north and south side. Is one of those short blocks, you know? With an alley behind it. I gonna go over there tomorrow and check it out. Is about a mile away. They say something about projects across the road; I'm not sure what that is meaning but I will find out."

"Take the bus to meet me in the morning and we will go together. Remember, you are supposed to be working at a bank so take an early bus west on 223rd and I'll meet you in the parking lot of Tartar's high school on Plaza del Amo."

"Ah, you say the sweetest things, *me amo*."

"Until the morning comes, my head will be filled with dreams of you." Gordon hung up the phone thinking of how ironic it was that two assassins, cold-blooded killers, could be as giddy as schoolchildren in love with each other. It seemed to break all the rules. Not the rules of society, the Scot had only had a grudging acceptance of them, but the rules of nature.

A couple of days apart lent credence to the old saw that absence makes the heart grow fonder but in this case it was not exactly the problem. Anastasia Viuda was a typically jealous woman. She did come by it honestly. She born into a patriarchal Hispanic society that measured success by how many women a man could support simultaneously without them finding out about each other. Gordon MacMaster was not a victim of the low self esteem that caused so many men to distrust their women. Gordon knew that if a woman was in need of more than one man then the best man available could not keep her from wandering. What worried him now was that she would take offense at some comment or amorous advance and kill someone. As high-spirited as the Scot blood made him, her temper was a step above his. He did not like leaving her alone in an area where so many different men would think they had a chance to bed her, and her refusal could turn so ugly, so quickly. She was a professional and would undoubtedly do her best to avoid unpleasant confrontations, but she was also likely to end any such situation that was deemed unavoidable in a terminal manner.

The four ounces of heroin that Gordon had purchased just north of the border would suffice to convince the leader of the South Alley Bloods that the Scot was serious about his proposal, but that might be unnecessary now, assuming the new intelligence was accurate. He didn't know about the amphetamines that Anastasia had acquired that morning. He also did not know the lure that said amphetamines had on the Argentine woman. She would never have touched them before; before the stun gun had deactivated the combat unit still buried in her brain. Before then she had more adrenaline than she could handle, more than she could ask for, but she had no idea how addictive it was. She had wanted the thing in her head to be gone but now she appreciated some of what it had given her. The adrenaline high was intense, almost orgasmic in its effect, and she missed it badly.

Potter Darnell had been an easy score since he was an independent and did not do business out of his house but had kept his stash there. He had practically hung out a sign saying ROB ME except that he had believed nobody knew what he was up to. Winslow Hardapple was not going to be such a walk in the park.

Winslow Hardapple liked to party and so his house had turned into a sort of crack warehouse and was always open. The police knew what he was up to, but he paid off the locals and they warned him about impending problems. His only real concern was the FBI or the DEA. The FBI knew who he was and where he was but was not that interested in his small-time operation. The watched him from time to time but knew he was going to bring himself down in time and just waited for the day when he could be convinced to turn on his suppliers for a lighter sentence. The FBI supplied the information to the DEA who would get to him eventually. They assumed he was going nowhere and they could take him down whenever they got around to it.

Winslow Hardapple may have lived in Crip territory, but he was not in good standing with the brothers. They saw his problem and knew he would rat them out when the time came. They allowed him to have his party house and knew he paid off the cops for their heads-up when the heat was coming down. He was going to be an asset until he got too strung out on the rock to be of any more use, and then they would take care of him permanently.

Jacob Vaughn, Winslow's lieutenant, may have sounded like a Neo-Nazi but was in fact half Japanese, a quarter German and a quarter black. His mixed heritage had left him with identity issues as a child and the attendant personality disorders. Jacob liked to fight, but he hated to lose. It made him one of the most savage and dangerous men in West Carson. His reputation was cemented one night as a seventeen year old when he bludgeoned three fully grown men to death with a crowbar.

Winslow's gang name was, as could be expected, Hardass. Hardass Hardapple lived in a townhouse off the 22000 block of South Vermont Avenue and he liked it there. A concrete wall surrounding a factory blocked access and vision from the east and a wooden fence blocked the same from the west. He felt secure from the prying eyes that drug dealers know are always trying to see.

Winslow sold crack though not the nickel and dime quantities that you could get on the street. Winslow sold ounces mostly. He would buy it by the pound and sell ounces as a cash only operation. Nobody got credit and nobody got a deal. From time to time, he would go on a bender and smoke a bunch of crack and drink bottles of Kirschwasser, a clear German brandy made from morello cherries. He had been on one such bender when Roberta had met him.

"What the fuck. Bad, we got some fool white boy standing in your yard with some tar." The man speaking had joined Winslow and Jacob for the day to help ensure the integrity of the customer base.

"That's who knocked on the door?"

"Yeah. He standin' there with a chunk a tar."

"Haul his stupid ass in here and let's find out what the fuck his problem is then."

The door opened and the tall blond man with the fist full of black tar heroin stepped inside. "Good day, gentlemen." he said with an exaggerated German accent.

"Who the fuck are you and what the fuck do you think you're doing in my yard with a chunk a shit in your hand?"

"That, my friend, is quite simple. I am to be your best friend north of the Mexican border. I can supply you with this product cheaper that any man you know." He tossed the heroin across the room at the man who was sitting on the couch. The guard at the door made the mistake of watching the drug fly across the room instead of watching the man who threw it. They had seen Mexican gangs come in force, and they had seen both Bloods and Crips try to invade territory, but they had never seen one white man come in swinging with a fistful of dope.

Terry reached inside his vest with his right hand and pulled his .38. He had intended to use it for crowd control but there was no controlling these men. As soon as the gleam of the stainless steel saw the light of day, the guard at the door was raising his AR15 from its vertical position. Terry had no option; he stepped back one step while snaking the revolver from his vest in a fluid motion. There was no time to aim, he simply pointed the stubby barrel and shot the man in the chest.

The one step backward saved Terry's life as the dead man's finger tightened on the trigger and the rifle, which had been modified to fully automatic, exploded its thirty rounds of ammunition in an arc from the floor to the ceiling. It made no difference that the weapon spit small rounds, anyone caught in that dead man's arc would be chewed to hamburger in a second.

The mistake Terry made was that he had not checked the hallway off the right side of the living room. The magazine had not finished emptying itself before the double barrel of a shotgun came around the corner and vomited fire. The shotgun spewed buckshot across the room and blew a hole in the door. One of the pellets caught Terry Kingston in the side. Kingston fell to his knees and the second barrel of the shotgun erupted, shattering the window behind him.

Hardass Hardapple was on his feet before the second blast from the shotgun tore through the air. He pulled a .44 Magnum from the back of his pants, but before he could take his first shot he caught a .38 slug in the chest. It fouled his shot and his eyes closed involuntarily. They opened in death as a second shot plowed between his ribs and burst his heart.

Deafened by the cacophony that had erupted in the room, Terry could not hear if the man with the shotgun had cracked it open or clicked it closed. He only knew that he had less than a second to take matters in hand. He vaulted over the pressed wood and glass table in the center of the room, somersaulted toward the couch and fired from a prone position. The shotgun pounded out its violence again, blowing a hole in the wall above him but it was the .38 caliber revolver that took the last victim that day. Jacob Vaughn never released the charge from the shotgun's second barrel. The bullet took him in the upper lip and drove upward through his sinuses and into his brain. The man fell like he had been hit in the face with a sledgehammer.

Terry took a long breath in through his nose, a grimace distorting his face. There did not seem to be any one else in the townhouse. He hoped briefly that there had been nobody home next door. Stepping forward, he found a paper bag on the couch, next to the former drug dealer, with eleven ounces of crack and four stacks of bills. He picked the heroin up from where it had landed on the couch and dropped it inside with the crack then, ignoring the pain in his side and the blood on the bag, Terry stuck his hand into the bag, still gripping his revolver and grabbed a dry part of the inside of the paper. The bag covered the gun and the paper managed to not fall apart and spill the contents all over the rug. He opened the door with the red rag from his back pocket and dropped the rag on the way out. Some people saw him but by the time the police got to the scene, everybody had forgotten what he looked like.

Gordon had hoped Anastasia would take an early enough bus that morning to miss the school children arriving for the day's classes. She did not. He had specified an early bus, perhaps she had not understood how early. Regardless, he could not sit in the parking lot of the school, in his enormous Cadillac, without attracting the wrong kind of attention. The parking lot of the business across the street was almost as bad, but the business had no windows facing the street so those inside were not involved.

The west bound bus Anastasia was riding finally dropped her off in front of the school and Gordon pressed on the horn to get her attention. She stalked across the street on her stiletto heels, making her hips sway gracefully inside the short black skirt. Her oxblood cherry lipstick had sparkles in it that caught the sun. MacMaster felt himself rising at the sight of her.

"*Aye, papi*, take this shit and get it away from me."

"Good morning to you as well. What have we here?"

"It is the crank. I took this from some *pendejos* in a trailer park. They were making the shit in the kitchen. I sat and looked at this shit all day Sunday and half of the night."

"Why? I've never known you to want drugs."

"No. Is not that I... I do not want to do drugs, but I need... Is something of the fire I need. Excitement that makes my heart pump. I know this shit will make my heart pump but it does not..."

"Let's get out of here. All I need to get my blood pumping is you but I think we can get you pumping too."

"Gordon, do not think that you do not excite me. I never have known a man like you. What I am talking about has nothing to do with the bedroom or the way I feel..."

"I know, my love. You want to feel alive and without the danger, you get bored. I can understand that completely. Let's go make some trouble."

Gordon piloted his automobile across the dividing line and back into Bloods' territory. He parked halfway down the block from D'arniel Jamiel's house, in the back alley where the garages sat. Neither he nor Anastasia knew whether or not he was home, so they waited.

The gate to D'arniel's yard never opened and the door to his garage never raised. By noon, Anastasia had gotten two hours sleep in the front seat, and Gordon decided that he had missed the opportunity. Anastasia awoke of her own accord and, after fixing her makeup, she was about to approach the house when a van pulled around them in the alley and stopped in front of the house next door. A man who looked like Bash Jamiel jumped in the side door of the van and it pulled away without delay.

After agreeing on what they thought had happened, Gordon pulled the car closer and Anastasia walked up to the gate. When she began to open the gate, she was greeted by the howls of dogs from within. She had no desire to play with any dogs, so she got Gordon to pull the car up to the wall that surrounded the entire property on the end of the block, and he stood on the hood of the car to get a look in the yard. Inside, chained with eye hooks in blocks of concrete set in the ground, were a dozen pit bull terriers. They were chained in such a manner as they covered the entire yard without being able to reach each other. Not a scrap of grass was visible in the yard but the ground was not covered with dog waste either. Someone cleaned the yard regularly, but it was obviously someone known to the beasts since it required intimate contact with the aggressive creatures.

As well organized as the dogs were, there was still a spot where they could not reach. At the back of the house was a path between the boundary wall and the wall of the house. No dogs were chained back there, but the only way to reach that spot was to vault over from the far side or to walk down the top of the concrete wall, and the top of the wall had been inset with the bottoms of broken bottles.

Gordon got back in the driver's seat and started the car. Traffic was still abominable but they were able to get out of the area and begin to head north toward the hotel. They spoke while they were stuck in traffic.

"It looked like a setup," Gordon began. "Like they knew we were coming. I don't think anyone lives in that house."

"I'm not sure but I think it was the man who came out of the house next door. The one who got in the van. We cannot go back to this place. They see us once and they think. They see us twice and they know. The job is not worth the money. We should just shoot him."

"No, we can pull this one off, but not there," Gordon said. "He has some sort of system in place there. I was not unduly impressed by him in person but he seems to have created something here that smacks of legerdemain."

"I do not know this. Explain."

"Old time magicians always used sleight of hand to convince people that they were pulling rabbits out of hats. If you can keep the audience focused on something else, they never see your hands tricking their eyes, Gordon said, rubbing his chin. "I'll get him to leave his comfort zone, somewhere he has less than three men standing with him, then we have him."

"This is all very good to say, but I think we should just shoot him."

"Perhaps when the interrogation is done they will let you finish him off."

"Phaugh. Why do you insult me? There will be nothing left when they are done with him. I do not want to shoot him for sport. I could go into the sewers and shoot rats if that was what I wanted. I think to prevent trouble we should simplify our plan."

"The job is to take him alive. Anyone can kill him. She hired us for our expertise. That is why we can demand the sort of money we do."

"Yes, you have told me and reputation is all we have." She said it as if bored with the subject. "But we got this job with no help from our reputation. We just walked in."

"Do you really believe that?" Gordon asked.

Anastasia looked at him for a moment and he smiled back. "There is too much you know about that woman."

"I never met her before in my life."

"If you take her to bed I will kill her."

"I've told you before that is not the remotest possibility. She is on our side."

"Yes, so you say. I do not like her."

The traffic cleared a bit and they were able to make their way to the hotel in Manhattan Beach. It was a fifteen-minute walk to the beach but swimming was not on the agenda. Anastasia wanted a shower and spent so much time scrubbing herself under the hot water that Gordon was forced to join her.

"So, Homer, what do you think of LA?"

"I'll tell you what, sis, this was worth it."

Homer and Jacqueline were having lunch at a sidewalk café in West Hollywood. Homer was dressed in sandals, shorts and a garish Hawaiian surfer shirt. Jacqueline was in business attire but they both wore sunglasses against the midday glare.

"I thought you'd like it out here. The apartment acceptable?"

"Yeah. I guess. It could be closer to the beach."

"I thought we agreed that you were going to lay low for a while. Whoever you got the money from is gonna want it back."

"Yeah, but they are in Miami."

"You don't understand. With all the technology in play today, they can find you from Miami. That's why I told you to stay out of Vegas. Every casino has hundreds of cameras, digital cameras that can transfer your face into their database. They have facial recognition software that can pick you out in no time. There are networks that do nothing but find people this way. The casinos don't sanction it but the IT crews and the security staff make a lot of side money this way. You need to stay out of casinos."

"You sound like that Glasgow dude."

"He got you here alive, didn't he?"

"Shit. I could have driven here myself just as easily."

"You're not being reasonable. Well, I should expect that. So, is the money safe?"

"Yeah. I put it in a safe deposit box."

"I want access."

"What are you talking about? That's my money. I took it and I'm going to spend it."

"I don't want your money. I got a thing set up here. It won't be long before I can retire too. I was just thinking that we need contingency plans in case something happens to you.

"Say you get kidnapped and I need to pay a ransom or you get arrested and I need to bail you out. I have a little money but not much. I'm working on a big score now, but I haven't pulled it off yet. I just think I should be listed as a backup on the box so I can access it in case of an emergency."

"Okay. I guess that makes sense." Homer did not look entirely convinced that he was doing the right thing. But, he conceded to himself, Jacqueline was usually right and she had always been smarter than he.

"Holy shit! Somebody shot you."

"Yes, dear, I think I knew that. I think we need to look at the fact that he was not a very good shot." Terry's nervous chuckle did nothing to set Roberta at ease; she was shuddering like a San Francisco earthquake.

"Well, we gotta get you to the hospital."

"No. There is no possibility of my going to a hospital. I don't care what you think about the subject, there is simply no possibility. I'll tell you what though, if you would be so kind as to set a towel on the bed we can keep from destroying the covers."

"Oh, shit. Okay. I… I…" Roberta got a towel from the bathroom and Terry sat on it.

"Now go to my bag and look in the side pocket. There is a needle and some nylon thread. Once you have that, boil some water in a pan would you?"

"You got a pan?"

"Bought some at the Goodwill. Under the sink. I haven't used them yet so make sure you get the water boiling well. Sterilize the needle and thread. I can't reach the hole in the back so you need to stitch that."

"Oh, shit. I ain't no nurse. You need to go to the hospital. Who you think I am, gonna sew up your bullet wounds?"

"Look, Roberta, I cannot go to the hospital. It is simply not an option for more reasons than I want to go into right now. This wound looks bad because of all the blood but it hit nothing of consequence, see? It went right through.

A lot of blood but no permanent damage. Now, take a washcloth from the bathroom and boil it. We can clean this off and stitch it up. Is there any more of that rum left? Good." Terry took a huge guzzle of rum straight out of the bottle and then lay back.

"Man, that looks like it hurts." She was still shaking slightly but the violent shuddering was gone.

"Oh, it does burn a bit. Don't tell me this is the first time you saw anybody shot."

"No. I seen plenty of men shot. Some women, too. They go to the hospital… or the morgue. They don't just go home and say 'Oy, let's have some of that rum while I wait to die.'"

"I'm far from dying, although I must admit it is starting to sting a bit."

"If I had some cocaine we could put it on the hole, uh, the wound and kill some of the pain."

"You know, that's not a bad idea. Why don't you look in the front seat of the auto. Bring in the sack that's in front." Terry began taking deep breaths through his nose. The pain in his side was beginning to get worse.

Outside Roberta shuddered at all the blood in the front seat of the car, but she was calming down a little from her initial panic. She grabbed the bloody paper bag and took it inside without looking at the contents. When she dumped it out on the bed, she could not contain herself. "Holy mother of all gangstas. What the hell did you do? Man. We got enough crack here to party all year. You got some tar and look at all that money. Terry, my man, you been a very bad boy."

For a moment, Terry feared that Roberta's assertion that she did not use drugs was a lie and that she would be smoking the rock instead of caring for his injury but his fears proved baseless. She took the ashtray and wiped it out, then dropped it into the now boiling water. When it had spent enough time in the seething pot she pulled it out with a pair of tongs that looked like they had been through a fire themselves. She used the butt end of a butter knife for a pestle and crushed half a dozen rocks in the improvised mortar. Once the drug was crushed, she added a drop of water and spread the paste on both sides of the wound. While it did not kill the pain entirely, it stopped the burning and made the stitching process much easier.

The one pellet that had struck him tore at the muscle of his side, just below the ribs. The entrance wound was a little darker than the exit wound, but there had been no fragmentation of the projectile so there were only two small holes to patch. Terry took care of the one in front and Roberta, after taking a shot of rum herself, sewed up the exit wound. Once the job of stitching up Terry's flesh had been accomplished, his new lover bent herself to the task of cleaning up all the blood he had spilled. She threw away the shirt, but he would not let her dispose of his vest until he had time to get a replacement. She washed the towels and his jeans in the shower and then went to work on the seats of the rental car. Much of her sympathy was gone by the time she was done there.

Roberta stepped inside and took another shot of rum. She was going to ask what he was going to do with the stuff when she remembered that along with a bag full of drugs he had brought a pile of money with him as well. "So, is this what you do for a living? You rip off drug dealers?"

"No."

"Well, come up with it then. I need to know what it is you won't tell me all this time. I can make a living for myself, you know?"

"Oh, yes. I know." Terry's eyes were clouding over from the pain.

"So what is it you do, bad man?" Her sarcasm was tinged with respect.

"I hurt people. People with lots of money pay me to hurt other people."

Roberta stood stock still not wanting to believe him but knowing that her savior was no angel and feeling that maybe he was a demon in disguise. "So," she began slowly, trying not to jump to any conclusions. "If you hurt people for a living... If you hurt people for a living, then what is with this bag of crack and all this blood soaked money?"

"Well, darlin', you remember I was asking you about this Bash Jamiel? Well, he is a very, very nasty man and a target but not to be shot." Terry's voice paused for a second as he remembered the crime scene photos of the mutilated young woman. The job involves kidnapping him. I thought I could get close to him if I had a big bag of something he wanted. It has worked for me in the past. Money, drugs and women make men do stupid things and I thought a bag of this stuff would get me close enough to put the finger on him."

"Is that what I'm here for? Are you using me to get close to this nigga? You gonna promise me to him too? You gonna give me up for the job?" The perceived threat sent her back into Rabbit mode as a protective reflex.

"No. At least that's not what I had in mind. I'd prefer to keep you out of it. You're not a professional, at least not in that sense of the word. I can't use you."

Roberta Cunningham was balanced on a knife edge. She was a step from running out the door again. She knew hurting people was a metaphor for killing them. It had been stressful enough so far for her but the revelation that Terry was a killer for hire was crushing. She had thought that she was getting away from the gangland lifestyle, but now it looked as though she was getting in deeper. His assertion that he could not use her was bogus in her eyes. A healthy, young woman was always worth something. She wanted desperately to trust Terry but he was making it impossible.

Chapter Eighteen
Crank It Up

A byword of the youth movement of the 1960s was that one should never trust anyone over thirty years old. The fact of LA gang culture was that a member seldom reached thirty without being incarcerated or killed. The gang members were recruited from the schools in the area while still impressionable and often written off by their teachers early in life. Philosophically, the schools never wanted to give up on a child. Realistically, if the student was drawn to the gangs as a youth, little could be done to change his perspective. It was often likened to smoking; if a child could be kept from smoking until they were eighteen, they would be free from the curse for life.

The same system that wanted to keep children out of the gangs and off the streets made it almost impossible to get government agents into the gangs themselves. The agents were simply not young enough to insinuate themselves into the hierarchy. The gang members had been members since the days when they were more interested in candy than women. They grew up with each other and they did not trust anyone they did not go to school with. Undercover operations took years and seldom yielded results of any importance. The agencies and the media crowed loud when they intercepted a large shipment of drugs from South America but they said nothing when asked about the thousand other shipments they missed. Government agencies tried to say they intercepted 10% of the drugs coming into the country but both sides knew this was a bold-faced lie. The police were only as efficient as they were allowed to be by law; their hands were tied and the gangs knew all the tricks of the trade. What the gangs had not been introduced to was an attack from the other side, except for the aborted reverse sting operations of the mid 1990s, when the crime lab was cooking cocaine into rock and including quinine in the recipe as a detector. The quinine would show up under black light when mixed with lemon juice.

The reverse sting operation was targeting small-time users and never had an effect on the problem. It was entrapment of the worst sort and eventually the courts labeled it so. Gordon MacMaster was not entrapping school kids; he was talking about going wholesale and using the South Alley Bloods as a conduit.

D'arniel "Bash" Jamiel called Gordon at eight o'clock on Tuesday morning and asked him if they could meet in Bubba's Barbecue at ten. Gordon pulled in the lot at five minutes before the appointed hour, and before he got the car parked a boy was knocking on his window. He opened the window and the boy said he would show Gordon where to drive.

This time they drove to a deserted tenement block on East 223rd street. The parking lot was chained off, but his was not the only car parked at the side of the road. The boy led Gordon under an overhang where there was a door that had been forced. The Scot looked quite out of place in his business suit and tie. A young man was standing in the doorway with a pistol in his belt. He asked Gordon's name, Gordon responded "Glasgow" and they proceeded inside. Upstairs was a room fitted out with discarded furniture and threadbare sections of rug. The door to the restroom was closed but the door was not enough to keep the stench contained. Sitting on one of the filthy couches was a teenage boy with a semi-automatic pistol in each hand. The situation would have smacked of ridiculous in most places but MacMaster knew that such was not the case here. The boy may not be an experienced marksman or a trained commando but he had enough fire-power in his hands to keep shooting till he hit something. He was what was known as a cowboy marksman.

The young man that joined the trio was also armed but his pistols remained in their holsters. "I gotta frisk ya."

"No, my young friend, you do not. I am in the mouth of the tiger and I will not surrender my weapons. I arrived in good faith and I will deal in good faith but I will not be disarmed."

"I don't think it was guns we lookin' for. You wired?"

Gordon removed his jacket, undid his tie, and unbuttoned his white shirt without unstrapping the holster from his shoulder. He pulled the bottom of the shirt up and displayed his bare chest and back. The young gangsters also got a look at the other revolver, stuck in his belt. Explaining what he was going to do, Gordon unbuckled his belt and dropped his pants. The youngster on the couch thought there might be something in his underwear so he dropped them as well. Once he had turned out his pockets, there were no more questions.

The oldest of the three took Gordon down the hall to another room. This room was furnished with the same sort of discarded furniture but it did not stink the way the other had. Sitting on the ratty couch was D'arniel "Bash" Jamiel dressed in clothing that was obviously supposed to emulate traditional African culture. He wore a colorful dashiki shirt over a pair of draw string trousers. His head was covered by a kufi, the brimless hat worn for special events in African Society.

"You've got a good spot here. The ball fields out back and the residential neighborhood across the street give you a good field, good view. Not that anyone can see inside here. I like your style and knew I could count on your discretion. I do have a request though. The man in the bathroom, the one with the gun pointed at me, do you think he could step off?"

Bash chuckled. "You not the same kinda suburban yuppie fuck that think he can come inta South Central an' make some money, isya?"

"I know none of the men you refer to but I must assume I am not one of them. I am a professional and I only deal with professionals and I chose you to deal with because I believed you were a professional. I see I am correct in my deduction."

"Oh, you correct. Bigdog, get outta that closet. We got a real man here." The man in the bathroom came out with the sawed-off double-barreled shotgun under his arm.

"Good. Now I have a couple of samples of what I have to offer," MacMaster continued. "This is a quarter pound of black tar from south of the border. I can get twice the wholesale north of here and twice that if I want it broken up and sold in little bits. That is not who or what I am. I am going to leave this with you and you will pay me the wholesale price for it in a week. I know you can make a year's wages off this in a week but I am not concerned with that. This one is a show of faith to cement our relationship. Are we clear?"

"So you sayin' you come back in a week and I give you four?"

"Six. You know you can't touch it for eight. I thought we had decided to treat each other as partners."

"Right. I call you in a week with the six and then what?"

"Then we're talking a kilo for forty-five," MacMaster said.

"I let you know."

"I'll let you know right now that you can't touch a kilo for less than sixty. You will be calling," MacMaster countered confidently.

"We see. We done?"

"No. I have something else I think you might be interested in." He pulled out the storage bag with the quarter pound of meth in it.

"That ain't crack."

"Crank. A shot of this and you'll be running for the border for three days. Crack is of no comparison against this lovely juice. Synthetic adrenaline, all day long."

"I know what it is. I grew up on this shit. This looks pretty good."

"Take a snort. See what you think."

The truth was that Gordon had no idea how good the chemical was. Anastasia had not touched it, despite an aching desire to give it a try. It was only her knowledge of the dangers involved that had kept her face out of the bag. Gordon would not know good stuff from baking soda, having no real experience with it. D'arniel knew crank however.

Laying a line out on the table he pulled a hundred dollar bill out of his wallet and rolled it into a tight tube. He took the first snort and his two associates each took a snort. The look on their faces said more than words could convey. Their eyes opened wide, their pupils became pinpoints, their nostrils flared and their mouths hung open. The young man who had brought him to the room actually shook, physically. Bash whistled and jerked his neck to the side, cracking the vertebra of his neck and knocking his kufi off his head.

"Man, this shit gotta fuckin' boot to it."

"Yes. Quality merchandise. You can't get this kind of purity anywhere for less than one-twenty. You know this and I know this."

"You talkin' a key?"

"Yes. I can get you a kilo of this quality, once a week, for sixty-five but I can't get this up front. The man won't do it for me. You know how meth heads get?"

"Yo. Look. I can see you on this but you gotta give me a couple a days. We cool?"

"I will see what I can do. He is cooking now but he does not invite anyone to his lab. We will meet in a house somewhere and I never know where beforehand. I can only find out the day of the exchange. If that is an acceptable term for you then I will make the arrangements."

"Yeah. We good. Leave the bag."

"I'm afraid this bag cost me five large. I have already demonstrated my willingness to trust you. Let us not strain our relationship so early in its inception."

"Yeah, whatever. Johnny Carson, give the man five gees and give me a cigarette." Bash was breathing very heavily and the boost the drug gave him was insisting he do something physical. If MacMaster was any judge, there would be a hot time in the old town tonight.

Gordon was escorted from the tenements; nobody had touched his car. The payback on the crank had almost covered the cost of the heroin. He had called it one way, thinking a good price on the Mexican narcotics would entice the gang leader but he had only been partially right. Bash's mediocre response surprised him. Anastasia on the other hand had called it right down the line. The crank was what Bash wanted and what had piqued his interest. Gordon knew he would be getting a call for that stuff soon. They had better be ready for it.

A few hours of genuine conversation, and half a bottle of rum, had opened up the possibilities for Roberta Cunningham. Her initial reaction to the news that she was shacking up with, not some middle-class white crusader but a genuine assassin, had calmed with time. Her feeling that she could make a life for herself outside the eternal cycle of the streets crumbled, however. She was starting to understand the attitude of the older women in the business; the fatalistic lack of expectations and acceptance of life's brutality. She took everything Terry said about setting her up in her own business with a bitter cynicism. Yet the more he spoke, the more she believed and the more she wanted to believe, but she had heard and seen opium promises before. They always seemed to go up in smoke.

Terry was looser than he had been in a long time. Roberta had convinced him to smoke some heroin for the pain, and he had knocked back half a bottle of rum. He was feeling sloppy and did not care if he was. He made himself a mental note to stay away from the heroin in the future. It made him feel too good and care way too little. He was pleasantly surprised that Roberta did not use any of the black tar or the crack that he had brought back. He did consider the possibility that as soon as he fell asleep that she would be out the door with not only the drugs but the rolls of money he had acquired. He was astonished at the feeling that he did not care if she did. That put the icing on the cake when it came to his smoking any more heroin. It put it out of the question.

"Damn, I went and got myself shot. That was not on my agenda for the day." The bemused expression on Terry's face made Roberta laugh through her hands.

"I'm sorry, I just don't know how to... I don't know what I'm supposed to do now." She was clearly amused by the change in his outward attitude.

"I'll tell you what, dear. Tomorrow you can go down to Carson and find out where the man they call Bash is. You do that for me and I'll give you this stack of bills." He held up one blood-soaked bundle. "Can I do that without becoming Johnny Australia?"

"I'm gonna need a cell phone," she said. "A throw away if you think that would be best. And let me take some of that crack with me. I guarantee them ho bitches would turn on their pimps for a couple o' good hits o' this."

"It's a deal. We go to the bank and set up a box in your name. I keep the key but the name is yours. We set it up so we can get in it together, not alone. Okay? That's the way we will do it. Then you can do your thing and I will do mine and we can get back to the money afterward. Okay?"

Terry was bleary and rambling and wanted to secure what he had stolen but did not know what to do about it. He was a little too far gone to drive.

"Terry, the banks are closed. They close early on Saturday and they aren't open at all tomorrow."

"Oh, bloody hell. There must be something I can do to secure this stuff. Rabbit, take this bill and go get another bottle of rum." The bill was a fifty.

"You promised not to call me that any more." She was clearly stung by the name.

"Of course, of course, Roberta. I'm sorry." Terry's eyes were about half open and he looked as though he was going to go out at any moment.

Roberta took the bill and headed for the door. She could tell he was going to be sleeping by the time she walked there and back. Hell, she could even pick up a trick on the way if she wanted. The thought half sobered her; it was not what she wanted to do and was a step in the wrong direction. Terry had picked up a stack of money and if she played her cards right, that money was hers.

As soon as Roberta was out of sight, Terry took the money and most of the drugs out the back door and locked it in the glove box of the old Ford station wagon. He had not told her that the old wagon was his and he had slipped the desk clerks a couple of bills for them to ignore it.

When Roberta returned to the room, he pretended to be sleeping, just to see what she would do. She poured herself another drink and sat in the easy chair watching television until he actually did fall asleep. He could not tell in the morning if she had looked for the contraband or not. She was ready for whatever he was going to do that day, though. She did not ask about the drugs and there was nothing missing from his wallet. She did not, however, return the change from the fifty.

Sunday morning went slowly. The churches and

restaurants were all that did much business before noon. Terry's appetite was poor that morning and his intake consisted of a couple of beers and a shot of rum. Roberta got some takeout, a bottle of hydrogen peroxide, bandages and antiseptic cream. For the pain, all she could get was over-the-counter stuff, but Terry insisted that he wanted nothing stronger. He had never liked doing drugs and had sworn to himself he would never get addicted. He even forced himself to stop smoking from time to time.

Roberta did not understand some of the precautions that Terry insisted she take. Why, she wanted to know, did she need to park outside of the area and take a bus into Carson? Why did she need to go through the trouble of establishing that she worked for a local escort service? Why did she need to risk angering somebody's pimp by pretending to recruit his women? Why did he want to know where the pimps were?

In the end, Roberta relented and followed Terry's game plan. His justifications seemed sound although her arguments still held weight. She drove the rental car to the airport in Compton and parked it in the short-term lot. From the airport a shuttle took her to the Horatio Hotel where she caught a bus to Doloros Street in Carson. There was nobody on the streets. She picked up another bus back to Main Street and had a bit better luck. Understandably it was still a bit early in the day for ladies of the night, but Roberta knew that addiction never took a break and that no good rock goes unsmoked. She found a likely subject in a place just opening up called Bubba's Barbecue on the corner of Main Street and West 220th.

Angel's real name was Angelina Gamez. She looked particularly hellish that morning. A fresh black eye contrasted with her deep tan and her pockmarked skin needed some make-up. Angelina's hair had not been washed in a few days, about as long as she had not changed her

228

clothes. Roberta was looking fresh and clean in comparison but, despite her feelings, she managed to reach a connection. Once she mentioned that she had some rock, their association was all but ensured.

It seemed as though Angel would have been happy to have smoked behind the local convenience store, but Roberta was not playing that game; she insisted they needed a secure area. While they were walking toward the house of a friend, Roberta underwent a subtle change. For days she had been reverting to Roberta but in a transformation that actually made her shudder, she became Rabbit once again. Her less visceral alter ego was confined to a corner of her mind where she watched the events unfolding with the reserved distaste she had maintained for the past few years. This was the way she had maintained her sanity and she reverted to it when it became clear that it was necessary.

When they arrived at their destination, Angel's friend Shaniqua was just getting out of the shower. She seemed less than pleased at seeing her associate, making it plain that she had no money to lend her. She relented a bit once she found out that she had come bearing gifts. While the woman of the house was getting dressed, Rabbit grilled Angel on the names of the pimps in the neighborhood. Angel did not seem suspicious about this but Shaniqua was a different matter. Her questions stopped when the rock and the pipe came out.

After a while, they started talking about their sisters in the business and as sure as night turns to day the discussion turned to men and the names of the pimps and the bosses and the losers and all the details on the various nefarious individuals came out. At one point, Rabbit needed to go to the bathroom to write down all the names she had heard because she could not have remembered them all. The real information she wanted was where Bash Jamiel did business. It took all of the crack she had and a couple of beers from the refrigerator before Rabbit plucked it from them. He used an office on the 400 block of Double Street, one that backed up to an alley off Grace Avenue. The women did not know the number.

The high from crack seldom lasts long, a failing of cocaine in general. It was not long before the women wanted more of what they did not have. Rabbit had the solution; she pulled out the black tar and let the others smoke it while she drank a beer. There was little more to be gleaned from her new associates and the afternoon was drifting into evening so she headed back to Main Street and caught a bus north to the airport. Terry asked her to bring him a pack of cigarettes and a six pack of beer on her way when she called him. She picked up the car from the lot and headed back to Van Nuys.

With his first cigarette in hours between his lips, Terry casually tossed a stack of bills to his partner who just grunted and stuck it into her bra, making it tremendously lopsided. He asked her if she could change the bandage on his back and she almost told him that sort of thing was extra. Her few hours on the street and the rock that she had smoked had hardened her attitude. It was going to take more work to warm her back up again. The hesitation was not lost on Terry. He might have been half drunk, and he said nothing about it, but he recognized the flinty exterior the streets demanded. It did not matter to him; he was going to take a couple of days to heal anyway and they could enjoy each other's company or not as she saw fit. He had most of the information he needed and didn't care to exert himself much at present.

Chapter Nineteen
Trail of Tears

MacMaster got the call on Thursday, early. D'arniel Jamiel wanted to see him on matters of commerce. The issue remained that the black tar heroin had not been paid for and that would be the first order of business. Gordon MacMaster would not allow the men he dealt with to believe he was an easy mark. It was too easy to end up dead that way.

Jamiel still did not trust his new connection enough to allow the meeting to occur in the office on Double Street. One needed to have dealt with him for a while before one was allowed to enter that location. Most of the local gang had grown up together from before they were in school.

The meeting was to occur in a motel room on Doloros Street. Bash warned his new associate to keep his head down; there had been more casualties in the ongoing war against the West Carson gangs. Gordon checked with Anastasia to make sure she was ready before pulling in to the parking lot of the motel. This one rented rooms by the hour.

It was clear that the leader of the South Alley Bloods had not slept in a while. His blood shot eyes were rimmed with swollen lids and he had not shaved. His nervous, birdlike motions gave up the fact that he had been dipping into his own stash and it was not the opioid narcotics. D'arniel was enjoying the heightened awareness shared by crank heads everywhere.

In contrast to the gang bangers, Gordon MacMaster wore a cream-colored suit with a matching hat and a brass-headed walking stick. He looked very much the carpetbagger in this heavily ethnic neighborhood.

"I'm assuming you found the product within the parameters of acceptability?" Gordon said with a smile.

"We up with that." Two of the three men in the motel room with him were at the windows, peeking through the curtains.

"I assure you I am alone."

"A man is never truly alone until he's in the grave," Bash said philosophically. "You might have company you didn't know about. The man always watchin'."

"Yes, but I took precautions. Besides, I am still unknown in this area. Before the constabulary has deciphered the manner of my business I will have put an associate in place to handle the business and I will have moved on. It is not the most profitable business model, but it is the most efficient. I follow the outline created by the British colonization of the Indian subcontinent." It was immediately apparent that his audience had no idea what MacMaster was referring to so he changed tack. "I have arranged for a kilo of the black to be delivered this weekend, but I cannot get the other on the cuff as I mentioned. I assume you have what you owe me for the tar I entrusted you with?"

"Bigdog, pay the man."

The man with the sawed-off shotgun pulled out a stack of bills, Gordon stuffed it inside his vest without counting it. The quantity was not as important to him as the business atmosphere the payment engendered.

"This weekend gonna be busy. I gotta bury some brothers. They gonna be burying somma theirs, too. I want more o' this ice." Bash repeatedly clenched his right fist.

"Ah, yes, well, I'm sure you know how difficult it can be to work with the chemists. It is right from the kitchen, as pure as can be found, but the chefs can be demanding."

"What is it you're saying?"

"They want to meet with the money man. In essence, they want to meet with you. They will kick me back a taste, but they will only deal in cash on the barrelhead. I cannot convince them of my trustworthiness when it comes to matters of faith."

"I have little faith myself. I'll send one of my lieutenants with the money."

"I do not think that will be acceptable to them. They know who you are. They want to meet you personally since they are going to be doing business in your area. They do not want to step on your toes but they are planning to flood the area with this very pure product. You know you cannot get this sort of quality from the Mexican cartels. I think it would be in your best interest to trust me on this."

"Why should I? How did you get to know these people anyway? You come in here sayin' I can do this and I can do that but nobody knows you."

"Let me assure you that I have been in contact with these people for a long time and I set them up, in a manner of speaking. They were going to use the house here and distribute in a different area until I convinced them that it would be best to allow you to have first crack at the product. If you will forgive the pun."

"Awright. We gonna roll. Two cars. Keep an eye out. Glasgow, you with me."

Both vehicles were late model Acuras painted in soft, neutral colors. Flashy paint jobs and hydraulic systems were good for some things but it was clear that anonymity was the order of the day. Gordon directed the driver to West 222nd Street and told them to park by the side of the road in view of the kitchen window. All four men clearly thought they were invited in, automatic weapons in hand, but MacMaster was adamant. D'arniel Jamiel would be going in the house and his associates would be staying in the cars. There was to be no further discussion.

Arquila Moses Khareem was as hard headed as could be expected. He did not want Bash going in there without him. RayJay backed Moses up on this one. The third man did not say a word.

There had been some difficulty convincing Anastasia that the plan was the best way to go. She preferred the less complicated methods of acquisition and repeatedly questioned the plan. She felt that the time for subterfuge was gone and that it would be so much easier and less messy if they simply shot everybody else and threw Bash in the trunk of his own car. In the end she relented and allowed that Gordon's plan had some merit.

Waiting inside the house on West 222nd Street was difficult, as waiting before a delicate operation always has been. She smoked a cigar in the kitchen, dropping the ashes down the drain as she sat on the counter. She needed no scope on the Savage, Hunter model at that range. It was not a real stopper, chambered for .243 caliber rounds, but the plan was not to shoot the men who came calling. There was however a row of shells sitting next to the sink in case she needed to do just that. The rifle was accurate and quiet and that was what they needed.

The expectation had been of flashy full-sized vehicles with huge rims and skinny tires but the group rolled up in commuter cars. Five men got out of the two vehicles and Anastasia had the hunting rifle trained on them before the doors closed. She was back, away from the window now, wishing she had chosen a repeater instead of a bolt action model. If Gordon had been disarmed, she would be hard pressed to take out two of them before disaster struck.

The hat MacMaster held up matched the cream-colored suit and she had thought it a waste to perforate it so soon after buying it but Gordon had insisted that the effect be one of accuracy and vigilance. She watched him explaining to the men clustered around him and then she saw him take the hat from his head and hold it up. She sent one round through the crown of the hat and had the rifle reloaded before Gordon had his finger through the hole. The projectile ended up imbedded in the wall across the street.

This was the moment. Either D'arniel was going to tell his men to get back into the cars or there was going to be a lot of blood spilled on the street. Anastasia centered the sights on Moses and breathed deeply. She saw the smile on MacMaster's face but knew it was artificial. If things went sour he would strike like an uncoiling spring. The moment stretched, clenched, and then eased and the tension flowed away like water. Bash signaled his posse to stay outside and moved to enter the home without them.

Anastasia kept the additional men in her sights until there was a knock. She set the rifle down, went into the living room and opened the door and the bars of the storm door. She was wearing no jacket and the shoulder holster was on the outside of her blouse. The gang leader was moved to express his appreciation, though silently.

It seemed to Roberta that Terry was more pissed off at himself for letting himself get shot than at the man who shot him. He told her it was no good getting angry at the dead anyway and she thought that a pretty good philosophy. It was also difficult not to respect a man who stitched himself up and was back on his feet two days later.

On Monday morning Terry took Roberta to the bank and set her up with a safe deposit box. She put the stack of bills into the box, kissed the key and slipped it into her panties. She was so used to men lying to her that she would never fully trust anyone. Terry was having some success at assaulting her defenses and he had initially planned to keep the key but did not attempt to retrieve it from inside her pants.

The alley that ran behind East Double Street was only eight houses long and did not have an official name. Those eight houses made up a third of the block. The problem, in Terry's eyes, was that the alley was too easily blocked. It was barely wide enough for two automobiles side by side. He spent a couple of hours on Monday afternoon parked at the dead end of the alley with Roberta at his side. She chattered about her family and childhood, the last time she had felt happy. He smoked, squeezed a hand exerciser and watched for activity. They left the neighborhood, once the children were out of school, and went to a bar instead. In the bar, Terry noted the looks Roberta was getting from just about everybody. They were far from her usual neighborhood and she knew none of the men in the bar, but the looks said it all. While parked in the alley, her clothes had been the perfect cover, but in a more usual social setting they were too extreme. On the way back to the motel, they stopped at a department store and Terry bought Roberta some outfits that were a lot less revealing than her current wardrobe. She had never worn business attire before but adjusted quickly and gracefully.

The business attire was for going to restaurants and bars. When the couple returned to Carson the following day they were not dressed for the office. Terry wore his vest and twin .38s over a plaid shirt and a crush hat. Roberta wore high heels and fishnet stockings with a short skirt and halter top.

Although it was legal to park on the sides of East Double, Terry was not comfortable there. He had been more at ease at the end of the alley but knew better than to park there two days in a row.

The street captain was looking a bit ragged when he arrived at his office on Wednesday. He had an entourage of three men dressed in baggy clothes and sideways baseball caps. They were all trying to look as dangerous as they could. Terry found them humorous until he remembered that he had been shot a couple of days earlier by just such men. That sobered him.

One man stayed on the porch constantly. There was no hope of trying the same antics that had gotten Terry into

Winslow Hardapple's apartment. There was also none of the traffic one would get at an established drug house. Bash was not retailing from his office. This was still the heart of the operations but showing up with drugs for sale would not get Terry in the door; it was more likely to get him shot. Again. His dangerous activities did not seem to have borne fruit. He marked the house and drove away, but he did not drive far.

The corner of East Carson Street and Grace Avenue was a strip mall set on an angle. The roof of this small commerce center was just that much taller than the surrounding houses and it had a flat roof. There was the usual assortment of businesses and Terry stopped by the convenience store for a half liter of whiskey. While in the store he casually asked if there was any problem with the roof, if it had developed any leaks over the years. The clerk looked at him stupidly, as if he had asked about plagues of locusts or blacktop whirlpools. Terry decided he was not talking to the right person so he asked who took care of the maintenance.

It turned out the maintenance man was white, which surprised Terry enough. The tired and bowed old man was found putting away his tools after a plumbing job in the basement. He moved slowly and obviously needed some encouragement. Acting as though he did not want to be seen, Terry screwed the cap off the bottle and took a quick shot. The gambit worked perfectly and the man was happy to show him the roof as long as he brought the bottle with him. The roof was white to reflect heat and studded with a row of air conditioning units. There were no rooms on the roof but the edge was a slightly raised rampart making for good cover. What was best was that the access was from the inside of the corner, downstairs. It was open to the public if the public had a good lock pick. The old man had opened it with a key he kept on his tool belt. The lock and the key had corresponding numbers stamped on them.

Terry sat on the roof with his new acquaintance for a while and finished off about half the bottle of whiskey before the heat drove them both downstairs. The maintenance office was air conditioned and had the basic amenities of civilized life. While the man who belonged there used the bathroom, the man who did not belong there stole the key to the roof. It would probably be a long time before it would be missed.

When he returned to the vehicle, Roberta was furious. After waiting a half hour, she had procured some Hennessy and gotten half baked in the front seat of the auto. He told her that she needed to learn some patience and that waiting for the correct opportunity may be boring but makes for a longer life. She swore at him and took another hit of cognac. He pulled off onto a side street and told her, in no uncertain terms, that she could be an asset or a liability and that he could dump her off at the bus station if that was what she wanted. She started crying and said that she was feeling too much, that she was not comfortable expressing her feelings, and it made her angry that he was forcing her to do so. Terry did not know what to say about that.

Rush hour traffic had the expressways jammed to a virtual standstill so the couple stopped at a bar in Torrance and without meaning to they both got falling down drunk and stayed there for the night. Wednesday they went to Redondo Beach and shopped and lay on the beach and watched the people. Terry did some mild exercising but stopped when his wound started bleeding. They stayed in a hotel on the beach that afternoon in a marathon of sexual congress.

It was midnight when Terry got back in the car and headed toward Carson. Concerned about her lack of patience, he left Roberta in bed, asleep. His rental was nondescript enough to cause no notice in the strip mall's parking lot and nobody saw him unlock the door to the roof. The Weatherby Mark V was in a canvas bag at his side but he was more interested in seeing who was coming and going than in popping any of them. He wanted a clean extraction, the pain in his side reminding him that, despite the way it looked, he was not in suburbia.

The guard at the door changed every two hours, rotating from within the building. Inside it looked like there was a card game going on. The guards looked as though they had been up for days, dopey and jerky at the same time. Terry wondered if they had slept since he last saw them. The only others to arrive at that time of the night was a man bringing a shopping bag full of liquor and a couple of women. The party lasted all night and the guard at the door was relieved by a new arrival at six. Terry had to give it to Bash, the man knew how to party.

It was about eight in the morning when six men got into three vehicles. Two of them were cookie-cutter foreign cars and the third was a low-rider style Buick Riviera. Terry saw them heading for the cars and scrambled for his own vehicle. He was only a block and a half from them but by the time he passed the place he had been watching, they were gone. He caught a glimpse of the Buick on his left as he hit Doloros Street and followed them to a motel a few blocks down. This provided him with the opportunity to get in close. He rented a room across the parking lot from where the cars were parked and settled down to watch. After more than an hour, a tall man in a cream-colored suit with a matching hat drove a full-sized Cadillac into the lot and went inside the room. Minutes later five men came out and got into the foreign cars; one of them was the man in the cream-colored suit. The two men driving the Buick stood outside and watched. It took every bit of brass Terry had to walk out that door and get in the driver's seat of the Ford. The remaining gangsters watched him drive off after the Acuras but did not seem to make a lot of it. They did not follow him.

The south side of West 222nd Street where Anastasia had rented her house was one continuous block from Moneta Avenue to Main Street. The north side was broken up into four blocks. When Terry saw the Acuras parked on the south side of the street, he pulled off onto Rashdall Avenue, drove down two blocks and turned around. Pulling to the side of the street in front of the second house north on that street gave him a good view of the cars and the three men in them. He pulled up a little and saw D'arniel Jamiel and the man in the cream-colored suit heading for the front door of a house. Hoisting his binoculars got him a look at the house.

"Wrangle and shear me!" he blurted. It was impossible but he could have sworn that for just a second that he had seen Anastasia Viuda aiming a rifle at the men in the cars. Then he realized that there were more Hispanics in California than any place north of Mexico. It had been an illusion. Then he saw a man's head, minus its cream-colored hat. It was a head covered with red hair. He never saw the man's face but the coincidence was too great to ignore.

"MacMaster, you flaming wallaby. How in the devil did you get inside this man's guard? Bloody hell, I wish I knew your plan so I can back it up." Terry felt his pulse quicken. Of all the freelance jobs in the world, how did he pick the same job as his mentor? What were the odds against that? Billions to one, unless they were being fed jobs by the same man. Terry had never considered that his contact in Michigan might be getting jobs through the same information conduit that supplied Gordon MacMaster. It seemed inconceivable. Was he jumping to an unwarranted conclusion? It was possible that his friend was protecting D'arniel. That gave Terry a start. There was a definite conflict of interest if that were the case.

"So, what do you need for backup? Can I give you backup without having the widow maker blow my bloody brains all over the street. What are you up to, you cagey old crow?"

Terry had barely finished his thought when the house they were all watching became a Hell on Earth. The explosions were not the huge conflagrations that occur when a gas main ignites; they were actually a series of blasts. The first set was a simultaneous ripping thunder that literally blew the roof off the house. Next there were eight small shots that, while coordinated, were not completely synchronous. They flattened the walls inward by kicking the bottoms off the foundations and folding the walls toward the center. Glass and wooden shrapnel flew out from the epicenter in every direction, pelting the nearby cars but not flying far. Most of the force was directed downward. A huge ball of flame rolled around the roof as it fell back to the ground and the flames roared as if they were a second explosion. The house was gone as was everybody in it.

Chapter Twenty
Rubble

Filming was essentially finished on "Blaze of Glory II"
and the editors and sound men were beginning their work.
There was nothing for Sean Warren to do now except
promotion. He would talk to Jay Leno and Letterman on
their late night spots and try to generate some interest in the
sequel. The studio had made it clear that if this one did well
in the box office then another one would be scheduled. Sean
didn't care much but his hero figure was very popular and he
was paid well for it.

It had been explained to him years earlier, by a
promoter and producer type, that Sean needed to live in a
mansion in Beverly Hills. It had brought up thoughts of an
old television show. It was old enough to have been filmed
in black and white. The man's words had proved prophetic
however. Once he became popular, he needed to obtain
housing far from the madding crowd, just to maintain his
sense of being. The fans and the paparazzi could be more
than just annoying; their intrusions were becoming the stuff
of legend. So Sean had gotten a mansion in Beverly Hills and
managed to keep it through two divorces, due to pre-nuptial
agreements. He had been uncomfortable with it initially but
it had grown on him. The high fence, elevated position and
large, treed lot kept unwanted visitors to a minimum.

"Hello, miss, this is Sean Warren. Is Archie there?"
"Mr. Warren, I'll patch you right through."
"Archie?"
"Sean, good to hear from you. Has any one contacted
you?"
"No. I think they know they will never get anything
more from me."
"So you just called for a briefing?"
"Archie, it's been almost three weeks and I have

nothing to make me feel any better. Have the men you hired done anything for me or are they having a beach party?"

"No, sir, no beach parties. We should expect results within days."

"I hope so. I'm busy Friday and I'm set to be in New York all next week. I paid good money for this and I'm getting a little sick of waiting around."

"I understand. I'll find out when this will all be wrapped up and let you know."

"Thanks, Archie. I knew I could count on you."

Sean hung up the phone frustrated and unsatisfied. He had paid good money to get this man and had gotten nothing. He began to feel that he was being taken advantage of again. His grief over Melissa welled up and tears ran down his face. He sat for a while alternately crying and growling, then went to his gun safe and took out a .44 Magnum revolver and a box of shells. He strode into the back yard where he had reproductions of famous Italian statues on pedestals, loaded his revolver and proceeded to shoot them. The .44 Magnum shells caused the plaster statues to explode upon impact.

As is true with most ballistics, the larger the round, the louder the report. A .44 Magnum round sounded like an explosion in the quiet of upper-class suburbia. It was not long before the police responded to the reports of shots fired, but they could not get in the gate. Sean calmed them down and told them he was blowing off firecrackers. It did not matter to him that they did not believe him, as long as they went away.

Waiting had been tolerable as long as he was working every day, but now he was consumed with grief, guilt and hatred. There was no way he could stand around waiting any longer. He called Ice Cream.

"Hey, Iceman."

"Sean, my brother. You still got my back?"

"Every day, Ice. Look, I'm starting to think I need to

try something different."

"What did you have in mind?"

"I say we go in big, shoot this guy's guards and take him ourselves."

"Sean, my man, you ain't thinking straight. As soon as you hit the city line you gonna be marked. They at war. They banging with the Crips in West Carson and if we made it halfway there it would only be because they wanted us deep inside before they tagged us. We can't go in big or we go out dead. That's the street man, that ain't no movie. I tol' you before man, I love you like a brother, but I ain't goin' in there. I already know I ain't coming back if I do. White man like you so big a target, you be the first one shot. The only way you go in is as a customer, not as a team leader. Get your head on straight."

"Okay, then, what do you suggest?"

"You can do what you want but only if you can get him out of Carson. Once he out, he got no network. Figure how to get him down on the beach and we got him. As long as he in Carson, we can't touch him."

"Thanks. I guess. I'm just so pissed off about this whole thing and I feel so useless sitting around. I'll be in touch."

"Yeah. I tell you what, don't you do nothin' stupid. You got a whole lot and throwin' everything away on a piece of shit from South Central ain't makin' a whole lotta sense. Give me a little while. I'm workin' on some things might pull the crab right outta his shell. Promise me."

"Yeah."

"I mean promise me. I got your back but I can't protect you down there, nobody can. If you start thinkin' you can go in there like a fuckin' cowboy and start shooting the place up, you gonna end up under a tombstone."

"Okay, I got the point. I promise."

The next call came to him and seemed both promising

and disappointing.

"Mr. Warren," Jacqueline's New York accent seemed unusually pronounced today. "Have you seen the news?"

"No. I have not been much for television lately."

"It broadcast at noon. You can probably find it on the internet by now. Do a search for explosions in Carson or something like that."

"All right. Give me a second. Sean accessed his browser on his telephone and found the story of a gang leader being caught in a gas explosion in Carson. The picture showed a house that had been completely demolished: the frame for the front door was in the street, bricks from the chimney were strewn all over the yard and the fire department was cordoning off the area.

"I got the explosion. Who said this Jamiel was in there? I think it's a trick."

"Archie is on it now. If it's a trick, we'll know about it. Sit tight and let us sort out what happened. I wouldn't do anything yet."

"That's all everybody keeps telling me. Don't do anything, sit tight, relax, we'll take care of it. I'm going nuts here. I need to do something or I'm going to freak out."

"Freak out? I didn't think anybody did that any more. Look," Jacqueline's voice took on a hard edge, "we will get you what you need or proof of an expiration date on the product, but you will need to let us do what you paid us to do. Are we clear?"

"All right. I'll give you until tomorrow."

"Mr. Warren, these things take time. We are working round the clock on this problem but it is not the kind of thing you can just say 'Pick up the laundry on Wednesday.' We will take care of you."

"I'll call back tomorrow." Sean hung up the phone and went to his study to research the explosion further.

The violence and fury that blew the walls of the cottage all over the street precluded anyone being left alive inside. Kingston was caught as much by surprise as anyone else. He saw the initial blast and watched the roof rise about four feet from the house, then the walls were folded in on each other like playing cards. There should have been no fire from this demolition, but something else was in play and the fire roared furiously.

The three men who had stayed in the automobiles got out and headed across the lawn, an act of futility. One of them kept yelling, "Bash, Bash." Terry thought he sounded like a sheep.

Kingston scanned the area behind the rubble with his field glasses. There was no possibility that anyone within the structure had survived so there was no need to look at the wreckage. He saw a weathered custom Chevrolet van pulling out of the driveway of the bungalow directly behind the carnage. Sometime in the 1980's the van had been given a custom paint job with a mural of a man holding a sword aloft and a half-naked woman clutching his legs. Terry memorized the mural. He would not have used such a distinctive vehicle himself but was grateful for the individuality.

For a moment, he considered shooting the three men but ended up leaving the gang members staring stupidly at the remains of the cottage. Terry put his Ford in gear and drove off. Nobody noticed him; all eyes were for the tragedy.

Half a mile west and a quarter mile north took the Chevy van to Route 110. It was late enough in the day to miss the morning commuters and early enough to miss them on the way home. It was over twenty miles to Archie's office but the van was easy to follow at a distance. Terry had too much respect to follow closely.

The serious conflict for Terry Kingston was his uncertainty of who he was following and where they were going. For all intents and purposes, the two men who had entered the home and the woman who was in it when they arrived were dead, blown to bits in the conflagration. There was no proof otherwise except for Kingston's heartfelt feeling that Gordon MacMaster would not die as a result of some accident. He realized that his vision may be unrealistic but he saw the demise of MacMaster as a blood-drenched last stand on some medieval battlefield with the bodies piled up around him like cordwood. He could not conceive of his dying in an accident. Assuming the destruction of the cottage was accidental. He kept reminding himself that he had not actually seen Gordon MacMaster either. He was proceeding on a supposition that followed an assumption. He did not know who was in the van, he did not know who had been in the house and he did not know if anyone had gotten out or not. On the other hand, he might be right.

Following at a distance is not difficult on the expressways, and as long as both vehicles are in the same lane there are no unusual maneuvers necessary. Terry followed the van onto Interstate 405 and north to Santa Monica Boulevard. Things became a bit more difficult there. Though he was certain they were heading for Archie's office on Melrose, he was not certain enough to take a different route and meet them there. He followed as far back as he could without losing sight of his objective entirely and almost missed it when the van turned north into the residential neighborhoods. That was where things got tricky. He was almost certain they had noticed him now. Why else were they taking this route? The possibilities swam in his brain, each a little fish in a school and impossible to concentrate on one for long. Boiled down like consommé, the ideas only led to two courses of action, he would follow the van or he would not. Fastening on this, Terry stopped second guessing himself and focused on following the van at a distance. He stayed as far back as he could without losing it but felt terribly exposed.

"I think, my love, that we picked up a follower."

"Really? One of the Acuras?"

"No. This man is white. He is in the dark car three places back. He wears a hat and sunglasses. I think I saw him on the other freeway and now he is on this one. I think he is following us."

"I doubt it. We pulled that one off impeccably. I must say your placement was perfect, though possibly a bit excessive," Gordon said, grinning.

"I learned explosives as a child. I remember my fingers smelling of gunpowder as I ate lunch. It is nice to work with Semtex instead of fertilizer and gasoline. And it was not excessive; it was perfect. The bungalow was destroyed yet nobody else died."

"This is our exit. I'm going to get into the back with shotguns. If our friend follows us onto Santa Monica, let him get close enough and I will punch his ticket right through the windshield."

"You could scrape away some of the stuff on the window, the stuff that makes it dark, so you can see through it." Anastasia said, already considering the shot.

"No, the reflective film is on the outside. I can see through it some. Just keep me updated. I don't want to shoot the wrong man." MacMaster stepped around the prone body on the floor, checked the breech of the shotgun and sat on the small couch next to the back doors.

"This guy is pretty good at staying away. He is still there but he is not trying to get close. It is almost as if he knew where we are going and he is just going to meet us there. Every time I slow for a yellow light he is already slowing down," Anastasia added.

"That's all right. I didn't want to shoot him on Santa Monica Boulevard anyway. Your left will be coming up in a few minutes. We will get him there, assuming he really is following us."

"Do you doubt me?"

"No, my sweet, never. If you say he is following us then he is following us," Gordon said hiding a smile.

"And I say yes. I do not know who he is but he is alone in the car and he is good at hiding in the traffic."

"But not good enough."

"No. He is not good enough."

"He's in that Ford? The fourth one back?" Gordon asked.

"Yes. I will turn the corner and we will start getting stop signs. When we get to where nobody is looking, I will wait for him. He will come to us."

There it was. There was no doubt he had been seen. The van had been three blocks ahead of him and then two. He had pulled the Ford to the side of the street halfway through the second block. The van sat at the intersection, waiting. Waiting for him. Terry felt as if he had a bull's-eye on his forehead. He ducked down in the seat. If they had been unsure before, they knew now for certain. He peeked over the dashboard, unable to keep from looking. The van had already backed halfway down the block. They were tired of being followed and were turning the tables on him.

As conflicted as he felt, there was no changing Terry Kingston. He had always been a man who reacted quickly and as soon as a decision was reached it went into effect. Terry seldom chose to run rather than attack, but this was one of those moments. He jammed the car into gear and screamed into a u-turn, the front wheels howling and the steering gear grinding as he hurtled around, jumping the curb on the other side of the street and tearing off through the stop sign.

"Well, look who showed up. I'm afraid we have no

more use for you." Jacqueline's obvious pleasure at telling Terry this was not just insulting, it was disrespectful and demeaning.

Terry did not let the receptionist's attitude affect him. "I'm here to see Archie."

"Well, Archie's not here. It's time you returned the rental. If it were up to me you'd be giving back the down payment too."

"Look, sweetheart," Terry's voice reflected a tired frustration. "I'm not here to play these silly games. There have been some unforeseen events and I need to consult with your superior to determine how to proceed."

"I already told you, he's not here."

"Call him. I know he carries a phone."

"He told me not to call. He's busy."

Terry rubbed the stubble on his chin thoughtfully and wondered why he had even taken this job. He had almost forsaken it more than once and was on the verge of doing so again. Then he remembered his Uncle Ginger's words, repeated often when Terry was in his teens. "You cannot buy a reputation, boy. The reputation you have is the reputation you earn and it takes a long time to change it. A good reputation is worth more than gold." If he walked away from the job he had been contracted for he would damage his reputation. If he killed this obnoxious woman, on the other hand, it would not damage him. The thought brought a broad smile to his face and reoriented his focus.

"Perhaps you could assist me instead. Have you contracted with a different party to achieve the same objective?"

"It's a competitive business. Given your actions, we decided that you were a bad investment and Archie authorized me to go a different route."

"Well, sweetheart…"

"Stop calling me sweetheart. I'm not your sweetheart."

The smile did not leave Terry's face. "Look, sweetheart, I don't know who you think you are working with, but you have thrown a wrench in the works. I think you got your objective blown to kingdom come."

"At least something was done. We were getting nothing out of you." Jacqueline's voice was tight and contentious.

"Sweetheart, I know what it is you wanted to get from me but that is not going to happen. I prefer my women not so expansive."

As he had expected, Jacqueline misunderstood the word expansive and took it as an indictment of her physical shape. He had learned how sensitive American women were about their figures. She stood, sucking her belly in as she did, pointed at the door and said "It's time for you to leave. Return the rental car or we will issue a stolen vehicle report on it and have you arrested. Your dubious services are no longer required and I never want to see you again."

He could not have told anyone why he enjoyed baiting this woman this way, but he did. There was something about her that set Terry off. She was young and attractive and volatile, the kind of woman that usually attracted him. He could not put his finger on what the problem was but from the first minute they had been in contact they had repulsed each other like magnets.

"Are we seeing each other then?" he asked. "I have had women tell me they did not want to see me any more but it was usually because we were seeing each other. I could lock the door and do you on the desk if you like, then we could say we were seeing each other."

Jacqueline sat down quickly and reached under the desk. Most people would have been caught flat-footed by the maneuver, but Terry was not most men. He stepped around the desk and as she pulled the pistol from its holster, he grabbed her elbow, slid his hand down to her wrist and immobilized the arm by pushing it across her chest. She gave a little cry as he wrapped his other arm around her and picked her bodily from her seat. He inhaled deeply through his nose, enjoying her scent and her closeness.

"Let me go," she demanded.

"So you can shoot me? I don't think so, dear. Drop the gun."

Jacqueline knew she had been outmaneuvered but what really surprised her was the fact that his strong arms around her made her want to stop fighting. She did not want this man. She had convinced herself that she did not want anything to do with him. He was a killer and a freak... and he was nuzzling her neck while she was trying to shoot him. She released her hold on the pistol and it clattered to the desktop and fell on the carpeted floor. "No, no," she said weakly.

"Ah, yes, yes," he whispered in her ear and then nibbled on her ear lobe.

She turned to face him, feeling herself getting wet with expectation. She did not want to want this man but in that moment, all she could think about was having him, right there in the office. She had never been overly promiscuous but at that moment she wanted to take him into her, right on the floor. Then the door opened.

Neither of them had heard the footsteps in the hallway, they had been concentrating on each other and the danger each represented to the other. When the door opened, they both turned to look as if they were guilty schoolchildren caught necking beneath the bleachers at a high school sports event.

Chapter Twenty One
Remains

"Hey, Roger!"

"Archie! What the heck." Roger looked at the uniformed officer guarding the perimeter and said, "Let him through. Retired LAPD."

"Thanks, Rog. What the hell happened here?" Archie limped forward.

"I was hoping you had something to tell me about it."

"I was watching the news at noon and I heard about this. They said a gang leader was in the house and I thought I might have something to contribute if I could get a little more information about the whole thing."

"Pretty much everything we know we got from the neighbor," Roger admitted. "As you can see, between the explosion and the fire there's nothing left. The evidence lab just got here but they got a hell of a mess."

Archie peered over the edge of the hole that was all that remained of the cottage. What had not been blown into the surrounding yards had burned into the basement and that had been doused by the Fire Department. A couple of feet of oily water with blackened timbers did not look as though it would yield any answers.

"So, I'm just watching these guys go through the scene. They're gonna toss you out anyway so we may as well watch from a distance."

"So, what's your call on it, Rog?"

Roger held the crime scene tape up while Archie limped under it. "Old age finally catching up with you, Arch?"

"No. I took one in the leg downtown. It might have something to do with this."

"I doubt it. These guys stay south of the four-oh-five. They got no hook downtown. From what I get, Bash Jamiel was seen going into the house just before it blew up. He has nothing to do with anything north of here from what we know. Hey, would you like to sit down? My car's right here."

"Thanks. I can't really tell you what the connection is. It's part of an investigation I've been contracted for. LAPD's been read in on it already." Archie opened the front door of the detective's car and sat on the bench seat.

Roger came around the front of the car and got in the driver's seat. "I haven't been read in on it, old man. Give me something I can work with."

"Can we go and get a drink?" Archie asked.

"In this neighborhood? You must be looking to get shot again. I know a nice Mexican restaurant south of here where you can get a beer and I can get some tacos."

"Speaking of tacos, you still banging that little Mexican cutie? What was her name, Angelina?"

"No. Angelina went back to Mexico to care for her mother."

"I thought you were gonna knock that up and marry it for sure," Archie jibed.

"Yeah." He breathed out heavily and looked pensive. "It wouldn't have worked out between us. The sex was great, explosive, but when we weren't in bed we didn't have that much in common. Plus her brothers were getting into smuggling; it's kind of the family business. It put me in a delicate spot."

"It was the delicate spot that got you there in the first place."

Roger breathed in through his nose. "Damn, shut up. I'm on duty."

"Shit, when did that start to matter?"

"Things are different now, Arch. You remember when Bobbie Sota got shot?"

"Sure. About two years ago. He was rousting some pimp in Lakewood."

"Officially. You know. What he was really doing was banging some whore on the hood of his cruiser. Off the record of course. They kept it quiet but things went to shit after that. Don't mention that to anyone, you hear."

"You know I never say anything."

"Precisely, but this time, if you have pertinent information, you are going to tell me. I would hate to have to run you in for obstructing justice."

"Get the fuck out of here. Run me in. Your mother obstructed justice when she didn't put a pillow over your face."

Both men were laughing as they pulled into the parking lot of the family restaurant. Minutes later they were eating enchiladas and Archie was swallowing painkillers with beer.

"This is the rundown. The neighbors say some *mamasita* moved in the house no more than a week ago. First thing you know, all the men in the neighborhood are sniffing after it like dogs. Today they got two cars pulling up in front of the neighbor's house. Foreign cars, the old woman thinks they were Toyotas. Two men get out, a white one and a black one. Woman obviously thought they were going in to get some, but I'm not so sure. You familiar with D'arniel Jamiel?" Roger asked.

"Not personally, but he's on my watch list." Archie said.

"Why?"

"You finish your part of the story and then I'll give you mine," Archie countered.

Roger grunted. "The woman knew D'arniel. The neighbor woman. She's lived in Carson all her life. She makes it her business to know every man woman and child in town. Nothing better to do. Living off her dead husband's insurance and SS. Anyway, she did not know the white man with the red hair who went in with the banger and she didn't see either of them come out. Obviously. There was a couple of guys waiting in the cars and they came out after the place self destructed. If you have questions for Bash the Blood, you're going to need to wait until you join him in Hell. Now, tell me a story."

It took little time to give his old associate the cut-rate tour of the situation. Everybody in the country knew about the murder of the rising young star and her mutilated body. Sentiment ran high precisely because she was an attractive, accepted actress and because she was engaged to a popular actor. There were no surprises there. It was the connection between the murder of Melissa and the explosion on 222nd Street that was in question. Archie was quick to assure Roger that he had nothing to do with the explosion, that it was most likely just a gas line damaged by one of the constant earthquakes.

Roger did not buy it. He knew there was no way Archie showed up on the scene to rubberneck, especially with a fresh wound in his leg. He knew that there was something more and he wanted to know what it was. He started grilling his old friend but Archimedes was not so easily intimidated. After all, he had used the same techniques on a thousand men.

Archie did admit that he had heard rumors of South Alley Bloods bragging about the killing and Roger corroborated it by saying that he had heard the same thing. What Roger assumed was that Jamiel had been executed for his involvement in the affair. That might have made Archie an accessory but the crusty old PI shrugged it off. He was as much in the dark as the police. He had never been anywhere near D'arniel Jamiel.

On their way back to the scene, Archie's phone rang.

The Governor of California was a movie star. California had a habit of making politicians out of movie stars and some of them had reaped great successes in the public arena after retiring from the private stage. Unfortunately, most of the commerce the inhabitants of California initiated was not subject to taxation. Most of the commerce was illegal. The film industry alone could not buoy up the state coffers enough to offset the illegal farm workers who were paid in cash and so contributed no taxes. There had never been a tax on the thriving drug trade.

Most people considered it obvious that legalizing marijuana was generations overdue and would provide the state government with enough income to eliminate its immediate debt. The problem lay with the fact that the Federal Government would not relent. In the eyes of the geriatric congressmen and senators in Washington, smoking marijuana was merely the first step toward a life of addiction to heroin. They had learned nothing from the prohibition of alcohol that had torn the country apart in the 1920s, and they refused to listen to the voice of the people. The summer of love was long over and the hippies had all grown gray with beer bellies and Volvos, and still nothing changed. The country had been in favor of legalizing that particular drug for decades and the entire country waited for the California vote.

Medical marijuana was legal, and a thriving business was being done in Humboldt County where 80 percent of the residents of the county had something to do with the growing and cultivation of the weed, so much so, the network news media ran stories on the product. Then the bill was placed before the Congressional Committee and Congressman Cabot voted against it, effectively squashing it.

A lot of people wondered what it was that made Congressman Cabot vote against the legalization of marijuana. His constituency was all for it. After all, he represented the south end of the San Joaquin Valley, currently wine country, but blessed with a deep rich surface soil that would grow a potent and healthy batch of hemp. All the indicators were in favor of Congress voting to legalize cultivation and reap the rewards of what he had sown, but he did not. His refusal to support the bill led to its being killed, and while it should have ended his career in the State Senate it did not.

Public opinion was about to squash the congressman like one of the grapes his constituents produced in such abundance. Polls showed Cabot had committed political suicide by voting against the legalization of marijuana. His opponent, John Pierce, former State Comptroller was clearly the winner by default until ten days before the election when he was indicted for embezzlement. Of course he denied everything but the Reno, Nevada bank account in his name had been the recipient of the funds transferred from the public coffers while he was the State Comptroller. The court of public opinion slammed the gavel down and he fell from favor in meteoric fashion. Congressman Cabot was reelected and began to work toward new legislation that gave the State Senate more authority in licensing the sale of marijuana. His argument had been that there was too little regulation for the good of the people. The truth was that his hand had been forced this once but he was never going to allow that again.

The man who had the sex tape had not wanted money; he had only wanted the correct vote on the marijuana issue. He had also assured the congressman that the opposition was going to have a political assassination pulled on him. The man had been smooth and respectful and had guaranteed Henry Cabot that he would be winning the election. Henry had been appalled. He had almost resigned but had seen the charade through to election time. To his own surprise, things had occurred exactly as the man had described and he was reelected by an unhappy constituency.

Henry Cabot tore into George Arridagio relentlessly until his assistant admitted to the whole affair. Henry knew that George had watched part of the tape, which was not an issue. George had set up prostitutes for his boss on multiple occasions. The congressman had forbidden George from taking any action on it. Somehow the message had not gotten through to Arridagio, however. George decided that somehow he knew the best thing for his patron. When he got to the part about Frank Hicks, the Henry Cabot's face got red as a beet. Of course, George had no idea that the congressman had contracted to have the owner of the studio killed. Henry got very quiet and told George to go through the whole scenario again. He did not want to miss a thing. One thing was for sure, Frank Hicks was the liability. That was why pirates killed the men who buried their treasures for them. Frank Hicks had buried a treasure and now he needed to be buried himself.

Henry Cabot had met many men of low principles while he went to the University of Michigan, before he had become a politician. They were not alumni of the school or even associated with Ann Arbor; these people lived and worked in Detroit. The true nature of the automotive downturn had not hit home yet, while Henry was there, and the union officials and members were sitting pretty back then. They would have been less willing to chance nefarious and underhanded deeds in those days, but now Detroit was full of men dreaming of glory days and wondering how they could get by. For a small consideration, these men of low character were happy to put Henry in touch with men who knew other men who would contact the proper mechanics. He had already done it once this year and had been so satisfied with the services rendered that when he called he insisted the same mechanic be put on the job. Monies were exchanged and communications made.

"Perhaps it would be better if you took a hotel room."

"Anastasia! I knew it was you." Terry was smiling but as subtly as he could he was also maneuvering Jacqueline's body between himself and the door. He saw the news magazine and that she had one hand inside it. He was happy and astonished to see her but he knew what she was capable of and he did not want to find out first hand. He was smiling, but the thought that her name was Viuda, Widow in English, kept him always wanting cover.

"Perhaps you two would like a few minutes?" the Argentine asked with a smile.

"Get off me," Jacqueline demanded. "This son-of-a-bitch attacked me."

"Oh, sweetheart! How soon we forget. It was your trying to stick something into me that I was worried about."

Anastasia licked her lower lip. "I remember having the same concern in the recent past. This woman is a bit quick on the draw."

"Not quite quick enough. There's a Glock 21 on the rug she was intent on burying in my ass. I wonder if she treats all her boyfriends this way?"

"Get off me!" She struggled out of his grip.

Anastasia let the folded magazine slide off her arm and kept her pistol pointed at the floor. Her smile, which had seemed genuine before, now looked more like that of a hungry alligator. It was impossible to know what was on her mind and given her history, Terry was certain he wanted to. He could not relax until she holstered her weapon.

"We thought it would be best not to call, because of the nature of our business. Is Archimedes here?"

Jacqueline was retrieving her pistol from the floor with exaggerated care, picking it up with thumb and forefinger. Terry's hand was sliding toward the inside of his vest and Anastasia was watching them both while holding her pistol with two hands. They were an uncomfortable triangle, three members of the same team, with the same objective, reticent to extend the slightest trust.

Jacqueline set her .45 on the desk and stepped back.

Anastasia looked Terry in the eyes. Terry smiled. Anastasia smiled.

Anastasia clicked the safety on her weapon. Terry moved his hand from the opening of his vest. Anastasia took her left hand from the grip. Terry dropped his hand to his side. Anastasia shoved the barrel of the pistol into the back of her jeans. Terry spread his arms wide in an embracing motion and they moved to give each other a tight squeeze and a kiss on the cheek.

Jacqueline looked at her pistol and then up, right into the eyes of Anastasia Viuda. There was no doubt but that blood would flow if she made any sudden move toward the desk. The only question was whose blood?

"So, you two know each other? What are the odds?"

"You advertised for professionals. There are only so many of us in the business. You know, true professionals. It stands to reason some of us would know others." Terry was visibly relieved.

"Again, Archimedes is not here, is he?"

"No, he is not, uh, Rio. Or should I call you Annie, Anistasa, Ani…"

"Just call me Rio. I need to see Archimedes. I think you have nothing to fear from this man, whatever he calls himself today. That is unless you try to shoot him again. That would be a bad move. You would be better to hire him."

A short bark of laughter jumped from Terry's mouth. "They did hire me, but you were a step ahead. I must say, blowing up that cottage was brilliant. Was that your idea? Yeah? I thought so. I must say it was a thing of beauty the way the walls fell into the basement; a work of art. The Scotsman's usually a bit more subtle but not always. He's blown a thing or two up in his time too."

"So, you need to call Archimedes and have him return to, uh, have him return. We have secured the package and require delivery instructions."

Terry lit a cigarette and Jacqueline gave him a dirty look. "You got the wog in the back of that fancy van?"

"In the parking lot."

"I knew it."

"It was you who was following the van?"

"Aye."

"You know we almost shot you?"

"I suspected that as well."

"You, woman, you will call Archimedes and tell him to come here." The contempt in her voice was plain. "Terry, would you stay here with her and watch that she does nothing stupid?"

"Of course, dear. Anything for you."

"I will be downstairs." She turned and walked out the door.

Jacqueline took another glance at her gun on the desk top, just before Terry scooped it up and slid it into his vest pocket.

"So, they call you Terry?"

"Never mind what they call me, sweetheart."

"Interesting."

It was seconds later the door burst open and the doorway filled with the massive form of Gordon MacMaster. Terry's hand had instinctively gone for his revolver but halted halfway there when he saw who it was. MacMaster entered with a thunderous laugh and threw his arms around his friend. The questions came hard and fast and were followed up with two more for every one that did not get answered.

Terry halted the torrent of *bonhomie* long enough to remind Jacqueline to call Archie. Jacqueline shook her head and dialed the phone.

Anastasia's former residence was thirty miles from the office of Prometheus Investigations and the time was such that nothing was moving on the expressways and wouldn't be

262

for a couple of hours. Rather than get stalled in the congestion, Archie hung around the crime scene waiting to see what was found. The Investigators wouldn't tell him anything but he thought they might have told Roger something more. They did not. When he left for more familiar ground he felt he had wasted his entire day. When he got to his office he found out he had not.

He saw the van running in his parking spot. Terry had parked a couple of blocks away so the rented Ford was not immediately visible. The woman he knew as Rio was sitting in the driver's seat when he pulled up, but she got out and met him at the back of the van. In response to the questioning look on his face she opened the door slightly, looking around to be certain they were alone. He stuck his head inside and saw the bound and gagged form of the erstwhile gang leader. She told him to go upstairs and speak with Glasgow about payment.

Upstairs there was one last bit of contention. Jacqueline Vandenberg was of the opinion that Terry had done nothing and had voided his contract. She isolated herself with Archie in his office and insisted that Terry had not supplied the objective and that he should not be paid anything. Archie understood her point and began to do some calculations in his own head. The money was in the safe but there was money enough for two contractors.

Archimedes had not survived as long as he had by being stupid. He knew he was stepping into deep waters and that the dangers were manifold. He knew that the sharks that swam in such deep waters were predatory carnivores that would not hesitate to eat him for dinner, but the lure of the liquid currency loomed large. He did not think about why his secretary was being so insistent about not paying the blond contractor. His mind was dulled with painkillers and his eyes were filled with stacks of bills. Finally he took half of the money from the safe and tried to give it to the men in his office. He knew better but he was not thinking very straight.

MacMaster did the talking while Terry sat on the secretary's desk, his feet on the seat of her chair. They made it plain that the negotiated contracts had been filled and both contracts would be paid in full. There would be no splitting of the money; it would be paid as promised.

Jacqueline watched disconsolately as the money she had been expecting to acquire walked out the door.

Chapter Twenty Two
Ice Cream

"It's time, Ice."

"What's it time for, my man?"

"It's time you sent a couple of your associates out for a chilly pickup. Look, I'm not comfortable with this cell phone. Can you meet me in the Steak and Grog on the corner of Sunset and Doheny?"

"In front of the hospital."

"Right. That's right. I need a couple of guys that don't ask questions."

"I'll meet you there. Goodbye." Ice Cream's usual jocular tone and playful banter disappeared. This was obviously business and he obviously took it seriously.

Lunch for the afternoon shift at the hospital always filled the Steak and Grog in the evening, but that was an hour in the past. Dinner hour seemed to end around seven o'clock most days. In all, it was so busy a place that most patrons were innocuous. Visitors to the hospital ate there so the clientele was changing daily. Sean, dressed more like his gardener than himself, had insisted on a booth in the back. Ice Cream sat down with him for a moment, got the location and the instructions and then left. Sean ordered another dark beer afterwards and stayed there for some rib tips.

The small box truck usually carried fresh seafood and the logo on the side said so. It was an insulated refrigerator truck, not usually a freezer, though the temperature could be dropped to the freezing point.

Ice Cream had owned several freezer-refrigerator trucks in his life and had gotten his name from one of them. He had parlayed his unusual interest into a mid-sized delivery business for regional frozen foods. The trucks were not always used for the sweet refreshment of a frozen confection on a summer day. Ice Cream had used his freezer trucks to transport other things as well.

Most of the humans that rode in the back of Ice Cream's trucks did not complain about the cold. D'arniel might have complained but for the duct tape covering his mouth. He was transferred from the relative comfort of the custom van to the all but frozen interior of the truck. He knew he would die in the truck if he stayed there long but he did not. There was no way he could tell where he was when the transfer was done. The van backed up to the truck and he was simply slid across and onto the icy surface.

"Technically, you know, you stole my job."

"Oh, come off it. That is what a free market economy is all about. To the victor belong the spoils. We had no idea you contracted for this job. Besides you got paid in full. We had no idea where you were. Then you show up in that office. Ana tells me you were just about to bang the secretary on the desk. Very unprofessional."

Terry grinned and shook his head. "I told you once, I was just trying to keep her from shooting me. I don't even like that one. I actually have a tasty piece up in Van Nuys. She's been taking care of me.

"I couldn't care less. It's just mixing business, you know?"

"And I could say the same of you. You and Ana are not exactly – what is it? – fraternal, no..."

"That's different."

"Oh, that's different."

"Look, we have more important things to discuss than who is banging whom. Once they determine who was behind the kidnapping, they are going to expect us to extract him as well."

"Extract him or eliminate him?"

"I don't know. It's so much easier for all of us if we just decommission the man and leave it at that."

"I agree. Well, we can always turn it down." Terry waved to the waitress for another beer. MacMaster was buying.

Anastasia was on her way back from the rest room and she ordered another rum and cola. All three of them were heading toward a memorable night though that was not apparent yet. The sun was down and the bar began to fill with softball teams that had played a game nearby. Half of them were exuberant because they had won and the other half were sullen. The drinking was unusually heavy for a Thursday night, but as the liquor flowed the inevitable camaraderie developed. The softball players started taking shots of some sort of German liquor and chasing it down with beer and as is the norm for this sort of thing, trouble followed.

A man attempted to engage Anastasia in drunken conversation as she returned from the ladies room. She told him that he needed to get away from her or she would send him his balls in the mail. He told her he had her special delivery and pinched her on the ass. She nailed him behind the ear with an oversized lipstick tube and dropped him like a sack of flour. The place went wild with laughter except for a couple of the man's closest friends, all of whom were drunk.

One team started taunting the other and it was only a minute later the fists began to fly. One man headed for Anastasia but was met by a couple of large and unfriendly foreigners. From that point, it was on. Gordon and Anastasia battled their way to the door. Terry stood in the middle of the floor and started to punch softball players indiscriminately. They were all dressed more or less the same so he was unable to tell who he should side with. He decided to side with himself and cleared an area around himself. The two teams exhausted themselves in a few minutes and with a sniff, Terry walked out the door. His knuckles were bruised and bloody and his side hurt but he had a huge grin on his face. In his opinion, that was just good old-fashioned fun.

They saw the police cars tearing into the area as they drove off. None of them were in any shape to drive far so they headed back to Terry's room in Van Nuys. Roberta was in a bad mood when they got there. She had been sitting there all day wondering what Terry was up to. He gave her a hundred dollar bill and told her to get them something fancy. She told him to get his new friends to run his errands for him and walked out the door. When she got back Terry was snoring, Gordon and Anastasia were making a lot of noise in the room next door and she consoled herself by drinking half the bottle of Napoleon brandy she had bought.

"Do you know who I am?"

"Yeah."

"Who am I?"

"You're Sean Warren."

"Then you know why you're here."

"I got no idea."

Sean took a drink from the glass in his hand and sniffed. He was wearing a black rubber apron, the kind butchers often used, over his street clothes.

"Your name is D'arniel Jamiel. They call you Bash on the street."

"So? What you want with me? You some kinda pervert, right? You got me down here in this basement buck nekkid and now you gonna fuck me or something?"

"Oh, I'm gonna fuck you all right." Sean turned around and picked up an angle grinder from a shelf behind him. "But don't worry, I'm gonna kiss you first. You took my beautiful little Melissa and raped her and beat her to death. Did you kiss her first?" Sean stared into his victim's eyes, almost surprised that he was going to relish murdering him.

"Man, I don't know what the fuck you talkin' 'bout. You fuckin' crazy. You let me outta here and I just gonna roll back where I came from and I'll never say nothin' to nobody about it. I…"

"Oh no. I paid good money to have you brought here and I'm going to get my money's worth out of you. Now, you are going to tell me who brought Melissa to you. There is no sense in trying to protect anyone else. Tell me now and I'll just kill you. I'll do it quickly and not make you suffer. Fuck around any longer and I will make the Gods themselves cringe at your punishment."

"What the fuck are you talking about man? You fuckin' crazy."

Sean had nothing more to say for a while. He plugged in the angle grinder and started stripping the skin from D'arniel's right calf. The blood and skin flew across the room as the abrasive wheel tore into the soft flesh.

An hour later Sean Warren stood in the shower upstairs washing the blood out of his hair. He could not believe how good he felt, how good it had felt to pull D'arniel's toenails out with locking pliers. The thought actually aroused him and the hot water pouring on his organ stimulated it. He became tumescent thinking about the screaming, the begging, the power he had over his enemy. He grabbed himself and did not even stroke it once before he climaxed so powerfully that it dropped him to his knees. It had never been that good with a woman.

Friday morning came around and MacMaster knocked on Terry's door. He looked surprisingly chipper for all the alcohol they had consumed the night before. Terry was not in such good shape.

The sound of Roberta in the shower covered the sound of the shower next door where Anastasia was bathing. Gordon's hair was still wet from his shower and he had a big cigar fuming between his jaws.

"Rather than be accused of stealing another job from

you, we are going to do this one together."

Terry clenched his fists and heard the cartilage cracking. The scab over one of the knuckles cracked open and oozed a single drop of blood. He shook his head and slapped himself a couple of times. "Is there coffee?"

"Come on, we'll get some."

The tavern next door was not open yet and the nearest diner on Sepulveda Boulevard was a couple of blocks away. Walking helped clear Terry's head. The food was nothing special but the hot black coffee was good.

"So, it took no time at all to get the names of the primary facilitators out of Captain Bash. I called this morning to determine if there was to be a follow up on that operation. It seems there is an organized crime figure who initiated the procedure and he was the culprit."

"Gawd mate, you sound like some bloody doctor. The primary initiator of the procedure was the culprit. Let me get through this cup of coffee before you start with that. I appreciate and understand what you're saying but my head hurts."

"Oh, does it hurt like shots of tequila?"

"That's precisely what it hurts like. So, is the culprit in this state?"

"Yes."

"In this city I suppose?"

"Ostensibly. His precise whereabouts are unknown; he's a sort of shadowy figure, right up at the top of the food chain."

The waitress appeared with the eggs and toast and apologized for having no marmalade. She refilled their coffee cups, took their orders for breakfast in a box and moved on.

Terry's hangover had not affected his appetite and he gratefully dug into a lumberjack breakfast. Gordon had a couple of Belgian waffles with syrup. Neither spoke as they addressed their respective plates.

"It does not look as though we have the time it would take to infiltrate this organization. These are professional men with years of experience. We would be weeks getting into anything like that."

Terry agreed. He remembered how long it had taken to infiltrate the Australian underground and all the tests and tasks involved with advancement. That had taken years and he had not made significant progress until Gordon MacMaster arrived in Sydney. The money would not be worth the time and work involved. The Sydney operation had been personal and the time involved was not a factor. This was business.

The waitress brought the take-out breakfasts and they walked back to the motel. The women ate, Terry took a shower and Gordon called the office again.

About ten in the morning Terry told Roberta he was heading back out and she started to voice her objections. She started to question why Anastasia would be allowed to go and she would not. He cut her off by telling her that Anastasia hurt people and Roberta did not. Roberta told him she would not be there when he returned. Terry smiled and handed her some money telling her to get her hair done.

It was less than twenty miles from the motel in Van Nuys to Archie's office on Melrose. They left the van in the parking lot of the motel and Terry drove them in the Ford. Anastasia was cramped and uncomfortable in the back seat.

In the reception area Terry gave Jacqueline her Glock back. She dropped the clip, saw it was empty and gave him an exaggerated smile. Archimedes Prometheus Chamberlain was a bit grumpy that day. Walking around at the crime scene had caused him no small bit of pain and he was downing painkillers and whiskey to dull the after-effects.

The folder on Archie's desk had pictures of Frank Hicks, directions to his mansion, a list of known associates, a list of offenses he had been charged with, few of which had stuck and a note saying that Mr. Hicks was off-limits due to an ongoing investigation. This had done nothing for Archie's mood.

"Mr. Chamberlain, I want to know for certain that you have contacted no one else in this affair. It is important is that we know of all the participants in this particular passion play. I almost shot an old friend yesterday because I did not know he was on the job or who he was. I thought he was an associate of Mr. Bash and needed an injection of lead. Fortunately for him, he is too good to be suckered into an obvious trap."

Terry lit a cigarette. "I already took one in the course of this job, I didn't need another."

Gordon and Anastasia both looked at him questioningly and he pulled up his shirt to reveal the bandage on his side.

"I will dress that properly later for you," Anastasia said. "In the means time I would like to get back to the subjects at hand. Do we kill him or do we capture him? I am in favor of a long-range rifle slug. We shoot him like a mad bull and then have a feast." She licked her lips and showed both rows of teeth in a savage smile.

Archie could not help but wonder if the woman he knew as Rio intended to stick a spit through Frank Hicks and roast him as well.

"My client wants him taken alive."

"He did not have enough of his blood lust sated by the one we delivered yesterday?" Gordon asked.

"I don't know anything about that. I never saw whatever it is you are referring to, and if it involves illegal activities I will deny it to the bitter end. Nor am I advocating that you break any laws today or in connection with any activities I may contract you for."

"Are you recording this?" Terry wanted to know. "Are you setting us up?"

"No, Mr. Indian, I am merely setting the ground rules. There are things I am unable to do, especially in my current condition and there are things I am unwilling to do. That is why I rely on men such as yourselves, and women of course, to handle them. The trail of evidence led to this man," Archie tapped the manila envelope, "as the director behind the entire affair. Once again, I can't involve myself directly. I need to be clear of the affair. If the LAPD links me to his disappearance they'll hang me. Remember, this man is the reason I'm limping around like a cripple. I want to see him pay as much as almost anyone."

Nobody seemed to think it necessary to threaten Archie. He had a firm grasp on the situation and understood the ramifications of betrayal. When they considered it, the double contract on D'arniel Jamiel had been more Jacqueline's doing than Archie's. He had been laid up in the hospital at the time.

"And now, to the pertinent business at hand." Archie got up and hobbled over to his wall safe. The painting masked the combination while he opened the door and retrieved a canvas bag with stacks of bills in it. Some of the money was cut into three piles and arranged across the face of the desk.

"Is this enough for a down payment?"

Both Anastasia and Terry looked at Gordon for acknowledgement. He reached out, picked up a stack leafed through it thoughtfully. He set the money back on the desk and picked the file back up.

"According to this outline, we are looking at one of the most senior members, if not the most senior member of the Mafia in Los Angeles," Gordon said. "I do not wish to debate whether or not the Mafia exists as such. I refer to the people who do the things that others do not do. I do not wish to debate whether or not I and my associates are to be included in that particular subset of society, it is clear that we are. As such, we have some small knowledge of the intricacies and difficulties involved with approaching this matter from the ground floor. The upshot of this is that we can do this job and very, very few others can. Securing a gang banger from Carson was child's play in comparison. This will not suffice for the munitions required let alone the expertise. I implore you not to insult us in this manner and to give us the credit we deserve for the skills we possess."

"I will need to contact my client and confer with him. I am certain there is something we can do that will be satisfactory to all parties involved. It may take longer than you would like since my client has some previous engagements, out of town."

"Confer my satisfaction with the previous arrangement and make certain of his. If necessary we will meet with him personally."

"No, Mr. Glasgow, that will be, not only unnecessary, but impossible. Call me tomorrow to finalize the details. I'm assuming I can expedite our business."

"'Til tomorrow then."

The three filed out the door and out of the office. Jacqueline refused to look at them. Anastasia asked why Terry had not satisfied her already to which he replied he might yet do so.

Back in the office Archie muttered, "Fucking highbrow prick."

Chapter Twenty Three
Bash

The two couples spent the remainder of Friday and the entire weekend playing at being tourists. They wandered around Hollywood and visited the beaches. Anastasia and Roberta went shopping in some of the high priced shops on Rodeo Drive where they got a chilly reception. Terry and Gordon got drunk in a bar very close to Venice Beach and passed out in the sand, giving Gordon a sunburn. Anastasia and Gordon rented surf boards and made fools of themselves in the water while Terry and Roberta rented skates and rolled up and down the streets until Terry's wound threatened to rip open. The couple sat outside a tavern on the edge of the beach and watched a glorious sea of tanned flesh. They saw Gordon and Anastasia frolicking at the water's edge. Terry thought to himself that he had never seen her looking so normal. He had thought about being with a woman like Ana but knew he would miss the moments such as this where she allowed herself to loosen up. He placed his hand over Roberta's and she smiled broadly. She had gotten over her pique at being left alone all day. The thought that he would be leaving her soon bothered Terry slightly; he could not tell if it would bother her. They did not make it to San Francisco that weekend, though they all said they wanted to.

Monday rolled around and the telephone call invited them back to the office where they got a mixture of good news and bad. Archie refused to admit that his client was Sean Warren though Terry had deduced that almost immediately. Archie merely indicated that the client was out of town for the week and though he had authorized the increase in payments, he was not on hand to physically deliver the remuneration. There was no way Archie was going to put up his own money; he refused to be any more involved than he was. This was already way beyond his normal purview.

Taking pictures of cheating spouses was his usual bread and butter and this job had already landed him in the hospital. Sean was due back in LA in a week and things would move from there.

The trio decided they would do some preliminary work and research, preparatory to any sort of physical action. For instance, they needed to know if somebody was already watching Frank Hicks and the extent of the indicated investigation. The FBI must be monitoring him at some level and probably the DEA was as well.

Anastasia found out that Frank owned warehouses in Los Angeles, San Francisco, Atlantic City and Belhaven, North Carolina. He owned partial interest in a shipping line that brought goods from China and another that brought fruit from South America. The file was by no means complete as far as the business opportunities that Frank had availed himself of. He was involved with a plethora of projects and owned several shell companies that routed investments in every possible direction. The gangster's file indicated he owned a mansion in Bel Aire where he kept his wife but he was rarely seen there himself. When he visited the mansion it was by his own private plane flown from Santa Monica Municipal Airport to the San Rafael Airport North of Bel Aire. He sometimes piloted the plane himself but he also had a pilot on call twenty-four hours a day. The plane was obviously on call for other runs as well, but was inappropriate for flights to the East Coast.

Frank had been indicted several times for racketeering, money laundering, smuggling and drugs, but it was hard to make any of it stick. Frank stayed away from the actual products of his nefarious activities. He would throw his girlfriends out if they did drugs and he never touched drugs himself, though it seemed common knowledge that he was a kingpin. Heroin from China and cocaine from South America were suspected but had never been proven. Raids by the DEA or local drug enforcement task forces had always come up empty, as if he had been warned of the raids before hand. Marijuana was almost a non-issue since it seemed inevitable that it would become legal in California. The drug enforcement agencies had more important things to do.

What was not as apparent from research was the fact that Frank was buying trucks, farms and vineyards. The indictments had taught him to distance himself further from his concerns so he had set up a shell company to finance the trucks. Their avowed interests were wine, grapes and juices from the San Joaquin Valley orchards and vineyards, but their dedicated trailers were specially modified. Frank's latest endeavor would flood America with marijuana. He was smart enough to know that as goes California, so goes the country. He knew that within a decade of the ratifying vote in California, the entire country would be smoking legal weed. The pharmacological concerns would fight it tooth and nail, as they had been for years, in conjunction with the insurance companies. They both knew marijuana was going to take huge bites out of the drug companies' profits and the insurance company executives would be suffering from the commensurate decrease in kickbacks from them, as well as accident payouts. In this instance, big business was at odds with the will of the American people and Frank was betting the people would win. He was poised to become the world's greatest producer and supplier of marijuana; he just needed a little more time to set himself up properly. Congressman Cabot was supposed to be going along for the ride. Frank had underestimated the politician, but he did not yet know that.

Security forces seemed a big issue. Frank never traveled alone. He kept an entourage of very bad men about him at all times and he insisted they remain in top shape. None of the fat, pasta-stuffing Italians of his grandfather's generation need apply. He wanted mercenaries, Navy Seals and Army Rangers. The lazy street thugs could do some of his dirty work but they would not be protecting him; for protection he demanded the best. When he traveled, it was by armored car.

Frank's wife and children were kept in grand style in the Bel Aire mansion: private schools, tennis, boating and riding lessons. It was the most obvious way to attack the man, but it was a path without honor. Gordon and Terry both subscribed to a code that would not allow women and children to be used as hostages. It was this code of honor as much as the money that had led both men to accept their current assignment as well as the previous one. Their targets were most often men without souls and while it was not a prerequisite for their services, it was certainly an additional incentive. Terry in particular was haunted by the pictures of the young woman, brutalized and murdered.

Frank's office, facing Cabrito Drive in Van Nuys, was a fortress. It had been a school, built in the early 1950s and declared obsolete in the 1990s. With the lower windows bricked up and bars on the remaining windows, it took on the look of a prison. The building was made safer by the railroad tracks on the other side of Cabrito drive and the fenced industrial buildings all around. Though by no means impregnable, the office would have required a larger team than was on hand to assault. Even if they had the team, there were other considerations as well. Taking down a man such as Frank Hicks would cause a lot of other men to be upset. In addition to the turf war, there would be very powerful and long-established men who would want revenge. The task required more subtlety than a SWAT attack. It was, after all, to be an extraction, not an assassination.

Terry was astounded that the newspapers seemed more interested in who was dating whom in Hollywood than who was killing each other. There was no mention of the explosion in Carson, no mention of the ongoing gang war in the same area. Sean Warren's interviews, intended to showcase his new movie, were entirely focused on the death of his girlfriend, and the media was ruthless. He was relentlessly pummeled by painful and personal questions to the point of sprouting tears on not one but two separate shows. The tears themselves became news and he got more bookings on New York shows. It was speculated that it was an act, but Sean had never been the dramatic type of actor; he had always been the action figure so his performance was not easily dismissed. They seemed to forget that he was a classically trained actor, and a good one.

When Anastasia logged onto an internet site at the local library, Terry was even more astounded at the banal and tawdry exploitation of this starlet's hair style and that actor's favorite brand of shoe. Real news needed to be searched individually and sometimes was not to be found. California's wealthy younger generation lived in a dreamland of digital images and adolescent interests that staved off the reality that was the streets for so many. Even the old aphorism 'If it bleeds, it leads' no longer held true unless it was on video. If an incident was recorded, it became national news on the social websites and quickly became news as well. If a girl got jumped in a bus station and some security guards did not break up the fight, it would never make a ripple. If the same incident was recorded and sent out on the internet, Happy Riviera on FOX News would be launching an investigation within hours.

It became easy to believe that the people did not care about what happened to the so-called minority populations in the South and East Los Angeles areas. Only the most dramatic of stories could make the front page. Sean Warren's fiancée had, of course, but none of the gang war victims even rated a byword. Women could become famous by marrying a rich man and thereby become richer while those who dedicated their lives to helping the disadvantaged were disdainfully ignored. The self-promulgating culture of glitter and wealth was like a tsunami washing everyone's lives before it and only those riding the crest of the wave were visible.

Frank Hicks tried not to ride the crest of the wave. His business was best kept clandestine and he knew it. Congressman Cabot, on the other hand, could not help but be front and center. His reversal of opinion and resultant vote on the marijuana issue thrust him into the limelight and got him almost as much press as the current Hollywood sweetheart's breakup. He needed to defend himself daily and did so with a veteran politician's panache and slipperiness. He did not say anything when he spoke publicly and did not reveal anything when questioned. Congressman Cabot had been reelected by the discrediting of his competition and had two years to regain the public's trust on the matter. The public wanted marijuana legal and Cabot could not stonewall them for long.

There was no way of linking Hicks and Cabot without being on the inside. A comprehensive examination would have led to the theory that they had something in common but that would be the extent of it. They deliberately insulated themselves from each other in the public's eye. Cabot was not insulated from his peers, however. He was hammered in public and in private for his vote. The governor himself called Cabot up and deftly told him that the next vote would be affirmative or there would be real trouble. The nature of the trouble was not clarified.

Late on Monday, Planned Parenthood got back to Terry and Roberta with a clean bill of health. Terry threw his box of condoms in the trash and they enjoyed each other the way sex was meant to be enjoyed, over and over.

By Tuesday morning the last of the gang members that D'arniel Jamiel had turned on was dead. In the basement of Sean Warren's mansion all gang loyalties were expunged in wave after wave of blinding pain. He had given up the names and addresses of every man who had touched Melissa, the man who had driven the car, the owner of the house where the murder had occurred and the boy who had delivered pizza while her ordeal was going on. Most of them did not survive the weekend, none lived past midnight on Monday. D'arniel had not survived that long.

Ice Cream handled the affair from a distance, through Coco Ali Marrakech an intermediary and made a good piece of money in the process. The money was not the main benefit of the action, however. Ice Cream was guaranteed a part in all the Sean Warren films and so, his career was ensured. By Tuesday morning he had photographs of the carnage as proof. As long as there was no way of connecting him to the murders, he was clean. By eight o'clock Tuesday night, Coco Ali Marrakech was wrapped in a sheet, weighted with chains and thirty feet underwater in the Stone Canyon Reservoir. Ice Cream was counting his cash and grinning like a fool.

"The job we have running is a complex and dangerous move, luv. I think it might be time to part ways for a little bit."

"You gotta be kiddin' me, Terry. You think you can fuck me like a sailor all night and then tell me to get lost in the morning?"

"Well, that's not really what I was…"

"What was it then? 'Cause I seem to remember getting down all night an' I'm sore this mornin' so tell me what that is. I know I didn't imagine it."

"You're not reading it the way I'm putting it out. I'm going after a very bad man and I'm concerned for your safety." Terry had expected some resistance but figured it was best for both of them if they parted ways for a little while. He wasn't trying to dump her, though it certainly seemed that way to her.

"Shit! I been walking the streets in South Central and now you're concerned for my safety? I think you just puttin' me back on the street. You had your fun with the black ho and now you gotta go."

"That's not it at all."

"Never mind. You go do what you gotta do and I'll be gone when you get back. I thought... I thought we had it better than that." She had threatened to leave before and had not, but Terry had not asked her to go before.

"Look. We're going after men that make Bash look like a cockroach. It's a complicated job and I can't afford to drag you along. Look, take the keys to the van. I'll set you up with another hotel room and you can wait there until we're finished with the job. After that, maybe I can help you get back in school or something, but until the job is done I need to be alone."

"What about her?"

"Rio? She's a professional. That woman scares me and she should scare you. She is unlike any woman I have ever met and, no offense, you will never be in the same category as she is. She's in a completely different class."

Roberta snatched the keys to the van out of Terry's hand and stalked out the back door. By the time Terry had gotten to the passenger door, it was locked. The drive wheel of the van left a long black streak on the asphalt of the parking lot as she left.

"She is not going to cause us problems, is she?" Anastasia was standing just outside the back door to her room with a long thin cigar smoldering in her mouth. Terry had not seen her standing there.

"No. I don't think so."

"It would be unfortunate if she did."

Terry thought briefly about the way Anastasia was playing in the water the day before, splashing and laughing.

282

The face she projected now was the polar opposite; a frigid, grinding determination that reminded him of a glacier.

Gordon MacMaster stepped through the door with a quizzical look on his face.

"I gave her the van," Terry answered the unspoken question.

"She didn't seem to think it was sufficient compensation?"

"Ah, I think she was beginning to make plans for the future."

Both Gordon and Anastasia looked down, nodded and stepped inside. The cigar smoldered on the outside window sill while the woman smoking it got a bottle of Coca-Cola from the refrigerator.

"I would have felt much better if we had put a bullet in her. I think Kingston is soft." The statement was delivered without emotion.

"I understand. Think though, that was a contact from a different operation and she was culpable, even though her part in the operation did not actually lead to its conclusion. I hope she remembers that," Gordon continued. "As for Terry being soft, he probably would find it difficult to decommission a woman he had been banging on all night."

"It would cause me no problem," Anastasia said coldly.

"I know that, my sweet little poisonberry tart. That's why I love you so much."

"Did you not hear him say he let her pimp live as well? Very sloppy."

"Well, maybe she wants to run back to him. I cannot fathom the labyrinthine twists of a woman's mind. I am but a man and Heaven has no rage like love to hatred turned nor Hell a fury like a woman scorned."

"A wise man said that."

"William Congreve. A playwright I believe, sometime in the late seventeenth century." He did not seem as concerned as she was and went back to examining the topographical map spread before him.

Anastasia digested her thoughts for a moment and calmly said that she would be happy to finish the job if Terry was unable or unwilling. Then she stepped out the back door with her bottle of cola and retrieved her cigar.

Chapter Twenty Four
Tourists

"No, listen to me. This one pays much better than the last. The buyers are from Detroit so there's no problem with local ties. I explained that you had done the Babbage job with panache and style, and they thought you might be the right man for the job. But they also have other connections and may want to use them instead, if I cannot secure results within their time frame."

The blond man stood on the strip in Las Vegas with the payphone to his ear, listening. He had been banking on a phenomenal run of luck that had turned suddenly and cost him a lot of money. It was not that he was broke, far from it, but he did not feel like losing any more money and could see no other alternative but to get back to work. He was wearing a white suit and wide-brimmed white hat, bought with his initial winnings, and was slightly upset that it was getting dusty. Jacqueline had stopped speaking, but Jerry Kragon had nothing to say.

"So, you'll take the job?"

"I'll consider it. I'm bored and need a little recreation. I expect you will have collected all the pertinent information for me to work with so I do not need to sanitize multiple locations?"

"I'll have everything you need. I'll see you at my place in a couple of days?"

"Decidedly. I'm looking forward to it." The man hung up the phone. He could be in Los Angeles in no time.

Jacqueline set the receiver of the phone down and looked across the table at George Arridagio. The restaurant was perfect for meetings because there was a telephone at each booth. George was much more at ease working with this woman than he had been working with Frank Hicks. For one thing, Jacqueline did not insist he strip down to his underwear as Frank had. He could not help but wonder how the congressman had slipped away and met with this woman without his knowing it. He knew everything Henry Cabot did; he was the one who made the congressman's schedule. George knew this was a test for him. He was astonished that Cabot had allowed him to come here and set this arrangement up. He took it as a sign of confidence and trust.

"That settles it then. He will be here for this job tomorrow or the next day. There is no changing your mind now.

"Remember, Mr. Arridagio, nobody knows anything of this and you are not to involve anyone else in any way. Discussing this with anyone will not only void our contract, it will create a new one. Am I making myself clear?" Jacqueline's gaze captured George's.

Suddenly George was less comfortable with the woman. He sighed deeply, broke eye contact, and looked at his hands. He had never envisioned this sort of thing when he took the job with Henry Cabot. Politics is devious enough, he thought, without the added stress of gangsters and prostitutes, let alone hit men.

"I will require the entire sum up front. My man does exceptionally good work and I will stress that there is a time frame to work under. You will be reading about Frank Hicks' unfortunate demise within days."

Jacqueline slid over and out of the booth. She did not allow herself a smile until she reached the street. One way or the other she was going to walk out of this affair with a pile of money. She did not have enough of a conscience to let it bother her which side of the equation paid her. It would not matter to them either, she thought with a smile, they would be dead. She knew it was a dangerous game, but the players did not know each other. Killers did not ask questions, they killed people, and that was what she wanted to see. She had tried to play the game with Terry Kingston and Gordon

MacMaster but those men, it turned out, did know each other. What were the odds of that? It must be astronomical. It wouldn't happen again.

"I forgot to ask him what to do with these boxes of clothing." Anastasia's lip curled with distaste.

"We can keep them until tomorrow in case she returns." Gordon looked up from the file. He was chewing on an unlit cigar.

"I say we burn them. They are probably diseased."

"Nothing in there you want to keep for yourself?"

Anastasia Viuda launched into a torrent of invective in a mix of Spanish, Portuguese and English that was almost impossible to follow but the sheer inventiveness of it caused Gordon to smile broadly. She finished up by calling down the curse of the mountain kings on all the whores in California so their pimps' balls would freeze and fall off. Then she asked God to forgive her and took a long drink of tequila straight from the bottle. By this time Gordon MacMaster was grinning like a monkey. She wanted to move the boxes of clothing outside, but he insisted that it was not practical because if any whores got murdered the clothing would look like evidence, even if it were not. He suggested they put the clothing in the Cadillac and she refused saying they were probably full of bugs that would infest the car. So Gordon taped the boxes more carefully and sat them in the corner. Terry had gone to a local hardware store for lye and soap to sanitize the location as they moved out.

On the surface it was easy enough to explain Anastasia's distaste for a prostitute's wardrobe, but Gordon could not help but ask himself if there was something else involved. After all, Anastasia and Roberta had gone shopping together, eaten dinner together, drank together and there had been no hint of the Argentine woman's distaste. It was not until the woman was gone that Anastasia's true feelings came out. This was so unlike her, she was not given to hypocrisy, that Gordon sat and contemplated it carefully. He searched his memory for clues to her motivation before asking if she was somehow jealous of Terry's little fling. This time there was nothing but scorn in her voice. She outlined how she had been humiliated by being required to keep company with a prostitute and how she had only done so for the sake of the mission. Then she told him she was going to take a shower. He reminded her that she had already taken a shower and she said without looking at him that she would take another.

Inside the shower she began to shake as if she was freezing. She reached up in the steaming cascade and felt the little scar on her scalp and remembered the dream, the memory that she had suppressed almost her entire life. The matron slapping her and telling her she must never cry, the operating table where they changed her life forever and the traumatic event that had brought the memory tearing back into her mind like a runaway train. Her legs weakened and trembled and she sat on the floor of the shower with the hot water streaming over her head and she found herself back in the jungles of Brazil, chained to the floor of a cabin. She smelled the rain, the garbage, the diesel oil, and the fumes of the rotting jungle floor. And she saw the man who had just raped her standing over her, pissing on her. She screamed.

Gordon MacMaster burst through the locked door as if it was cardboard. In his hand he carried the loaded Serbu assault shotgun. He had not thought before reacting or he would have known there was no danger in the bathroom. He heard his woman scream and he reacted instantly. The door burst open and then the sliding glass door to the shower. The thing that came out of the shower looked so little like his woman that Gordon almost shot it. His first impression was of a harpy from the bowels of Hell. Her face was contorted with all the hatred of a hundred generations of slaves and her hands were the clawed talons of a demon. The apparition was so dramatic and so patently furious that Gordon punched out with his left fist and smashed his woman in the eye.

Anastasia went down, sprawling back into the shower, but came right back up again. This time it was not the disorganized and ferocious attack that had first ensued, this time it was the calculated assault of a trained fighter. She struck at Gordon's balls, his throat, his nose. Fortunately for him, Gordon MacMaster was as fast and as well trained as his woman and was able to fend off her assault. He dropped the shotgun, grabbed her wrist and twisted it over her head. He grabbed her other arm with his bear-like hands and held her immobile from behind. He backed to the wall to keep her from heel-kicking him in the groin and growled her name in her ear.

She fought a few seconds longer, wild-eyed and out of control, but she could not escape his grasp. She soon collapsed into his embrace and after verifying that she was not faking, he laid her on their bed. The episode reminded him of the effects of the device implanted in her head when she was young. This was different though. The implant had increased her strength and speed but had not turned her into a raving lunatic. It had turned her into a killing machine but whatever had affected her this time had driven her mad.

The device had conferred the benefit of warning Anastasia of impending danger as well. It caused a buzzing in her head prior to the adrenaline rush allowing her a short bit of time to excuse herself from a dangerous situation before going into all-out attack mode. As soon as Gordon remembered this, he grabbed the shotgun from the bathroom and checked the windows front and back.

Terry had liked the motel because the rooms all had a front and back door and the parking lot was away from the road. Gordon agreed, as long as there was a team of at least two to watch both sides. Watching the road and the parking lot alone was impossible. He walked from one to the other to try to catch a glimpse of the danger that had set Anastasia off but he saw nothing. There were no police, no men in dark suits with bulges in their jackets, no street thugs with whatever street thugs favored these days; it was just another sunny California day coming to a close.

Anastasia did not sleep long but sat bolt upright after ten minutes. Now Gordon had both windows vulnerable while he watched to see what she was going to do. She ran her long fingers through her wet tangled hair and asked, "*Dios mio*, what in the name of God just happened?"

Gordon moved to the back window and peered between the casing and the shades. He could still see nothing but had learned to respect the unusual abilities Anastasia had possessed in the past. The device had been short-circuited by a stun gun and had been quiescent ever since but stranger things had happened.

"Don't move, love. You've had an episode of some sort," Gordon said quietly. "We were discussing the boxes of clothing and you started having a go at every prostitute in the country and you went to take another shower as if discussing it had made you dirty. In the shower you started screaming so I came in like a fool to rescue you and you damn near clawed my eyes out."

"So you have seen something? There is danger?"

"No. Nothing so far. I was recalling what triggered your episodes in the past and was attempting to remain vigilant. Either the thing in your head is coming back or you're having some kind of flashback. Did you do a lot of drugs when you were young?"

"Drugs? No. Not drugs but there is much that I do not remem... I... *Ai, Dios mio*. I am having memories from my past that were not there before. I have forgotten much that is painful and *degradando*, uh, embarrassing. In the jungle. Things were bad in the jungle. No, do not touch me. I need to take a shower."

"That was how it started before. You got in the shower."

"I need to take another shower."

This time there was no flashback, no memories of torture or tragedy invaded her mind. The hot water brought her back to reality instead of divorcing her from it. She stepped from the shower feeling better than she had in a long time. She did not even towel dry but stepped dripping into the bedroom where her man was still alternately looking out the front and back windows, and announced that she was ready for hot, sweaty love. He looked at her incredulously, certain she was going mad, but he had never turned her down before and would not disappoint her this time either.

Chapter Twenty Five
Flashback

MacMaster and Viuda had not slept well the night before despite the epic sex. They had each spent time watching and listening for something that had not appeared, and before morning came, they decided it was time to find a different place.

When Roberta Cunningham knocked on the door to Terry's room both assassins jumped for a weapon but calmed down quickly once they saw who it was and told her to come inside.

"Damn, woman! That big fucker blackened your eye?"

"I cannot say it was his fault. I think I did this for myself."

"I wonder how many times I heard that. Shit, I said it myself." Roberta's voice changed. "Velvet put a beatin' on me and I said, 'Oh, it was my fault. I didn't cook his eggs the way he like 'em'"

"Roberta, I tried to kill him."

Roberta looked in Anastasia's un-swollen eye and saw nothing but cold steel. The assassin had a pistol stuck in her waistband, and there was a shotgun peeking out from under the pillows. Roberta ran her tongue around the front of her upper teeth and said, "Remind me never to go for a three-way with you two."

Gordon barked laughter and Anastasia smiled briefly, stepped over to her, took Roberta's jaw in her right hand and kissed her on the mouth, slowly, savoring the moment. It took Roberta's breath away. It also furrowed Gordon's brow.

"Where's Terry?" Roberta asked after a few seconds of embarrassment.

"I'm sorry, dear, he went for supplies," Gordon said. The truth was that he was not sure where Terry had gone that morning.

"Is he hiding from me? I can't believe it."

"No. He had some things to pick up."

"Y'know, I could help with whatever you got going. I'm not just a... a sex object."

"Where are you staying, I will send him over there."

Roberta was crestfallen. She had been angry, but she had expected Terry to be there that morning. She grabbed a box of clothes and headed for the van. She could not help but think that it was typical for a man to use her and then ride off into the sunset. It should not have affected her as much as it did; it had been this way all her life. She had hoped this one was going to be different, but she knew, even when they were together, that it was unlikely to be so. She took a deep breath, accepted the situation and prepared to move on. She wrote the address of the long-term motel she had taken a room in and left without further conversation. A single tear ran down her cheek as she drove off. She could not decide if it was Terry she was crying for or herself.

"What was that all about then, eh?" MacMaster was unwrapping a cigar.

"What do you mean?"

"I mean yesterday you did not want to sleep in the same room as the woman's clothing and today you were kissing her on the face. Maybe you did not get enough last night and wanted a little strange this morning. I could have left the two of you alone."

"It had nothing to do with that. Last night, in the shower, I had a dream, I think."

"I think you were in the shower all day yesterday."

"I was back in a place I do not wish to discuss, with men that are no longer alive. I learned things there that I had wanted to forget, but I did not, could not forget. There are many women in the world who find themselves in situations they did not want. These women are slaves and they will always be slaves. I can be away from this... this thing, but I cannot forget it. This woman reminds me of it. I pity her."

"So?"

"So, *nada*. I needed to remember and I needed to cry for them. I remembered."

"But you did not cry for them; you attacked me instead."

"I apologize for that again, my love. It will not happen again. Let us clean this location and move on. I am no longer comfortable here."

In addition to changing locations that day, Terry got in touch with Archie and told him they needed a team for an action related to the job they were after. Archie suggested he work with a group of retired police officers, causing Terry to chuckle. Retired members of the law enforcement community would not be appropriate for the sort of work he would be doing. Archie told him he understood and contacted Sean Warren. Sean put him in touch with Ice Cream.

Thursday was wonderful for Anastasia. She discovered that without Roberta at her side, the clerks in the upper-class boutiques fawned all over her. She eventually determined that they thought she was the wife of a Mexican drug kingpin and said nothing to disabuse them of that notion. She bought an expensive, matching white outfit with a wide hat and high heels, a close-fitting vest over a blouse and a short skirt. She actually had a woman ask her if she was a movie star after the woman took her picture. The woman was less than thrilled when Anastasia took the camera and threw it under the wheels of a passing truck. To prevent the tourist from calling the police, she slipped her some hundred dollar bills and gave her the name of a popular Mexican soap opera. The woman was distracted enough for Anastasia to slip away without further incident.

Dinner was a complex and ornate affair at an

overpriced restaurant and they went dancing afterward. Anastasia ended up with a blister from the new shoes, but they both went to bed in fine spirits in an upper-class seaside hotel. In the morning, they drove to San Francisco.

The drive on the Golden Gate Bridge was an experience, but it was that, or go all the way around the bay to get to Bel Aire. The mansion on Midden Lane was guarded by a strike team and a wrought iron fence. Midden Lane itself was a dead-end, accessible only through a gate and clustered with cameras. It was not an impossible target, but it would take a coordinated team. There had to be a better, easier way. The couple conferred and neither of them liked the prospect, so they continued out of the neighborhood and this time actually did travel around the bay to rent a hotel room in Vallejo. Their best chance to take Frank Hicks alive looked like the airport, but that was a highly exposed area. There were too many witnesses at the airport, too much security and too many innocent civilians that might get caught in the crossfire. Also, there was no good escape route from the airport.

Gordon visited the docks on Saturday morning while Anastasia went to the library and spoke with a young man who was more than willing to help her find a method of checking on incoming freight from certain companies. Both Gordon's visit and Anastasia's probing were methods of familiarization since they did not expect to find anything coming into the San Francisco docks. Frank might have had a home in the area but his freight all off-loaded in Los Angeles. The deeper water port was friendlier to the container ships that departed from the Asian coast. A project was underway to deepen the San Francisco Port's draught capabilities but it was slow going. The water depth in Los Angeles was 35 feet and San Francisco only managed 26 feet.

Both adventurers found the Coast Highway to be a lovely drive. They stopped from time to time to soak in the ambiance. They were disappointed when they reached the populated areas again.

Anastasia was in the Platt branch of the public library on Victory Boulevard, using the account she had created in San Francisco, when she picked up on a shipment to a shell company that did no actual manufacturing, warehousing or distribution. Quing-Xai Distribution was to receive a container full of decorative fan-fold paper streamers on Monday. It would be picked up by truck and delivered to a warehouse in Ontario. The entire arrangement looked false since there was no final destination listed. Most of the containers that came in from overseas were loaded onto rail cars and sent east by train. The containers were off-loaded in rail yards in Kansas City, Saint Louis, Chicago and points east. The cost of warehousing colored paper would never allow a return on investment and transporting it anywhere by truck would yield the same results. If you looked at this sort of transaction all day, five days a week, you might never consider the situation shady but Anastasia picked it out after studying manifests all day. Looking deeper into the load she found it was authorized for an armed guard. That container held more than fancy paper. She took down the number. This would be the first load they hit. If it was nothing then they would hit another.

When she found her lover he was reading Huckleberry Finn and was surprised at how quickly she had picked out a suspect. Neither of them had known how long it would take and had expected to be looking for days. He slid the American classic back into its spot on the shelf and the two of them left for champagne and sorbet in a nice restaurant. The container would not be moved until Monday. The day had been long and filled with a useful education.

There was no competition in the stamina department on Sunday. Anastasia could run longer and farther than her paramour regardless of the surface. She would never have tried him in the strength arena, but she left him behind in the long run up the beach. She told him he needed to give up cigars but he said he was having nothing of it. She beat him on the way back down as well but not by as much. He seemed able to pull reserves of energy from somewhere within his muscular frame.

"This is it, a semi coming from the docks to somewhere. The cab will be locked and the tanks will be full so the driver won't be stopping. We need to take it at a stoplight or something but we can't have Joe Shmoe seeing us and calling the cops. You read me, mate?" Terry was talking to Ice Cream.

"Piece of cake. You think this is the first time something fell off the back of a truck in LA? What's the cargo? What kind of truck? Is it a reefer?"

"No, mate. I told you, off the docks it's one of those convertibles you pull off the wheels and put on a ship. It should be Chinese AK47s hidden behind a front of some dollar store stuff."

"So, it leaves the docks and goes where?"

"I can't be sure yet. It may not be going where the manifest says it is, which is the town of Ontario. You know a regular warehouse won't be uncrating automatic weapons, but they may unload them. It's best to hit the truck before it gets where it's going."

"That's why I'm asking. It doesn't sound like you thought this one out very well. Maybe you need to go back to your friends and ask them where, when and what. I already know why." Ice Cream was still uncertain he wanted to work with his new associate. There was any number of things that could go wrong even if this was a legitimate job. He would not be going along on the job anyway. He had a new career in the offing and working with Sean Warren would get him other parts as well. He was insinuating his way into the Hollywood crowd where the real money was. His gangster days would soon be history.

"I'll know all that tomorrow. I need to know if you are ready to make a lot of money and move a lot of product on Monday. If I need to find someone else, or do it alone I can do that, but I would rather you helped." Terry was only half bluffing but the plan would be changed too much if he had to do it alone.

"If this turns out to be a set-up, a jack-up or a fuck-up, you get the first round, right through the heart. I'll kill you like a cockroach. You got me, mate?" Ice Cream's cold and aggressive attitude was actually a relief to Terry. It helped convince the Australian that he was dealing with a serious man. He still had concerns, however.

"No worries, mate. This is a tip of the iceberg. Play this right and we end up rich and living next door to the Beverly Rednecks."

"Play it wrong and we end up dead."

"There is that possibility."

"When do we roll?"

"Monday."

Chapter Twenty Six
Hijack and Attack

The run up to the Oscars and the annual ceremony had been tense and Sean had not wanted to go. He had not been expecting to get an Academy Award for a sequel but had been invited to the ceremony and that was almost as good. He had seen many of his old friends and received the condolences of a long line of A-listers. Even the most jaundiced of the Hollywood crowd had given him credit for getting back on the set and finishing what could not be considered that important a film in his career.

The 767 set down at LAX on Sunday night with Sean Warren in the first-class compartment. He was sick of fielding questions about his poor dead fiancée. He had been so tempted to tell the entire viewing audience that he had already taken hooks and hot pokers and tortured the soulless bastard who had done those horrible things to her. He had cried openly on more than one late night, New York, television show but he could not let them know that the tears were the bitter tears of retribution and that he was having men murdered, in LA, in the name of the same cause.

A large automobile was waiting for Sean when he got out of the terminal. He did not want a limousine since it would attract too much attention. He was traveling more or less incognito and he had attracted little attention as he made good his escape. His lawyer was in the driver's seat of the automobile, and they drove up the San Diego Freeway and East on Melrose. Sean spent a short time on his phone, telling someone that he was back and that he had already made the financial arrangements.

When they reached Prometheus Investigations, Sean stayed in the car and his lawyer delivered a suitcase to the office. They stayed there no longer than they needed to and no one could identify the action star as having been there at all.

Monday morning was another perfect California day, despite the earth tremors that had punctuated the night. The power grid had not been affected, there had been no falling buildings and the morning commute was as annoying as everyone expected.

Terry was pleasantly surprised by the apparent professionalism of Ice Cream's crew. Once they had a job in the works, they took it seriously. They had arrived early and looked fresh. Nobody was flashing weapons or bragging. Nobody had asked unnecessary questions. Now they were in various locations along the route between the docks and Ontario International Airport. Frank's warehouse was between South Bon View Avenue and South Campus Avenue, west of the airport. The warehouses themselves were never subject to investigation. The stock going into the airport was where the scrutiny was concentrated.

The watchers first picked up the truck as it came off the West Ocean Boulevard Bridge on Monday Afternoon. Gordon was disguised as a photographer trying to get the perfect picture from Santa Cruz Park. He finally got the picture he wanted and made a phone call.

Golden Park is just north of Santa Cruz Park on the west side of Route 710. Anastasia Viuda put down the novel she was trying to read and picked up her field glasses. There it was, heading north on the expressway. Within seconds she was in Terry's rented Ford and pulling onto the concrete.

Route 710 hits Interstate 10 in East Los Angeles proper and to drive a truck through there in the middle of the afternoon could only be considered madness. Most truck drivers would have pulled off in a Whale Mart parking lot or some deserted street and let the volume of traffic diminish for a while. It takes a hardy left leg to keep working the clutch over and over again in bumper to bumper LA traffic.

The driver of this particular truck was paid to drive straight to the warehouse from the docks, without deviation. He was paid extra for his efforts and his passenger was on hand to make sure there were no side trips or piss breaks.

It was simple to shadow the truck north on Route 710. The Ford was innocuous and traffic was heavy. Once Anastasia got directly behind the truck, she tucked in tight to the bumper and the driver could not even tell she was there. She could have jumped on the back bumper and opened the doors if she wanted to and nobody would have been the wiser. By the time the truck reached the exit for Route 10, it had picked up a couple more tails as well. Ice Cream's crew was on the job. Hijacking a truck in bumper-to-bumper traffic would be easy, the driver couldn't go anywhere without plowing through the cars around him like a rampaging elephant but the thieves had the same constraint. They could jack the truck and wait for the police to arrest them or they could play the waiting game.

Instead of traveling east in the wake of the truck, Anastasia headed west on Route 10. She had other business to attend to and had completed her part of this operation.

Frank's warehouse was well over thirty miles east on Route 10. In rush hour traffic it took the truck two and a half hours to reach the exit onto southbound Euclid Avenue. Four blocks south of the expressway, on the corner of Euclid and Fifth Avenues is a stoplight. By the time the truck had reached that stoplight, low-riders and pickup trucks had surrounded the truck.

Terry watched from the driver's seat of a Ford F150. The bed of the pickup truck had a ladder rack on it and the bed was full of drywall tools. It was good cover in any residential area during the day. He watched the truck in question pull up behind a minivan that was sitting at the light. The light turned green but the minivan did not move. After a few seconds a woman got out of the vehicle. She was not what might be expected to emerge from the driver's seat of a minivan; this was no soccer mom. She was black and wore a halter top that barely covered her enhanced breasts, a mini skirt and high heels. She wobbled back to the door of the truck, looking a bit distressed and a little drunk but not dangerous. Against the wishes of his bodyguard, the driver rolled down his window to talk to the woman.

As the window came down a pickup truck made a right turn from Fifth Avenue and stopped adjacent to the cab. A tall, thin black man threw off a canvas tarp that was covering him in the bed of the pickup truck and stood with a sawed-off double-barreled shotgun in his hand. The window had not opened all the way and it shattered as the buckshot from both barrels chewed through it. The shot took out the driver's face and head as well. The blast did not kill the bodyguard, however, who immediately thrust the barrel of his own shotgun out the window and discharged a deer slug into the chest of the attacker. The man with the sawed-off double-barrel was thrown from the pickup and onto the pavement. The guard opened the driver's door and kicked at the dead driver, trying to push him out of the seat but his seat belt was still attached so he sagged, half out and half in. The seat was not clear and the door would not close. Before he could release the seat belt a spray of 9mm slugs chewed into him, turning his torso to hamburger.

As quickly and efficiently as possible, the attackers released both bodies from the cab of the truck and left them lying in the road. A block back, both lanes of southbound Euclid were blocked by an old Chevy station wagon. The man who jumped into the gore-soaked seat of the truck had a commercial driver's license and had driven every sort of truck, van, crane and earth moving equipment there is. The woman moved the minivan and the truck was once again mobile. That truck was the only thing to get through that intersection for a couple of minutes and any good Samaritan who may have wanted to follow the truck was dissuaded by the crew that blocked it. When the crew dispersed, they went in every direction.

East on Fourth Avenue brought the truck back to Route 10 and it headed east again until it turned north on Route 15 and then off onto Foothill Boulevard and into an empty lot on the corner of Etiwanda Avenue. There was a different truck idling in that empty lot. Two men dropped the legs on the hijacked trailer and disconnected the cab. The driver pulled the cab off to the side and did not even shut it off, just evacuated, locked up, jumped into the new cab and hitched it up. The two men hooked up the wires and air lines, raised the legs, and then jumped into the new cab. This truck had a sleeper so they were hidden from view as the driver headed back toward the expressway.

Back on Euclid, the fallen comrade had been tossed into the bed of one pickup. Terry had been watching from the side street, ready to run interference if necessary. It was not. Of course there were witnesses, drivers trapped by the station wagon in front of them and the median that separated the northbound and southbound lanes. One or more of these well-meaning individuals had called the police but said officers were unable to reach the scene until well after the action was completed. The station wagon was found to have been stolen, and it was the only vehicle left on the scene by the time the police arrived.

"Sydney?" The Scotsman's gravelly brogue sounded expectant.

"Aye. Project Backgammon is complete."

"You have maintained your integrity, I assume?"

"If you mean the continuity of my skin, I will say yes."

"Does it look successful?"

"I've not got a look at the load, but it had the armed guard so I assume it was important. I'm coming to join you now."

"You know where I will be."

Terry hung up and headed west. Instead of the Hollywood Freeway he took Route 5 north; he was not sure why he did it but knew that predictability bred disaster. Traffic had eased considerably and he turned west on the Ventura Freeway after Griffith Park and north again on the Hollywood Freeway.

"I don't know what's been done, but someone has disturbed this anthill in Van Nuys." The tall blond man was watching through a high-powered scope from across the railroad tracks.

"We have an unexpected issue," replied the woman's voice on the cell phone.

"Jacqueline, my dear, you know I don't like unexpected issues."

"I understand, but it is unavoidable. It seems that you are not the only man interested in the subject today."

"Perhaps I should let them take care of the job and be on my way."

"No, this is impossible. These men are contracted to extricate the subject."

"Extricate?"

"Is that not the proper word?"

"I suppose. So, they are here to take the prize from under my nose?"

"Precisely."

"Will there be any issue with sanitizing them when I sanitize the location?"

"That is what you have been paid for, right?"

"Assuredly. I assume, however, that you have no better information on the object's exact location, so that I may be hunting snipe here."

"No. The subject is probably there. Just do what you

were contracted to do and you'll get the remainder of your fee upon confirmation. As I explained before, time is of the essence and even more so now. If you fail to eliminate the subject and he is extricated, I cannot be responsible for the repercussions."

"Very well. I do not like doing this on such short notice, but I will be in touch." Jerry Kragon punched the button to hang up his cell phone. The purse on this job was too juicy to allow another man or team of men to beat him to the wire. He had not intended to move so quickly, but he was ready to do what needed to be done. It looked as though it needed to be done right then and there.

Frank Hicks was beside himself. He had been sitting in his office monitoring the tracking device installed in the container that had come into port the week before. It had not been off-loaded until Sunday and had been set on a frame and hitched to a truck on Monday morning. Customs had examined the paperwork and the agent in charge that day had rubber stamped its contents and certified it for input. Frank had been elated when he saw the signal leaving Terminal Island in the afternoon. He knew there was an armed guard in the cab.

It was the second bit of good news that day. First had been that the customer had finally gotten the purchase price together for the women. All his schemes were coming to fruition. He had lit a cigar and cracked open a bottle of fine champagne. He had a thirteen-year-old Philippine girl engage herself under his desk as he watched the truck's slow and steady progress through Los Angeles. The girl was gone and the cigar was smoked by the time the truck took an unexpected turn. It was almost to the warehouse when it headed off in the wrong direction.

As soon as the truck started away from the warehouse, the claxon sounded and men began to suit up everywhere.

Half a dozen dangerous men in business suits took off from the warehouse in Ontario. Though they would undoubtedly be too late to facilitate aid, half a dozen men were deployed from the school-turned-office building in Van Nuys. Four men scrambled from a high-end stereo shop in Gardena. Five men put down their forks and left their dinners uneaten in La Verne. Half a dozen men left the historic business district of Orange and headed east. It turned out that the only direction that was not covered from Ontario was to the east and that was where the signal was headed, down Route 10 toward Arizona.

Frank could not believe that anyone would be stupid enough to jack his shipment. It was understandable that someone would want to. It was a huge load of China White, one of the biggest that had ever come into America. It was worth billions and on top of it being protected, the idiots were driving the load east on Route 10. Everybody knew that the immigration checkpoints were set up there.

Frank smiled tightly. He had immigration people on his payroll. He got on the phone and roused one man from bed. The man usually worked the night shift and had only had a couple of hours sleep but snapped to when Frank Hicks called him. Within minutes he was dressed and heading for the checkpoint. More phone calls verified that the men from Ontario were already on the expressway, just ahead of the men from La Verne. That put ten men immediately on the trail with half an army coalescing behind them.

"No, I am certain that he has not left the structure. To be sure I have not seen him at all, but the report does indicate that he has quarters within the building. He has come to Los Angeles and this is his headquarters; I think it is safe to assume he is in there."

"I'm surprised at you, Rio. We both know where

assumptions will lead us."

"Glasgow, my love, if we expect to pull this operation off in such a limited time frame we are in need of such, how-you-say, leapings of faith? I am objecting to this but I will always be there for your back."

"Aye," he breathed, sounding like a condemned man exhaling his last cigarette.

"Half the guards are gone. The parking lot is almost empty. I have the two men on the east side in my scope. The wind is minimal. The shot is a hundred and fifty meters. I could take his sunglasses off without hurting his nose if I wanted."

"Yes, dear, I know. Are they done scurrying about?"

"It appears so."

"Then I'm going in." MacMaster sounded fatalistic.

"I repeat, that is a very bad idea. At least wait for Terry."

"Take the shot, woman. The man is here and I'm going in."

The school had been built after the rail line was decommissioned, and then sat unused after the railroad was revitalized by growing industry in the area. It had been perfect for Frank Hicks' needs because it was surrounded by warehouses, and he immediately refitted it for other uses. The ground floor literally could not be seen from any street. Of course there had been questions regarding the need for so many armed guards on the premises, but the local police had been paid off and Frank had dirt on more than just Congressman Cabot. The congressman was almost like a cherry on the top of his sundae.

The problem with limiting the view from outside is that you also limit the view from the inside. Surveillance cameras had been installed, but they are only as good as the bored men observing them, and day after day of the same nothing happening leads to complacency. It was not like a casino, where something is happening every minute, it was more like staring at a wall where observing a spider capturing a fly would become front page news. Normally two men manned the cameras, a rotating position, but today one of them had been sent after the disaster in Ontario. Although that event was miles away and he would never reach the hijacked truck in time, it was Frank's decision, so the man just went, along with half the office security staff.

Gordon MacMaster came around the corner of the warehouse, and waited the one second it took for the man Anastasia shot through the neck to realize he was dead. The other man did not have enough time to react before she shot him in the chest as well. MacMaster strode to the door, recognizing that he needed to work quickly. A .357 round makes a lot of noise so the Scotsman was wearing automatic electronic headphones. The door was card activated but had never been replaced from the time it was a school. The school windows had been bricked up, but the doors were still glass panes set in aluminum frames. He shot the door and it erupted inward in a spray of lethal fragments. A guard stepped out of a cubicle inside and MacMaster shot him as well. The man on the outside, who had been shot in the chest, sat up gun in hand. He had on a bulletproof vest under his uniform but it did not save him. As soon as he sat up Anastasia put a rifle round through his head.

Gordon had turned off his telephone to prevent it from sounding at an inopportune time, so Terry was unable to reach him. Anastasia's phone was right in front of her on the roof of the warehouse. It vibrated once and she pushed a button. Terry was calling to tell her that he was still nowhere near the location but that he was on his way. She told him that Gordon had already gone in to secure the objective alone and that he was not going to make it out without help. Terry snarled a curse about chowder-headed Scotsmen, thanked her and went back to driving. Without missing a beat, she shot the one man who was running down the front of the building from the middle entrance. She had seen that the guard on the side had been wearing a bulletproof vest and she did not have a clear chest shot but took him through the shoulder. The trajectory of the round was downward. A soft round might have been deflected by the scapula or a rib but the full metal jacket on the rounds she was shooting ensured penetration. She took him through the heart with one shot. The other man who had been guarding the front door stepped through that door and out of her line of fire. Nobody came around from the other side of the building, even though she knew there were at least two men on that door as well. Those men were out of her line of fire.

Now nothing was moving outside the old school. The silencer on her rifle had prevented unwanted attention from the warehouse she was lying atop, but it had not kept the guards from knowing they were under attack. The magnum rounds made certain of that. When the whole thing was over, she vowed to herself, she would punch Gordon MacMaster in the face with everything she had. After all the hours of lectures she had heard from him on the art of preparing for an operation, he had gone in the building like some kind of Hollywood cowboy. If he made it out alive, she was going to make him suffer for this.

Inside the air-conditioned structure, MacMaster found that the ground floor rooms were all storage space. He was there to remove a man, not to go through the inventory of who knows how many years of God only knew what. The distraction caused by the stolen truck had worked better than could have been expected. He breathed a momentary thanks to Anastasia's powers of observation. There was no way he could have picked out the proper load to hijack without some extensive training he had not had.

Ducking into what had been a classroom at one time and blocking the door open allowed Gordon to hear the two men trying to sneak down the hall. They should have taken off their shoes. The sound of their footsteps rang on the tiles and was reflected by the ranks of metal lockers still adorning the walls. The electronic headphones amplified the soft footsteps. The men no doubt saw the door blocked open and swung in, pistols first, but had no target. MacMaster had secreted himself behind a pile of boxes full of files and records of some kind. He heard the expelled breath of the killers. They had both been holding their breath as they came around the corner. As soon as he heard their outward breath stop he stepped out from behind the pile and fired both pistols, two shots each. Four shots in an old brick classroom would have deafened anyone and Gordon got a new appreciation for the electronic headphones that had amplified the sound of the men's breathing but cancelled the sound of the gunshots.

There was no doubt that his presence had been announced. One of the two men on the floor was still moving slightly so Gordon shot him in the head for good measure. He was a good-sized man and his blood spattered bulletproof vest was large enough to cover MacMaster's chest. He availed himself of it and then reloaded his revolvers.

Peering around the corner of the door jamb and down the hall that ran the length of the building, Gordon saw a flash of movement at the far end. Someone was heading up the stairs. Both ends of the hall had glass guard shacks but there had been no motion from there. Logically he could have expected three guards to be on the far end of the hall but there had been no movement from that end during his initial assault, so he deduced that they were either waiting for him at the far end, coming around the outside of the building or had moved upstairs.

Three sets of stairs split the hall, one at each end and one in the center. The center set coincided with the short hall leading to the front door. It had seemed as if the two men at his feet had come from the front door. With a revolver in each hand, MacMaster stepped into the hallway trying to keep his armored chest and back in the lines of fire but there was no movement and no sound came from the enhanced earphones.

The guard shack at the front door was empty. There was no movement on the ground floor. Moving quickly MacMaster ran down the hall to the door he had entered.

Chapter Twenty Seven
Shortcut

Terry was driving like a teenager that had just stolen his first car. Traffic had eased some from the peak of the rush hour and was flowing better now. He could not believe that MacMaster had elected to go into the office building alone. He would never have sanctioned anyone under his charge doing the same. It was the act of an amateur or some cocky fool who fancied himself a one-man army. It might have taken a couple of days and a few phone calls but they could have gotten a tested assault team in time. For that matter, a bit of cash could have hired a Mexican-American gang that would have come with an arsenal already in place.

A new Lexus was driving too slowly in the right-hand lane and cars were passing it as they could. Terry took to the shoulder and floored it. The truck was no hot rod but it held its own as drivers honked their horns, yelled and made obscene gestures. Terry was immune to their comments on his rude behavior. He had a place to go and was not about to let a little thing like traffic law prevent him from getting there as fast as possible.

An inspiration came upon him as he approached the railroad tracks, still tearing down the shoulder of the road. The tracks had a service road that ran down the length of them. The trail had no name and was not officially a road of any sort. It did not cross the bridges but it led directly to the Cabrito street offices of Frank Hicks, with some notable blockages along the way.

Terry tore off the Hollywood freeway at the Burbank Boulevard exit, pounded up the dirt access road the maintenance crews used and raced down the cinder track bed, lava rock flying from his tires. From the exit to the building was just under seven miles. Only a madman would even consider taking the run but Terry felt more than a little mad.

The first bridge came at Buena Vista Street and without missing a beat Terry jammed the brake, then the gas and tore the back end of the truck around so he ran almost directly at the rail. The front tires held as he bounced the driver's side wheel onto the ties and he pounded his way down the tracks. The truck was beating itself to pieces on the railroad ties and tools were flying from the back of the truck.

It was incredibly difficult to get the beaten truck back off the tracks at the far side of the bridge and the front wheel was wobbling badly as he raced down the maintenance track. Terry did not think the truck would make it to the office building this way. When he approached the bridge at Hollywood Way he knew the truck would not survive a repeat of the stunt. He saw his opportunity just before he hit the bridge and cranked the wheel to the right coming down off the elevated track and into a construction yard, through the fence and onto West Empire Avenue.

The truck looked like a junkyard nightmare enveloped in a cloud of concrete dust with the wheels wobbling, the ladder rack swaying and the horn blowing. He could not help but run the stoplight at the speed he was going and he did not look back. Empire Avenue had few through streets since it followed the berm of the railroad tracks; the through roads cut under or over the tracks. West Empire turned into a paved service road after a couple of miles and Terry chose to continue down it, though he suspected it would dead-end before long.

The service road ended at Vineland Avenue, adjacent to the Burbank Glendale Pasadena Airport. A short jog north, a cut through the hole in the fence under Vineland Avenue and Terry was back in business. The residential structures were gone now and the truck plowed its way down the dirt path between the tracks and the warehouses. A couple of loading spurs had to be negotiated but he made better time than he could have on the streets.

The trail ended again at Sherman Way and Terry tore down the embankment, under the tracks, over the curb and into the northbound lane, heading south. He only ran a hundred feet before swerving into the center lane, roaring across the southbound lane, over a curb and onto a dirt lot. The curb was the last call for the truck's damaged front axle and it folded over sideways. The back end of the truck rose its own length in the air and came crashing back to earth sending the ladder rack flying into the road. Tires smoked and squealed as commuters came to an immediate panicked stop.

Bob Feeniman did not stand a chance as he screamed to a halt in his F350. He was an able construction supervisor and ready to confront employees who thwarted him, but he could do nothing when Terry Kingston tore open his door, pulled him from the truck and threw him face first in the street.

Terry turned the truck around, all four rear tires screaming and smoking. He roared off to the south, keeping the tracks in view. Southwest on Sherman Way led to north on Whitsett Avenue and then off onto Raymer Street. Once again he was paralleling the tracks but now on the south side of them.

Raymer Street ended at one of Los Angeles' huge storm drains. There was a slat fence covering the edge that was no match for an F350. The one-ton truck pounded down the angle of the storm sewer but was unequal to the task of riding up the far side. Halfway up the angle, it rolled over twice and ended up on its side. Terry Kingston came flying out of the top door, actually the passenger side, and ran up the angled concrete wall. At the top, he found himself on the other piece of Raymer Street. Warehouses dominated the area and diesel engines throbbed their lonely idle song of waiting. The first one he came to had no one in it and no trailer attached. Within seconds, it was in gear, and Terry was roaring bobtailed down Raymer Street. The road came to end but the increased ground clearance of the semi truck cab was more than a match for the railroad tracks, and the bridge at Woodman Avenue was in the rear views in no time.

The cell phone was almost impossible to operate as he pounded down the tracks but he managed to pull up Anastasia's number. He told her he was coming and blew the air horn so she could get a fix on him and lead him in.

The upper floor of the building contrasted with the stark utility of the lower floor. The ranks of short, stacked lockers were replaced by full sized metal locker doors and the ubiquitous half-glass hardwood doors were opaque with curtains. The floor was still ceramic tile and the ceiling still sprouted fire extinguisher nozzles, but the walls above the lockers were freshly painted a pleasant light blue rather than the industrial green that dominated the walls downstairs.

The true folly of his brash attack began to sink in as Gordon stuck his head out of the stairwell for a brief second and pulled it back again. With his enemy on the alert and an unknown number of assailants in unknown locations, he had set himself an impossible, suicidal task. Then he heard the sounds that did not make any sense to him. He knew he was alone in his assault yet he clearly heard the pfut of a silenced weapon that was not directed at him. There was no accompanying concussion as a bullet contacted the wall or floor. A bullet fired into the door of a locker would have woken the dead. The sound was repeated twice, this time followed briefly by a scream that was cut short by a third iteration of the pfut. Someone with a silenced gun was systematically eliminating the inhabitants of the second floor. There was a joker in the deck.

Puzzled and challenged, Gordon stuck his head out and pulled it back. There was no one in the hall. There must be access between the old classrooms other than from the hallway. Dialing up the sensitivity on the headphones brought little help. He could hear no footsteps. Whoever it was that was firing the weapon must be on the far end of the hallway. There seemed no way of telling which side of the hall, however.

Holstering one of his revolvers, MacMaster stepped into the hallway, up to the first doorway, opened the door wide and stepped back. No bullets tracked him, the room seemed empty. Stepping inside confirmed what he had thought he saw; the classroom had been converted into a bedroom with silk and velvet on the bed and Persian rugs on the walls. There was indeed a door leading to the next classroom, on his right as he entered, partially blocked by the open door. Unlike the hallway door, this one was a full, two-panel hardwood door. Gordon was about to open the door when he caught a slight movement of the covers at the side of the bed. He turned to fire and saw the terrified face of a girl peek out briefly and then pull back in under the bed.

There has been endless debate in the camps of soldiers and mercenaries about the efficacy of leaving witnesses alive. The consensus of opinion is that it is a bad idea and that sanitizing the area is the best way to prevent any involved from telling tales, but the ethical dilemma had never been fully clear one way or the other. In the heat of battle, it is common for men to shoot first and ask questions later and only the most dispassionate of killers can actually choose for themselves. MacMaster's mind flashed to a different day in a much different place where he had been driven to the brink of madness and had butchered every living thing in a small village. He had tried since then not to succumb to that ravening, overwhelming bloodlust.

The tiny whines of the girl where barely audible, even with the enhanced hearing the headphones had given him. Gordon thought briefly that the girl was probably used to hiding as he grabbed the mattress and tossed it off the bed.

The little girl looked Asian but with a slightly darker cast to her skin than most Chinese. He did not know enough about the inhabitants of Asia to pick out an original country of origin. The little girl froze. She looked about ten years old. MacMaster put a finger to his lips in the universal sign for silence then pointed at the open door. The child needed no second invitation and ran out the door and down the stairs.

Opening the door between the rooms revealed a classroom, just as it had been when it was in operation. The children's chairs were made of wood and the desks were separate, with hinged tops for access to the interior. The teacher's desk was clear except for a bottle of sexual lubricant. A large blackboard dominated the front wall and somebody had written *I will not suck cock in class* on it a number of times. There was no one in the room. The door to the next room was locked. Gordon could hear whispering behind it but not clearly enough to tell if it was male or female. Then he heard the smashing of glass down the hall and a male voice protesting that he was only the janitor. It did not seem to matter as the silenced weapon he had heard before silenced the protests.

Halfway down the long hall, a wide stubby branch of hallway cleft the building front and back, dividing the floor roughly into quarters. Whoever was going room to room and killing the inhabitants would not be able to avoid coming out into the hallway once he had sanitized the quarter he was in. Gordon ran the remaining distance and ducked into the branch that ran toward the front of the building. There was a large window, the central stairs at the end and doors on either side. The south branch included what looked like the entrance to the upstairs janitor's closet. Putting his back to the window, he waited.

The silence rang in the old school like a bell, much worse than any noise. Always a patient man, MacMaster had visions of his objective lying in a pool of hot blood. He already regretted the imprudent invasion which would have been difficult enough without the addition of a wild card. Whoever else was sneaking in here represented as much a danger as the men who were already here, and there was now a question of when the men who had left might return. Crouching and sliding down the wall that had no lockers on it, the Scottish assassin reached the corner and came around before he could second guess himself.

The man was tall and blond. He had a handkerchief tied around the lower half of his face, obscuring his mouth and chin. He looked very much like Terry Kingston which caused Gordon to hesitate for a critical second. Anastasia had told him to wait for Terry but he had not known how far off the Australian was. He felt certain the guards had dashed off in response to the truck being hijacked but here was a walking contradiction. Then the blond man turned his silenced pistol toward the Scot, and Gordon knew that he was mistaken. For a fraction of a second, MacMaster saw the angel of death.

Both men fired simultaneously though the noise of the Smith and Wesson revolver overpowered every other sound in the building. Neither man shot the other, and the bullets ricocheted down the hallway as both men dove for cover.

Thoughts raced inside Gordon's mind, trying to make sense of the scenario. He knew the man he saw was not one of Hicks' thugs. This man was killing everyone he ran into. He could only conclude that he was here for the same purpose as MacMaster, to secure Hicks. Was he alone or was there an entire team in the building? If there was a team, MacMaster was in a lot of trouble.

The headphones itched under Gordon's ears where he would have been growing a beard. He smiled as he realized how much of an advantage the headphones would give him. He peered around the corner and down the hall. There was no one there. He could not be sure what side of the hallway his new opponent had gone to, but there was no time to waste. The man had already been through the southwest quadrant, the one on Gordon's left, so that was where the Scotsman ducked. He saw the body of a man sprawled on the floor. The man had greasy looking gray coveralls on, but he was not moving and was probably dead. There was not much blood and no blood spatter. Gordon concluded that his opponent was using a relatively small caliber gun, probably a 9mm. He had not been able to tell in the hall. The silencer had confused the issue.

Next to the janitor's body was a push broom. Gordon picked it up, glanced back down the hall and saw nothing. He listened carefully and heard nothing. He could not wait. For a second he considered evacuating the building and leaving Frank Hicks to the tender mercies of the other intruder but he quickly decided not. This was his job and his payoff and he would be damned if someone was going to come in at the last minute and get his payoff.

Stepping quickly across the hall, Gordon swung the business end of the broom into the window of the first classroom door. Nothing happened. He looked inside. It was an office with four old-fashioned wooden desks topped with computers. There did not seem to be anyone inside. He did not enter.

When he shattered the next window he received a reply. The aged, varnished wood of the door exploded outward, demolished by a shotgun blast. Nothing moved for a second. Gordon stood still, waiting to hear the rack of the shotgun loading another shell but the sound did not come. The next sound was that of a door being thrown open and banging against the wall behind it. There was a scream and another shotgun blast erupted but not into the hallway.

MacMaster's mind raced but to a single purpose this time. Two rounds with no rack meant a double-barreled shotgun, empty now. Somebody had been shot but there was no way of knowing who. The blond man or an accomplice had beaten him into the room. There was only one way to pull the job out of the crapper now, and he took it. With a revolver in his left hand he swung around the door jamb and fired two shots into the room, in the general direction he assumed the door between the rooms was. Then he jumped back. There was no return fire.

Though the door had a large hole in it, and a shattered window, it was still locked. Gordon could not risk reaching through it into the interior, so he ran down the hall to the next door which was not locked. He had seconds or less. Maybe it was already too late.

He burst into the old classroom and through the smoke saw his blond opponent's silhouette through the doorway between the rooms. He had a silenced pistol in his hand, pointed downward. Without hesitation Gordon shot the man in the back. The figure spun around and up against the wall but never went down. Gordon felt two slugs take him in the chest like sledgehammers. The bulletproof vest saved his life but did not stop the rounds from kicking, hard. He shot the man again, this time in the chest and the figure went down.

Inside the room, Frank Hicks was on the floor, trying desperately to reload a double-barreled shotgun with one hand. His right arm hung limply at his side, dripping blood on the floor.

"Frank," Gordon said. "Your only hope of survival is to come with me."

Frank did not acknowledge that he had heard the Scot and Gordon quickly enough realized that he had not. The gunfire had all but deafened the man. There was no time for sign language. MacMaster holstered his revolver, grabbed Frank Hicks by his lapels and hauled him to his feet, knocking the shotgun aside. He threw an arm around the small of his back and propelled him into the other room, out that door and down the hall. When Frank got halfway down the stairs he collapsed on the landing. Gordon threw him over his shoulder, grunting at the pain in his chest and bodily carried him to the ground floor and out the front doors.

Outside there were two separate sirens competing with each other. Someone had called the police from one of the buildings nearby and a patrol car was pulling into the parking lot with its lights on. Another was a couple hundred yards behind it. There was the deep foghorn sound of a diesel truck's air horn coming from beyond the parking lot.

The first patrol car slid sideways as it came to a halt and the two officers jumped out. One had a shotgun in hand, the other was running forward howling for MacMaster to set the victim down and get to his knees.

"There's a madman with a gun in there," MacMaster cried and continued toward the idling patrol car.

The lead officer pulled his pistol and ran to the doorway of the school; the one with the shotgun racked a round into the chamber and took over yelling that the Scotsman was to put the man down. He would have been better off responding as his partner had. Anastasia saw the cop with the shotgun as an immediate threat and shot him through his right shoulder. The man collapsed as the second cruiser pulled into the parking lot. Suddenly an apparition from some mechanical Hell pounded off the bed of the railroad tracks, belching diesel fumes, howling its air horn and sending cinders flying. The trailerless cab of a truck, its engine and transmission screaming as its drive wheels left the ground launched itself into the parking lot like some modern leviathan. It bounced once as it contacted the ground and lurched into the front end of the second police cruiser, tearing the front end off the cruiser entirely and smashing it into the other patrol car. It did not stop until it had pushed its load of twisted steel into the corner of the brick building. The only officer in any condition to do anything began trying to yell instructions to everyone to get down on the ground.

Anastasia was lining up her barrel to take the final officer down when the door shattered behind him and he fell, face first on the tarmac. The tall blond stranger that Gordon had shot in the chest was standing in the doorway with his silenced pistol in a two-hand hold. A split second before he shot either Gordon MacMaster or Frank Hicks, Anastasia Viuda shot him dead center and dropped him.

Terry jumped out of the crumpled cab of the truck, a little worse for wear, and followed Gordon as the Scot carried Frank Hicks out of the parking lot and shoved him into the trunk of the Cadillac.

MacMaster admitted he had overreacted when he saw so many leave the parking lot. He thought the building must have been all but deserted. He had not counted on the number of people who drive to work together. Then he remembered the girl who had been hiding under the bed and the whispering voices in the locked room. He asked if anyone else had left the building but Anastasia said that she had seen no one else leave. It seemed unusual that a man as careful as Frank Hicks would share a building with prostitutes or worse, slave women. Perhaps they were his personal harem. If the girl had not left, perhaps she had no idea where to go. Human trafficking from Asia was a huge issue on the West Coast. He shook his head and decided that it was in the hands of the authorities now. Frank Hicks, however, was in their hands.

A telephone call reached Jacqueline at Prometheus Investigations. The secretary did not seem surprised they had gotten their objective already and simply told them that the proper parties would be contacted and that she would call them back.

Jacqueline sat at her desk, grinning. In her locked desk drawer was the other half of Jerry Kragon's commission, the congressman's money. With the other team having secured Frank Hicks, Frank would disappear like smoke in the breeze and that money was hers. Sean Warren was remarkably free with money after the team had delivered him D'arniel Jamiel. His lawyer had delivered another case of money. Archie had never seen that case. And then there was Homer's stash in the safe deposit box. Before the week was over Jacqueline was going to have quite a nest egg.

After the good news had been relayed to Archimedes, Jacqueline went back to her desk. He was already calling

Sean Warren who was ready for the call. To say he was happy was the wrong description; he was in more of a conflicted mood. He was about to do something inhuman, something that would have physically sickened most people, but he was unaccountably anticipatory about the act itself.

Sean hung up after getting the news from Archimedes and called Ice Cream. Ice Cream was watching the news and asked Sean if he had seen the latest. Sean turned the television on, the story had shot through the local channels and gone up the news channel rankings as high as CNN. The whole country was watching the footage of the forty-five young Philippine girls being taken from the damaged building. The newscast included the truck that had smashed into the building and the four police officers that had been injured. They were still uncertain as to how many other men had been killed and with normal American Puritanism, the regular channels did not show the carnage though they did show some of it on Univision, the Hispanic station. The Hispanics had less compunction against broadcasting dead bodies.

There was no mention of the fact that Frank Hicks owned the building though. Officially it was owned by a shell company that was a subsidiary of another shell company. The trail had not yet been traversed but the story was so big, at least until something bigger knocked it off the top, that Congressman Cabot would not be able to quash it.

Sean was a little confused but his black friend assured him that the story was relevant and it was going to put Frank Hicks on the FBI's top ten most wanted list. He had gotten sloppy and it was going to bite him. Sean told Ice Cream that it already had and that he needed some butter and white bread delivered to the mansion. He wasn't sure what brand yet but it would be a prepaid delivery so he needed to be sure the check cleared. There was no ambiguity in the message for Ice Cream who simply said he had a truck ready.

The California Highway Patrol was all over the Cabrito Road location. They knew they could not stall the FBI forever but they were doing their best to sanitize the location before federal agents arrived. With typical distain for the local departments, they did not interview the downed officers immediately. All four local officers had been taken away by ambulance, two with gunshot wounds and two with head wounds from bouncing around the interior of their cruiser.

The local precincts were buzzing like hornets. Their men had taken the bullets and they wanted some retribution. They wanted the shooters alive, unlike Congressman Cabot's hand-picked cover-up team. One of the downed officers told a close friend on the force that the shots had come from the east side rooftop across the tracks. The local police were in there like lice on a stray dog, asking questions, hampering production operations and pushing people around. The local captain was pushing for surveillance camera footage when he got a call from a young officer who told him about a parking ticket he had written. There had been a Crown Victoria, the same model the Highway Patrol used. He had initially thought it was a stakeout, but when he found no one in the car he had written a ticket. The car was registered to a rental agency on Melrose. It took less than an hour to get a couple of detectives on the job. When they found out who had rented the car, Detective Broward, a friend of Archie's, went to Prometheus Investigations while his partner got the immediate location of the vehicle.

It was Archie's worst nightmare come true when Detective Broward started asking about the Ford. It was the discretion of the operators that had been emphasized when he hired them, and he had repeatedly emphasized that discretion was the name of the game. They had gotten sloppy and now the entire operation was going to blow up in his face. Conspiracy to commit murder carried a five-to-nine year sentence but the actual term was irrelevant. Archie would be living with the men he had been putting in those cells as a thirty-two year veteran of the force. He would never survive the first year.

Broward had known Archie for fifteen years. Tales of Archimedes Prometheus Chamberlain had been passed and embellished by the departmental personnel for years so he was already a larger than life figure when Broward joined the department twenty years earlier. Many of the legends were exaggerated and Archie was the first to tell you that, but there had been much to admire about the man when he was on the force. The fact that he was now in the private sector had done little to damage his reputation. Until now.

It was obvious to Broward that Archimedes was being evasive. He did not need to be a detective to know that the PI was hiding something. Finally Archie admitted that he had hired a third party to watch Frank Hicks' Van Nuys offices. He had already seen the film footage so he knew enough to say that he suspected the man of running a child smuggling and exploitation ring, but Broward wasn't buying it. He knew that private investigators only did things when they were paid for it; they did not do the LAPD any favors, even if they were former members themselves. Archie refused to tell who the client was and insisted that he thought the rented Ford had gotten stolen.

If there had been nothing but a hit-and-run or a breaking-and-entering charge, Detective Broward may have let the whole matter evaporate right then, but there had been citizens killed and four cops were injured, one of which might die. This was bigger than anything he had ever been involved with and he was sinking his teeth in and not letting go.

Archie was becoming desperate. He would have given up his sainted aunt to stay out of prison, but he had so little actual information that he was beginning to wonder if he really could get a deal. He did not know the real names of the assassins. The only man he really knew to be involved was Sean Warren and given the nature of the job, there was no way to prove it. Money was exchanged, but all transactions were liquid; there was no paper trail. There was really no proof of his story, and he had really been no more than a facilitator. The affair that had gotten Sean's fiancée killed had even been covered up to some degree. The case was still open but there was almost hope of the police finding the perpetrators. No one in law enforcement knew that the job had been done privately and Archie could never tell them without promises of immunity. Until more information came out or suspects were captured, Archie clammed up. He had seen too many people get in trouble by talking too much.

Detective Pardee, Broward's partner, called him on the instant access phone. They had a location for the Crown Victoria. Broward told Archie that he was not to leave town making himself sound like some prime-time television detective. Broward must have forgotten who he was talking to. No sooner was he out the door that the PI was on the phone with Terry Kingston telling him to dump the car and to meet him on Osborne Street by the Hansen Dam Bike Path.

Terry relayed Archie's message. There was no discussion, no questions and no dissention. Gordon opened the trunk of the Cadillac and Anastasia took a can of lighter fluid from its glove box. Frank was force fed a pint of water to keep him from expiring in the trunk and the lid was closed. Rather than to try going back down the way they had come, they left the Ford burning behind them and headed further north. The cluster of bungalows in the shadow of Sugarloaf Mountain had no name and was not large enough to hide anything in. Gordon turned the Cadillac west at Lopez Canyon Road and began the climb up the mountain. There was a switchback at the top of Sugarloaf that encompassed almost 180 degrees and they were about to drive down the far side of the mountain when Gordon saw Indian Canyon Road.

Indian Canyon Road was unpaved and did not look as though it was well used. In a wetter climate it would probably have washed out at the switchbacks, but in Southern California it was still a viable roadway. There would be no high speed antics on a trail such as this, but there would be almost no traffic and it would not be watched as a first choice of fugitives. If there was a roadblock they would be forced to shoot their way through, there was no turning around, but as it was, there was no difficulty.

The Cadillac was halfway down the mountain when the Detectives and State Police reached the raging fire that had been a Crown Victoria on Kagel Canyon Road. They immediately radioed for a roadblock on the south end of that road and one on the south end of Lopez Canyon Road, but Indian Canyon Road was not on the map. If they had taken a second to pull up the electronic version they would have seen it, but they stuck with the laminated paper version and missed it. Gordon piloted the Cadillac past the roadblock, almost within sight of it. A low rise of dirt prevented the police from noticing their vehicle as it inched its way back to Route 210. Instead of pulling onto the expressway, they took the underpass and went down Osborne Street to the bike path. They were less than two miles from the hornet's nest of helicopters and police cruisers that was swarming the burning Ford.

Chapter Twenty Nine
Fallen Star

Hansen Dam had been built in 1940 to control floodwaters. It was not the usual kind of dam in that there was no water against it and nothing running down the spillway. It was like a bridge to nowhere except when the spring rains hit and even then it was much too large a dam for the little bit of water it needed to contain.

Ice Cream had never been to Hansen Dam so it was no surprise that he looked confused when he pulled into the bike path parking lot. The massive structure seemed to sit alone, like a modern pyramid or a monument to some forgotten past.

Terry Kingston was sitting on a guard rail smoking a cigarette. The lot was lined with cars adorned with mounted bike racks. There was no sign of the van that Ice Cream had picked up Bash from.

Terry moved to the passenger window where Ice Cream was sitting. The question was simple. Did the up and coming star have the agreed upon payment?

Ice Cream grinned and opened the door. Not one but two briefcases were transferred to Terry's hands. Waiting a moment for a couple to finish loading their bicycles onto their racks and ride off, Terry opened the cases, one at a time, right next to the truck. Ice Cream did not stop grinning.

"I'd say, mate, that we got a bit more than the contract called for."

"I'd say a shitload more. That, smoker, is payment for services rendered and a bonus from the truck job."

"I'm assuming it was lucrative then?"

"We was thinking guns. We got China White. A whole fuckin' truckload of it." The rapper couldn't stop grinning.

"Drugs?"

"Yeah, man, fuckin' drugs. That's your cut. You ever

get a tip like that again, I'm in. You read me?"

"Certainly. I'll bear that in mind. Now, you are going to want your delivery."

"Yeah, I'm expecting some white bread."

"Drive this way a half mile, take a left down San Fernando Road. Pull off on the right when you see the steel horse on the left. Clear?"

"There's a steel horse. Is that like a train or like a real horse made of steel?"

"It's a horse. There will be a man I believe you met before. He will have the delivery."

"I don't like it. How do I know you're being straight with me?" Ice Cream made no move himself, but Terry knew there were at least two men in the back of the truck as well as the driver.

"You can take one of these cases if you want." Terry said tossing his cigarette but to the ground and affecting a look of unconcern.

Ice Cream thought about it for a second and decided that Terry had been straight with him all along and that most of the money was his anyway. Their short association had been and would continue to be tremendously profitable and it was not something he wanted to waste. He instructed his driver to head south on Osborne.

Back in the parking lot, Terry thought he was being generous when he offered a man two hundred dollars for the man's bicycle. The man was rude and told Terry to take a walk, that he had paid fourteen hundred dollars for the bike. Terry watched as the man loaded it and left. He was perplexed that anyone would have paid fourteen hundred dollars for a bicycle.

A couple of families came off the bike path and loaded up, Terry did not approach them. He lit another cigarette and waited. A younger man pulled in a beat up, older car. Terry had no trouble buying this man's bike for fifteen hundred dollars and he got the distinct impression he had overpaid for this one. The bike was nice enough and even better, it had a pack rack over the back wheel with a bungee cord on it. Terry fastened the suitcases to it and prepared to ride it across the top of the dam.

The man he had bought the bike from was expecting others to join him so he traded places with Terry on the guard rail.

A man pulled in without a rack on his car, causing the Australian to question why he was there. The driver had Ace bandages around his chest when he got out of the car. The trunk lid popped open but it was clear that there was no room for a full-sized bicycle in the trunk. Terry got on his new transportation and was riding away when he saw the new arrival pull the shotgun from the trunk and level it at the man sitting on the guard rail. It was clear that there had been a mistaken identity and if Terry wanted to survive this bike ride he was going to need to move a little bit faster. When he heard the shotgun blast he hoped that the young man had not just been killed though he suspected he had. He did not turn around to look.

When Ice Cream pulled off San Fernando Road he found himself at the top of a deserted quarry. There was a Cadillac parked, facing him. The large red-haired man was the same one who had delivered the previous live shipment. There was a minimum of conversation. The truck backed up to the rear of the Cadillac and the trunk lid opened. The transfer was done in no time and the small freezer truck drove off with the still bleeding Frank Hicks in the back.

"Look here, you insolent little cunt, I've only got one more favor in me. I hit the target as planned and even put one in 'im. Then this other team shows up and I took three in the chest. Only reason I'm alive is I'm fuckin' good, so don't even try it. If you can't get me to the target, you become the target." The man's voice was as cold and dry as a Bond martini.

"I'm sorry, Jerry, did you not go to Hansen Dam?"

"Of course I went to the dam. There was no Cadillac and no Frank Hicks."

"Then you must have been late. Is that my fault?" Her sarcasm was clear even over the phone.

"You saucy bitch. I'm considering doing you on general principles."

"Wait, wait, wait. There's no need for this. Frank has disappeared and he will never be heard from again. That should validate your, um, action." Jacqueline was beginning to sweat. She had been certain either Jerry Kragon would be killed, or the other team would be eliminated. She had not been particularly choosy which it was.

"Don't try to pull me off. Tell me where he is. The deal was for the ring finger, remember? I was to secure the ring finger with the diamond ring on it and that was my ticket. My paycheck so to speak."

"Well, that's not possible now."

"Oh, yes it is. You are going to tell me where my paycheck is to be found or I am going to come to your house in the middle of the night and I'm going to cut your tits off. Are we still clear?"

There was silence on the line for a moment then addresses: no name, no small talk, no directions, just the address of Sean Warren's house followed by George Arridagio's. Then, thinking it would make Jerry more comfortable, she told him who George worked for. She had told him that George would be paying him upon receipt of the ring finger. George had made no such demand and had, in fact, already delivered the balance of the cash which was still locked in Jacqueline's desk along with the money Sean's lawyer had delivered.

Forty five minutes in the back of the freezer truck had all but done Frank in. By the time he arrived at Sean's Beverly Hills estate he was more dead than alive. He was taken to the basement and handcuffed to an old brass bed. Sean grudgingly fed him some chicken soup and cleaned his bullet wound.

Ice Cream left without having much to say. He had stitched his future to Sean's rising star and they were going to the top together.

Sean fixed himself a drink in the living room. Frank's being wounded had not figured in his plans previously. It was almost fortuitous that he had been; it set the man up for a longer and even more painful ending.

The scotch was smooth and warm and Sean poured himself another. Sean had enjoyed burning and tearing D'arniel Jamiel's flesh. He licked his lips as he thought of peeling the man's skin off. More than just revenge was moving him then, it had been some sort of inner compulsion. Sean was going to enjoy doing the same to Frank Hicks but first he was going to gain the man's trust. He was going to share a cask of Amontillado with his Fortunato.

Smiling to himself he went into the pantry where he located a first aid kit. He had cleaned Frank's wound but had not dressed it. It looked as though the bone was broken and that would make for a long and painful rehabilitation. Sean had given the staff the day off so he knew he was alone in the house. He may need to fire them all to cover the time. He was not going to do this thing quickly.

In the basement, Frank was naked and almost unconscious but breathing steadily. It seemed likely that as long as infection did not set in, the man would live a while. Sean chattered to him as he bandaged the bullet wound.

"So Frank, I gotta tell you I'm not sure I can save you but I'm all you got. You got lots of men out there that want to see you dead. Not me, I'm your friend but there are others who are not. I'm gonna see what I can do about getting you outta here. We need to be careful, there are people watching, looking for you. I need you to stay here for a while so they don't find you. If it were clear, I'd let you go now but there are too many dangerous men around." Sean so began his plan to trick Frank while he healed and to then betray him. He was not being particularly inventive about it since it was more of a spur of the moment plan than anything else. The gangster had been close to comatose; it would have taken little to kill him, but Sean had moved beyond the revenge stage, now. Killing the man would not satisfy him, now. Sean did not admit it to himself but killing ten men would not quench the fire that had flared in his chest.

It caused Sean no little consternation that, when he returned to the ground floor, there was the silenced barrel of a pistol shoved into his eye. He had no idea who the blond man with the odd accent was that was standing in his living room, only that he was there and wanted to know where Frank Hicks was being held. It only made sense that it was one of Frank's men here to save him from what he deserved.

"Who are you? I don't know what you're talking about. What are you doing here? I have security and they'll be here any second."

"You mean that bloke at the gate? I don't suppose he'll survive. You'll forgive me if I'm a bit coarse today. I've been frustrated at every turn. What promised to be a simple and lucrative contract has turned into a complete balls out mess and if you cannot assist me you are of no earthly use to me. You will be my next victim."

"No, no, no. I can get you what you need. Don't worry. We're on the same side. Here, I have some twelve-year-old scotch, let me fix you one." Sean moved to the sideboard where the crystal glasses and some decanters sat. "Do you take ice?"

Jerry was amazed that Sean had gone from astonished to smooth and friendly in a heart beat. He almost liked the man for his capable attitude. He thought they might actually be able to work something out until Sean turned around, not with a glass of scotch but with a .44 Magnum. Jerry shot him through the lung.

Sean stood there, his mouth working like a beached fish, trying to get a breath. He looked at the hole in his chest and tried to get the pistol back to shooting level again. Jerry Kragon shot him again, this time through the eye. The back of action film star Sean Warren's head graced the mirror above the sideboard and dripped down into the crystal glasses.

Downstairs, Frank Hicks was looking almost as bad as his host. His wound had been dressed, but he had lost a lot of blood and he needed a doctor. He never got that doctor.

"I'm telling you, he made a deal with Hicks and he's coming there to kill you and Cabot."

"What? How can this be? I paid him. That is to say I paid you. You have the money."

"No. I paid him. I gave him the contracted money but he made a deal with Frank Hicks and he is coming there to kill you first and then Henry Cabot."

"What the…?"

"Shut up and listen. I'm telling you he made a deal with Hicks. Hicks is alive and you are going to end up dead unless you do exactly what I tell you to do."

"What?"

"Do you have a gun, George?"

"Yes, I have a skeet gun."

"No pistols?"

"No, ma'am."

"Well, we're going to need to make do with what we have. Load it with the heaviest rounds you have and wait for him. He's tall and blond and has a really nice tan. He should be getting there soon. As soon as he steps in the door, shoot him. And don't miss or he will take you down in a heartbeat. This man is a killer and he is going to be armed to the teeth so you can't give him a chance to kill you. You need to take him out first."

Jerry's chest and back still felt as though he had been kicked by a couple of large horses and it was not getting any better. A couple of ibuprofen tablets from Sean's medicine cabinet and a swallow from the one bottle not covered in blood and brains had dulled the edge slightly, but it still throbbed. He patted his pocket where Frank's ring finger was wrapped in a handkerchief. He thought, "*All this dramatic bullshit is more than I wanted to deal with, but it's not the first time I've had to prove I was the man on the scene.*"

A cursory inspection of the mansion revealed a lot of nice things: paintings, statues, crystal and cut glass. There was a wine collection covered with dust in a basement alcove. Jerry suspected there would be a safe somewhere in the house but he did not find it. There were no loose briefcases full of money either.

Jerry tried to take a deep breath and began to cough. It hurt horribly and he was sure he had broken at least one rib. He cursed the big redhead who had shot him and silently swore that he would shoot that big bastard if he ever saw him again. Jerry additionally swore he would never work without a bulletproof vest again. He was wearing one when he walked up to George Arridagio's front door.

The thing about bird shot is that it will kill a man at close range if he gets shot in a vital area such as the throat. Bird shot will do nothing of merit against a bulletproof vest except perhaps aggravate the wearer. Jerry Kragon had already had enough of being shot that particular day so when George Arridagio stuck a shotgun barrel out the door expecting to cut him in half with it, it was all he could take. He shot George nine times, the silenced pistol making no further racket in the neighborhood. It did not take long to determine that the remainder of his payoff was not in the house. If there had been women and children in the house they would have suffered as well. Jerry was in a truly foul mood now.

Sitting at the kitchen table, assessing his current situation, Jerry realized that there was only one person who could have set up this impromptu and incompetent attempt on his life.

George had some more powerful painkillers in his medicine cabinet and Jerry took two of those and swallowed them with some cheap white wine from the refrigerator. Then he drove to West Hollywood.

By the time Terry Kingston had reached the far side of the dry dam he had decided that bicycles were no longer for him. His father had bought him one when he was young but it had been all but useless at Uncle Ginger's farm and he had quickly outgrown it. That had been the last time he had ridden a bicycle and his muscles were unused to that activity. It was a surprise to him that he was suffering from the action.

After half an hour of recuperation, he spied the Cadillac approaching. He undid the jackpot from the back of the bike and joined his partners on the trip out of town. They left Los Angeles with almost no regrets.

It was past closing time for Prometheus Investigations and ordinarily Jacqueline would have closed up for the day but there was too much in play. The woman's thoughts raced like chipmunks through her mind. She had sent an assassin to Frank Hicks' office. She had sent an assassin to Sean Warren's house. She had told Jerry about George Arridagio. She had rented the Ford. She had hired the team to kidnap

Frank Hicks. She was at the heart of the entire situation and the only way she could survive the encounter as a free woman was to get the hell out of town and change her identity. The identity part would be easy for her, she was a programmer after all. She would write herself a life and insert it into the databases of the world. She thought about Terry whom she still thought of as Indian and wondered why she had wanted him while being simultaneously repelled by him. She had not yet raided Homer's safe deposit box either. She was not leaving town before doing that but she needed to hide somewhere nice and quiet. The enormity of the situation and her swirling thoughts made her feel like she was being dragged down a huge drain. She began to try to concoct plausible stories for the police but the stories did not even seem reasonable to herself. She had waited until Archie had left for the day and had put the bundles of cash in the hidden safe in his office. She did not know why she had done that, it just seemed that it would be safer there. She had once seen a man juggle running chain saws, the vision of it came to her now.

Jacqueline saw him step in the door without knocking, a pistol in his hand, and she reached under the desk for the Glock in its hidden holster. The first two shots were fired from that level. The first missed, the second shot went right through the outside of the man's left thigh, twisting him and dropping him to the floor. He howled more in rage than in pain and began firing back.

The first round hit Jacqueline's knee and traveled up her leg. The second round caught her square in the crotch, tearing through the soft tissue of her vagina and rectum before exiting through her lower spine. The third shot perforated her small intestine and glanced off her pelvic bone. One more involuntary shot from the .45 under the desk hit nothing of importance.

Jerry stood with difficulty and shot Jacqueline three

times in the face. He had been getting progressively more annoyed all day. Everybody he met was trying to kill him and he had not yet been paid. A quick examination of the office revealed the same. One dead victim but no bag full of money. The gunshots from the Glock had undoubtedly alerted the good citizens of the area, and LA's finest were no doubt on their way. There was nothing he could do for it, he needed to leave and there was only one more place he could go to get his payoff.

Henry Cabot had no idea how quickly events had stacked upon each other once he gave George the connections and the money to eliminate Frank. He thought that sort of thing would take a long time.

The sun was down in the west when he first met Jerry Kragon and it was an unorthodox introduction. Jerry was sitting in his bedroom, bleeding on his bed, when the congressman entered to get ready for sleep. The pistol that was leveled at the congressman's guts left no room for negotiation. Henry Cabot thought the intruder insane, ranting quietly about killing Frank Hicks and George and getting paid for it. Henry had only a cursory idea what he was referring to and was totally unprepared for the invasion. He did not yet know that George was dead. He had made the money available but had not been told that the contract had been made. After all, it was in his best interest not to know. Plausible deniability was almost as good as diplomatic immunity.

Jerry took a deep breath and attempted to explain one more time to the shaking politician that George Arridagio had contracted with him to kill Frank Hicks on Congressman Cabot's behalf but poor communication had resulted in George being dead and Jerry not getting paid. He paused and asked if Henry understood that.

After letting it sink in for a minute, Henry replied that he did.

Jerry then asked Congressman Henry Cabot if he was willing to pay for the services rendered, aware by this time that there had been no conscious contract with him.

Henry Cabot did not answer immediately. He licked his lips and nodded, but it was obvious to Jerry that the rabbit was about to bolt for a hole. Henry spun and reached for the door handle. Jerry shot him once, through the hand that was reaching, surprising himself at the accuracy of the shot. Henry howled like the legendary banshee and continued to scream until Jerry knocked him across the head with the silencer on his pistol. He fell to the expensive, plush carpeting with a moan and lay there trembling.

Jerry asked again if he was willing to pay for the services rendered and he got the desired answer that time. The knock came on the door moments later as Mrs. Cabot hurried to inquire over the screaming. Jerry opened the door, reached out and grabbed the woman by the hair, throwing her to the floor.

"Good evening, marm. Allow me to explain the current situation." The words were courteous but the tone was far from it. "In the course of your husband's business interests, I have shot almost a dozen men and women today. Ordinarily I would have been paid for this service and be sunning myself on the beach. I, myself, have been shot five times today and this has made me a bit testy, as I'm sure you could understand.

"I am here to collect the money I am owed for the wet work I performed on your husband's behalf and that is all I am here for. When I have it, I will leave. But, I have no problem with leaving you both lying in pools of your own blood. The fact that you are a woman makes no difference to me. I shot the last woman who crossed me in the cunt. Have I made myself clear?"

Mrs. Cabot was unable to even answer the man. Her husband was bringing himself back into consciousness, but he did not scream again, only moaned loudly.

There was no more resistance from this point. All three went downstairs to the library where Henry Cabot revealed a safe hidden behind a row of false book labels. Once the safe was open, Jerry did not even wait to see what was inside. He had waited long enough and put up with way too much trouble by this time. Despite his assertion to the opposite, he shot both Henry Cabot and his wife through the head, dropping them like slaughtered beef.

The inside of the safe proved to be a treasure trove of cash, bearer bonds and some truly lovely diamond jewelry. Jerry took the valuables, leaving only what appeared to be keepsakes and heirlooms. He considered he would probably need to leave the country now that he had slopped his bloody DNA all over three murder scenes, but there was one more target to strike before he left. It was pure spite and a personal hit but he swore to himself he would kill the big redheaded man who had beaten him to the punch. Jerry reasoned that it had been that man responsible for all the trouble he had been forced to contend with that day. He did not know the man's name but he considered it worthwhile to find out. The man had been good and had caused him untold pain. Before Jerry Kragon could consider himself the best, something he long had, the redheaded assassin needed to die. He took a deep breath through his nose and exhaled through his mouth. His chest ached and his leg was stiffening up. He needed some nursing and some recovery time before he was going to be killing anyone else, but once he set his mind to it, it would get done.

Archie could not understand what had happened. He did not know why his secretary had been shot or why the rented Ford had been reported near the scene of the Cabrito Road massacre. He was never charged in the killing of his secretary; he had been drinking in a bar at the time. There was no evidence he was culpable in the killings of Sean Warren and Frank Hicks, only the Ford his secretary had rented was a speculative connection. The Warren and Hicks murders were eclipsed by the killing of Congressman Cabot and his wife the same day as George Arridagio was murdered. The newspaper headlines read "Bloody Monday". Archie was not remotely involved with that either. He answered the questions, gave a statement, grieved for a few days and announced his intention to retire. When he was allowed back into his office, he found that his little safe behind the painting was packed with cash. He did not know how it had gotten there and he did not question it much. Whatever Jacqueline had been up to had gotten her killed. He decided he would keep the cash for his trouble. He took the money home with him, wondering what to do with that much cash. It felt dirty and with the impending investigations, it looked suspicious.

While the reputable newspapers carried the story of the murdered congressman, Sean Warren's picture was on the front page of the National Investigator along with the headline "Fallen Star".

Roberta Cunningham never saw her knight in shining armor again. It did not surprise her; men had been lying to her, using her and deserting her as long as she had been alive. She did not know what to make of it when a courier delivered the key to a safe deposit box to her motel room address. There was no return address on the package and the bank was thirty miles away.

The money would be spent but the note in the safe deposit box would remain with her for the rest of her life. It read, *This should be enough to get you a four year degree. I'm sorry I couldn't be there to see you graduate. The keys are for a station wagon in the parking lot of the motel in Van Nuys. It doesn't look like much but it has what it takes. You will always have my love.*

Terry